PRAISE FOR

FEAST
of
SORROW

"In her addictively readable first novel . . . the food lore is fascinating and the time period is inherently dramatic. . . . Aficionados of all things SPQR will eat this up."

—*Kirkus Reviews*

"Through the lens of a slave in ancient Rome, Crystal King illuminates a realm of seemingly impossible gluttony and excess, along with every other deadly sin. In the household of outrageous gourmand Apicius, he of extraordinarily decadent mores, one man, a slave, Thrasius, provides the sole ethical center. *Feast of Sorrow* is impossible to put down."

—Randy Susan Meyers, bestselling author of
Accidents of Marriage

"Crystal King's debut is a feast for the senses, bringing ancient Rome to dark, vibrant life. Politics, intrigue, danger, and passion mix deliciously in this tale of a young slave vaulted into the corridors of power as personal chef to the ancient world's greatest gourmet. Not to be missed!"

—Kate Quinn, author of *Mistress of Rome*

"Sometimes you just want a big, fat, juicy read, and Crystal King's debut novel fits the bill. . . . Romance, power, politics, and mouthwatering meals described in detail . . . We think we've just discovered the Food Channel's first miniseries."

—*The Huffington Post*

"Crystal King's debut novel, *Feast of Sorrow,* tells the story of Apicius, the notorious gourmand of ancient Rome, from the viewpoint of his slave and cook Thrasius. It's a dark and engrossing read and provides an evocative new perspective on the rule of Tiberius."

—Emily Hauser, author of *For the Most Beautiful*

"Crystal King has written a delicious feast of a book, one that allows us to not only see but also taste ancient Rome in all its dark and varied appetites."

—Yael Goldstein Love, author of *Overture*

"King's descriptions of the food and entertainment are exquisite, her characters are beautifully drawn, and events and people of the times are deftly woven throughout. . . . A delight to the senses, King's debut novel is to be savored and devoured."

—*Library Journal* (starred review)

"The historical world of *Feast of Sorrow* lives and breathes, and it is a delight to follow its characters' struggle for happiness and survival amid the simmering peril of Rome's great houses. Even if you're not a foodie drawn to novels of ancient Rome, this immersive, sensorily rich page-turner will take you for a delicious and unforgettable ride."

—Tim Weed, author of *Will Poole's Island*

"An engaging foray into the treacherous world of Claudio-Julian Rome from a fresh perspective. Who knew that the gourmand Apicius was larger than life? King deftly serves up intrigue, scandal, and heartbreak with lashings of exotic sauces, mouthwatering recipes, and the occasional drop of poison. Highly recommended."

—Elisabeth Storrs, author of the series Tales of Ancient Rome

"Finely paced . . . The novel combines exotic menus with the melodrama of a Greek tragedy. King's debut is a compelling historical drama with an appetizing center."

—*Booklist*

"The ancient Rome of Crystal King's *Feast of Sorrow* is filled with delectable dishes and astonishing injustice, deep loyalties and stunning loss. By the time you're done, you'll want a sip of honeyed water alongside some fried hyacinth bulbs. An engrossing read."

—Marjan Kamali, author of *Together Tea*

"Ancient Rome comes alive with a remarkable degree of immediacy and authenticity. I savored every page of this compulsively readable novel."

—Lisa Borders, author of *The Fifty-First State*

"King excels at researching a historical period, and her knowledge of the culinary life of early imperial Rome is second to none. When Thrasius cooks up a particular recipe for one of Apicius's extravagant dinners, the reader's mouth waters, even when the ingredients are unfamiliar. By re-creating Apicius's famous recipes, the world of ancient Rome comes to vivid, sparkling life."

—Bookreporter

FEAST
of
SORROW

A NOVEL OF ANCIENT ROME

CRYSTAL KING

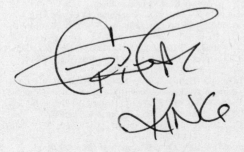

TOUCHSTONE

New York   London   Toronto   Sydney   New Delhi

Touchstone
An Imprint of Simon & Schuster, Inc.
1230 Avenue of the Americas
New York, NY 10020

First Touchstone trade paperback edition April 2018

TOUCHSTONE and colophon are registered trademarks of Simon & Schuster, Inc.

For information about special discounts for bulk purchases,
please contact Simon & Schuster Special Sales at 1-866-506-1949
or business@simonandschuster.com.

The Simon & Schuster Speakers Bureau can bring authors to your live event.
For more information or to book an event, contact the Simon & Schuster Speakers Bureau
at 1-866-248-3049 or visit our website at www.simonspeakers.com.

Manufactured in the United States of America

1   3   5   7   9   10   8   6   4   2

The Library of Congress has cataloged the hardcover edition as follows:

Names: King, Crystal, author.
Title: Feast of sorrow : a novel of Ancient Rome / by Crystal King.
Description: First Touchstone hardcover edition. | New York : Touchstone,
2017. |
Identifiers: LCCN 2016025828 (print) | LCCN 2016034508 (ebook) | ISBN
9781501145131 (hardback) | ISBN 9781501145148 (paperback) | ISBN
9781501145155 (ebook)
Subjects: LCSH: Apicius—Fiction. | Rome—History—Augustus, 30 B.C.–14
A.D.—Fiction. | Gastronomy—Rome—Fiction. | Gourmets—Rome—Fiction. |
Cooking, Roman—Fiction. | BISAC: FICTION / Historical. | FICTION / Sagas.
| FICTION / Family Life. | GSAFD: Historical fiction.
Classification: LCC PS3611.I5723 F43 2017 (print) | LCC PS3611.I5723 (ebook)
| DDC 813/.6—dc23
LC record available at https://lccn.loc.gov/2016025828

ISBN 978-1-5011-4513-1
ISBN 978-1-5011-4514-8 (pbk)
ISBN 978-1-5011-4515-5 (ebook)

Excerpts from *Apicius, A Critical Edition with an Introduction and English Translation* by
Sally Grainger and Christopher Grocock © 2006 Prospect Books, reprinted by permission of
Prospect Books, Devon, England.

For Joe,
who always saves me

PART I

1 B.C.E. to 1 C.E.

TRAVELER'S HONEYED WINE

A long-lasting honeyed wine, which is served to travelers on the road: you put ground pepper with skimmed honey in a small cask instead of spiced wine, and as required, you pour out as much honey and mix with it as much wine as is to be drunk; but if you use a thin-necked vessel, you put a little wine in the honey mixture. Add enough for the honey to pour freely.

—*Book 1.1.2, Mise en Place*
On Cookery, Apicius

CHAPTER I

Marcus Gavius Apicius purchased me on a day hot enough to fry sausage on the market stones. It was the twenty-sixth year of Augustus Caesar's reign. I was nineteen and I'd been put up for sale at the slave auction in Baiae after three months under Titus Atilius Bulbus, a fat, swarthy beast I was glad never to see again. I thanked the gods for the day Bulbus realized that a good cook was worth ten times his weight in denarii and decided it was more advantageous to sell me than to sleep with me.

Midmorning, the slave master, a heavy man with a barrel-shaped torso supported by birdlike legs, shuffled me toward an empty pen at the end of the slave platform. He brought a stool so I didn't have to sit on the dusty ground as two haggard old women scrubbed my naked body until not a trace of grime lingered on my skin. They trimmed my hair and scraped off my beard, leaving me cleaner than I'd been in months.

From my bench in the new pen, I heard my future master before I saw him.

"Ah, Master Apicius," the slaver said in a simpering voice unlike the one with which he usually barked out commands at his slaves. "I am glad you are here. I have two others inquiring about the cook. I hoped you would arrive first."

"Where is he?" Apicius asked, his voice a smooth baritone.

There was a rustle of tent flaps and the slap of sandals on the hot stones. I scrambled to my feet as they rounded the corner and came into view. Apicius looked about a decade older than me, with dark hair and

3

an aquiline nose typical of a long Roman bloodline. An extraordinarily tall Egyptian with wick-black hair and biceps the size of ham hocks hovered in the background. I surmised that he was Apicius's body-slave—the personal attendant who accompanied him everywhere.

The slaver opened the door to the pen and yanked me out to stand in front of Apicius, who took appraisal of my naked body, noting with his eyes that my head was bare. "No cap." He nodded his approval. The lack of a slave cap meant the fat slave master would guarantee me for six months. It also meant I was worth more.

Apicius lifted the bronze plaque around my neck, freshly polished and etched with my credentials and history of ownership. I would wear it every day of my life as a slave. "Free of illness. Does not steal. Good, good. Thrasius, eh? That's a Greek name."

I nodded, unsure if I should speak.

"You were the *coquus* to Flavius Maximus?" Apicius let go of the plaque and it slapped against my chest. "Interesting. I dined with Maximus a few months before his death. We had sausages of pheasant, sweet melon relish, and a *patina* of small fry. Was that your doing?"

I gathered my courage and hoped my voice did not shake. I remembered that patina—an egg custard of which Maximus was quite fond. "Yes. The sweet melon relish was something new that I was trying."

"How long did you work for Maximus?"

"I ran his kitchen for a year before he died. He was fond of entertaining." My mind raced. Apicius was certainly interested in my cooking but what if this man was as cruel as Bulbus?

Apicius raised an eyebrow at me. "Can you make roasted peacock?"

"Yes. I have a recipe for peacock with damson raisins soaked in myrtle wine. It works equally well with partridge or duck. I'm sure you would find the dish to your liking." I wiped sweat off my brow.

"What do you consider your specialty?"

"There are three," I answered, raising my voice in order to be heard over the din of the market. "My ham in pastry, with honey and figs, has often been praised, but I have been told it is equaled by my truffles with pepper, mint, and rue. I can also make you a dish of roasted salt belly pork with a special mixture of *garum*, cumin, and lovage."

Apicius smiled and started to ask another question. But the slave master was growing impatient. "The boy will make you famous," he whispered to Apicius. "With him cooking, you will have clients and friends lining up in the morning, begging for a spot at one of your *cenae*!" He paused. Apicius glowed.

The slave master continued, "His talents go beyond that of the kitchen. He can read and write, he is excellent at figures, and he speaks several languages. This is the coquus for you!"

"Famous?"

The slave master cocked his head and smiled. "Most definitely."

I expected Apicius to ignore the slaver's words. Yet he asked my price of the slave master and the answer shocked me. Twenty thousand denarii! Slaves rarely sold for more than a few hundred denarii.

"Sotas!" Apicius beckoned to the body-slave. Disapproval briefly flashed across Sotas's features as he stepped forward with a bag.

Apicius opened the bag to reveal several gold aurei, then laid the heavy pouch in the slaver's dark calloused hand. "The *argentarii* know me well," he said, gesturing in the direction of two men standing under a small canopy at the corner of the slave market. As representatives of the Roman bank, the argentarii were responsible for officiating over the larger sales, verifying credit, and making sure transactions went smoothly. "They will sign my letter of credit for the rest."

The slave master grinned. He had profited heavily.

I would later learn that my selling price was more than all the other slaves sold that morning combined.

After the slave master had removed my shackles and thrown a threadbare tunic at me, Apicius motioned for me to follow. Sotas followed behind.

As we made our way through the Baiae streets, I could sense unease in my new dominus. Perhaps he was having second thoughts about the high price he paid for me.

When he spoke it was with impatience. "Tonight I'm having a small *cena* with a few close friends. Tell me what you will make for the meal."

I faltered at my new master's words. I gazed up at the laundry lines strung between the *insulae* we walked past, with colorful *stolae* hanging out to dry. The sun was already past its apex.

"I am unsure of the staples in your kitchen." I kept my eyes down. My stomach churned as if I had eaten a rotten apple.

Apicius stepped around a small group of boys playing a game of knucklebones. "Never mind that. If you had any ingredient at your disposal, what would you make?"

"You said it was a small dinner?"

"Yes," he affirmed.

"In that case, I would begin with a *gustatio* of salad with peppers and cucumbers, melon with mint, whole-meal bread, soft cheese, and honey cake." I tried to draw on my memory of one of the last meals I'd made for Maximus.

Apicius licked his lips. "Yes, yes, go on."

"Then pomegranate ice to cleanse the palate, followed by a *cena prima* of saffron chickpeas, Parthian chicken, peppered morels in wine, mussels, and oysters. If I had more time, I would also serve a stuffed suckling pig. And to close, a pear patina, along with deep-fried honey fritters, snails, olives, and, if you have it on hand, some wine from Chios or Puglia."

"Perfect. Simple and the flavors would blend nicely at the beginning of a meal. Good."

Apicius led us across the square to the altar to Fortuna Privata, the goddess of luck and wealth. I had been right in thinking my new master was worried about his purchase—it was the only reason he would need to ask the goddess for a divination. On the way to the altar, we stopped at a grocer's stall to purchase offerings: a live goose, fruit, and honey cakes.

The altar was between two buildings on top of a tall stone platform that housed a richly adorned statue of the goddess. Sotas handed the goose to Apicius, who brought it toward the priest waiting next to the altar. My heart pounded. This divination was about me, about how I would affect the Gavian household. An unlucky reading would place doubt in Apicius's mind, and the last thing I wanted was for Apicius to return me to that filthy slaver. He would beat me within an inch of my life for cheating him out of such a fortune. The gods only knew who I might end up with then—the slaver might decide to send me to the salt mines, which would be a death sentence. Few slaves lasted more than a year or two cutting salt.

The priest, a bald man with heavy-lidded eyes, wore red robes that, despite their color, could not hide the dark blood stains of his trade as a haruspex, one who gave divinations by viewing the entrails of sacrifices. Apicius handed the squawking goose to the priest, who sprinkled it with salted flour, poured a few drops of wine on its forehead, and said a blessing. He placed the goose in the copper bowl resting on a low side table and abruptly ended its cries with a quick slash across its neck and a push of the knife down its belly. Scarlet flooded the feathers and flowed into the bowl in a rush.

There was no struggle, which bode well for the divination. The haruspex rolled the goose over and pushed upon it until the entrails fell into a viscous mess in the bowl. I observed my new master, wishing I knew what thoughts were going through his mind. An ironlike smell wafted up from the bowl.

A few more cuts and the haruspex set the carcass into a second bowl off to the side. The goose meat was payment for his services. He pushed his hand through the goose guts, pulling aside intestines and organs. Last, the priest singled out the liver, heart, gizzard, and gall bladder. He turned each organ over in his hands, searching for spots and abnormalities by which he could discern the goddess's wishes. As a cook I had seen the insides of hundreds of geese, but I still didn't understand what a haruspex saw when he examined the blood and guts.

After many long minutes, Apicius was unable to take the priest's silence any longer. "Well?" he asked as he twisted the thick gold wedding ring around his finger.

I was just as impatient. What if the divination said I was a terrible purchase? Would I be back on the slave block before the end of the afternoon?

The haruspex cocked his head at Apicius, one eyebrow raised. I imagined he had seen the same look in the eyes of the wealthy before. He cleared his throat. "The goddess Fortuna smiles upon you in some ways but, I fear, not in others."

Apicius wiped his palms on the folds of his toga. I held my breath.

The priest pushed around the entrails. He lifted up the liver. It was larger than normal but very smooth. "In this I see a life of indulgence and prosperity. You will win many hearts and bring pleasure to many people. You will have much to love in your life." He examined the gall bladder. It was swollen and no longer green as it should be, but a bright, angry red.

A whirring noise engulfed us as several hundred flapping pigeons swirled through the air. Apicius cursed. "Damn pigeons." He glanced upward. "Perhaps I should have sought an augur to read the birds instead of a gut gazer." I had to wonder as well; so many birds appearing at that moment must have great significance.

The priest didn't look up. Apparently birds meant nothing to him unless they were sprawled open under his knife. He slashed the gall bladder open and pulled it apart with the tip of his blade. It was filled with hundreds of yellowish-orange pieces of gravel. He grimaced and my stomach lurched. What did he see?

"This is most unfortunate. A healthy liver and a rotten gall bladder. You will feel the blood of life mingling with the pang of death. Your good fortune will be as a disease throughout your life. The more you work toward success, the more your sky will darken." The haruspex jabbed a fat finger toward a particularly large rock glistening with bile. Two larger pebbles stuck to its sides. "See that? Beware! For every success, greater failures will cluster to the sides."

The priest ignored Apicius's sharp intake of breath. He put the gall bladder aside and turned to the rest of the entrails. He lifted the gizzard, a double-bulbed organ, and cut it open carefully, exposing a cavity full of grass, rocks, and other debris. "Look here," he said, pointing to a piece of rounded pale blue glass amid the slimy debris. "This means unusual judgment."

"What do you mean?" Beads of sweat stood out on Apicius's brow.

"It means that, ultimately, you will be judged in the Underworld by how our world and the world of the future perceive you."

The haruspex picked up the bowl and turned away.

I felt sick—it had been a dismal fortune and surely Apicius was bound to march me right back to the slave trader.

"I see," said Apicius, looking perplexed.

The statue of Fortuna glowed in the early-afternoon sunlight. Her eyes, painted blue, stared at me.

As he rose, Apicius repeated the priest's words over and over in a whisper: *"Judged in the Underworld by how the world sees me now and in the future."*

I glanced at Sotas, but the body-slave only bowed his head. I wished that I could ask Apicius what he intended. Would he send me back? I looked toward Fortuna and dared to stare into that aquamarine gaze. I thought back to my time with Bulbus and how he abused me in ways no person should have to endure. *Please, my lady, grant me your favor. Please. Do not send me back to a beast like Bulbus. Please . . .*

After the divination, Apicius was agitated. There was no more friendly discussion on the way back to his *domus*, which was a short walk outside of town. I was glad for the silence. It gave me time to think about the whirring of birds still spiraling in my mind. The last time I'd seen birds fly in such a manner was the morning my previous master, Maximus, had fallen dead as his slaves were helping him don his toga. If birds foretold death to Maximus, what did the flock of pigeons mean for Apicius? Did they mean anything for me? Terror held court in the circle of my heart.

This terror took new form when I saw the vastness of the estate where I was to work. Apicius lived in a grand domus that rested on a high ridge with sweeping views of the Tyrrhenian Sea. It was larger and more elaborate than any I had seen, despite the fact that I'd been owned by three different patricians, each among the very rich. I was not prepared for the opulence of the house that lay before me. Apicius led us through a labyrinth of painted corridors that sometimes opened toward the ocean and the beach below. We passed through the peristylium, and I almost gasped aloud. The courtyard was immense, and laden with fountains and small running streams. Flowers bloomed everywhere and the rich smell of thyme permeated the air as we crushed the growing herbs against the stones beneath our feet. In an unusual design for a domus, one side of the peristylium was open toward the sea, and specially rigged gates could be closed to create a wall against the elements if the need arose. The size of the house was massive. I tried to imagine how many slaves worked for Apicius. There must have been hundreds.

"Sotas, take the boy to the kitchen and start him working," Apicius ordered.

A sour taste rose in my mouth. "But, Dominus, I need more time to . . ."

As soon as the words escaped my mouth I knew that I should not have said them.

Apicius whirled around. "Do not question me. Sotas will take you to the kitchen, where you will cook me the cena meal you described, with two exceptions. I don't want Parthian chicken. Instead, you will cook me your 'specialty' ham in pastry and there will be lobster instead of mussels."

Then his tone changed. "Eat no food tonight you did not prepare by your own hands. If you must partake of food other slaves have made, make them taste it first. And under my explicit instructions, you are not to touch any food that one of my guests asks you to taste, understand? Find another slave to taste but you are to take the utmost care for your own well-being."

What had happened to the last cook? A lump of panic rose in my throat.

Apicius put a hand on my chest and thrust me in Sotas's direction.

"How did I anger him?" I asked Sotas when Apicius was out of earshot. I had to look up to meet his eyes—the top of my head came only to his chest.

"It wasn't you. It was the haruspex."

"Why did he want to buy me so badly?"

Sotas gave me a crooked smile. "Because you're a good cook, or at least you were the night Apicius ate at Maximus's house. Apicius still talks about that meal. He wants that for his own table. He wants someone who will help him become gastronomic adviser to Caesar. He is expecting you to be that person. As for money, you'll find he has a lot of it and he spends it freely."

"I don't understand. The reading for the haruspex was terrible."

Sotas laughed but it was a bitter sound. "Didn't you notice what he was whispering to himself the whole way back?"

I remembered only Apicius mentioning the part about judgment in the Underworld and I said as much.

"Exactly. Apicius heard what he wanted to hear. The part about success, what was it . . . ?"

"The more he works toward success, the more his sky will darken. Sounds like failure to me."

"Yes, that. He's angry and worried now, but by morning he will have convinced himself the failure part was never said."

I remained silent.

Like the domus itself, the kitchen was the largest I had ever seen, full of bustling slaves preserving food, cleaning pots, and cooking on the three large hearths. The fresh, sweet essence of honey cakes wafted through the air, mingling with the acrid smell of vinegar and the rich aroma of smoking meats. The kitchen was loud and hot despite the ocean breeze drifting through the open windows. A red long-tailed hound lay in one corner, asleep with his tongue hanging out one side of his mouth. A large sundial in the garden was visible through the kitchen window. I had only a few hours to prepare an elaborate meal.

I counted fifteen kitchen slaves. They all appeared to be cooking, not serving, and I guessed there must have been at least a dozen more elsewhere who served the courses of the cena. A few prepubescent youths wandered in and out of the kitchen, likely errand runners. I could barely breathe—by the gods, how was I going to manage all these people? I knew how to run a kitchen, but only a small one, with three slaves and three servers—nothing on the scale of what appeared to be expected of me in the Gavian household! My moment to worry passed quickly, for after we entered the room, Sotas rang a large bell on a shelf next to the kitchen door and all the slaves stopped their work, their faces shining in the heat. He pushed me forward into the room and presented me to the kitchen.

"That the new coquus?" an older, mostly toothless woman asked from her post at a low counter where she was pickling parsnips. Her long gray hair, streaked with white, was loose and cascaded down her back. I wondered how much of it found its way into the food.

"He's your new boss. Don't make him angry," Sotas warned, and headed back into the depths of the house.

I watched him go, unsure of what I should do. The kitchen staff waited for me to speak but I could not find a thing to say. A huddle of women plucking chickens and pheasants kept working, looking from me to the birds and back again. The dog lifted its head expectantly. After an uncomfortable silence, the toothless woman spoke up. "Are you mute, boy?"

The words of my former master Maximus came back to me. He had always said that there would be certain times, despite my status as a slave, when I would need audacity and sheer brazen nerve. In those moments I should assume that all around me understood that I knew best. For the first time, I understood the truth of Maximus's words. If I didn't speak and react with authority, I would never have the respect of the staff, and given all the money Apicius had spent on me, I had better gain that respect fast.

"Mute? Unfortunately for all of you, no, I am not." I strode to the center of the kitchen. I gazed at each of them as I spoke. "I am Thrasius but you will call me Coquus. I run a smooth kitchen and I expect the best out of my staff. You there"—I pointed to the old woman—"what is your name?"

She arched her brow, deciding whether she should answer me. I stood my ground, staring intently at her until she blinked, her black eyes disappearing behind wrinkles of skin.

"Balsamea."

"Balsamea, who is second to the coquus in this kitchen?" My eyes scanned the room, refusing to betray my fear to the other slaves. Most were older than me and that would make gaining their trust even harder.

"That would be me, Coquus," said a man standing near a large jug of garum in the corner of the room. I noted the stamp on the vessel, from Lusitania, one of the finest garum factories in the Empire. Good garum, a sauce made from the entrails of little anchovies, was one of the most important flavors in a dish. I was glad to see I would have access to the best.

"I'm Rúan." The man stepped forward, wiping his floured hands on his thick kitchen tunic. He was young, still in his teens, with an unusual head of red hair and striking green eyes. I wondered if he was from Hibernia, the large isle off Britannia.

"Rúan, I have a menu which Dominus has instructed me to prepare for tonight's cena. Have you slaughtered any pigs recently?"

"There is fresh ham from this morning stored in the cellar," Balsamea spoke up. Rúan glared at her for answering on his behalf, but she didn't look away from the vegetables she was slicing.

"Good." I glanced around the room. "Who bakes the best pastries in this kitchen?"

"Vatia has won the praise of Dominus Apicius," Rúan replied, pointing to a young woman standing behind a low table on the right side of the room. He was Hibernian, his accent so thick that I had to concentrate to understand. Vatia stopped kneading bread long enough to nod her acknowledgment. Her dark, shiny hair was pulled back in a tight knot, which pleased me. Before the end of the night, I planned to tell Balsamea that imitating Vatia would be in her best interest and that she would no longer have the liberty of keeping her greasy locks free in my kitchen.

"Have you prepared the honey cakes?"

Vatia pointed to a nearby pan filled with little cakes ready to slide into the oven. Good. One less thing to worry about. "There are two more tasks for you this evening. You will prepare fifteen rounds of dough, which I'll use to wrap the hams. I also want you to cook the fried honey fritters for the *cena secunda*. It seems you are already at work on baking the bread." I assumed Apicius had invited guests according to tradition, meaning there would be nine guests, symbolizing the nine Muses. Still, I could be wrong and being prepared for accidents was wise. Additionally, there were often uninvited guests, "shadows" or "parasites," who sat at the ends of the couches and would need to be fed.

"If we do not have on hand melons, saffron, morels, chickpeas, pomegranates, lobster, oysters, pears, and snails, you'd better send the fastest boy we have to the market to get them," I said to Rúan.

A cry rose from the back of the room. "I'll do it, I'll do it!" The voice came from a blue-eyed boy dressed in a ripped tunic, waving his tanned arm around wildly. The boy moved forward. Rúan opened his mouth as if to say something when the boy tripped and crashed into a table. The kitchen slaves shouted as the table toppled, taking with it a dozen brightly colored glass goblets. Several of the slaves lunged to catch some of the glasses but no one was swift enough to save them. They crashed into the tiles, shattering into a thousand rainbow pieces. I closed my eyes and took a deep sigh to keep calm. No doubt those goblets were precious.

"Pallas! You fool! Out! Get out!" Rúan yelled at the boy. Balsamea took him by the shoulder and led him away.

The broken glasses were the least of my worries. Despite the gravity of the situation, I could not stop thinking about Apicius's last words to me—the instructions not to eat any food I hadn't directly prepared. I watched the slaves hurry to clean up the mess: Rúan, the ruddy Spaniard with the broom, the girl with the unusual blond hair picking up shards of glass, and all the others milling about. I regarded each of the fifteen slaves, wondering who among them might want to poison me.

CHAPTER 2

It was a massive task. The water clock in the corner of the kitchen showed that I had less than four hours to prepare for dinner. Still, I could not take my mind off that flock of birds we saw, or Fortuna's unreadable stare. Despite the lack of time, I knew I must have more spiritual guidance. I asked Balsamea where the family's Lares shrine was located, suspecting her to be one who held to tradition. Approval flickered in her eyes. Rúan, however, snorted and shook his head. It was clear that he thought little of our Roman gods.

Still, he had Balsamea remain in the kitchen and he himself led me to the atrium. He pointed at the tiled recess in the wall that housed several tiny statues of the Lares and Penates, the household gods and family ancestors. Sunshine filtered into the open area of the atrium and glinted off the polished bronze and gold of the statues. I removed a small stick from the wooden box next to the shrine, lit it from the torch flickering nearby, then lit the lump of incense sitting in a golden bowl in front of the statues. The smell of myrrh filled my nostrils. I knelt.

"Whether You for whom this house is sacred are a god, or a goddess, I wholeheartedly pray to You, O holy Lares. Please grant me success today and in all the days following and I shall offer You a honey cake each day I am blessed in the house of Marcus Gavius Apicius."

I didn't linger long. Rúan waited for me at the edge of the atrium and together we hurried back through the labyrinthine corridors. For extra measure, I said a few additional prayers to myself as I walked: to Sors, god of luck; to Fornax, goddess of the ovens; to Cardea, goddess of thresholds; and again to Fortuna.

15

A voice stopped us. "You there!" The command was loud and shrill.

We turned, unsure who the command was directed toward. An elderly woman dressed in rich yellow silks strode toward us, anger etched in her eyes. She looked as if she regularly bathed in unhappiness. Her visage resembled a gorgon, with a nose hooked like a vulture's beak and dark, squinty eyes. A black wig sat slightly crooked on top of her head. Several strands of wispy silver hair poked out from under the edges like little weed snakes.

She drew near. "Who are you?"

Rúan had fallen to one knee. I too bowed low in deference. "Thrasius, the new coquus."

"I thought as much. Stand up."

No sooner than I had, she cuffed me across my chin with the back of her hand. Pain accompanied the scrape of a ring as it cut open my skin.

She stalked off.

I stood there in stunned silence for a moment, wondering what had happened. I stopped the blood with my hand, grateful it was only a scratch.

I felt Rúan's hand on my shoulder. "Apicius's mother, Popilla."

"I don't understand."

He shook his head. "Not here," he whispered. "Come."

Once we were back in the kitchen, Rúan handed me a basket and told me that he wanted to show me where everything was located, then led me past the other slaves to a storage room adjacent to the kitchen. I was shocked at the display on the shelves, momentarily forgetting the bruise rising on my cheek. I gaped at the beautifully wrought glass goblets of all shades and sizes, stacks of dishes imported from many parts of the world, trays full of spoons with pointed handles, and sets of woven napkins. I had never seen so much wealth gathered in one place.

"Napkins and spoons?" In most houses a guest brought his own to dinner.

"Apicius spares no expense."

"I see." The throbbing had begun anew. "Why did Apicius's mother hit me?"

Rúan curled up his lip in disgust. "Because she can. Expect her to abuse you regularly. You have the attention of Dominus and she will despise you for it. She hated the last cook too. I am certain she drove him to his death."

I stopped myself from cursing aloud. Of all the people I had to worry about, it would have to be Apicius's mother. It made me wonder again about what Apicius had said before he left me in the kitchen. "Dominus warned me not to eat anything I hadn't prepared with my own hand. Do you know why?"

Rúan grimaced. He glanced toward the small barred window in the back of the room where the sea breeze occasionally gusted inward. "Probably because Dominus doesn't want you to die."

Goose bumps surfaced on my arms. "So that's what happened to the other cook."

"Aye. Most of us think Popilla had him killed. She hated Paetas. Stay away from her."

"I don't understand."

"Two months ago, Dominus Apicius was visiting his villa in Minturnae and Domina Aelia was on the other side of Baiae taking care of a sick friend. With both of them gone, Popilla had dinner alone in her room. She complained about her soup and demanded Paetas try it and tell her what he thought. He tried the soup and agreed that it shouldn't taste so."

Rúan's eyes darkened with the memory. "Paetas went back to the kitchen, dumped the soup, and sent a fresh bowl to Popilla, which she ate with no complaint. By the time she went to bed, Paetas was complaining of dizziness and that his heart was beating too fast. His face turned red and he started vomiting. Soon he was gasping for air, and before morning arrived, he was gone." Rúan shuddered.

I wondered if any of the slaves felt loyalty toward Popilla. I endeavored to keep my face devoid of emotion in front of my new second-in-command. "Why would she have wanted to hurt Paetas, or me, for that matter?"

"Nothing she does makes any sense."

"Did anyone accuse her of Paetas's death?"

Rúan shook his head. "How could we? Fortunately, Domina Aelia had returned. She stayed with us through the night. We waited with Paetas until he died, promising him we would send his ashes to the sea.

Balsamea thinks it was yew powder because it takes a while to work. Paetas didn't feel ill until Popilla had long since retired and the soup had been thrown out, so we couldn't test it on one of the chickens.

"Domina believed us but what could she do? Popilla is her husband's mother. The only thing she could do to punish Popilla was to tell her that without the cook, the staff couldn't be trusted to make anything besides barley soup. We served soup and apples until Apicius returned a month later." He lowered his voice and looked toward the door to make sure no one would hear. "Popilla is so stupid she never realized Domina let us eat normal meals when Popilla took her bath or left the villa to eat with friends, which, after the first few days, was nearly every night. Popilla hates barley soup."

"What does Apicius think of his mother?" I asked.

"He barely puts up with her. He avoids her when they are both at home. I once asked Sotas why Dominus doesn't send her away. He told me Apicius had promised his father he would take care of her. When Gavius Rutilus died, he gave Apicius everything and Popilla nothing. I've heard it was well over one hundred million sestertii! I think that makes it clear what he thought of his crazy wife. Apicius would love to find her a husband. I hear her dowry is huge, so someone will probably take the old sow off his hands soon."

The conversation was beginning to run long and I started to worry about the meal. I surveyed the glassware and cutlery before me. I took the basket from Rúan and motioned at the shelves.

"Those glasses that Pallas broke, did Apicius pick them out especially for tonight?"

Rúan shrugged. "I don't know. They were delivered earlier today. They could have been a gift from a client, or Dominus could have had them ordered. If something new arrives we usually use it the same day."

"Let's hope they were a random gift." In their place we put aside a set of glass cups colorfully painted with vivid pictures of powerful animals—bulls, cheetahs, and horses. If Apicius asked, I would explain the broken glasses, but in looking at the collection before me, I had a feeling he wouldn't miss them.

We finished packing the basket. When we emerged, I found myself coughing as kitchen smoke filled my lungs. I had never been in a kitchen with so many ovens—three of them along one wall. Dozens of amphorae of oil and wine lined another wall, while shelves filled with bronze pots and baskets of vegetables took up space along the wall closest to the door.

I barely had time to set the basket down before Apicius burst into the kitchen, Sotas trailing behind. Apicius was already dressed for dinner in an off-white toga. His leather shoes were dyed red, another symbol of his patrician status. They set him apart from other rich, noble citizens, equestrians, who did not have the family ancestry that marked them as elite.

He didn't notice me. "Thrasius!" he bellowed across the kitchen.

"Yes, Dominus?" I moved around the table past Balsamea. He fixed his gaze on me.

"I received word Publius Octavius will be joining us tonight. He will be critical of every aspect of this evening's cena. Octavius is a man who believes his cook to be the best in the Empire. You will prove him wrong. Do you understand?"

"Yes, Dominus." I tried to keep the fear from my voice.

I opened my mouth to ask him more about Octavius but Sotas shook his head in warning. I took the hint—Apicius's foul mood would only find fuel with my words.

"If you are successful, I will give everyone in your kitchen an extra holiday this month."

A murmur of excitement reverberated among the slaves who had quieted to hear the conversation. Many masters did not afford their slaves holidays. Thankfully, the words of the mighty philosophers such as Cato the Elder touted the need to give hardworking slaves regular days off from work, swaying many slave owners who wanted to moderate unruly slaves.

"Thank you, Dominus, that is generous of you."

Apicius glared at me. "Don't thank me yet. If you fail, each of you will lose two holidays this month."

The kitchen was silent, then erupted into a sudden clamor of knives beginning their chop, logs being thrown onto the fire, and the slaves rushing back to their tasks.

I spoke up, taking a chance at my master's wrath. "Dominus, I too saw the birds fly this morning when you prayed to Fortuna. I believe they were a sign—"

"It had better be a good sign," Apicius cut me off. "Remember, make no mistake this evening. You will not tarnish my reputation as a host."

Sotas dipped his chin at me and followed after our Dominus.

"Coquus?" Vatia waved at me to come to her table. Rúan stood next to her. He ran a hand along her arm as he made to return to his own station, a casual but intimate gesture. I made a mental note; sometimes romance in the kitchen was a lucky thing but sometimes it only hindered work at hand.

"What is it?" I was irritated, assuming that she had been distracted. "You are only now rolling out the dough?" I bit my tongue so she could explain, reminding myself that anger would not be helpful under such circumstances, despite Apicius's dire warning about Octavius's expectations.

"My apologies, Coquus, but dough holds its shape better if given time to chill." Her voice shook and she stared at me with wide brown eyes. I realized she could not be much older than Rúan.

"Chill?" I asked, wondering how anything could be cooled in the blistering summer heat, much less with the heat the ovens generated.

"Under the domus there is a snow chamber," she said. "You will never want for cold in this kitchen. We had a shipment this morning."

When I worked for Maximus, I'd ordered snow to be delivered only a handful of times. I couldn't help but stare in amazement whenever I saw the hard-packed ice chunks, usually delivered in thick, straw-padded barrels buried under a wagon full of hay. The barrels, harvested from the hills of Mons Gaurus, west of Rome, each cost a small fortune.

Vatia was no longer looking at me; she was rolling a round of dough around one of the hams, which had been scored, smeared with honey, and stuffed with figs. Her method was precise and the dough formed perfectly around the meat in a way I had never been able to achieve before.

"I see what you mean about chilling the dough," I said, amazed.

"This is what I wanted to show you." She directed my gaze toward a few strangely cut pieces of dough in front of her.

"I don't understand."

"Watch." She picked up the pieces and attached them to the pastry-wrapped ham, her thin fingers carefully sealing the pieces of dough to the ham by dipping them in water. In a few moments she sat back.

"It's a pig!" I exclaimed, pleased with the ears and snout she had added to the ham.

"I hoped you would like it," she said, her voice filling with pride. "I had the idea when you first told me what we were doing. I had a pig pictured in my mind and thought it might be pleasing to guests if I could re-create it."

"Do you think they will bake without issue?" I asked, worried.

"They should. Also, I thought I would brush them with egg so they are shiny when they come out of the oven."

"Please do." I could not take my eyes off the little pig. It was brilliant and I wished I had thought of it. I patted her on the shoulder. "The gods are smiling on you! Show me the secret. I'll help you finish." I let her demonstrate how to cut the proper shapes out of the dough, thanking Fortuna for sending me someone like Vatia to make my first meal extraordinary. This attention to detail was what truly made my heart sing, and to find someone else who had such an eye felt like a relief amid the chaos.

When I surveyed Rúan's work during the final meal preparations, I asked why Apicius hadn't let him run the kitchen. He seemed to be both capable and willing to learn.

"I'm only sixteen. Plus, it wouldn't be good luck for Dominus." He smirked, shaking his head of wild red hair. I should have realized that Apicius would never let a barbarian run his kitchen.

I probed a little further. "Sotas told me that our Dominus wants to be gastronomic adviser to Caesar. Do you know why?"

"Aye. He wants fame. He wants the world to know who he is. The thing is, he has no talent for anything. He'd make a terrible senator, orator, or lawyer. He thinks too much of himself to go into the merchant trade. So he needs to tie his star to Caesar. The only thing he knows how to do well is eat and, to some extent, marry flavors together. That's where you come in—your job is to make him famous."

I thought back to my purchase. The slave trader had seemed to know that about my new master. *"The boy will make you famous,"* he had said. He had said a few other things as well, but it was that word—*famous*— that had caused Apicius to spend so much money on my purchase.

• • •

A little before sundown, an hour before the cena was to start, someone called my name. I looked up from the final preparations of the hams and found myself staring into the green eyes of a young woman with plain features who stood on the other side of the worktable. She wore a rich red silk *tunica* layered with a patterned red and yellow stola. Her chestnut-colored hair was piled high atop her head, leaving dozens of curls to frame her face. Around her neck rested a shiny golden necklace with inlaid garnets and pearls. The matron of the house.

I was covered in flour, with smears of wine and honey wiped haphazardly across my kitchen tunic. Embarrassed, I bobbed my head in greeting, keeping my eyes low.

"No, please do not look away. I'm Aelia," she said. I looked up, surprised by her jovial tone. "I wanted to greet you personally. Marcus was in a mood today and I fear he may have been unduly harsh with you about his expectations for tonight's meal. Normally he's quite involved with dinner preparations but I thought it might be best to keep him out of your way on your first day with us."

"Thank you for your kindness," I stammered, unsure of what else was expected of me. In other households where I'd served, the matron of the house rarely paid me any mind unless something with a meal had gone wrong. Instead, here she was, telling me she was protecting me from the whims of my new master.

She walked around the kitchen, peering into bowls and tasting from the dishes with the tips of her fingers. The rushing slaves slowed when she came near and hardworking scowls turned into smiles of pride when she commented on their work. When a blond wisp of a girl from Germania dropped a basket of apples and they tumbled across the floor, Aelia bent to help her pick them up. She waved off the slaves who came to her side, talking gaily as she and the girl placed the apples back in the basket. "Give the bruised ones out to the other slaves," she said, winking at the girl, who bowed her thanks repeatedly.

Aelia plucked an apple from the top of the basket and brought it to Balsamea, who thanked her profusely and slipped the apple into her pocket. Aelia closed her eyes and breathed in the aroma of the kitchen.

"Thrasius, if your food tonight tastes half as good as it smells, you are well on your way to earning great respect in this household."

"I hope everything will be to your liking, Domina," I mumbled. "My apologies if it seems simple or rushed."

Aelia grinned at me. "I'm sure it will be fine. Marcus has been bragging to me all afternoon about how fortunate he was to find you for sale," she said. "Could you do me a favor?" Aelia cocked her head slightly as she spoke.

I was in awe of this young woman. For all the rapport I had had with my previous Dominus, he still commanded me as any master would a slave, as did his wife, who used to bleat instructions at me through thin puckered lips and the bar of her yellow teeth. There were never any "favors" to be given, only service demanded.

"Of course, I am pleased to serve," I said, motioning for Vatia to take over the task of brushing egg yolk across the dough before the hams went into the oven for their final stage of cooking.

"Marcus will love those pigs." Aelia smiled, motioning to the tray with her hand. "So will Apicata, but I am sure she'll be more interested in playing with them than eating them."

"Apicata is your daughter?"

"Yes. That's why I came by. To meet you, but also to ask you to have dinner ready for her in a short while. She's sleeping now but will be up soon. Maybe some cheese and fruit?" Aelia curled a strand of hair around her finger as she spoke. "Rúan came by with her supper earlier but she had fallen asleep amid her dolls. We played all day at the ocean and she was tired."

"Yes, Domina. The sun and sea do tend to wear you out." I myself was pleased to be near the water and already looked forward to my first day off so I could wander the beach below the house. All day the smell of the sea had invigorated me every time a breeze blew through the open kitchen windows.

"I'll send Passia along to fetch a tray. May Fortuna and the Lares of this house shine upon you tonight!" Aelia pulled her stola close around her and left the kitchen, the *tink-tink* sound of the gold links of her necklaces and earrings becoming fainter as she moved through the corridor beyond.

I instructed one of the younger slaves to put together a plate for Apicata and returned to the task of organizing the slaves who were serving the cena courses.

"Remember to count!" I instructed the six serving slaves as they left the kitchen and crossed the threshold into the outdoor *triclinium*, where the guests rested on couches in the late-summer sun. Despite the frenzy in the kitchen, I'd managed to find a half hour in the afternoon to help the slaves practice the way I wanted them to serve the meal. It was obsessive, but I could not help myself. When the spectacle of the food arrived in a fantastic way, it made the pleasure of eating the meal all that much greater.

I watched as the slaves reached the diners, stepped together in perfect time, and simultaneously placed trays of food on the tables before each guest. The servers removed polished spoons from their aprons and newly bleached napkins from over their shoulders and presented them to the guests. I breathed a sigh of relief that the slaves followed my instructions and stayed in step with one another.

The cheese flowers that accompanied the bread made the ladies squeal with delight, but it was the look on Apicius's face that pleased me most. Throughout the meal, Apicius beamed, his face glowing more from pride than it did from the light of the fading sunset over the sea.

When I returned from the triclinium, where the guests were finishing their honey cakes and drinking from jeweled goblets of pear juice, a woman entered the kitchen from a side door.

Out of all the surprises I'd had that day, she was the most surprising of all. The vision of her dark eyes, waves of auburn curls, and the sylph-like curve of her hips would haunt me in the days to come.

"I came for Apicata's meal," she said. Her voice floated across the room, undulations of sound washing over my skin. This was the woman Aelia had said would come for the tray. Passia. The name glittered in my mind as I made the connection.

"Is that it?" She pointed, one long finger tipped with carefully curved, pink-pale nails. I had been standing like a statue, stunned by my close proximity to what I thought might be the physical manifestation of Venus herself.

"That's the plate, yes, over there. There." Suddenly I wished she would leave. If not, all would be lost. I wouldn't be able to complete the cena, wouldn't be able to direct the servers, and would end up under the lash as the result of my gloomy failure to live up to Apicius's expectations. Inside my head, I said a prayer to Venus that Passia would go, but in the same breath, I begged the goddess that Passia would remember me, as I knew I would remember every sumptuous detail about the moments she stood before me.

Thankfully the goddess was paying attention. Passia didn't give me a second glance. She skimmed across the room, her arm brushing my hand as she leaned over the table to take the tray. In the span of a dove's breath, she was gone.

Balsamea noticed my agitation. She flicked a bit of water at me with the end of the spoon she had been using. "Looks like there is more than dough rising in this kitchen, wouldn't you say?"

If I had felt heat on my cheeks earlier, it was tenfold with that statement. I glared at her, wishing I could hurl a lightning bolt in her direction. I chose not to answer, but instead turned back to my counter to finish shucking the last of the oysters.

CHAPTER 3

Rúan and I stood in the doorway between the kitchen and the outdoor triclinium, looking toward the guests and the sea beyond. I tried to ignore the rumble in my belly. I'd taken Apicius's warning about being poisoned to heart and hadn't eaten anything that day save for some radishes I'd pulled from the garden and small tastes from various dishes I myself had prepared.

Apicius and his guests chatted merrily, enjoying the cooling salt breezes, marveling at the pomegranate sunset over the ocean. A three-sided couch, or triclinium, held nine guests to represent the nine Muses, as tradition dictated. Each diner lay on his side propped up by one elbow. A square table rested at the center of the couch, laden with hard-boiled quail eggs, grapes, olives, and little treats to whet the appetite. The guest of honor that night, in unusual form, was a woman. She lay laughing in the coveted position on the far left of the middle couch, next to Apicius.

"Who is that?" I whispered to Rúan. I was grateful for his willingness to help me navigate the politics of Apicius's household.

"Fannia, an old family friend of the Gavii. She recently remarried but you'll not meet her husband anytime soon."

I was about to ask why but Rúan continued, gesturing at the man who sat between Fannia and Apicius's mother. "I don't know the name of the man at the end of the couch but I think he's another money-hungry lawyer interested in Popilla's dowry."

I leaned back into the kitchen and indicated that the next set of servers should deliver the lobsters and oysters to the table. I held my breath until the slaves set the snow- and shellfish-laden platters down and turned back toward the kitchen after an exaggerated bow.

Rúan chuckled as Popilla immediately reached toward the tray to snatch the largest piece of lobster tail on the plate. We watched the diners extract the oysters from their shells with the pointed handles of their spoons.

"That's Trio and Celera." Rúan indicated a young couple reclining on the other side of Fannia. Trio was a handsome man with thinning hair and a jawline characteristic of the long Caelius line of Roman patricians. Celera seemed about fourteen or fifteen and appeared to be with child.

"Apicius said that Publius Octavius would be in attendance. Is that him on the other side of Fannia?" I asked.

Rúan pulled back to let one of the slaves pass by. "Yes. His father was a senator but Octavius doesn't seem to be following in his footsteps. Instead he spends his money on parties and his time on sucking up to people close to Caesar. His wife is the one with the red hair."

"Is he from Baiae?"

"Nay, from Rome. He has a summer villa here. I've never been to Rome, but I hear the summer is unbearable."

Rúan was right, summers in Rome were said to be miserable. As a result, Baiae had become a hotspot for the wealthy to bask in the sea breezes and spend time on the beaches in the summer.

He continued, "Apicius doesn't like Octavius, but he always says to keep your enemies close. I think they used to be good friends, but now everything between them is a competition." Rúan rubbed his hands together. "Should I get the hams ready to go?"

"Yes. I want them still hot when they arrive at the table."

When the hams were presented, Aelia laughed at their golden-brown bodies and the pastry snouts and ears.

"I'm not sure I can eat this! What a marvel, Thrasius!" She reached forward and carefully detached one of the pig ears from its body and popped it into her mouth. She closed her eyes, savoring the crunchy pastry. "Well, perhaps I can!"

I smiled and motioned for the scissor slave to start cutting up the rest of the hams into bite-size pieces.

When the slave had finished cutting the meat and the diners were delighting in the dish, Apicius waved me over with one tanned arm high over his head. Turning back to his guests, Apicius gushed, "I must introduce you to my new coquus! Come here, Thrasius."

The smile he wore belied his earlier dour mood. He indicated a nearby stool and motioned for me to bring it to the table in the center, uncharacteristically closing off the U shape of the triclinium, a request that surprised me. The delicious smell wafting my way reminded me of my hunger and started my belly rumbling.

"So this is your new acquisition," Octavius said, eyeing me up and down. A little shiver ran down my spine. "I didn't expect him to be so young. How many tricks can someone that age have up his sleeve?" He snickered.

I said nothing and kept my eyes firmly fixed on a couch leg carved into a lion's head and paw.

"Yes, do tell us," Popilla agreed, her tone caustic. "You can't be more than fifteen. How do we know that this isn't the only dinner you know how to prepare?"

Apicius shot his mother a look that could have turned a basilisk to stone. The tension grew thick with the implied insult to her son. The eyes of the would-be suitor at her side grew wide at the exchange.

"He is nearly twenty, mother. Thrasius, tell them where you learned your skills." Apicius smiled at me but the warning note in his eye was clear.

I drew in a breath. "I learned from Meton, the coquus to Flavius Maximus before me. I was in his kitchen for seven years. He took me under his wing when he saw that I had a talent for understanding spices. He taught me everything, but I always wanted to experiment. He was very old and as the years passed I did more and more of the cooking in Maximus's kitchen. After Meton died, Maximus made me coquus. I was called coquus in his kitchen for eighteen months." I did not add that Meton and Maximus were both like fathers to me and that I still greatly mourned their passing.

"I've heard of Meton!" Trio exclaimed. "Remember when your sister stayed with us, Celera? She was raving about him. Said that he was the best cook she had ever encountered. Her husband was very jealous."

"Her husband was quite a gourmand, was he not?" Aelia asked.

Apicius's irritation had turned to delight. "One of the best palates in all of Rome, if I recall, right, Celera?"

"Yes, may his genius live on—my brother-in-law is well missed."

To my relief, Fannia changed the subject. "This ham is delightful! The pastry is perfect, so crisp and flaky." Her smile highlighted the wrinkles that lined her face. She was heavier than the other women and her dark reddish-brown wig was worn high on her head with curls that puffed out, making her head look as big as an overstuffed pillow. "I must have the recipe for my new cook. If I send over a wax tablet, could you have it transcribed for me?"

"I have tablets, Fannia. And this boy can write the recipe himself. Isn't that true, Thrasius?"

"Yes, Dominus. I would be happy to write out the recipe."

"Who taught you how to write?" Popilla asked me, her mouth full of pork, and her tone accusatory.

I had met women like her. No answer I gave was going to satisfy.

Popilla eyed me, waiting for an answer. "Well?"

I struggled to keep the revulsion out of my voice, finding it easier to look at Aelia as I spoke. Her calm demeanor diminished the horror I felt knowing that Popilla likely had arranged for the murder of my predecessor. "Maximus had me schooled to read and write Latin, Greek, Egyptian, and Spanish. I can also understand a little Persian. He thought everyone in his household should be educated." I lowered my eyes to avoid Popilla's critical stare.

"I know some people are opposed to educated slaves. . . ." Aelia leaned forward on the couch. Her eyes flickered toward the edge of my tunic, which I was twisting nervously in my hands. I stopped the twisting and sat up straighter, determined not to let my nervousness show through. She continued, "But I agree with Maximus's way. There are many advantages to schooling every member of the household. I suspect Rúan can teach you a bit of Celtic. He's from that island just off of Britannia."

Octavius plucked off the tail of his pig and waved it at me. "So he is Hibernian? Ha! Well, then, Thrasius, I imagine he could teach you how to be pretty fierce as well!"

Octavius was at least twice the age of his wife, with graying hair and a paunch that was evident despite the folds of his toga. "What a wonder it would have been to see such a creature painted blue with that mess of red hair coming at you, spear in hand!" His wife giggled a soft, girlish laugh. She herself wore a red wig, but red was a common color for wigs. To see someone like Rúan with naturally red hair was quite unusual. I imagined it was often a subject of conversation at Apicius's parties.

"I don't think he ever wore paint or carried a spear," Aelia reprimanded with a smile. "He came to my family when he was just a boy. His father may have worn the blue war marks but Rúan was too young."

"You have a bunch of youths running your kitchen, it seems, Apicius. How honed can this boy's sense of taste be?" Octavius's question cut through the laughter.

I looked up, then back down to the lion carving. "I might be young, but cooking has always come easily to me," I said, hoping my voice didn't waver. I raised my eyes again, but not my head. "I have always had an intense palate. When flavors blend well, it is like harmony in the mouth. I think about how the components can come together to make each dish sing."

Fannia murmured in approval but Octavius wasn't impressed.

"Did you think that the abundance of sand in my oyster would make my dish sing?" He turned to Apicius. "If you like, I can send my cook, Herakles, over to show your slave how to properly shuck them. Even Caesar has commented on the skills of my coquus. I think that Corvinus himself is jealous of Herakles's skills."

I didn't know who Corvinus was and I didn't care. But he was lying about the sand. I had inspected each oyster myself.

"A thousand pardons," I said, my voice quavering and my blood boiling.

Apicius began to speak but his wife interjected. "Oh, Octavius, it was just a mistake. My mistake, in fact," Aelia said. What in Jupiter's name was she doing?

"Apicius, dear husband, I was in the kitchen this evening and I fear that it was I who distracted the poor boy preparing the oysters. He must have missed one when I was talking to him."

Octavius squinted at me. "Slave, wouldn't you have inspected each oyster before it went out?"

I opened my mouth but Aelia again came to my rescue. "He intended to, but in the interest of expediency, I told Thrasius that I had looked them over and then I had the boy put them in the snow room. We have not had him long but I imagine he wouldn't dare disobey me, would you, Thrasius?"

"No, Domina."

"Good. Please send out some new oysters for dear Octavius. We mustn't have him leave unhappy."

"No, no, do not concern yourself," Octavius said, his jowls shaking. "I'll be fine."

Aelia winked at me and Apicius dismissed me with a small wave of his hand.

I was disconcerted when I left, and was several paces away before I realized I had gone in the wrong direction. Sotas tsked softly when my error took me close to his post near the door. He waved me over to him.

"Thank the gods for Aelia!" he said, leaning down so I could hear.

"Is that man always so unbearable?" I watched as Octavius licked his fat fingers of ham sauce.

"Always. And he knows what to say to get under everyone's skin. That mention of Corvinus, for example. He has the post that Apicius wants—cultural and gastronomic adviser to Caesar."

"I see."

"Clearly you made Octavius nervous or he wouldn't have made that jab. Look at Apicius. You can still see the irritation on his brow."

I turned my attention to my master. He did seem to be brooding, saying very little while his guests chatted around him.

"I've heard all the ways that Dominus would like to rid the world of Octavius—dumping him in boiling water, slashing his neck with a dagger in a dark alley, infusing his wine with oleander. The list is endless. I'm sure you'll get a sense of it soon enough."

Aelia's body-slave was perched on the edge of a huge flowerpot between us and the diners. She paused for a drink of water and then picked up the lyre once again. Sotas smiled in her direction. "That's Helene," he said simply, but longing was evident in his voice. I changed the subject.

"I've not met a body-slave as well spoken as you. Where are you from?"

He paused for a moment, as though considering if I were worth the story. "I'm Egyptian," he finally said, confirming my suspicion. "My father died before I was born and my mother was forced to sell me into slavery when she could no longer afford to feed me. Apicius's father bought me and brought me to Rome. He had me trained for several years to be a body-slave to Apicius. I was educated, much like you seem to be."

"Do you advise him?"

"Sometimes. But I'm not his adviser."

Something about his manner said he wasn't interested in continuing that line of conversation. I looked back at the diners. "Why does Dominus Apicius dislike Octavius?"

Sotas snorted, his massive chest lifting with the gesture. "Dominus met him six years ago, when Octavius was summering in Minturnae. Octavius took him under his wing, teaching him about politics, parties, and Rome. He's the one who convinced Apicius to buy the villa here in Baiae, where he could meet influential Romans who came down for vacation. Octavius was a mentor at first, but over time he became ambitious and jealous, acting more as a rival than a friend. He's an arrogant, name-dropping fool. Fannia keeps telling Dominus to stop inviting him over, but I know that he won't. He will keep him close."

That surprised me. "Fannia tells him what to do?"

"Yes. Fannia Drusilla has been like a surrogate mother to Apicius since he was ten years old. She used to live next door to the Gavii in Minturnae. Dominus never saw much of his father and, well, when you get to know Popilla, you'll understand why the two of them aren't close."

"Do Popilla and Fannia get along?"

"Ha!" Sotas scoffed. "No, Fannia and Popilla are always going at it. Apicius never listens to Popilla. It's one reason Popilla has become such a bitter old shrew. She is constantly vying for her son's attention." He tilted his head in their direction.

Apicius's voice rose as he became more animated. "Fannia, remember the time when Mother held that big cena for Consul Calpurnius Piso?" He patted Popilla on the shoulder in a bit of lighthearted, but obvious, pity. Popilla shrugged his hand off. Her eyes were black and hard.

"Yes! That cena was a shipwreck," Fannia teased Popilla. "Poor dear, you didn't know the first thing about throwing a dinner party. The wine was plonk from Surrentine, the shrimp were tough, and you didn't even serve a gustatio to start the guests out!" Fannia waved her spoon as she spoke. "I had to take things into my own hands for the next party! Thank the gods Apicius was a quick study!"

Popilla seethed, concentrating on the plate before her, scooping up tidbits of ham and pastry with her fingers. Her would-be suitor had shifted a few more inches away from her over the course of the conversation.

When Popilla spoke, it was to pose a barbed question to Fannia. "Where is Pulcher this evening?"

Popilla's question left a sheen of tension in the air as thick as a temple curtain. Celera drew in an audible breath and Apicius seemed to bristle. Fannia was the only one who seemed unperturbed. "Pulcher is in Macedonia negotiating a new trade line of wine." She turned to Apicius.

"Would you like me to put in an order for a few amphorae of the latest vintage? I imagine you have room in one of your cellars."

Popilla delivered her own perfect, hemlock-edged smile. "You and Pulcher make such a sweet couple. I imagine you miss him very much. Will he be home in time for the Saturnalia festival?"

A large flock of seagulls flew overhead with a raucous noise, turning the diners' attention away from Popilla's question. Excited conversation broke out as the guests tried to contemplate what the sign meant. Popilla looked so angry at the distraction, I thought she might burst.

Sotas chuckled softly next to me. "Serves the old witch right."

"Who's Pulcher?"

"Fannia's new husband, Quintus Claudius Pulcher. Her first husband died a few years ago and recently Fannia was forced to marry Pulcher by her cousin, Livia. You know, Caesar's wife?"

I coughed with surprise.

"Yes, that Livia," Sotas continued. "When Livia was made to divorce Tiberius Claudius Nero in favor of Caesar Augustus, she was more devastated than most would guess. Especially when Fannia started sleeping with her ex-husband."

"I imagine that would make Livia a little angry."

"Quite angry. She and Fannia used to be close until that happened so the betrayal was even more of an affront. There was no proof, only widespread rumors from her slaves, so Livia had to be creative in her revenge. You know that rule, the one Caesar put in place that men and women need to be married?"

"Yes, I know it. Dumb rule, in my opinion."

"Most would agree with you. At any rate, Livia suggested to Caesar that Fannia marry Pulcher, and Caesar made it so."

I saw Rúan appear at the doorway on the other side of the triclinium. He saw me and waved his arms.

"What's so bad about Pulcher?" I asked, knowing I should go but wanting to hear the rest of the strange tale.

"When Fannia was young, Pulcher's family and Fannia's were once close and often vacationed together. Rumor has it that on one of those shared holidays, someone raped and strangled Fannia's older sister and dumped her body into a fountain. There was no proof but Fannia has always sworn it was Pulcher.

"Jump forward fifteen years and Fannia, who was newly widowed, makes the mistake of sleeping with Livia's ex-husband. Livia was furious. She bided her time and when Pulcher's wife died, she exacted her revenge and made sure Fannia was the one to remarry Pulcher. The one thing that Livia didn't count on was that Pulcher is always traveling, meaning that Fannia barely sees her husband. They despise each other and he stays far away."

The sun had set and the last red and pink streaks had begun to fade over the distant ocean. Apicius snapped his fingers at one of the slave boys to light the lamps.

"Go back through the house." Sotas jerked his head toward the hallway behind him. "That way you don't have to cross in view of everyone."

I nodded and slipped behind him toward the corridor. There was a cluster of boys playing dice in the hall.

"You! Tycho! Now! Go light the lamps!" Behind me Sotas's voice was low but cutting. A young boy about the age of seven, with a mop of dark curly hair, rushed forward while the other boys followed him to illuminate the diners.

I stopped one of the boys before he could get far and had him guide me through the halls back to the kitchen, where Rúan was frantic, wondering if the next course should go out. It would have been just my luck if I had gotten lost in the labyrinth of corridors in the domus.

The rest of the evening passed almost without incident. Apicius did not notice the missing glasses, Octavius begrudgingly agreed that the meal was delicious, and Popilla excused herself early because she was "tired."

When the last of the meal was delivered and the wine was opened up, I leaned on the doorway and watched the plates of olives, grapes, fine cheeses, and honeyed almonds go out to the guests.

Apicius was talking with Trio and his wife, Celera. Celera reached for the just-delivered morels in wine. "When are you coming to Rome?" she asked Apicius.

"Not just yet," said my new dominus. "I think we want to wait a couple of years until Apicata is older."

The corners of Octavius's mouth curled upward slightly. I thought it interesting that he was pleased Apicius would not be coming to Rome anytime soon.

"Besides, look at this view!" Aelia extended her hand toward the darkly glittering sea. "Why would we want to give this up? Even if I had a house in Rome, I would still want to be here!"

"True, true," conceded Trio. "However, there is much to be said about Rome. The people, the parties, and, oh, the games! You must visit soon and we'll take you to the races, or to see the gladiators! There is no finer sport than watching the gladiators!"

"I care little for the gladiators." Aelia wrinkled her nose. "So barbarous!"

"Ahh, but I bet you might like the meat!"

She opened her mouth in a horrified O. "From the gladiators?"

The group broke out laughing.

"No, no! From the animals!"

My interest was piqued. What I wouldn't give for some of the rare meat distributed after a match! Meat from bears, tigers, rhinoceros, and other exotic animals killed in the height of battle was highly prized due to the heated blood that ran through the veins when the beast perished. I wanted the chance to serve up such delicacies.

"I have an in with the right people at the games," Octavius bragged.

"Of course you do," Apicius said dismissively. "Trio, do you go to the games often?"

"I do! If you come to Rome I can promise you excellent seats, not far from Livia and Augustus!"

Apicius smiled widely at his Roman friend, ignoring Fannia's small groan of derision at the mention of her cousin's name. "I would love to go to the games with you, Trio. I would absolutely love to."

"All this heavy food has made me weary," Octavius said loudly, interjecting himself into the conversation. To me he didn't look weary, only bored.

His body-slave rushed forward to help Octavius off the couch. He took his leave of the party and Sotas stepped forward to escort him out of the house. Before he left he turned his head to where I stood in the kitchen doorway. Subtly, so that Apicius and the rest of the dining guests could not see, he raised his hand slightly and gave me a one-finger salute. I instinctively tucked my body back into the kitchen, and quickly sent a prayer off to Jupiter, for protection from that terrible envy, Invidia.

When I glanced back, he was gone. My heart hammered within my chest. I had only just met the man but already he felt angered and threatened by me. It seemed the rivalry between Apicius and Octavius was deeper than Sotas had let on.

PART II

1 C.E. to 2 C.E.

PEACOCK MEATBALLS

Peacock meatballs rank in the first place, provided they are fried until they burst their skins. Pheasant meatballs rank in the second place, then rabbit third, then chicken fourth, and tender young pork ones are fifth.

—*Book 2.2.6, Meat Dishes*
On Cookery, Apicius

CHAPTER 4

We didn't see Octavius much in the following years. He went to Rome, where he quickly climbed the patrician ranks, which irked my master to no end. But I had a bigger concern—Popilla. She took every opportunity to make my life miserable.

She kept the worst of her torments for when Apicius was not around. She was fond of having her lackey, a burly house guard whose name I never learned, administer the lash.

Seven months after my purchase, Apicius went to his villa in Minturnae for a few days. On the fifth day he was gone, Popilla decided that I did not add enough garum to a dish of lamb.

"This is the most miserable piece of meat I have ever eaten!" she screamed, picking up the pieces on her plate and flinging them across the triclinium. The scissor slave who had been cutting up her meat backed away and cowered in the corner.

I stood in the corridor ready to send in my serving boy, Tycho, with the next course. At her scream, little Tycho tilted the plate of mustard beans he was carrying and they skittered in slimy trails all over the floor. He immediately burst into tears, terrified of the beating he might receive. I took the plate from his hand.

"Back to the kitchen, hurry," I said, just loud enough for him to hear. I did not want him to be the one to receive the lash.

I stepped around him and entered the room, wondering if this night would be my last. Each day of Apicius's absence Popilla had grown even bolder.

"You! Not only are you a terrible coquus but you are a clumsy oaf too! You can't even hold a plate steady. Are your hands broken? No? Perhaps if they were you would have an excuse for your mediocrity!"

I saw her chin jerk toward her guard and next thing I knew I felt the lash upon my back. The plate crashed to the ground, and when I fell, the terra-cotta shards tore into the skin of my chin and chest. The guard kicked me. I felt the lash tear into my back again and the world swam for a second, then went black.

I did not see or hear what happened next, but, fortunately for me, and for my hands, Apicius had come home early. A screaming match ensued as well as a few brutal slaps to Popilla's harpy face. Rúan told me about it the next day when he came to see me as I lay curled on my pallet, bruised and sporting many cuts that would turn to scars. It was a week before I could return to the kitchen. I hated Popilla more than I had ever hated anyone and I wished every day for her disappearance from the earth.

Aside from the troubles with Popilla, my time in Apicius's kitchen passed as fast as an eastern wind over the ocean. My work was hard but I felt very alive then, more so than I ever had. Rúan and I became fast friends and his presence by my side at each meal was part of my early success. We seemed to inherently understand each other and his love of cooking was surpassed only by mine. Some of my most classic dishes were developed with his collaboration.

Rúan greatly missed Hibernia, his country in the north, which he called Ériu. While I had only ever known life as a slave, he was captured as a youth and his desire to be free was still strong within him. Sometimes we would daydream what it would be like to be the master, not the slave.

"But who would cook?" I once asked. "I do not think I could trust a slave."

Rúan laughed, his deep chuckle reverberating through the kitchen. "Aye, you are right. We have high standards, my friend. Who on the gods' green earth could cook a meal as fine as ours?"

Our meals were fine indeed. I often cooked around a specific theme, whether it be only foods from the sea, foods that began with a certain letter, or perhaps those that came from a certain region. I was adamant that the servants who delivered the food were both pleasing to the eye and able to serve the dishes with incredible precision and flair. The music that accompanied the meal had to create a specific ambience. The actors and acrobats I hired were elegant even when comedic. But the centerpiece of everything was, for me and for Apicius, the food. And while my master loved my cooking and believed I worked hard out of loyalty and dedication, in truth, it was my own pride that drove me in the kitchen. I was only a slave, but in this I knew I had great power. I experimented ruthlessly, tweaking recipes to highlight and bring out the finest flavors. I wanted, perhaps too much, for everything to be perfect.

It was not long before Apicius's parties became the talk of Baiae. His couches were always full. I took great pleasure when I would walk to the market to make a purchase and overhear a passerby talking about how very much he would like an invitation to dine with Apicius. My dominus began to brag about my skills in the kitchen to all he knew.

I had asked for success on my first day and for that I kept my promise to the Lares. Every day I offered up a honey cake for their favor. It's a promise I held to for many years, until the day I knew beyond all doubt that the haruspex's words had not been false.

I had a greater devotee than Apicius, however, in his little girl, five-year-old Apicata. She was bubbly and vivacious, with a head of chestnut-brown curls that always seemed to be in disarray, and she loved the little animals I carved for her out of radishes and parsnips. Every time I saw her she asked if I would make her some new animal with her next meal. I was only too happy to oblige. I saw her nearly every day, which meant that I saw Passia every day as well. When I saw the flash of her stola in the entryway, my heart would beat like a temple drum.

Passia! Her name was a song in my mind. Whenever she came into the kitchen I thought I might faint with desire. Everything about her was perfect. Her long auburn hair was perfect against her tanned skin. Her eyes were a perfect ebony brown, her wrists perfect and delicate, her voice a melody that I wished I could hear every waking moment of my life.

She wanted nothing to do with me.

Months passed, and no matter how often I tried to strike up a conversation when she came to the kitchen to eat or to pick up a tray for Apicata, nothing I did or said could convince her to share more than a few words with me. If I saw her in other parts of the domus, she walked by, eyes on the tiles. I stopped her once on my way back from the Lares shrine, but she only glared at me and turned in the other direction.

I tried to casually ask Sotas about her but he saw right through me. "Give up now, Coquus. She is the dream of every slave in this household. In her mind you are no different. She wants nothing to do with any of you."

Eventually I stopped asking her questions. I spoke to her only when she spoke to me or I needed to tell her something about the food she was taking to Apicata. I carved her roses out of radishes every day and placed them on every plate she picked up. She said nothing. She too thought I carved them for little Apicata.

Apicius saw the roses as a complement to the dishes I cooked and soon was asking me to carve more elaborate designs out of gourds and other vegetables. He often remarked on my talent with the carving knife. However, despite the success of our banquets, it wasn't easy working for Apicius. I made a few mistakes early on, like dropping a platter full of fritters all over the kitchen floor when he made a surprise visit, or forgetting to add salt to a dish. In the beginning, my dominus was very harsh with me. I discovered that he was prone to wide shifts in mood. One moment he would be kind and giving to everyone around him and the next he was instructing Sotas to administer the lash. I didn't speak much at first, preferring to err on the side of caution, but as I grew to know my dominus better, I learned how to discern his intent and how to avoid scars on my back. Eventually he became more forgiving even when I did make mistakes, provided they weren't any that might embarrass him in front of others.

The first time Apicius joined me in the kitchen was disconcerting. It was late afternoon, a few hours before the evening cena. I was preparing a date sauce for a roasted lamb shoulder. I had just begun chopping up the onions, carrots, and parsnips when my master arrived in the kitchen. He strode over to my table and gave me a big grin.

"Pass me a knife, boy."

I backed up a step.

"No, no." He laughed. "Close that mouth, you'll catch flies. I don't want to kill you; I want to chop those carrots."

I couldn't believe my ears. My master wanted to help me chop carrots?

Apicius laughed. "Hand me a knife, Thrasius."

I pushed the knife I had in my hand across the table. He picked it up and began chopping the thick white vegetables as though he had worked in a kitchen all his life.

"Don't just stand there." He gestured with the knife. "That onion isn't going to chop itself."

I chuckled nervously, took up another knife, and started to chop.

"You are wondering why I'm chopping vegetables with you." It wasn't a question.

"The thought had crossed my mind, Dominus."

He pushed the chopped carrot to the side and took up the parsnips. "When I am in the kitchen, making food, it is as though the gods are with me."

"What do you mean, Dominus?" I was not accustomed to asking my master questions, but Apicius seemed to be inviting conversation.

"I feel a sense of calmness, of true competence, infusing me. The same energy fills me when I am chopping and stirring, or when I discover a new wine vintage. Such culinary experiences bring me great pleasure."

"I think I understand," I said. I wasn't lying. I did know that sense of flow. It overtook me too when I cooked.

"I used to cook often with Paetas, when he was alive."

"I am honored to have you cook with me," I ventured, unsure how my words would be received. Was I being presumptuous?

"What's next?" he asked.

"We need to grind some pepper." I pushed the mortar toward him, then poured a generous handful of peppercorns into the stone basin.

"And silphium?"

I gave him a genuine smile then. Silphium was a precious herb I used in many of my dishes, but in recent years it had become quite scarce and costly. It had a taste that was reminiscent of leeks, garlic, and fennel, but smoother and more aromatic. It was one of Apicius's favorite flavors.

"Definitely silphium."

After that time in the kitchen, Apicius came to work with me often, usually on days when guests had not been invited to cena. He loved to cook nearly as much as I did and cared not what anyone said of him. He even occasionally bragged to his guests of his skill with a knife or how he was looking for the perfect way to meld the flavors of a new sauce. He seemed happiest when he was cooking, and there was a kindness to him that was not as evident when I served him outside the kitchen.

"Ambrosial!" Apicius said to me yet again one afternoon as we chopped beets for the evening meal.

The knife revealed dark rings with every slice. There was something precious to me about black food—sinister yet seductive. Oh, how the beet juice would look in glass goblets, the torchlight glinting off the black surface! Apicius loved beet juice, and the rumors about its powers as an aphrodisiac were always a wonderful source of conversation with his guests.

Apicius's voice jolted me out of my thoughts.

"Popilla . . . she's left you well enough alone?"

I hesitated, trying to find the words to be judicious. While I knew that Apicius also did not like his mother, I was a slave, and to be critical of any matron was not wise. I didn't dare mention that when I did cross her path she called me vulgar names and told me all the ways she'd cursed me.

"I try to stay out of her way," I said truthfully. "She complains about most of the food sent to her room even though she eats half of it before she sends it back."

"I don't understand why someone doesn't want the ridiculous dowry I have offered up. Do so many others know how awful she is?" he muttered as he sliced the beets with a vengeance.

"Watch your fingers, Dominus!"

He slowed his chopping. "You can't trust her. Be careful." He set the knife down. "I have another matter to discuss. Thanks to you, I now have a new problem to manage."

A knot of worry took hold of my stomach. I prided myself on not inciting more of my master's wrath than a cuff on the back of the head. Apicius was mostly fair, but I learned early on that it would not do to cross him; in that regard he was similar to his mother. Only a week before, one of the slaves carrying Apicius's litter had stumbled on a rock and Apicius had Sotas beat him in public in the center of Baiae. I ran through last week's menus in my mind, trying to remember if anything had gone wrong.

I wiped my hands on a towel. "Dominus, I work hard to do your bidding. I have never wanted to be a problem to you. Please tell me what I can do to be better in your service."

Apicius smiled. "You mistake my words. My problem is a happy one. You see, I have to figure out how I can keep track of the long list of clients and associates wanting a dinner invite! Everyone is talking about you. I can't go anywhere without someone asking me what new succulent dishes my coquus has devised!"

The pressure in my chest eased.

"I want you to help me manage my clients. Up until now I've not needed to worry. I know my secretary could help me keep track, but I think that you, as the keeper of my kitchen and the source of my guests' delight, should have a say in helping me make the right determinations. In my mind the coordination of the guests is as important as the coordination of the food. I know how you work. Your mind is strong and nothing escapes you. My secretary is good at figures but not at the nuances of understanding people, food, and feast. We'll start at the *salutatio*. I'll inform him that he will train you."

Apicius was asking me to take on one of the most important roles in the household—advising him about clients during their morning visits.

"Are you sure, Dominus? I have never served in that capacity before. I'm just a cook."

Apicius raised an eyebrow at me. "You are more than a cook. You are the key to my success. It's time for you to demonstrate just how much."

I gripped the edge of the counter to steady myself. For a master to give so much credit to a slave was unheard of. While a part of me was pleased, another part was terrified at the task he was suggesting.

"Rúan can manage the morning meal. On feast days one of my secretaries can step in to advise me so you can be in the kitchen, but on most mornings, I want you by my side."

I wasn't sure what to say. I was surprised at how happy I was at his words. I knew managing his client affairs alongside meals would be a great deal of work, but it seemed to me more of a reward than I had ever had before.

For the first time in my life I thought there might be something greater in my future than working hard as a kitchen slave, toiling for my monthly *peculium* until I turned thirty-five, and would, at the mercy of my master, be eligible for manumission.

"I am honored, Dominus." I didn't trust myself to say anything more.

"Good. I feel good about this, Thrasius."

After we sliced up the rest of the vegetables, I showed Apicius one of the recipes I had in mind, beet leaves stuffed with a mixture of chopped leeks, coriander, cumin, and raisins, bound together with a bit of flour and water. Together we tied up the leaves into small bundles, which would be boiled when it was closer to the dinner hour. At the evening's convivium, they would be served in a sauce of *liquamen*, oil, and vinegar.

When we had finished tying off the last of the beet bundles, Passia came into the kitchen, Apicata in tow. My heart raced.

"I'm hungry!" Apicata declared. Her dark hair was pulled back into a braid and tied with saffron-colored ribbons, her blue tunica marred by smudges of dirt. I smiled. Even children of nobility liked to play in the mud.

"You are always hungry!" Apicius said, his deep voice booming. "It's as though I sired a bear, not a daughter!"

"I'm not a bear!" She placed her hands on her hips.

I couldn't help but chuckle. "I know what will help," I said, picking up a nearby radish. I began carving it into a rose with delicate petals. Although they had seen me carve vegetables before, Apicius, Passia, and Apicata sat in rapt attention as I turned several of the radishes into flowers.

"A beautiful lady should have beautiful flowers." I placed a small cluster of radish flowers in Apicata's hand. On impulse, I presented one of the radish flowers to Passia. Much to my disappointment, she handed it to Apicata.

Apicata was delighted. "Are you sure I can eat these? They're so pretty!"

"Eat up, sweet one. And if you ask, I am sure Thrasius will make a pear patina tonight." Apicius's voice always held a special warmth when he addressed his daughter.

"Please, Thrasius! I love it when you make the pears pretty!"

I laughed at her description of the fruit, honey, and egg dish. I always added an extra layer of pears on top, and I had to admit, they did look pretty once they were cooked and shining with oil. "I would be pleased to make that for you, little Domina."

Spontaneously, Apicata ran around the table and gave me a big hug. She ran back to Passia and together they left the kitchen.

"She likes you," Apicius observed. He took off the apron protecting his tunic and laid it on the counter.

"She is charming," I replied, though I wished Apicius had been talking about Passia. "She reminds me of my sister." Or at least she reminded me of what I thought I remembered about the little girl whom I was separated from so long ago. I was a twin, born to a slave woman who died in childbirth and whose name I never knew. My sister and I were raised by another slave in a respected domus in Pompeii until we were four. When that patrician died, the household slaves were willed to several different relatives and we were separated. I don't know what happened to her.

"And you. You like Passia." Apicius fingered one of the carved radishes that hadn't fit into Apicata's hand.

I froze, unsure of what to say.

What Apicius said next shocked me more than if Jupiter himself had appeared in the kitchen.

"I will let Passia know she is to make herself available to you as you desire."

I dropped my knife. It clattered to the floor with a noise that caught the attention of a few nearby slaves.

"Careful there. You wouldn't want to stab one of your feet, or something worse," Apicius said with a hint of amusement in his voice.

"You are right, Dominus," I said, bending to pick up the knife. "I'll be more careful." I could feel my face on fire.

I did not sleep with the other slaves in the high reaches of the domus. Instead I had my own *cubiculum* on the ground floor not far from the kitchen. It was one way that my master doted on me; he always said that he wanted me well rested, not kept awake by whispers and snores of other slaves. It was why I was startled that night when the door to my cubiculum creaked. I was not accustomed to the sounds of others in my room. I slid my hand under my pillow to grasp the knife I kept there. I opened my eyes to the soft light of an oil lamp piercing the darkness.

Passia. I let go of the knife. My heart pounding, I sat up.

She shut the door behind her and put her lamp on the table next to my bed. My every nerve tingled with anticipation upon seeing her closer in the lamplight, her hair cascading down around her face.

Wordlessly she lifted her thin shift up and over her head until she stood naked before me. I was light-headed. She was far more beautiful than I had imagined all those nights in the dark, alone with my hand beneath the blankets. Her body was shapelier than any statue of Venus, breasts firm and taut, with hardened nipples that stood out from a swirl of dark amber. The heart of hair between her legs beckoned me, and when she moved toward the bed, my body responded. All my limbs seemed to reach toward her, desiring to twine around and through her, to converge in a haze headier than any opiate or honeyed wine.

She pulled the blankets down to the end of the bed and looked me over. Then, slowly, her face devoid of emotion, she leaned down and her hand reached out to touch my chest. A shudder of pleasure swept through me. Surely I was dreaming.

She ran her hand across my chest and between my legs, where I was already hard and willing. I gasped when she curled her hand around my penis. I reached up to touch her but she pulled back so that her breast was out of reach.

"Please, come here," I breathed, holding out my hands, willing her to move toward me.

She did not.

Despite the intense pleasure that was radiating through me, I also felt an underlying current of sadness. She didn't want me to touch her.

Apicius's words came back to me. *"I will let Passia know she is to make herself available . . ."*

I leaned forward and put my hand over hers, stopping her movement. It took everything I had not to let her keep going. The flickering shadow of her breast on the wall nearly did me in.

"Stop." My voice wavered.

Hesitantly, she pulled back and perched on the bed beside me. I sat up and gathered up the blankets to pull around her lithe, enticing frame.

"I don't understand." Her eyes were dark and unreadable.

"Apicius sent you, didn't he?"

"Yes." She lifted her hand to move a strand of hair out of her eyes.

I wished those fingers were touching me once more. I struggled to imagine her with her clothes on. I tried to think of carving apart pigs, or to imagine myself standing in a pit of snakes . . . anything to lower the level of my desire.

"Do you want to be here?"

She crinkled her brow, just for a second, puzzled by my question. I thought she would tell me that she did, that she would lie, because she was here by the will of Apicius and it was her duty. I was wrong.

"I do not."

She leaned over and picked up her shift. I didn't stop her. I longed to touch the curve of her spine, feel the skin beneath my fingers. But in the space of time between my last and next breath, she was gone.

Oh, Lady Venus, I prayed, *please do not let her have slipped away from me.*

The next morning at the salutatio, Apicius jostled me in the arm when I took my place standing next to his chair. He winked at me and I returned the look with an awkward smile.

At that moment, thank Fortuna, the first client arrived, one of Apicius's neighbors, a balding man who I remembered owned swaths of vineyards east of Baiae. I was glad for the interruption; my anger was such that I was sure to have said something that would have warranted punishment for disobedience.

As a patron, Apicius was the benefactor to many individuals, each of whom looked to him for advice, protection, loans, or political connections. In return these clients, a mixture of *equites* and *plebs*, would provide important political votes and support, information, hard goods, or favors of all kinds. Every morning all across the Empire, patrons met with their clients at the salutatio to discuss whatever business was at hand.

My first salutatio was the easiest, as I had no real duties other than to watch and learn. Apicius's secretary did all the work, reminding Apicius of the history of various clients, advising him about decisions that might affect his relationships with other patricians, and helping him decide who would have a seat on his couch for the cena that night. Sometimes he would advise Apicius to instruct certain clients to fulfill particular favors, such as running errands, casting votes on bills in the local senate, or bartering items needed for the household. In some cases, Apicius handled the meeting without assistance. Each client was shown in to meet with Apicius in turn, for five to ten minutes and no more.

At the end of the salutatio, I was overwhelmed with the enormity of what was being asked of me. Sotas had been dismissed while Apicius went to take a bath and he sat with me while I went over the books with the secretary.

"Looks like you might rather be back in the kitchen?" Sotas teased.

"How can I be expected to keep track of all that?" I said, collapsing into Apicius's open chair.

"Do not fret," the aged secretary said to me, squinting as he finished taking notes on his wax tablet. "Apicius wants you to advise him primarily. You will have secretaries like me to take notes and inform you. Afterward, we will meet to go over what transpired and you will decide what actions need to be taken."

I thought the old man would be perturbed that his position was being partially usurped, but instead he was relieved. It turned out that he wasn't fond of the role. "I'd much rather be behind the scenes," he confided. I wondered if perhaps I would too.

"It gets easier," Sotas reassured me after the secretary left.

"It's the same fifty or so people, and once in a while one of Apicius's clients from another town will pop in with a request. You'll get to know each of them and their quirks pretty quickly."

"I hope so," I said, but I didn't feel hopeful.

"I have names for them all," he whispered, picking up the goblet of wine that Apicius had left behind and downing it with a single quaff. "When your duties are to stand next to Apicius all day you have to make a game of it."

Sotas gazed off across the atrium as he remembered who had been at the salutatio that morning. "The first one, the guy with the grapevines . . ."

I consulted my list. "Arvina?"

"You mean Gator Mouth."

I laughed. Arvina had a mouth full of teeth that looked a bit too pointy to be real.

We continued to banter about names until the bath slave came to tell Sotas that Apicius was asking for him.

"Do you have a name for Dominus?" I asked as he stood to leave.

I had never seen Sotas look offended, but in that moment, he truly was. "May Fides strike me down, no."

I watched him go, shocked at the depths of the loyalty he held for Apicius. What slave held his master in such high regard?

After the salutatio, I returned to the kitchen to help Rúan start preparations for the rest of the day. I was carving flowers and animals for Apicata's *prandium,* the lunchtime snack, when Passia walked in.

I caught my breath at the sight of her, dreading the awkwardness that I expected to follow in the wake of the previous night's encounter.

She came right to the table where I worked, ready to retrieve the tray, just as she did every day. I set it in front of her. My heart beat so hard that I was almost sure she could hear it.

"Thank you, Thrasius."

She looked at me then, her dark eyes locking with mine. It was the first time she had ever said my name. Then she turned away, tray in hand.

"Wait! You forgot this," I said, placing a large radish flower next to the plate on her tray.

She smiled at me, a small but genuine smile, held more in her eyes than on her lips. She nodded her head at me then departed.

That afternoon, before the cena, I ran to the temple of Venus in the center of town and left a honey cake at her feet.

A few days later, I awoke to the sound of women wailing in a distant part of the house. I scrambled from my bed and threw my clothes on. When I reached the commotion, I found Sotas and a handful of other guards in the hallway before Apicius's bedchamber, waving curious slaves back to their duties. Passia stood in the corridor, her face a mask of worry. Before he sent me away, Sotas indicated that I should cancel the salutatio. He was too busy to explain further.

Passia fell into step with me on my way to the kitchen.

Surprised, but pleased, I asked her if she knew what had happened.

She nodded her head and folded her arms close to her body as she walked. "Domina miscarried. It's the third child she has lost."

Then I understood the shrieks of grief, which were likely not from Aelia but from her mourning slaves. I hadn't even known Domina was pregnant, but suddenly I understood some of her strange food requests of the past few weeks.

Passia spat into the flower bed lining one edge of the atrium to ward against the evil eye. It was a strong gesture that I did not expect from someone like her.

"It's Popilla. She cursed Domina. I know she did. She's trying to force Apicius to put our Domina aside for not giving him an heir. She never thought Aelia was good enough for Apicius. No one is ever good enough. I bet there is a leaden scroll stuffed in the cracks of Popilla's family crypt, filled with curses of hate and loathing for the people in her son's life."

"Do you think she'd do that?" I thought of the curses that flew in my direction every time I had the misfortune to run into her.

"I believe that with all my heart. She knows nothing but hatred."

"It is strange to see such jealousy in a mother toward a son."

"Her husband never loved her." Passia wiped tiny beads of summer sweat from her brow. "When he was a child, Apicius was desperate to please his father and he emulated him in every way, including loathing his own mother."

"So she is in conflict," I mused. "She is desperate for Apicius's attention, and yet she would do anything to destroy the things he loves."

Passia nodded. "It's made her easy to hate. Everything she does is dark and mean and petty. Personally, I think she gave her soul to Discordia. She desires nothing more than to wreak havoc on all those around her. She's a selfish, bitter woman."

Venom laced each of Passia's words.

"You hate her even more than I do," I said, venturing a guess. I marveled that she was talking to me at all and I wanted desperately to keep her attention.

"She killed my mother," she said in a low, bitter voice.

I was shocked. I stopped and ushered her into the little chamber that often served as a breakfast area so we could be away from the prying eyes and ears of passing slaves. "What do you mean, she killed your mother?"

Passia looked away, her eyes scanning the painted garden frescoes on the walls. She seemed to be considering whether she wanted to continue the conversation.

"Apicius's father purchased me and my mother when I was three. It was hard growing up in Minturnae with the Gavii. So hard, in fact, that for much of the time when I was young, my mother went out of her way to hide me. I spent most of my time keeping the slave chambers clean or helping out in the vineyards."

She turned back to me. Her eyes held none of the hardness that used to be there when she looked at me. "My mother died when I was six, before Apicius took command of the domus. Popilla was angry that my mother had failed to bring her the correct wine. She had my mother beaten so severely that several of her ribs broke and her lung was punctured. She died that night."

I could feel the sadness radiating from her. After a short, uncomfortable silence, I reached over and took her hands, squeezing them in comfort. "I'm sorry. May Pluto and Proserpina keep her safe."

She let me hold her hands for a moment, then pulled them away. "It's hard to think back to those times. I haven't spoken to anyone of my childhood for many years. It's better not to think of these things. I do not like the darkness that comes when I do."

Passia left then. I watched her go, the wisps of her yellow tunica fluttering against her legs as she walked.

My own hatred toward Popilla had increased a thousandfold.

CHAPTER 5

"Don't leave me!" Aelia lay propped up by dozens of silk-encased pillows. Her voice was shrill despite her weakness, her eyes red with sorrow and her hair greasy and lifeless. It had been five days since she lost the baby and she was still despondent. Her body-slave, Helene, was itching to get Domina into the bath as soon as her strength would allow. That morning I brought some broth for Aelia to sip, but when I made to leave, Apicius commanded me to wait for him. I went to stand with Sotas next to the door, where we faded into the background as Apicius paced the room, instructing one of his new Gallic slaves on what to pack in the large trunk next to the door.

"Please, husband. I need you now. Do not go away to Rome. The signs are all wrong. Lightning broke apart our tree in the courtyard earlier this week. And a crow landed on the windowsill yesterday!"

Apicius looked at his disheveled wife and sighed. "I must. I am expected in Rome for an important convivium that I dare not miss. Fannia invited Consul Messalla Corvinus. You know I want him to commend me to Caesar Augustus. I cannot miss this opportunity."

I was alarmed at my master's lack of empathy. Aelia had been sick for days, and only in the last two had rallied back toward some semblance of her old self. No longer fighting to live, she was free to mourn the loss of her child. Already the slaves were wagering on how soon it would be before Apicius divorced her. He needed a male heir and she didn't seem to be capable of providing one.

"I have been here for you, night and day," he continued, sitting down next to her. "You are getting well, my love, and will be on your feet soon enough. You yourself said you had a dream about a gazelle last night. See? Swift travel is in my future. And when I return, there will be plenty of time to try for another child."

Aelia laid her head on Apicius's shoulder, sobbing as he held her tightly. I exchanged a glance with Sotas. I was glad to see the tender, if rare, side of our dominus.

Apicius stroked her hair. It was hard to hear his whisper. "I promise you, Aelia, I will never leave you or send you away from me. I love you and will be home to you in a fortnight. I go to bring the name of the Gavii greater fame and fortune, all to benefit our family."

Aelia wiped away the tears from her cheeks with the back of her hand.

"Come," Apicius said to me, Sotas, and the slaves who had helped pack his trunks. "We should make haste. It's a long journey ahead."

I groaned when I realized that the reason he had asked me to stay with him was that he meant for me to attend him as well. Since I had taken on his morning salutatio duties, he seemed to want me with him more and more often, much to my chagrin. I did not want to leave Baiae, or, more important, Passia. I wished Aelia's dream of a gazelle would be prophetic, but traveling with Apicius was rarely swift. Apicius's roofed carriage, called a *carpentum*, was especially heavy, adorned with gilded statuary on each corner post and bedecked with thick red curtains. Because of the weight, instead of mules, a team of oxen pulled it on the open road. A small contingent of slaves dressed in bright colors waved red and gold flags ahead of us, clearing peasants out of the way. Armed guards flanked the carriage and protected the party. It was always a spectacular ordeal to travel with Apicius. I was sure it would be slow and arduous for all except my master, who would be ensconced in the carpentum, gambling or listening to poetry by the clients who always found ways to hitch a free ride when he traveled to Rome.

The journey was as I feared. A trip that normally took two days took four. On the first night, it rained heavily, leaving several slaves who slept on the wet ground feverish in the morning. The second day was even worse.

The ambush came in the afternoon, when the sun was at its highest point. The robbers seemed to come out of nowhere, cresting over the hills on horseback, waving their swords in warning.

"Stop the carpentum and put down your weapons," one of the robbers yelled through the cloth that masked all but his eyes. His accent marked him as one of the peasants who lived on the back side of the great mountain Vesuvius.

The carriage rolled to a stop but none of the guards put his weapon down. The slaves who had been walking, including me, huddled against the carpentum in fear. Apicius's guards circled around us, their long rectangular shields forming a wall to hold us safe within.

Apicius had given Sotas a kindness and let him sit in the carpentum for a few miles. When he stepped out of the carriage, an audible gasp arose from the robber closest to me. Sotas was always an imposing figure, but when he traveled, he kept a monstrous *spatha* at his side. The sword was longer than a typical *gladius*, and was used by gladiators in the ring. I had never seen a spatha as large as the one that Sotas carried and it seemed that the bandits had not either. Apicius's guards parted their shields to let Sotas pass through. He held his sword out in front of him.

"Ask me to put my weapon down again," he boomed.

The bandits hesitated, their horses dancing nervously. Then, without warning, one of the robbers spurred his horse forward, intending to slash at Sotas as he rode by. It was not the move of a professional marauder.

Sotas effortlessly cut the man's hand off and the sword clattered to the ground, the hand falling away when it hit the dirt.

"Who is next?" Sotas pointed his sword at the robbers.

Two of them immediately turned and rode off, and the others did not hesitate long before following suit.

"Are they gone?" Apicius sounded bored. He peered through the curtains.

"They are gone, Dominus," Sotas assured him.

"Good. All of us, we must make haste!"

Apicius pushed us hard, making us run for much of the distance until we reached the next way station five miles away. He hired extra soldiers to accompany us but the intrusion had left everyone on edge.

When we arrived in Rome, we all were weary except for Apicius, who was oddly rejuvenated.

Fannia greeted us warmly at her villa on the Caelian Hill. Apicius's clients had already departed—they had secured their ride to Rome and would seek him out again only for the return. Apicius dismissed most of his slaves into the care of Fannia's steward. Sotas and I both longed for the reprieve that the other slaves had while Apicius was in Rome, but instead we found ourselves standing on one side of the atrium while Fannia caught up with Apicius.

"Some honey water will refresh you." She flicked a finger toward a Nubian slave.

Fannia wore a white tunica with an emerald green stola that complemented her auburn hair, piled high upon her head with far too many ringlets framing her face.

Apicius took a seat on the couch opposite his hostess. The midday sun streamed through the atrium overhead.

"You've repainted!" Apicius said with delight as he gazed upon the intricate frescoes decorating the atrium walls. "But aren't you treading a bit on the scandalous?" He gestured at the depiction of Bacchus with his wine-bearing nymphs. I wondered the same thing myself. The cult of Bacchus was not well accepted; Caesar didn't like how rowdy the god's festivals had become.

Her laughter rang through the room. "What the world needs is a good old-fashioned Bacchanalia, I say!"

"Shame about that pesky little decree against them," Apicius teased.

She snorted her derision. "We don't have to call it a Bacchanalia, now, do we?"

Apicius laughed.

"Tell me about Aelia. Is she well?"

"She is. She's most excited about me bringing new furniture home. The list she has for me is leagues long. Couches, tables, and rugs! You must come to visit soon. I know she will be delighted to show off all the new finds I'm going to bring back for the domus."

I forced myself to keep my expression neutral. It wasn't the first time my dominus had lied and I was sure it wouldn't be the last. I closed my eyes and prayed to the gods to get me through this trip and back to Baiae. I longed to see Passia. She had just begun to talk to me a little more each day and I savored every moment. Each day since I had left felt too long.

When I opened my eyes, the Nubian woman was standing in front of me, holding a tray full of glasses of honey water. I was shocked. Slaves were often overlooked and I had expected to remain thirsty until we were dismissed later that day. I took the glass, a tall, pale blue shaft painted with the face and name of Cosmus, a gladiator who was well ranked and beloved by the people. The honey water was sweet and cold. The slave could see the weariness on my face. She set the tray down on a nearby table and went to fetch me and Sotas stools. Fannia's kindness toward her slaves was well known but I had not believed it to be quite so true.

"While I'm in Rome, Fannia, I'm also hoping you can recommend me to a few good toga makers. I'm considering buying several for gifts for my Saturnalia cenae this year. What do you think?" asked Apicius.

"Certainly! Everyone would talk about your generosity!"

Generosity was an understatement. Togas were expensive. Giving them as gifts would further indebt Apicius's key clients.

Apicius leaned back on the couch and sipped his honey water. "Also, do you have a source for Cyrenian silphium? Thrasius has some new sauces that suffer when he uses that wretched asafetida. The taste is not the same." He glanced over at me.

"They are starting to restrict sales. My supplier just came back from Cyrenaica. He told me about another experiment to farm it, but of course it didn't work. Our goddess Ceres is determined not to let anyone but her cultivate it. I strongly suggest you buy as much as you can now. Oh, how I wish it were possible to make a little go far."

Apicius chuckled. "My dear Fannia, let me tell you one of Thrasius's secrets. Take twenty or so pine nuts. Place them in a clay jar with a sprig of silphium, stopper it up, and leave it for at least a week. When you need a taste of silphium, crush up the pine nuts and add it to your dish! It will last for as many weeks as you can keep the nuts fresh—much longer than the herb would itself."

"Brilliant!" she exclaimed. "Oh, the gods were looking down on you the day you found your cook. Is he taking good care of you, Thrasius?"

I nodded my assent and raised my glass in toast.

"I make sure he has all the latest tools for the kitchen and have given him the use of a slave who has caught his fancy." Apicius twirled one of the couch's pillow tassels as he talked, a nervous habit I had learned to identify. "I've even asked him to take over as my aide during the salutatio. I know it is unusual, but I want him to become familiar with my clients—my parties will be all the better when we cater to specific guests."

Fannia patted Apicius on the arm. "Once again, my little caretaker, you have made me proud. Such cleverness!"

She smiled at me and I forced myself to smile back. I was still bristling at Apicius's offhanded mention of giving Passia to me. I so desperately wanted to protect her. I could only hope that Apicius would not consider "giving" her to another.

One of the door slaves entered the atrium and handed Fannia a parcel. The slave withdrew and she opened it, removing a card with flowery script.

"Bastard," she said, scowling.

"Is everything all right?" Apicius sat up in alarm.

"It's from Messalla Corvinus. He is bringing Livia and Publius Octavius with him tonight. He knows you are dining with us but begs I do not invite any others. How presumptuous! Now I have to disinvite people."

My stomach lurched at the sound of those names. I was not anxious to see Octavius again, but it was Livia who gave me pause. I had never met Caesar's wife. Many thought of her as the model Roman matron, and women across the Empire tried to emulate her. The thought of being in a room with someone so renowned filled me with both curiosity and fear.

Apicius also paled. "I wonder how they found out about the cena."

"No doubt someone asked Corvinus where he would be tonight. He can't easily lie to Livia. I'm sure she's coming because of Octavius. He seems to have curried her favor. I heard in the baths today that Octavius is rumored to be on Caesar's short list for gastronomic adviser now that they finally—eight years later—have decided to replace Maecenas. Livia is forever trying to antagonize me. She will do anything to remind me that she will never forgive me for sleeping with her ex-husband. But why would Octavius come here? To show you up?"

"Maybe."

Fannia stood up and shouted for her slaves. "I'm sorry, my dear friend, but I should attend to these changes, starting with notes to the other guests. Please, feel free to use my baths, or, if you like, go visit the public baths or the market. I can have one of my servants guide you through town. Nasia will compile a list of my most trusted vendors for you." She waved a hand at the Nubian woman.

"Thank you, Fannia. I'll be fine. Are you sure you don't want my help? Or Thrasius's?"

She shooed him off. "No, no, no. My cook is already cooking from the recipes Thrasius gave me when I last visited. Go enjoy yourself and rest up."

Apicius rose from the couch. I was hoping he would give us the afternoon to ourselves but I knew he would want to keep me close to discuss the situation. I had heard of the rivalry between Livia and Fannia but had never been unfortunate enough to witness a direct exchange. And Octavius—what were his motives? He was a man who did nothing without cause and often that cause was in direct opposition to my master.

"Sotas and Thrasius, let us go."

We took one of Fannia's litters, as oxen, mules, and horses were not allowed on the city streets. "What will I do?" Apicius asked the second we were ensconced inside. "I have always hoped to avoid Livia until it was advantageous to me. This could be dreadful! I will never have a chance at becoming gastronomic adviser if she knows how close I am to Fannia." He twisted his toga in his hands as he ranted. What if he fell ill? What if he paid men to kidnap Livia? No, those wouldn't do. He must have angered one of the gods, but which one? I had no answers for him.

"This is a disaster! I should have stayed home with Aelia."

Hindsight was much clearer, I thought.

"Oh, Apollo, tell me your truths, what could Livia want with Fannia? And what role do I play in this farce?" Apicius lifted his eyes skyward. I too crossed my fingers, hoping for a good omen. I wanted to go home.

After the baths, Apicius decided we should meet with the vendors Nasia had marked on a slim wax tablet to take his mind off the night ahead. By the end of the afternoon all of Apicius's slaves were loaded with goods, ranging from fresh togas to game sets of ivory knuckle-bones to jewelry and silver statues of Fortuna and bronze likenesses of Apollo.

In addition to the gifts he bought for clients and for future cenae, Apicius also ordered complete sets of new furniture and bedding for the villa in Baiae as well as the villa in Minturnae. "What we have now can go to the slaves," Apicius declared. "I'm sure you could use new blankets, eh, Thrasius?"

I agreed, but I was shocked by the cost of the new goods and by my master's lack of concern for the waste of the old items. Wouldn't it have been better to sell much of the furniture for a profit? It would be a healthy profit too, enough to give a small gift to all his slaves and have enough left over to justify some of the cost of replacing the furniture with new items. When I first started as his coquus, I thought that one day I would get used to how much money Apicius spent, but over time I found I was becoming only more appalled by the incredible waste.

On the way back to Fannia's house, Apicius requested a stop at the Capitoline temple to Jupiter, Juno, and Minerva. Sotas and I followed him into the vast great court of the temple. I was amazed at the glory of the building. Everywhere I looked there was gold. The floors were marble, with intricate mosaics of every color. The ceilings were so high that I could not imagine how men could have painted them with so many stars.

I wished I could gaze upon the massive golden statue of the god but only priests were allowed. We waited near the doors of the temple while Apicius spoke to the priest and gave him the offering that would be left on Jupiter's altar. "The last time I was here was seven years ago," Sotas said to me in a low voice. "It is still just as beautiful. I wish we had time to visit the temple of Fides as well."

Sotas had always been enamored of the goddess of fidelity, which made sense for a slave, but few believed in her power to reward those who remained loyal. I always wanted to ask, but the way he spoke of her made me feel like I would be intruding on something private.

When Apicius returned to us, I noticed he was missing the large emerald ring he had been wearing on one hand. He had left a generous sacrifice. As we exited the temple, Apicius handed each of us an amulet and instructed us to wear it that evening, tucked beneath our tunics. The charm he gave Sotas was heavy, made from thick gold, fashioned into the shape of a hand with an eye in its center. It was designed to protect against the evil eye. He hesitated for a moment before he handed me mine, which made me wonder. It was a slim golden disk with the shape of a leaf on one side—the precious silphium leaf. The other side was etched with an elaborate evil eye with a blue lapis lazuli stone in the center. It was beautiful, and so appropriate that Apicius must have commissioned it and brought it with him for a blessing. The import of such a gesture was not lost on me. We slipped the expensive charms around our necks. I felt proud, and in a small way a little powerful, that my dominus desired so much to protect me.

When we returned to the domus, Apicius convinced Fannia to let me guide her cook in making an asparagus patina for Livia.

"This is my chance, Fannia," Apicius said as she led us to the kitchen. "Livia will marvel at every bite she takes. And if she likes it . . ." He trailed off.

"You hope that she will set Octavius aside. It may not be so easy as that, Apicius, my dear," Fannia said, patting him on the arm.

"It is a start. She knows nothing of me and now she will."

Despite Fannia's command, her cook did not seem pleased for me to teach him how to make the patina. He was an older man with a brow full of worry lines. Only begrudgingly did he let me into his space and allow me to borrow his knives. If Apicius and Fannia hadn't been standing nearby gossiping, I think he might have outright sabotaged my efforts.

I cut up the asparagus tips and instructed him to add them into a mortar with pepper, lovage, coriander, savory, and onions. Once they had been thoroughly ground, I added raisin wine, garum, and olive oil.

He looked at the mixture, skeptical. The lines in his forehead deepened. "This will not work." His voice was gruff.

"Not like that, certainly. You need two of these," I said, cracking eggs into the mixture. "Once you beat those in, you can put it into the oven to bake. When it is firm, take it out, cut it into wedges, and sprinkle with pepper."

The old coquus was about to say something else when Fannia came over. "Make sure to follow his instructions exactly," she told her cook.

"We must make Empress Livia proud. The meal that comes out of this kitchen today must be your finest work."

"I have seen his technique," I said, hoping to make peace with the man and also to prevent him from spitting into the food. "It is no wonder you hired him for your kitchen, Fannia. I think there is much that he could teach me."

Apicius laid a hand on the man's shoulder and squeezed in approval. "Fannia has always had impeccable taste!"

The man beamed.

Before the guests arrived, Fannia and Apicius met in a cubiculum off of the atrium where a small set of couches was arranged. Sotas and I stood in a corner with four other slaves, ready to attend to our masters if the need arose. Fannia carried a glass of Roman absinthe in her hand as she paced the room.

"What on earth could she want?" She took a sip of the bitter drink. "She wants to shame me somehow."

Apicius took a seat but didn't recline. He sipped his glass much more slowly than his hostess. I wondered how quickly those glasses would disappear when the guests were introduced. It was not customary to drink before dinner and women were never supposed to drink.

"When was the last time she dined with you?"

Fannia's voice quavered. "She has never dined with me. She wouldn't stoop so low."

"Think hard. What could she want?"

Fannia paused. "She wants me dead. I should have thought twice before I bedded that old ex-husband of hers."

Apicius shook his head. "You exaggerate. I don't think she wants you dead. And if she did, I don't think she would have you killed in front of me, nor would she do it herself."

"True. She enjoys tormenting me too much." Fannia resumed her pacing. "Let's see. . . . Well, I know she wants me to leave Rome." The late-afternoon sun was starting to disappear and the atrium was losing its light. She waved a hand and her slaves rushed to light the lamps.

"Does she have any way to force you to move?"

"No. She knows I hate my husband—which I'm sure gives her great pleasure. I have no child so she cannot threaten my family. Blackmail will not work; I have lived my life in the public eye as truth. She could not pin me with scandal before, nor could she now."

They continued to discuss scenarios that would explain Livia's intent, but when the door slave came to announce the guests' arrival (and to whisk away the absinthe), they were no closer to understanding. Fannia and Apicius hurriedly popped mint and anise seeds into their mouths, chewed to mask the smell of alcohol, and spat the seeds into a nearby planter moments before Corvinus and Octavius escorted Livia Drusilla Caesar into the triclinium.

Time seemed to stop when Livia entered the room. I'd never imagined that one day I would be in the presence of the most powerful woman in the world. Caesar's wife was as the rumors said—radiant with strong features, clear skin, and ocean-blue eyes. Her graying hair was threaded with tiny glass beads and piled high upon her head, with two curled ringlets falling to each side, cradling her high cheeks. She wore a stola of yellow, pinned by two simple small ruby and amber brooches in the shape of lions. Her arm was linked in Corvinus's arm. Octavius followed. I thought he was a pig in comparison to the empress, with a protruding belly and tufts of hair growing from his ears.

"Livia! Corvinus! Octavius! What a pleasure to have you dine with me tonight!" Fannia stepped forward to greet them, the jewels adorning her stola tinkling with the movement.

"You look lovely as always, Fannia." Corvinus kissed each cheek.

"Cousin, thank you for inviting me." Livia politely bestowed a kiss on Fannia, and then looked in askance at Apicius, who stood a few feet behind his hostess.

"And this must be Gavius Apicius? I have heard much about you."

Apicius bent to kiss the delicate gold ring on Livia's hand. "I hope they are songs of praise!"

Octavius reached out and shook hands with Apicius. "Rest assured, old friend, our ears have merely been tantalized with stories of your provincial feasts."

"I am flattered." Apicius ignored the insult. "I hope one day, Empress, you will join me and judge for yourself."

I was beginning to understand the intent behind Octavius's visit—to put Apicius in his place.

Fannia led the group to the Lares shrine, where she gave each of the guests a cluster of grapes to sacrifice to the gods of the house. Sotas and I followed behind with the other slaves. Fannia passed a vial of wine to Livia and let her pour the libations to Edesia and Bibesia, goddesses of feast and of drink. We knelt in prayer and I silently asked for an extra boon of protection. Fannia sprinkled some wine on the ground for the spirits of the ancestral dead, the Lemures, who took their sacrifice off the floor of the dining area. When food fell to the ground, the Lemures expected it to remain. The slave who was responsible for cleaning the floor in Apicius's Baiae villa and burning the remains on the Lares shrine was an unlucky girl, always falling, breaking dishes, or having some other form of bad luck for thwarting the Lemures from their sacrifices. No slave wanted to be the one to clean the floor in a triclinium.

When the guests had settled onto the couches and the first course of eggs, olives, fig tarts, whole bread, and fried oysters had arrived, the conversation became more interesting.

"Fannia, where is your husband tonight? It's been so long since I've seen him," Livia asked before she slipped an oyster between her reddened lips.

"Thank you for asking, cousin." From her tone one would never know how much Fannia hated her husband. "He is in Gaul right now, negotiating for transport of the slaves from the armies in the region. He handles the transactions and takes a small portion of the profit from the soldiers who capture the slaves. I am fortunate to have a husband in such a lucrative trade."

Livia appeared amused. Fannia was always clever when it came to subtle retorts.

Corvinus seemed anxious to change the subject. "Apicius, I understand that Officer Sejanus is related to your wife?"

Apicius's nostrils flared. I wondered why the name Sejanus bothered him. He plucked an olive from the plate in front of him and considered it as he spoke. "Why, yes, Corvinus, they are cousins. I imagine you know a few of my wife's relatives. Her father, Lucius Aelius Lamia, is one of Caesar's cavalry officers."

"I do know Lamia. He's a good man who will go far. He has found much favor with Caesar," said Corvinus. "And Sejanus seems to show promise as well."

Fannia diverted the topic by motioning for the gustatio to begin. The slaves brought goblets of pomegranate juice mixed with honey, and platters of boiled eggs, as well as lentils, onions, and mustard beans.

It was a quiet dinner with only a flutist for accompaniment. Fannia likely wanted to be hospitable but not offer up any reason for the meal to go on longer than necessary.

I was alarmed to see that Octavius remembered me. He kept moving his eyes in my direction. Why would he care if I were there? Sotas noticed as well, nudging me with his elbow after one prolonged look. I wished I could have disappeared, the stare disarmed me so.

What did Livia and Corvinus want? We were all still waiting to know.

When the main course arrived, the conversation turned toward food and drink. Apicius, once more in his element, did not hesitate to talk about his culinary loves. He described a recent trip to Sicily, where he'd discovered a special recipe for olive relish. He promised to have it sent to Livia. Octavius, rising to the occasion, had a story to rival each of Apicius's tales. To counter the relish, Octavius offered to send Livia honey from Spain. When Apicius said he thought the best cheeses were from Gaul, Octavius disagreed, saying that aged cheese from Bithynia was the best. Livia nodded politely, not seeming to care much about the topic of conversation.

"How is your son, Tiberius?" Fannia asked Livia, being careful to distinguish between Livia's son and her ex-husband, who shared the same name. She seemed to be trying to steer the conversation away from the increasing rivalry between Octavius and Apicius, though it was another jab. Tiberius's withdrawal from politics was rumored to be an embarrassment to both Livia and Caesar.

Livia didn't give in to the bait. "He is well, cousin. I visit him often. The isle of Rhodes is a beautiful place and his villa has astonishing views of the ocean."

"Julia must miss him," Fannia said, referring to Tiberius's wife (and Caesar's daughter by his first wife, whom he forced to marry Tiberius). All of Rome knew how much Tiberius hated Julia. There was increasing gossip about her attendance at nightly orgies and drinking parties, so much so that it wouldn't be long before Caesar would no longer be able to ignore the rumors.

"Not as much as you must mourn for your lost son." She reached across the couch and patted Fannia's hand.

Fannia snatched it away. Livia knew how to wound her cousin. Fannia still lived with the pain of losing her only child to fever at age ten. Sotas had once told me he thought it was part of the reason she had taken to mentoring Apicius, to feel solace for the son who was gone.

"I hear your grandson, Drusus, is growing up quite fast," Apicius said to Livia in an attempt to change the subject.

"Why, yes, he is." Drusus was Tiberius's only son from his first wife. "He's sixteen and is learning the sword already. I suspect he'll make a fine commander in Caesar's army one day."

The asparagus patina came out and Fannia's scissor slave sliced the egg dish into wedges for each guest. "This is a recipe from Apicius's kitchen," she said with pride.

Livia took a bite. "This is exquisite." She seemed to be addressing Octavius, who smiled and dipped his head.

"It is indeed," he said between mouthfuls. I was surprised. I expected him to be more contrary.

She dabbed at the corners of her mouth with her napkin. "Apicius, everyone I know who travels to Baiae says an invitation to one of your parties is most desirable. After tasting this, I know why."

Warmth flooded me and I felt momentarily dizzy. The empress liked my food!

Apicius too was pleased. "Thank you, my lady. I am humbled by your words."

"I see you brought your coquus with you," Octavius noted, waving his spoon toward me.

All eyes were on me. My heart leaped into my throat, lodging there like a too big piece of radish.

"Octavius says that he has made you quite the star in Baiae."

It was strange to hear that Octavius would say anything nice about his rival. Nor did he seem perturbed by Livia's words.

Apicius didn't have the wherewithal to be humble. "Why, yes, Thrasius has certainly helped me raise the bar when it comes to entertainment."

"Octavius would like to buy him from you," she said.

My mouth dropped open in surprise.

Octavius delivered an oily smile at Apicius's hesitation. "I realize he must be quite valuable. I assure you, I am willing to pay whatever price you name."

There was an uncomfortable silence. I said a small prayer to Sotas's goddess, Fides, promising to be faithful to Apicius if she would keep me from being sold.

"Well?" Octavius asked, his brow furrowed in irritation.

"My friend, while I appreciate your offer, I cannot part with Thrasius, not for any amount of coin. He has become part of our family and to lose him would be devastating to all of us."

"I see." Octavius's tone was abrupt and threatening. "I promise you, Apicius, at some point you will be most inclined to change your mind." He glanced at Livia, as though he expected her to back him up, but she only arched her eyebrow at Apicius.

Then she smiled, glancing at Fannia as she spoke. "Family is important and should be highly regarded. It is admirable of you to protect and respect yours, Apicius." She gestured to her body-slave, who rushed forward to help her up and into her cape.

"Fannia, thank you for a lovely meal. Apicius, I am glad to have met you. I trust that you will seriously consider Octavius's offer. May Mercury protect you on your journey home." Her voice was flat and held no hint to what she might truly feel.

As soon as the door closed, Fannia barked an order to her slaves to bring back the absinthe. "You, my dear friend, have just made yourself a powerful enemy in Octavius. Be glad he did not fully curry the favor of Livia. She could have forced a purchase today if she had desired. In the future you may not be so lucky."

Apicius wasn't anxious to return home and ordered a stop at the villa in Minturnae, where he spent his time brooding, drinking, and bedding the female slaves. His temper was short and he made Sotas administer many beatings during our visit.

"Please, Dominus Apicius, we should return to Baiae. Surely you miss Apicata?" I said one day, in an attempt to reason with him. I was desperate to see Passia with every passing day.

The look on his face told me everything I needed to know. I dared not move as he strode toward me and slammed his hand against the side of my face. His heavy rings smashed against my temple and I could see stars through the blackness. I fell to the ground, clutching my head in pain.

"We go when I say we go. Next time think hard before you question me." He turned back to the window and left Sotas to gather me up and escort me out.

I reeled with his words.

I stayed away from him after that, sharing only the barest of words when asked at meals. A month passed before his mood shifted and we returned to Baiae.

Aelia came out to the gates to meet us. Her hands were on her hips and the look she bore was that of a woman deciding whether to give her lover a second chance. I looked for Passia but she had not come to the door.

Apicius hurried to his wife and wrapped his arms around her as though he were afraid he would never see her again. "Oh, how I missed you!"

She held him for a spell, then pulled away. "You were gone for much longer than you promised. Why didn't you send a messenger?"

Apicius bowed his head. "In truth, my little dove, I was so busy I didn't think of it."

I wanted to kick him.

"Well, husband, what kept you so busy that you didn't have time to think about your wife?"

Though the scorn in her voice was evident, Apicius was excited to show her all he had acquired in his travels. He shouted at the slaves to start bringing in the furniture.

"All this, dear wife."

Aelia's mouth fell open and her eyes widened. I knew her well enough to guess what she was feeling—amazement at her husband's inability to comfort her and astonishment at the purchases being unloaded from the many wagons.

"You are replacing *all* of our furniture?"

Apicius grinned. It was as though he were eight years old and showing a favorite toy to his friend. "I hoped to cheer you up. I bought new furniture for the villa in Minturnae as well." He pulled her close once more. What he couldn't see but Sotas and I could was the look of sadness and resignation on Aelia's face.

CHAPTER 6

After we returned from Rome, Passia was a different person toward me. Much to my delight, she would often appear in the kitchen with Apicata in the late morning when all was quiet. We would tell Apicata stories and sometimes take walks with her in the garden. We talked only a little to each other at first, with most of our conversation centered on Apicata.

Over the months that followed, the walks began to include longer conversations. Six-year-old Apicata would run ahead and Passia and I would sit on a bench and talk. I longed to touch her, to reach out my hand and place it against hers, but I did not. Instead we let our words touch and entwine. We talked about what life would be like if we were not slaves. We shared house gossip, gave each other advice on how to handle Apicius, and discussed Aelia's sadness.

"I try to keep Apicata from Aelia when the darkness consumes her," Passia said to me one day, almost a year after the night in my cubiculum. I was pulling radishes up from the garden and she was helping me by wiping off the dirt and placing them in a basket. Apicata was drawing in the dust with a stick at the other end of the garden. One of the house cats was batting at the stick in play.

"It's not good for her to see her mother so depressed," she continued. "It fills her with sadness and no little girl should feel that way." It sounded like she was remembering her own childhood.

"She should have more children her age to play with," I said, pulling hard on one of the radishes. "Apicius should not be so narrow-minded. He should let her play with the slave children."

"I asked Sotas to help me convince Apicius to let one of the girls be a little handmaiden to her but Dominus refused. He did not see the need for her to have two slaves at her age."

Rúan appeared at the end of the row of radishes. "Popilla is looking for Apicata," he said, waving at Passia. "She wants to have lunch with her."

"May Pluto take that old goat," Passia muttered.

We watched her take Apicata by the hand and pull her away. "Pluto won't help her," Rúan said as they disappeared into the house.

"You're always so certain that our gods are worthless," I teased, but only half-heartedly. In the three years I'd known him he had often been dismissive of the gods. I had never understood. "How can you be so sure? We don't scoff at your Tuatha Dé Danann. We even have temples to your own goddess Epona."

Rúan sniffed with disdain. "In this the Romans are stupid. They would rather believe in everything than make a choice."

"But who are we to say what gods may decide our fate?"

Rúan picked up the basket. "Men decide their own fate."

"I don't know if that's true. I think that the gods step in and change our fate. We can ask them to help us."

"Believe what you will, but no god has ever helped me get what I want. If they did I wouldn't be standing here watching you sit in the dirt pulling up radishes."

When he left, I thought about his words. I didn't believe him. I couldn't. I had to hold on to hope that Venus would bring me Passia and that Fortuna would bring fame to Apicius and in turn to my food and my kitchens. Otherwise I had no purpose, I would be just like so many other nameless slaves, worked to the bone until they died, alone and with no stone to be remembered by.

That evening, Apicius intended to hold a small cena. I had planned an ocean theme, with a wide variety of morsels fresh from the morning's catch.

When my dominus found me, I had just finished filling a basket of snails plucked from the *cochlea* where they had grown fat on a specially mixed milky porridge, then boiled and cooled. The snails, nearly as round as a baby's fist, were ready to be fried and served with salt, oil, pepper, cumin, and a bit of silphium.

"There you are!" Apicius's voice rose over the din of the kitchen. He wasn't yet dressed for dinner and wore a red tunic that appeared to be simple at first glance. But as he came close, the intricate border of the tunic became apparent, a thin patterned line of gold along its edges. I could not help but grin. Opulence should have been Apicius's cognomen. Sotas crossed the kitchen with his master but moved beyond to stand against the wall where he could easily survey the kitchen. He smirked at me.

"Snails, I see!" Apicius said. His voice was bright and his enthusiasm was infectious. When his mood was high my world always felt a little lighter.

"Part of the gustatio." I was pleased he approved.

I set the basket of snails down on the table next to Vatia. "Shell these, please. You can use the pick in my knife box."

Apicius picked up one of the snails. "What else is on the menu?"

"I was thinking of an oceanic theme. Sprats in white wine, salt fish balls, stewed eels, oysters, mussels . . . perhaps a patina of sea nettles."

Apicius frowned. "These snails aren't from the sea."

"I know." I chuckled, moving out of Vatia's way so she could slip by and get the shell pick out of my personal box of knives, which I kept in the area of the kitchen designated as my work space. "But they seem as though they should be from the sea, do they not?"

"I suppose they do." Apicius laughed. "Now tell me . . ."

Apicius was cut off by Vatia's scream, a piercing cry that stopped everyone in the kitchen.

I turned from Apicius to see Vatia swinging her arm hysterically. A small snake hung from her hand.

Another cry rose from the table next to where I stood with Apicius. "No!"

It was Pallas, the slave who'd broken the glasses on my first day in the household. I had moved him from the kitchen and now his job was mostly in the laundry, washing the napkins, the seat cushions, and the costumes the serving boys wore. His scream mixed with Vatia's shrieks of fear and pain. Pallas stood there, a look of horror on his face.

Vatia slammed the snake against the table. She snatched up a nearby knife and slashed at the snake, missing and cutting deep across her wrist. Blood poured from the wound and across the head of the viper. Eventually, it relaxed its hold and thudded against the tiles. It had happened so fast that most of the kitchen was too stunned to move. The snake lay there for a second before slithering along the floor toward Apicius.

The blood-spattered serpent was marked with shades of dull red and two dark stripes that began at the eyes and extended down the body. A white wavy pattern crisscrossed its scales. When it was three foot lengths from Apicius it paused and began to make a terrible rasping noise. The whole kitchen knew that sound, the snake was a deadly asp.

"Jupiter, protect me," Apicius whispered.

"Don't move!" I yelled to him, although it was clear my dominus was too scared to do anything but stand there, frozen.

Keeping my eye on the viper, I reached back to the table next to me, feeling for the basket Vatia had emptied of the snails. I began to lift it off the table, trying to keep my movements slow and steady.

My effort at subtlety was futile. The rasping sound stopped and the snake began to move. This time I moved much faster. I pulled the basket off the table and slammed the reed vessel down over the viper one second before it would have sunk its fangs into Apicius's ankle.

Apicius fell backward, his head narrowly missing the thick acacia-wood legs of the kitchen table. He pushed himself away from the basket, while the creature hissed beneath.

I pointed at the pale boy. "Grab him!" I yelled at Sotas and another burly slave standing behind Pallas. They responded with the same urgency, lunging forward to grip the boy by the wrists and shoulders, preventing his escape. Pallas tried to struggle but gave up after Sotas slapped him across the head.

Vatia was on the floor. Rúan reached her first.

"Vatia, oh, Vatia," he crooned as he took her in his arms. Tears brimmed in his eyes. She was as white as a freshly bleached toga. Her breathing was heavy and she stared past Rúan.

Balsamea rushed forward with an armful of towels with a swiftness that belied her age. She knelt and wrapped up Vatia's arm. I watched in horror as the blood soaked the towel in less than a minute. She quickly snatched up another towel and tried again to stanch the flow.

I could not help them. Apicius was still sprawled on the floor. I reached out an arm to help him up. He took my hand and, shaking, got to his feet. Then I turned back to the cluster of slaves standing around watching. "Get that snake out of here, now! Kill it once it's out of the house. Now!"

Apicius touched me on the arm. "Who is he?"

I looked in the direction of his gaze. Pallas's head hung low, his dark hair covering his face.

"He's from the laundry," I told Apicius. "And I think he knows what happened."

"Is this true?" Apicius said, moving toward the boy.

Pallas looked up. His mouth formed a wet O, but no sound came out.

Sotas tightened his grip on the boy. "Tell your dominus what you know!"

Pallas fixed his eyes on the ground. "Popilla . . ." he managed.

Apicius gasped.

"Popilla what?" I asked, moving forward to grab the boy by the tunic.

"She, she, she . . ."

"Did you put the snake there?" Apicius asked.

"Yes." The boy began sobbing. Snot dripped out of his nose and over his thin lips.

"What did she offer you?"

The boy struggled to speak. "One hundred denarii and, and . . ."

"And what?" Apicius's voice rose.

The boy's watery eyes were rimmed with red and full of despair. "Safe passage to Cyprus."

I winced. What a fool. "Safe passage" was more likely his being handed to a slave trader bound for Egypt, where the boy would serve its Roman governor. The one hundred denarii would go right into the trader's hands in return for silence.

"You'll get your safe passage." Apicius flicked a hand at Sotas.

Sotas responded before the boy could, sliding out the knife in his belt and raising it to Pallas's neck. He was deft, cutting the throat and twisting the boy down to the ground in one movement, directing the gush of blood across the floor. I watched the blood pooling on the tiles around Pallas's crumpled body. It wasn't the boy who deserved to die. He would have been as much of a victim if he had refused the task. The person who deserved to die was the woman who had motivated his actions.

Apicius seemed to be of the same mind. "Come, Sotas. And you too, Thrasius. We have another matter to attend to." He led us out of the kitchen, past Vatia, unconscious in Rúan's lap with Balsamea and the other slaves trying desperately to stop the furious flow of blood from her arm.

"She won't live," Apicius said as he strode through the corridor away from the kitchen. "I once watched Caesar Augustus order a man to die by asp. They tied him to a board and let snakes crawl all over him. After he'd been bitten several times they took the asps away. Then they made shallow cuts all over the man's body. After the asp bites, a man will no longer hold his blood. Death is swift and painful."

Sotas and I were silent. I knew Sotas thought very fondly of Vatia. She was a dear friend who always had kind words for him. As for me, I could not imagine Vatia being absent from my kitchen. By the blood of Apollo! Only the day before I had convinced Apicius to give her a raise in her peculium. It was a small increase, but for Vatia it meant she had been that much closer to earning her freedom.

We stopped in front of Popilla's chambers. Apicius didn't knock. He pushed on the door but it was locked. He didn't need to motion to Sotas. Sotas steeled himself, then slammed one shoulder against the door. It gave way on the first try.

Apicius stormed into the room. Popilla sat on the couch in the corner reading a scroll. She looked up at her son. Her slaves took one look at Apicius and rushed out of the room.

"Get up or I'll have Sotas get you up."

Popilla's eyes held concern as she set aside the scroll. "What is wrong, my son?" Her voice was syrupy. "Did you really need to break down my door?"

"*Get up!*" Apicius roared, causing the veins in his neck and forehead to bulge.

Popilla stood in a hurry. I wondered if she had ever seen her son so angry. I know I hadn't. I had no idea he was capable of such wrath.

Her voice shook. "What's wrong?" she asked again, even though it was plain she knew the answer. She looked at me, her eyes pleading. I could only scowl.

"Kneel, you lying, conniving bitch of a woman. *Kneel*." Apicius signaled Sotas to come forward.

Popilla dropped to the floor, wincing with the crunch that sounded from one knee as she landed. Sotas moved to stand behind her.

"You have betrayed me, Mother." Apicius glanced at Sotas, who grasped her by the hair and pulled her head back.

"What do you mean? What have I done?" she wailed.

Apicius looked like a madman. "Tell her," he said to me, not taking his eyes off his mother, who was raking Sotas's hands with her fingers.

Looking at this gorgon of a woman, I knew true hatred. I was so angry that for a moment I found it hard to speak. When I did, it was with a vitriol I had never before known. "Vatia is dying from the bite of an asp. You meant for that snake to kill me. And now a boy, the slave Pallas, has died for helping you make the attempt. You promised him freedom, but you gave him only lies."

"I don't know what you are talking about!"

"You were named by the boy," Apicius said simply.

"What boy? I have not spoken to any boy."

Apicius paused. Then I noticed a small box under Popilla's couch. I crossed the room to retrieve it.

The box had air holes like those one would buy at the market for snake offerings to the god of healing, Asclepius. Inside was a rolled-up scroll. I handed it to Apicius.

"My son, you must listen to me," Popilla spluttered. Her hands pulled on the arm by which Sotas held her hair.

My master unrolled the scroll and read it. A vein on his neck began to pulse. He handed it to me. "It's a curse. Make sure this is destroyed."

Suddenly, he tore the snake box from me and threw it at his mother. It hit her in the chest and she screamed. Sotas pulled her head back farther.

"I am exercising my rights as the paterfamilias, Mother," Apicius said. "With your actions you have destroyed your worth. You are my property and I do with you what I will."

"No!" Her howl was piercing and I resisted covering my ears.

Apicius looked at Sotas. Like he had with Pallas, Sotas drew the blood-stained knife across Popilla's throat.

I turned away before she hit the floor.

That night, Apicius had Pallas's and Popilla's bodies weighted with rocks and taken out to sea. Vatia died within the hour. While the other slaves made preparations for her cremation, I took the scroll my master had asked me to destroy and set it on fire without opening it. I feared the evil Popilla had captured within its folds.

A heaviness overtook the villa. Rúan wandered around directionless, inconsolable. Aelia took Apicata and visited friends in Pompeii for weeks. The slaves spoke little and obeyed without question. It was not unheard of for a patrician to exercise his rights as paterfamilias against a family member but it was far from common. Usually when a patrician had a family member killed for his or her actions it was a sibling or a spouse, not an elderly matron. It made us wonder, if Apicius was angry enough that he would kill his mother, what would happen to the rest of us?

I dealt with their deaths in a different way. I became jumpy. I think that I thought the ghost of Popilla was still among us. Balsamea noticed and she spoke to me one day when we were preparing the evening meal.

"You need to let go," she said in a soft voice. "She is in the Underworld."

Confused, I put down my knife and looked into her dark eyes, almost hidden by the folds of her skin.

"Let go of your fear, Thrasius. No one will try to kill you now," she said.

I smiled despite myself. She was right. Since Popilla's death I had become even more nervous—about snakes, about my food being poisoned, about whether someone might jump out from a hidden corner. I even threw out the knife box and kept my knives visible and within reach.

"I know, I know. But once burned by the fire, won't you go out of your way to make sure you are never burned again?"

She smiled. "Yes, but how can you be burned if there is no fire?"

I didn't respond. I picked up the knife and a partially chopped head of lettuce and with careful precision slipped the blade through the leaves.

A crow cawed at the window as the lettuce fell in half. In that small, seemingly unimportant moment, I thought I caught a faint smell of smoke.

PART III

3 C.E.

BEETS

Chop leeks, coriander, (mix with) cumin, raisins, and flour. Put the mixture in the middle (of the beet leaves); tie up and (boil). Serve in a sauce of liquamen, oil, and vinegar.

—*Book 3.11, Vegetable Dishes*
On Cookery, Apicius

CHAPTER 7

My relationship with Passia bloomed slowly over many months of comfortable conversation and subtle flirting. I thought often back to that evening when she touched me in my cubiculum, and longed to have a moment like that again. But despite my desire, I did not push her. She was a strong woman, with many ideas and opinions, but there was a part of her that was distrustful.

One unusually hot night in early June, after I had dismissed the kitchen slaves, I invited her to join me in a little library in the back of the house. "I want to show you something," I told her.

The library shelves were empty but the floor was haphazardly covered with baskets full of scrolls and parchment. Apicius had finally decided it was time to move the family from Baiae to Rome and the domus was in disarray from the packing.

On the empty desk I rolled out the scroll that I had been working on for weeks.

"What is it?" she asked.

"Look and tell me what you think it is." I had been teaching her to read, and while I was excited about my project, I didn't want to ruin a perfect teaching moment.

"Sss . . . auce for cr, cr, craane, duck, or chick, chicken."

I was proud of her progress. At the last Saturnalia, after we listened to Apicata read to us about the great goddess Diana, Passia asked me to teach her. "I'm sad," she said, "that a child can read such beautiful words and I cannot." From that night on we practiced every evening after the slaves had finished the cena and Apicata was asleep.

"Keep going, you are doing well."

"Pepper, dr, dri, dried onion, cumin, love, love, love . . ." She fought to say the word *lovage*.

In our practice, I would have helped her finish the word, but at that moment, hearing her say what I was feeling was almost too much for me to bear.

"Lovage!" She smiled at me, her eyes glittering in the lamplight.

My heart filled to bursting. "Yes," I managed, not trusting myself to say more. I wanted desperately to take her in my arms then and pull her to me.

"It's a recipe." She unrolled the scroll further. "Oh, Thrasius, are these all recipes?"

I took a breath. "Yes. I thought that I would make a book of them. So many of Apicius's clients keep asking for recipes for their own cooks."

"What a wonderful idea. Dominus Apicius will be very pleased."

"I hope that is so." I looked down at the scroll, which contained many hours of hard work. I had been testing and perfecting the recipes over the past year, painstakingly writing down the results and making changes here and there until I was sure of each dish. While it was true that Apicius's clients wanted the recipes, I thought of this book as my own true legacy. When I died, my food would live on. I savored the idea of someone making my recipes hundreds of years later.

"Would you take a walk on the beach with me? It will be our last chance."

By the gods! I warmed with the thought of walking next to her on the shore. We had walked the beach many times, but never by moonlight. And she was right. There were no beaches in Rome. I would miss the sea and the sand.

"I would like that very much." I hoped she couldn't hear my heart hammering against my ribs.

The marble stairs to the beach were well lit by the bright light of the full moon. At the bottom we stopped to remove our sandals, leaving them on the platform that led back up to the domus. The sand felt good beneath my toes.

In my mind I said a prayer of thanks to Venus, my hope rising.

We reached the shore and together walked south, toward the great pier on the farthest end of the beach, brightly lit by dozens of torches.

The salt water licked our toes with each long reach up the sand. In the distance, closer to town, several fires had been lit; the beach was a favorite place for parties after tourists had spent their day soaking and gossiping in the famous Baiae mineral baths.

"When will you show your recipe book to Dominus?"

"I'm not sure," I confessed. "When I have the courage. I don't know if he will like the idea of telling the world how to cook in his style."

She giggled. "Ahh, but his ego will have the better of him. If you write it all down, there will be no doubt of a recipe's origin. If not, one of Apicius's clients could tell their cooks to try to copy you. I think that he will be quite pleased with your book."

Suddenly she reached over and took my hand, squeezing it. "I can't wait until I can read it all by myself."

I knew I must be smiling like a fool but did not care. I squeezed her hand back as we walked. "It won't be long. You are a fast learner."

She moved closer to me. I put my arm around her, marveling at the smoothness of her skin.

"Thrasius . . ."

"Passia?"

She paused, and I realized that she was gathering her courage to speak. "That night, in your cubiculum, I . . ."

I took her hands and held them together between my own. "It's all right, Passia. You don't have to say anything."

"You surprised me," she blurted out.

"I surprised myself. It took everything I had not to keep you there with me."

She leaned forward until our faces were close. "I know."

There was nothing to do but kiss her, with all the passion I had harbored from the moment when she first appeared in the kitchen on the day of my arrival. Her lips were soft, and sweet like fresh Iberian honey. I ran my hands along her back and up into the tangle of her hair. My thumbs stroked the flesh of her neck and cheeks, and when they pulled away, her lips.

We fell into the sand, twining together our summer-tanned limbs. Our hands roamed up and down the length of each other, slowly removing each article of clothing. I delighted in feeling the way the measure of my passion made my skin tingle with desire from head to toe.

"Apicius always says you are the answer to his prayers. I think he is wrong. I think you are the answer to mine," she whispered in my ear before I entered her and we both cried aloud. The sound was washed away by the crash of waves beyond us.

The next morning, I woke to Apicata shouting in my ear.

"Thrasius, get up. Get up!"

Something soft and giving slapped me across the back, forcing me to disentangle myself from the blanket. On the next fall of the pillow against my head, I snatched it away from the wielder.

"All right, Apicata! I'm up!" I squinted and saw the six-year-old smiling with satisfaction. Through the window behind her I saw the first peach shades of sunrise breaking apart the blue night. By Jove, she was up early!

Then I noticed Passia standing in the doorway. The memories of the night before came flooding back to me. She had returned with me to my cubiculum and we had made love until deep into the night. When I fell asleep she must have slipped out to return to her pallet at the end of Apicata's bed. Her smile told me everything I needed to know. It had not been a dream.

"Come on. We don't have much time. Get up!" Apicata clapped her hands loudly for additional effect. That's what Passia did to waken her from a nap. "Please, will you take me to the market today? I want to say good-bye to Prokopton!" In my haze it took me a minute to remember we were leaving for Rome that day. "I made sure I got up early. Rúan let me tie up one of the roosters outside my bedroom window."

I sighed. I had heard the bird. Her alarm worked like a blessed augury, and I remembered thinking to myself I would have that bird roasted at the first opportunity, then I fell back asleep.

"I don't think we have time," I protested.

"If you hurry, you will," Passia said. "I'll let Aelia know and I'll tell Rúan he's in charge of preparing breakfast this morning. But don't dally. Apicius will want you to help greet clients."

"All right. We can go to the market," I told Apicata.

Apicata cheered. "Can we get some honey ice while we're there?"

"We'll see." I hoped she would forget by the time we reached the market. Honey ice would cause her to dawdle.

I took a deep breath and thought about the day ahead. Today was the last day we would have in the beautiful sea-swept Baiae villa for some time and it made my heart ache to think of it. I loved Baiae. I loved the water, the little market, the sound of the bells that tolled when ships entered the harbor. I was excited about the opportunities in Rome but it was hard for me to fathom living there.

As it was unlikely Apicius would return to the villa before next spring, the salutatio would be long. Apicius had many clients and political supporters in Baiae. There were still many who wanted a last audience so they could secure future visiting rights to Apicius's new domus on the rich and exclusive Palatine Hill. Apicius was likely to be irritable and impatient to be on the road, not to entertain a long line of guests.

The walk to the market filled me with conflicting emotions. So many things had gone well for me since I'd come to Baiae from Maximus's villa in Pompeii. Apicius increasingly turned to me for advice on his affairs, even outside the kitchen. Aelia and Apicata had become as close as family. The kitchen slaves respected me and worked hard to gain both my favor and Apicius's. My love for Passia had bloomed in the sun of this festive town. Truly, I thought, I had found a form of Elysium here in Baiae, made all the more sweet by the fact that at any time it could have been swept away—as a slave nothing was guaranteed. I had years before I turned thirty-five, the age at which I could legally receive my freedom. Apicius could die the next day and I could be back on the block again.

Baiae was beautiful, the clay and brick buildings shining in the dawn sunlight. The breeze carried the scents of jasmine and the sea. Apicata raced ahead of me, her dark curls bouncing against the back of her blue tunica. In her fist she carried a handful of violets and periwinkles picked from the side of the path near the villa. She was determined to give Prokopton a gift, and I suspected he would have an even larger one to give back to her.

Prokopton was a merchant who specialized in everything nonedible. Whatever you needed he always seemed to have on hand or, if not, could readily procure. Over the last three years, I had purchased cooking utensils, everyday pottery, silver serving platters, and even furniture from Prokopton. Apicata loved the big bear of a man. He always had small toys to share with the girl, whom he called "little bird." After we moved to Rome, I kept the pet name for her; it was fitting.

That morning Prokopton gave Apicata a tiny wooden wind-up bird, a gift that shocked me. The bird was most likely quite costly. It was delicate, with wings that moved and legs that carried it forward. Feathers had been carefully painted on in a rainbow of hues. Due to their rareness, wind-ups were not for children. They were entertainment pieces meant for the adult table and could often sell for many thousand denarii.

"Prokopton, are you sure about that gift?" I asked, looking up at him.

The merchant's plump cheeks reddened. "I am. It was my wife's. I have no children to pass it on to. Please remind her of me when she grows. I will be sad not to see her every week."

I left Apicata with Prokopton so I could say farewell to other merchants I frequented. The market was still coming to life and each stall in the large two-storied building was in a varied state of preparation. In the central atrium, a young slave girl sorted baskets of flowers into pretty arrangements. The smells of sausages and melted cheese tickled my nose as I passed by the food stalls. Chickens ran underfoot and dogs slept on the tiles, not caring that they were being stepped over. I made my rounds and said my good-byes, some of them tearful on the part of the shopkeepers. I would miss the market of Baiae, busy and varied but not so big that I didn't know most of the people who worked there. Rome would not be so comfortable.

On my return, I found myself walking behind a small cluster of drunkards, not an unusual sight in Baiae in the summer. Baiae was well known for its festival atmosphere and many came down from Rome to take part in the carefree lifestyle.

There were three nobles, still in their fine evening wear, and two prostitutes, identifiable by their cheap wigs and overdone makeup. It was likely they had been up all night in wine-infused orgiastic bliss and were now looking to find an open *popina* to serve up breakfast.

My ears perked up when I heard the tallest man speak.

"Look at that sweet girl." He motioned down the street to where Apicata sat on a bench playing with her bird. Prokopton was tacking bolts of silk on the shelves next to where she sat. "What I wouldn't give to break that little girl! She would tremble beneath me and learn to beg for more! Come now, let's look closer!" His friends laughed, one of them stumbling in his mirth and almost pulling one of the women to the ground. She helped her companion right himself and the group ambled their way toward Prokopton's stall.

Heat rose to my face. Rage infused me but I dared not act. I was a slave and there were consequences. Relations with children happened from time to time but such effrontery toward a child of the nobility was beneath any refined Roman. Apicata was clearly not a slave child; her dress and style of hair easily marked her as a member of the upper class. She was not to be used or given to anyone other than by her father. If a slave made lecherous comments toward a patrician's child, he could be put to death.

I raced ahead to reach Apicata before the drunkards did. I swooped Apicata up and wrapped her in a dark brown shawl from a nearby shelf. I did not want her ogled any longer nor did I want her to see what was happening. I shushed her worried questions and protests that I was crushing her bird, breathlessly telling Prokopton the story. Prokopton, a freeman, had far more leeway than I did when it came to protecting the honor of the girl.

The drunkards arrived at the stall, stumbling and laughing. Prokopton looked the group over as he leaned casually with one hand against the handle of a well-worn ax. I knew Prokopton was ready to use it if need be.

"I think it would be best for the lot of you to keep moving," he growled.

The man who'd first eyed Apicata had one arm draped across the shoulders of one of the whores, who had a chipped tooth and wore a cockeyed black wig. His blue eyes were a bleary red. He was what I supposed women would consider handsome. He had dark hair and a perfect Roman aquiline nose. The noble was in his midtwenties and his silk *synthesis* indicated he was a man of money. His mouth stretched into a drunken grin.

"We mean no harm," he said to Prokopton. The scent of wine was heavy on his breath despite the fact that we stood several feet away. His voice was deep and rich and most likely he had seduced many women. "Is that your lovely daughter? We were remarking on what a pretty little thing she is."

Prokopton started to speak but in my anger I cut him off and answered the man myself. "Any more remarks and you'll be apologizing to Marcus Gavius Apicius yourself, on your knees begging for forgiveness for the lecherous insults you bestowed upon his child. You are not presenting your best face today, and I suggest you sober up and regain your honor."

"You don't say!" The man laughed, his dark hair falling away from his face as his head tilted back. "Apicius has a daughter! Well, well, that's as much of a surprise as if Juno turned me into a cow." He lurched toward me and I took a step back. Prokopton intervened, ready to use the ax.

The man started laughing but stopped abruptly when he saw the shine of Prokopton's ax. "You are right, my good man! It's best we be on our way. I will have to pay dear Marcus a visit soon!"

"He's leaving for Rome. You missed your chance," I lashed out. I was shocked at the audacity of the noble. Even Fannia didn't casually use Apicius's praenomen of Marcus. Only Aelia had the right to be so intimate. My heart was pounding. The last time I had experienced such rage was on the day Popilla had killed Vatia.

"Ahh, even better. I can look for him at leisure when I return to Rome myself!" He pulled his friends away, chuckling as he left us standing bewildered and enraged.

"Did you know him?" I asked Prokopton. I unwrapped Apicata from the shawl and set her down.

"Why did you have to cover me up? You hurt my bird!" Her voice was loud and I shushed her with a quick finger to her mouth.

Prokopton shook his head and came close enough to talk quietly without the girl overhearing. "Keep her safe."

I wasn't sure how someone in my station could do much of anything save cook a good meal. "I will try, my friend. I promise."

We arrived back at the domus to find the house bustling with activity. Many of Apicius's clients had arrived early and were loitering outside the gates, waiting for their patron to receive them. I pushed past them, ignoring questions about how long Apicius planned on keeping the tiny crowd waiting. Apicata had whined the entire way home, upset because we had to leave without honey ice and because I kept a pace her little legs could barely match. Once she tripped and almost crushed her wind-up. Despite her protests, I had to take the bird from her to keep it safe on the walk home.

Apicius was waiting in the vestibule, ready to receive his clients. He wore one of his best togas and in his hand he held a large scroll. He must have been going over the list of clients in my absence—something we usually did together before we opened the doors to welcome the many Baiae citizens who turned to Apicius for protection, advice, food, and favors.

Sotas sat on a bench on one side of the room. He sighed and shook his head when he saw me. It meant that Apicius was in a foul mood—the kind of mood where you didn't want to go anywhere near him. I steeled myself for the worst.

"Where have you been?" Apicius scowled when he saw us. Then he saw Apicata's reddened, tear-stained face. "By Ceres!" he said, invoking the goddess who looked after the Empire's children. "Apicata! What is wrong?" He rushed to hug his daughter.

"Thrasius didn't let me have any honey ice! He took away my bird and he made me run home!"

I handed the bird back to Apicata. She took it without looking at me and then buried her face in Apicius's shoulder. Her tears blossomed up in full force, one of her best offensive moves. Apicius hated seeing his little girl cry. I groaned inwardly at the irony of the situation.

"There'd better be a good explanation for why you are late to the salutatio and why my daughter is upset," Apicius said, looking up. His eyes betrayed his thoughts—a tempest raged within.

"There is." I signaled with my head and eyes that I wanted Apicata to leave before I gave an explanation.

He pulled away from Apicata, wiped her cheeks with his fingers, and smoothed back her curls. "My sweet flower, go find your mother. She will want to see your new bird."

Apicata brightened at the mention of showing off her new possession. She dutifully kissed her father on the cheek and ran out of the room.

He turned his attention to me, arms crossed and brow knotted. He reminded me of lawyers I saw in the city, stern and demanding, waiting for but never believing the truth. I told him, the entire scene unfolding in front of me once more.

Apicius's expression was unreadable, except when I mentioned that the man claimed to know him. Then a line of worry extended across my master's brow. He made me describe the man in detail but, strangely, it made him even angrier than before I'd begun the story. I could see his fist curling into a ball inside the folds of his toga.

I finished my account and stood silently, waiting for my dominus's response. When Apicius spoke, it was clear he was struggling to keep his temper in check. He paced back and forth in front of his receiving chair as he spoke. "You were late to the salutatio. My clients have been kept waiting. My daughter is upset. On top of all this you dare tell me a ridiculous story about a drunken equestrian in order to make up for your lateness?"

How could Apicius think I was lying?

"Dominus, I have always spoken truth. What would I have to gain from lying to you now?"

The wound of Apicius's doubt pricked me deep beneath my breast. In the four years since my purchase I had been the model slave, truthful, dependable, and unwavering. Apicius was often disappointed in other slaves, but rarely did he seem displeased with me.

"To keep your reputation unblemished, I suspect. You knew how angry I would be that you were late for the salutatio and you wanted to escape my wrath! Out of all people, Thrasius, you know how important my last day in Baiae is!"

"But, Dominus! I swear on my life it's true!"

Apicius sat in his receiving chair. He poked his finger at me. "We will speak of this no more. Punishment will be five lashes and you will walk with the house boys behind the carts—the entire way to Rome. You will also apologize to my daughter." Spittle flew from his lips. When he finished his admonishment, he snapped his fingers and pointed to the floor next to his chair. "For now, stand here and advise me in today's salutatio." He gestured at Sotas to open the front doors.

Confused, I did as I was told without further complaint. I advised Apicius on all the clients who came to pay their respects, reminded him of names, suggested favors to ask such as recommendations to relatives in Rome, advised about the payments to poets and writers who might write and sing Apicius's praises, and took note of those who hoped for an invite to the villa in Rome.

When the salutatio was over, Apicius made good on his promise, forcing me to submit to the whip.

Sotas strode to my side and took me by the shoulder. He squeezed me gently, and I knew that was his way of telling me he was sorry. He pushed me down until I was kneeling on the stones in front of Apicius. "Remove your tunic."

I pulled it off and closed my eyes.

"Count them." Apicius's command was cold.

The first lash landed squarely on my shoulders and I let out a cry.

"I said, count them."

"One," I said, gritting my teeth.

"I couldn't hear you. We'll start again. Five lashes, Sotas."

Sotas cracked the whip down against my skin again.

"One!" I felt the rush of warm blood trickling down my skin.

The whip landed again, and again. I counted, five times. I know that Sotas was as kind to me as he could be, but that did not diminish the pain—or my humiliation.

When it was over, Apicius rose. "We leave in an hour. I hope you packed an extra pair of sandals. You'll need them."

He strode from the room and I fell to the tiles, confused, angry, exhausted, and bloody, unable to rise for many minutes. "I'll send Passia," Sotas said, touching me on the head after Apicius turned away.

I lay there till Passia came, wondering how a day that started so beautifully could turn so sour.

CHAPTER 8

I was surprised at how much I liked Rome. I had thought that leaving Baiae behind would dampen my spirits but instead I found that the chaos of the city filled me with energy. The Palatine Hill was quieter than the other hills, filled with villas of enormous size surrounded by beautiful gardens and walkways. Below the Palatine was the famous Roman Forum, with its vast temples, shops, and city buildings. The Forum was the true life of the city. Everywhere one turned there was something new and amazing to see. People from all over the world came to live in Rome—or as slaves, had been forced to serve in Rome—and walking down the street it was not unusual to hear dozens of languages being spoken. I was particularly pleased about the markets, of which there were several, each with a specialty.

The first few months of our time in the new city was spent readying the house for upcoming banquets. Apicius had new triclinia made and designed every detail of those rooms to be as sumptuous and impressive as possible.

"I will have dozens of new clients in no time," he said when he first surveyed the massive triclinium in the garden that would accommodate eighteen people. Since our arrival, Apicius had been obsessed with building his client base. In the city such connections were more important than ever, for protection, to procure influential votes, and to secure the right invites to the right parties. "And to recommend me to Caesar," he added. "It won't be long now, Thrasius."

I did not share his confidence.

• • •

It was four months before we were ready to open the doors to guests of our first Roman cena. My master was delighted to be entertaining once more, but not all of his slaves were as enthusiastic.

"I don't want to fight with you. Please, Balsamea. It's such a small thing for me to ask." I placed a white scarf on the table in front of her. Lately she had decided that she no longer wanted to pull her hair back.

"I like it the way I used to wear it, before you." The aged slave stared at me.

I didn't understand this new defiance of hers. Her age was catching up to her and of late her behavior had become more erratic. I tried a different tactic. "It's a big night for Apicius and we've no time to waste. Don't make me wish I had left you in Baiae."

I was determined that this night would run smoothly. I pushed the scarf toward Balsamea once more.

Balsamea reluctantly reached for the cloth. "Dominus is fretting a bit overmuch," she grumbled as she began pulling back her hair.

"I know. But he wants to make an impression."

"By getting them all drunk? Some impression."

I had to smile. "Everyone loves to get drunk, isn't that true?"

"Not everyone loves to clean it up." She looked at me square in the eye, a small warning that she would not be pleased if that was what she ended up doing. She knotted the scarf around her hair.

"Thank you."

Balsamea grunted and returned to the task of weaving laurel leaves, roses, and hazel flowers into the many wreaths we would need for the evening.

I spent a few minutes directing other slaves preparing for that evening's *commissatio* before taking up my own knife to chop up the bundles of lovage, dill, thyme, and sage. The aromas wafted up as I chopped and lost myself in the rapid slices of the knife.

I thought about the party ahead. I agreed with Balsamea's concerns. At first, I was nervous about Apicius starting out in Rome with a drinking party instead of a traditional dinner. While imbibing was something of a pastime in the tourist town of Baiae, I assumed that Caesar

Augustus's austerity would hold more sway in Rome. But Apicius wanted to invite as many people as possible. He had many potential clients in Rome as well as a few of his own patrons. Narrowing down the guest list to nine or eighteen would have been nearly impossible. Not that it was difficult for me to change my mind once I started thinking of all the possibilities for the party.

We decided to hold a commissatio with wine and amusements, but also a special treat, a gustatio that would let visitors sample the dishes of which Apicius and I were particularly proud. While it was somewhat unheard of to mix the courses of wine and food, eventually I was able to convince Apicius to serve small bites of food before the commissatio. My argument was that if the visitors sampled the dishes, Apicius would be able to gather clients and patrons who would look to future seats at his table. Apicius had agreed, especially after I explained how I would dress the young boys as cupids and the girls as nymphs. I made a sticky mock ambrosia cake from honey and apples, to be served by one of the prettiest slaves, dressed as a handmaiden to Venus. I hoped when people left they would be raving about both the atmosphere and the food.

"I came to go over the menu," Apicius said, jolting me out of my thoughts. He was like an eager child just given a fresh plum. Sotas settled onto a stool near the door and raised a hand in greeting.

"Of course. I can make a variety of dishes and cut them up for easy sampling. I wanted to start with roasted hyacinth bulbs, some soft cheese drenched in raisin wine with bread, and slices of sow's udder with garum and lovage. I thought we could serve the Lucanian sausage I made earlier this week. And remember my hard egg mice with the almond ears and the clove eyes? I think those might go over well."

"Perfect! The mice will delight the ladies!" I was relieved to see he was in a good mood.

"What about those delicious fried hare livers you make? Send one of the boys to the market if you need hares."

I pushed the cut herbs into a small bowl. "I can do that. What about the cabbage?"

At the mention of the cabbage, Sotas shifted in his chair and the scraping noise caused me to look over at the big slave. He waved his hand in front of his nose in disgust. I had to agree. Apicius had been obsessed with cabbage of late and had combed all of Rome for recipes

I might test and modify. In the last months the two of us had cooked more cabbage than I ever cared to see—or smell—again. Plus, I wasn't sure the ages-old belief that cabbage would prevent hangovers held any truth.

"Of course!" Apicius went to the vegetable baskets on the shelves and selected five cabbages.

Together we chopped up cabbage and discussed the wine service. "Who will you choose as *rex bibendi*?" I asked, wondering who Apicius had in mind for the honored position of Magister of Revels. The Magister was an important figure at any party, responsible for diluting the wine, leading the libation hymn, and watching the quantity of alcohol consumed by the guests, making sure no one got too much or too little. The Magister was also in charge of directing conversation, deciding if games got too out of hand—in short, keeping the peace. "You need someone who can be both merry and diplomatic in guiding the conversation."

"Yes. It's a tough decision. There are too many people attending to decide by throw of the dice." Apicius dropped a handful of cabbage into the crackling oil.

"What about Aelia's cousin Lucius Aelius Sejanus, for example. I know him not but Domina speaks well of him. Would he make a good Magister?"

Apicius wrinkled his nose, as though he were recalling something distasteful. I wondered if I had somehow made him angry. Finally, he said, "It's rumored that he likes to enjoy his drink at parties. I may not want to confine him to such a role. Let's not worry. Fortuna has been kind to me thus far, and I think she will be again. I'll consider it later."

When Apicius talked of Sejanus the tone of his voice had changed, taking on a worried lilt. I glanced over at Sotas. The big man shook his head in warning. Clearly Sejanus had not been a good suggestion. I wondered why.

Apicata burst into the kitchen in a squeal of laughter, a swirl of colored ribbons braided into the dark hair flying behind her. Sotas stood in deference to the young mistress but she sailed by him without a glance. Passia smiled at Sotas, patting his arm as she passed through the doorway into the kitchen. She was breathing hard, likely from having run the length of the house trying to catch up to Apicata.

"Father, Father, can I come to the cena?" Apicata stood at the table on tiptoes, looking up at us with wide doe eyes.

"I'm sorry, Dominus. I did try to explain it was a party for grown-ups," Passia said.

Apicius reached over the table and affectionately tweaked Apicata's nose. "It's not a cena, my little one. It's a commissatio. Guess how many people can come to a commissatio?"

"Ummm . . ." Apicata held her tongue between her lips as she thought about the answer. "Nine?"

"No, not nine. That's a cena."

I shook my head and flashed my hands open and closed behind Apicius's back, trying to indicate there would be many people.

"Ummm. Twenty?" she said, looking uncertainly at my hands.

"Maybe twenty, maybe more. A commissatio doesn't always have a certain number of people who can come." Apicius's eyes hardened. "However, little one, I'm not sure it is the right place for a sweet maiden such as you."

Apicata was crestfallen. The corners of her mouth turned down and her lip jutted outward in a pout.

"You shouldn't frown," I said in mock warning. "A bird will come perch on your lip!"

Apicata ignored me. She knew how to tug at her father's heartstrings. "But, please, Father?" she said with a quiet squeak. I tried hard not to laugh. She was too transparent.

Her father sighed and gave in. "All right, you can come for an introduction, but you cannot stay. I'll let you meet a few of my friends, but then you will have to go back to Passia. And you have to promise me you will work extra hard tomorrow on your Greek lessons."

"I promise! Can I have a wreath too?"

"Come here, child, I can make you a wreath." Balsamea held up a handful of hazel flowers and waved them toward Apicata. The girl skipped over to her and climbed up on the bench to help weave the flowers together.

For a few minutes we watched Balsamea show Apicata how to layer the laurel and hazel leaves. Passia came over to the table. "Did you show him?" she asked me, her eyes wide.

"Show me what?" Apicius asked with a mixture of curiosity and suspicion.

My heart began to pound. I wasn't sure I was ready to show Apicius what Passia was referring to. My palms sweating, I went to a cupboard in the corner of the kitchen, removed a large scroll, and brought it to Apicius. Passia thought it was time I should show him my cookbook.

"This."

Apicius pondered the scroll for a second. "I don't understand." Slowly he unrolled the scroll. The words "On the Subject of Cooking" were written in large letters at the beginning.

"It's a recipe book. All the best recipes of your kitchen. I'm not quite finished, but thought you would want to see it. I wanted to find a way to commemorate your legacy for generations ahead."

Apicius stood there, silent, his eyes running over the Latin script. After several quiet minutes Passia and I exchanged a worried glance.

I begged the gods for my master to say something.

When Apicius looked up, there were tears in his eyes and a crooked smile on his face. "Yes! By Jove!" He laughed and it was a happy, strange laugh.

The mixture of relief, happiness, and pride that mingled within me was as great as it was the day I first kissed my beloved Passia. Oh, how I wished I had a stool to sit upon! My knees felt like bent straw.

I leaned over to point at different parts of the scroll, unrolling it across the counter as I spoke. "See, here are recipes for shellfish, patinae with fig peckers or with chicken, a few of our cabbage recipes, and tips for the cook. I added your trick about using eggs to help make cloudy wine clear, instructions on how to preserve oysters, and even Fannia's recipe for how to make wormwood liquor. I thought about how many cooks don't have the right information or knowledge. I wanted to help bring the same level of standards to other households that you have in yours," I continued in a rush. "It is far from finished, as you can see."

Apicius clasped my shoulder with a firm hand. "Thrasius, you have made me proud. Buying you that day was one of the best moves I have ever made. Have you shown Aelia?"

I shook my head. "No, not yet."

"I must show her! She will be delighted!" He gathered up the scroll. "I'll check later to see how the cabbage turned out." He patted Apicata on the head and left. Sotas stood, saluted me, and followed Apicius out the door.

"That went well." Passia came around the table to wrap her arms around my neck.

"Better than I had thought. I hope his mood holds. It always tends to sour the closer we get to the start of a party." I brushed my lips against the side of her cheek, close to her eye, feeling the smooth skin warm to my touch.

At that moment, we were jolted by a shower of petals and leaves from a wreath crashing into the sides of our heads.

"Ow!" Passia exclaimed, jumping back. We looked down to see the remains of a hazel and laurel wreath at our feet.

"Not here in my kitchen," Balsamea said from the table where she sat with Apicata, who was laughing.

I was amused at her audacity. "You mean *my* kitchen." I pulled Passia close and planted a hearty kiss on her lips.

Many hours later, I went to find Apicius to finalize a few questions I had about serving the meal. Sotas knelt outside the door to Apicius's bedchamber. The door was cracked open, but Sotas waved me over to the side.

"He's in a foul mood. You may want to wait until the moment is right," he warned me in a whisper.

I sighed. As I'd predicted. "Can I wait with you?"

Sotas nodded. "Listen for a while, then decide if you want to stay. Let Aelia calm him."

I crouched down next to him as Apicius's voice rose.

"Be gone!" His dress slaves rushed out the door, anxious to be away from their master.

Sotas leaned over to me. "Dominus snapped at them the entire time they were layering his toga."

I shook my head.

Aelia's voice wafted from the room. "You like the white stola? Are you sure the yellow silk wouldn't be better?"

"Aelia, please stop worrying. You look beautiful. We've had large parties before and you haven't been nervous." There was the clink of cosmetic pots and bottles of nard used to perfume the forehead.

"I wasn't nervous until you mentioned Ovid would be coming," Aelia said.

Aelia was not alone in her love of Ovid's poetry. Passia had read every word the man had ever written. He was considered to be one of Rome's experts on both love and beauty, and most women I knew owned several of his books. When Passia heard he would be in attendance I thought she might swoon.

There was the ruffle of a scroll being unraveled. "Could this be one of the sources of your concern? *Women's Facial Cosmetics*?"

I remembered the book. Apicius had bought it and other Ovid titles for Aelia two years earlier as a Saturnalia gift.

"I know, I shouldn't worry. But if he didn't know so much, how could he write it down? It is as though he were the mouthpiece for Venus herself!"

There was the soft sound of a kiss.

"Aelia, you are the sort of woman Ovid writes his poems about. That mirror cannot show you what I see."

"I think you exaggerate, husband."

"No, I do not. At any rate, you know many of the people who will be here tonight. Fannia will help you navigate through all the family names. You know Trio, Celera, and Publius Octavius, and Gaia too."

Aelia's voice turned sour. "I don't know why you invited Octavius. It's always such a competition between the two of you. Don't you get tired of showing each other up?"

Apicius was silent. More clink of pots.

"I talked to Apicata about Numerius Cornelius Sulla," Aelia said, changing the subject.

"Did she understand?" His words were full of concern.

"I think so. She liked the idea of wearing the flame veil and the 'pretty' belt, as she described it."

I eyed Sotas, who nodded his head. A flame veil referred to the traditional Roman wedding veil the color of saffron, and the "pretty" belt was a knotted belt to be untied by the husband on the wedding night. It seemed that Apicius had betrothed his daughter. In truth, I was somewhat surprised he had not done so earlier. Many children of Roman patricians were betrothed at very young ages, to seal family commitment and build relationships.

Apicius chuckled at his daughter's reaction. "It is a shame that he could not be here to help us celebrate."

"It's just as well," Aelia said. "Sulla is so much older than you are. It might have confused Apicata to see him."

There was a long silence, then Aelia spoke up.

"Did you deliver an invite to Sejanus?"

"Yes, I did." I heard Apicius moving toward the door. I stood and backed away.

"It will be good to see him again." Her voice sounded far away.

"It has been a while," he said, emerging from the room into the hall where we waited.

He saw me and scowled. "What do you want? Shouldn't you be in the kitchen?"

"Yes, Dominus, but I wondered . . ."

"Wonder it later. I have too much to do to worry about whatever it is you want. I don't need to hold your hand. Just take care of things!"

I sucked in a breath, shocked to hear such venom after he had spoken so tenderly to Aelia.

"What was that about?" I asked Sotas after Apicius dismissed us. "He was fine earlier."

"Did you notice when his mood changed? During his conversation with Aelia?"

I picked up the pace to keep up with the big man. I thought back to the conversation. "When Aelia mentioned Octavius and Sejanus."

Sotas slowed and glanced around.

"What I tell you must not become gossip in the house. You must be silent. If you are not, I fear for how Fides will punish me for misplacing my trust and betraying the secrets of my dominus."

I knew he feared the wrath of his goddess more than he feared losing his life. I clapped a hand on his arm—his shoulder was a bit high for me to reach. "Fear not, Sotas. I won't let you down."

"Dominus wants to avoid Sejanus," he said, his voice low.

"But why?"

"Hard to look in the eye a man you've bedded when you discover he isn't the whore you thought he was."

I caught myself before I exclaimed aloud. I don't know what I thought Sotas was going to tell me but I certainly didn't expect that.

"He slept with Sejanus?"

Sotas grunted. "It was nine years ago and we were summering in Pompeii. Dominus met Sejanus at the baths. Sejanus was maybe fourteen, so Dominus would have been about twenty-three."

Sejanus was a year older than me. I had been living in Pompeii then and we could easily have been at the baths at the same time.

"You've been to the baths there, right?"

"I have." The baths were small and always packed tight like anchovies in oil.

"Right, everyone sits so close together. I noticed Dominus staring at one of the boys. He was what some might call handsome, I suppose. He was fit, with muscles that looked like they could have been sculpted by that famous sculptor, what was his name?"

"Pheidias," I supplied, looking around to make sure we weren't overheard.

"Yes, him. Anyway, the boy came and sat next to Dominus. He didn't say much but he listened to all of our dominus's stories. He didn't have a body-slave with him and he was by himself, so we assumed he was a pleb.

"The boy followed him through the *frigidarium*. They dressed together, still talking. When we left the bath, Dominus propositioned him. I remember gasping aloud. Dominus elbowed me so hard I had a bruise for days after."

I couldn't believe what I was hearing. Apicius spoke disparagingly of his friends who had a penchant for young boys. He thought Greek love was vulgar!

"Anyway," Sotas went on, "within an hour the two were holed up in an inn above a loud popina. You know how much he hates taverns."

"A popina? I can't even picture it." I was amazed at the story. It was out of character for our dominus.

"I ran ahead and secured the room. Thrasius, the amount of money he gave Sejanus for just an hour! Dominus paid him as much as he would have for a new slave. I had to stand outside the room and guard the door, hearing every grunt and groan. I was glad when we left. But then the next day we met him there again."

"Again?"

"Yes. We met him several times over the course of that summer. Always at that popina and always for an exorbitant amount of money."

"He didn't know Sejanus was Aelia's cousin? And an equestrian?" No wonder Apicius was embarrassed. If other nobles discovered the tryst, it would be shameful indeed. Having sex with slaves and plebs was one thing, but with a patrician—that was a line that was not to be crossed.

Sotas shook his head. "No, he didn't. He truly thought him a pleb. He identified himself as Lucius and didn't give his full name. At the end of the summer, Dominus asked him if he could deliver a package for him. The boy agreed. We returned the next day with a parcel. He took it and that was the last we saw of him that summer."

"But you saw him again at some point?"

"Yes, but that's not the worst of it."

We paused until a trio of laundry slaves had passed. When they were out of earshot, he continued. "The parcel was damning."

"What was in the parcel?"

"A vial of poison, a letter with instructions, and money. A great deal of it, meant for an assassin."

I covered my mouth for fear I would exclaim aloud. "Whom did Apicius intend to have killed?"

"Publius Octavius."

I couldn't believe my ears. "Octavius? Are you serious?"

"I told you that Dominus has hated him for years. Dominus told him once that he wanted to become the gastronomic adviser to Caesar. Not three weeks later Octavius announced his own intent to find favor with Caesar. That angered Dominus to no end."

"What happened?"

Sotas grimaced. "One night not long after, Tiberius—yes, that Tiberius," he said, noting the question in my eyes. Tiberius was Livia's son and Caesar's stepson. "He was visiting Octavius at his villa. He had with him a young man who was said to be one of Tiberius's oldest and closest friends, a soldier from his military days. During the meal the man complained that his tongue was numb and that he was growing very cold. He was dead within fifteen minutes."

"It sounds like wolfsbane," I breathed. I had been taught at an early age how to distinguish the leaves from that of the radish, as they looked very similar. The poison worked fast. Every part of the plant was extremely deadly and the juice of the plant was said to have caused the death of many a senator over the centuries.

"Tiberius flew into a rage and had his men execute Octavius's cook and the entire kitchen staff."

"What about Octavius? How was he spared from having to go to trial for attempted murder?"

"I know not. Perhaps he trusted Octavius, or maybe Octavius convinced Tiberius that his kitchen had been infiltrated."

"By the gods." The muscles in my neck tightened.

Sotas gazed down the hallway toward the peristylium, his eyes as cold as flint. "It was a year until we saw Sejanus again, in Rome at Aelia's mother's funeral. We were listening to the priests give the blessings to guide Amelia Lamia to the Underworld, and Dominus raised his head, looked across the old woman's body, and saw him. The gods have frozen the moment in my mind. I can smell the cassia and frankincense. I can hear the chants of the priest. I remember the ancestral masks lining the room. Domina was crying. And the boy, whom we knew only as Lucius, was staring at us.

"Lucius walked next to Dominus and Domina during the procession to the cemetery outside the gates of the city. I walked behind everyone so it was easy for me to see he kept eyeing Dominus. Many hours later, after the fire from the pyre had begun to die down and they were starting to collect the ashes for interment, the boy appeared. Neither of us expected him to reach over, put his arm around Aelia, and hug her close. I remember he told Aelia that Ceres would watch over her mother and make sure her journey across the Styx and to Pluto was safe.

"She said thank you, then introduced him to Dominus as her cousin, Lucius Aelius Sejanus, whom she hadn't seen in years. He leaned in and whispered to Apicius words I still remember to this day. 'I delivered the poison, but kept the letter and gave the instructions directly. I suggest you treat me well in the years ahead. You never know when I might need a favor.' Then he returned to his place in the procession to walk with his family. Dominus was horrified."

As was I. "How could that letter be traced back to him?"

"Dominus used to leave notes with the proprietor of the popina to let Sejanus know when to meet again. Nothing salacious in those letters but they were fastened with his seal. I saw Dominus write the letter of instructions for the assassin. He mentioned Octavius by name."

I thought about Apicius's distinctive flair with the stylus. His writing was as rich and dramatic as he was. Anyone who had seen his writing, even once, would instantly recognize it. Even without his seal. "Why wouldn't he have disguised his handwriting?"

Sotas shrugged. "I think he thought Sejanus was of no consequence. Plus, back then Dominus himself was not in the public eye."

I shook my head in disbelief. The story seemed nearly too incredible to be true. I tried not to think about what might happen if he was found out. What would happen to me, to all of the slaves, if he were discovered.

I wasn't sure how to absorb this new information. Lost in thought and not paying attention to where I walked, I managed to bump into a table and knock over a vase full of white roses. Sotas caught me as I lost my footing in the slick water coating the tiles.

"Thanks, Sotas. Hopefully I'll be the only one you need to catch tonight."

"I hope so too," he said grimly.

CHAPTER 9

I was passing through the atrium when Fannia Drusilla arrived. A slave showed her in and a quick glance at the water clock revealed that she was early.

"I cannot tell you how happy I am that you will be by my side tonight." Apicius clasped his mentor's hands in his own. "I need your advice and good fortune to guide me this evening."

Fannia had lost weight and looked ten years younger. "Good fortune indeed! I do bring a bit along with me tonight. Now tell me, did you consult a haruspex?"

"I did. My first sacrifice was unworthy—the liver was full of spots. The next one was fine, but he warned me I should watch for conspiracy. I have been fretting, I must admit."

"No, do not fret." She patted his arm. "I consulted with an astrologer before I came. He said nothing untoward would happen this evening, though he did say that something occurring tonight would have far-reaching consequences for the future. Perhaps someone will recommend you to Caesar?"

"We'll see. What about you, Fannia? It could pertain to you."

"I had a priest paint an evil eye on my stomach before I came. I don't want my cousin showing up tonight! But the good news is I think Livia is growing bored with tormenting me. The graffiti has lessened."

After Octavius and Livia had offered to buy me, Fannia had begun to see graffiti in her neighborhood, graffiti naming her as a woman cursed by Pluto himself. In the last two years, not more than a fortnight went by before new markings appeared. When she saw fresh scrawls, she always sent a slave to scrub them clean, but the emotional damage had been done. Daily, she made a sacrifice to Hera, asking for protection, for both her and Apicius. "You're in Rome now!" she would say, telling him she made the sacrifice so he wouldn't be vulnerable to the complex and violent politics of the Forum and the palace. I imagined that it would take more than a painted tattoo and a few sacrifices to protect him.

One of my serving girls arrived with glasses of pomegranate honey water. The girl was blond, and dressed in a long, white, diaphanous slip that hid nothing—even I had to avert my eyes from the dark buttons of her nipples and the soft triangle between her legs. She would cause a stir in such a half state of clothing, which was precisely what Apicius wanted when he'd instructed me to find twelve slaves to be given as gifts to some of the night's lucky guests. I disliked the duty of finding these women but I took comfort in the fact that I could protect Passia. I therefore suggested they should be exotic because I didn't want Passia to be considered. While she was striking, Passia was of Greek birth and thus her features were quite familiar. Instead the slaves given as gifts were from the farthest reaches of the Empire, from Germania, Cappadocia, Galicia, Britannia, and other provinces.

"Beautiful girl. I have half a mind to ask you for her hair! I could use another wig." Fannia took the glass goblet from the slave and nodded at Apicius approvingly. "Now back to my astrologer. His name is Glycon and I think you should take comfort in his words."

Apicius took Fannia by the arm to escort her to the dining area. I had not yet been dismissed so I fell into step behind Sotas.

"What else has he predicted true for you?" There was hunger in Apicius's voice.

"He told me my damned husband would return early from Alexandria last month. I took heed and went to Herculaneum to visit my sister. Sure enough, he did and I was able to avoid him."

They reached the peristylium and lay down on the sumptuous pillows on the couches. I knew there were numerous duties awaiting my attention, but I hesitated in the shadows beyond, wanting to hear the rest of the conversation. I could see my master and his friend through a slit in the curtain that covered the door. Sotas sent the rest of the slaves away, but when he saw me lingering in the shadows, he smirked.

The peristylium was lit with lamps hanging from poles along the wall, with more small lamps placed on a high, water-free platform in the upper part of the center fountain. Apicius had spared no expense. The couches were covered in cloth dyed the most expensive Tyrian purple and studded on the edges with hundreds of tiny rubies—many of which I expected would be pocketed before the night ended. Dancers dressed like nymphs waited in the next room, ready to float through the crowd, twirling and bending and twisting to the flutists.

"He also told me I would take a lover." Fannia winked at Apicius. Her face had a girlish glow.

"He did? Have you?"

"I have! It's positively scandalous, of course, so you must be discreet. He's strong and dark with a body that . . . mmm." She paused and licked her lips. "Glycon also told me the very day I would meet my new lover and, sure enough, on that day I met Florus at a beach party in Cumae. I am serious. You should consider hiring Glycon."

Apicius set his empty glass on the small tripod table next to his couch. "I'll think about it. Having extra guidance would be good."

Her face darkened. "You mean now that you are here in Rome with enemies."

"Yes, that's part of my concern. And I worry about Popilla," he admitted.

"She can't touch you here. Even if she were a ghost who wanted to haunt you, you are a hundred and fifty miles from where her shade might be. Rest easy."

Apicius gazed down at the tiles. "I suppose. But there are other reasons too."

"Sejanus will be here tonight, won't he?" Fannia said.

Apicius curled his lip into a distasteful snarl. I was surprised that Apicius had told Fannia about the relationship with Sejanus, but, then again, she had always been his closest confidante. I wondered if she knew about the accident that killed Tiberius's friend.

"Yes, damn him to Tartarus. And Octavius too. Why I was ever moved to invite him, I don't know." From the folds of his toga, Apicius pulled out the amulet he'd had blessed at Jupiter's temple. He held it to the sky. "May Jupiter and Vesta protect me this night in my own house!"

Fannia raised her glass in solidarity. "Sejanus won't do a thing," she reassured Apicius. "He doesn't want anyone to know he was sleeping with you. Worry not—he can only delight in making you uncomfortable. Don't give him the satisfaction."

"I have much more to lose than he. Not only did I sleep with my wife's cousin, a damned equestrian, but I also committed adultery, which is punishable enough on its own if the emperor decided to enforce the law—"

"Unlikely," Fannia interrupted.

"But those letters . . ." he continued, his voice dropping. "I was so stupid to include my seal on the notes to him. He could decide to give them to Octavius at any time! Worse, he could do it in front of me! Or worse, he could show Tiberius and my life would be over without a trial—he could have Caesar order my death." His voice lowered into a barely audible hiss. "I killed his best friend!"

Fannia patted Apicius's hand. "It might not go as bad as that."

"Are you mad? Tiberius would not spare me. Oh, gods, I wish I knew what Sejanus wanted. He's clearly biding his time, but for what? Pluto, I beseech you, take him now!" He punched the back of the couch with his hand and several rubies fell into the cracks. When Apicius pulled his hand back, there was blood. I passed a cloth I kept on my belt to Sotas and he rushed forward to help stanch the blood. Apicius took the cloth and waved Sotas off.

Fannia was unperturbed by his display of anger. "Oh, I've no doubt that he'll attempt to blackmail you at some point. I'm sure you are right. He's waiting until he knows exactly what he wants in return."

"I wish I could get those blasted letters back." He pressed the cloth to his hand. His face was twisted into a scowl.

"Have you had any run-ins with Livia?" Fannia asked, changing the subject.

"No, not at all. But I dined with Caesar's gastronomic adviser last week and he told me she's been traveling with Caesar Augustus. It was the first time I had seen him since the night at your house."

"Ahh, Corvinus." Fannia tapped the edge of her glass with her finger. "What else did he say?"

"I asked if Livia bore me ill will for refusing to sell Thrasius to Octavius. He didn't think so. He thinks she's forgotten all about it."

"Don't trust her. She harbors grudges for years, then strikes like a cobra. Always be wary. But Octavius . . . he is ever more dangerous. Unlike Livia, he is more desperate. Why did you invite him?"

"I want to know what he is up to. Besides, I have Sotas to protect me." Apicius turned in our direction and I pulled my head away from the curtain, hoping he didn't see me.

"True. You would not want to meet Sotas in a dark alley. Your father did well when he bought him."

I looked at Sotas, agreeing with Fannia. He was large enough to pick me up and hurl me across the room with ease.

Apicius grew quiet, returning to the subject of his mother once again. "Do you really think that Popilla is not able to follow me here?" It was one of the few times when I heard true fear in the voice of my master.

"Absolutely not. Besides, you performed the rites at Lemuria this year, didn't you?"

He had. I still had in my mind the image of him wandering the Baiae domus at midnight this past May, his voice low and dark. He tossed black beans into every corner of the house as he chanted, "I send these; with these beans I redeem me and mine." He walked the length of the domus nine times. When he was done, all the slaves erupted in a cacophony of noise as we crashed bronze pots together and sang, over and over, "Ghosts of my fathers and ancestors, be gone!" nine times. If that racket hadn't scared off the ghost of Popilla, I'm not sure anything could. But Apicius didn't look convinced.

The slave with the gossamer gown entered from the door across the peristylium, this time leading a couple into the garden. Fannia patted Apicius's shoulder and told him not to worry about Popilla. He nodded and straightened to meet the guests, Trio and his wife, Celera. The party had begun. I rushed to the kitchen, chastising myself for being pulled into such ridiculous intrigue. I was worse than Balsamea, listening to conversations that were not my own.

Back in the kitchen, Rúan presented me with a large square of framed wax and a wooden stylus. The tablet had been my idea. Finding a way to explain the dishes was important given the unusual manner of presenting food during the commissatio. Apicius had arranged couches for those who preferred a more formal presentation, but guests could also mingle and partake from slaves who wandered among them, offering up morsels on silver trays. The wax tablet, which would describe the menu, was to be placed on a table at the entry to the peristylium.

I inscribed the names of the dishes onto the tablet. Fried hyacinth bulbs, sow's udder, Lucanian sausage, hard egg mice, fried hare livers, oiled cabbage, fried carrots, milk-fed snails, honey ricotta sliced bread, apples, mussels, and peppered truffles.

"Are you sure about this?" Rúan asked me. "There is no surprise for the guests."

In truth it was an experiment, but I thought it a good one. "I think that guests might appreciate a choice."

"Mayhap, but it seems odd to show people what we're serving."

I was about to respond when Tycho, who had become one of my most prized serving boys, piped up behind me. "Will Dominus be pleased?"

He waited with four other serving boys, ranging in age from eight to twelve. They were dressed in silver tunics with tiny feathered wings strapped to their backs. Their hair shone with silver flecks, a trick Passia had come up with—how she managed the effect, I hadn't asked. The boys' lips were reddened with the finest colors from Egypt, purchased that morning from the peddler who brought cosmetics to Aelia.

"Oh, yes, Dominus will be very pleased." They were so charming, I was sure each of them would be lent out before the evening was finished. I tried not to think about that aspect of their duties. I kissed each of them on the head and bade them to go make their evening offerings to Vesta before the party started.

Not long after the serving boys returned from their prayers, I was helping Balsamea carefully plate the last of the hard-boiled mice—clove eyes, chive tails, and almond-slivered ears—when Rúan came to inform me more guests had arrived. "I served them honey water, but Dominus requested that we bring out the food," he said.

"The plates are ready to go, as are the boys." I waved to Tycho to bring his troupe over to start gathering serving trays.

Passia entered the kitchen, sweeping past Rúan and dragging Apicata with her. The girl held her new puppy, a thin gray creature, one of the smaller hound breeds. It held its tail between its legs as though it had just been whipped.

"Maybe you can talk some sense into her," Passia said, her brow wrinkled with exasperation. I wanted to reach out and hug her worries away. Our little mistress had recently begun to assert her independence more frequently and Passia had often been frustrated. Apicata behaved as a perfect angel when Aelia was anywhere near, but as soon as she was sent back into Passia's care, the girl turned into a baby Hydra. You never knew which head you were going to get when dealing with Apicata.

"What's wrong now?" I knelt down to be on her level.

"I want to show Perseus to Father's friends!"

"Apicata, I'm not sure a party would be the best place for Perseus. He might be frightened with so many people milling about."

"He wasn't afraid when we went to the market the other day."

I stifled a deep sigh and tried another angle. "Have you asked your mother or father?"

She pushed her sandal along the tiles, moving a fallen piece of carrot around with her toe. "I can't. They are already with their friends. That's why I want to go show them!"

I pushed a lock of hair behind her ear. She looked at me with wide hopeful eyes.

"How about we do this? Let's go to the peristylium. Passia will escort you to your parents and I'll stand by the door with Perseus. Ask your father what he thinks, and if he is happy to let your dog play with his guests, have him give me a thumbs-up. If he's not, you give me a thumbs-down and I'll take Perseus back to your room."

Apicata didn't look happy with the suggestion but she nodded. Looking over her shoulders, I saw her ball up her thumb between her fingers behind her back in the sign of the fig. I tried hard not to smile. Many young children used it as a lucky sign, not knowing the gesture had sexual implications. I put my hand on her shoulder, happy we were able to come to a compromise. Together we walked to the peristylium, the squirming puppy in my arms.

When we reached the wide-open doors, I saw many guests had arrived, far more than we had anticipated at such an early hour. The women in their silk stolae made a colorful contrast to the men in their white togas. They stood around, talking and sampling food from the trays the slave cherubs held in their young hands.

I waited at the door while Passia brought Apicata to the couch where her parents sat. My view was blocked by Passia, so I watched carefully to see who would give me the agreed-upon wave of the hand. Several moments passed as the conversation turned toward Apicata. I strained to hear but the nearby fountain burbled too much for me to make out any words.

Suddenly the sea of people parted. Passia moved to the side and I saw Apicata with her arms outstretched, waiting for me to release Perseus. Apicius gave me the thumbs-up and as I set down the hound and released it, I realized Apicata stood in front of a man in his midtwenties. His hands were on her shoulders, and his face was twisted into a conniving smile.

I thought my heart might stop.

The man holding Apicata was the same man we saw at the market that morning in Baiae five months ago. Then I understood, all the pieces coming together in a mad rush. The man had to be Sejanus.

He saw me and recognition flickered in his eyes. He gave me a two-fingered wave and smiled down on Apicata, who was ruffling her pup's ears.

When I returned to the kitchen I could hardly focus. I left Rúan in charge of the next course and went to seek out Sotas in the shadows of the peristylium.

He sat on a tiled bench, watching the guests mingle. The night was steamy and I brought him a cup of wine in which I had slipped some precious snow, a treat not typically afforded to slaves, but no one would notice; in the unusual heat of the October evening it had already melted.

I slid onto the bench next to him. Sotas was looking in the direction of Sejanus, who was talking with Apicius, Fannia, and Aelia. Apicata played with Perseus beneath their feet. Sejanus was more charismatic than the day I saw him drunk in Baiae, his features even more finely chiseled, his eyes a touch bluer and the smile more devious than I remembered.

"Bastard," Sotas said. "He remembers me. You watch him, and tell me what you think. Even if that day hadn't happened, there is something *wrong* about him, something underhanded and wicked."

"He's the man who wanted to accost Apicata at the market in Baiae."

Sotas stared at me, his eyes widening. "Are you sure?"

"As sure as you are sitting next to me." I seethed. "He said that Apicius owed him a favor. I tried to warn Dominus but he wouldn't listen.

"Tell me, Sotas, if Sejanus has such evidence on Apicius, why hasn't Apicius tried to kill Sejanus?"

Sotas cocked an eyebrow at me. "You mustn't talk of such things."

"Why not?"

"Apicius hates Sejanus but he's on his way to becoming a Praetorian—the best of Caesar's guards. If anyone would die in an attempt to stop him, it would likely be him for even thinking it. The investigation into his death would be relentless, and the consequences painful and deadly—to all around Apicius."

He turned back toward the party. I watched with him, marveling over the web that the Fates wove for us—it was truly tangled.

At length, the flutists moved off and I could hear the conversation.

"Your daughter is delightful!" Sejanus was saying to Aelia. I gripped the edge of the bench and bit my tongue as he spoke. "She is a living testament to the good looks that seem to follow the gens Aelia."

Aelia smiled. "Cousin, you flatter me."

Sejanus had set the tone for the evening with the clear slight against the Gavia clan. "It's only a shame I share the name through adoption—not blood—or who knows how much more attractive I might have been!" Nearby guests laughed at the joke but to me it seemed the true intent was to point out that Apicius had, at least at one time, found him attractive. Sejanus looked at Apicius directly as he spoke, a smile on his face.

Apicius gave away nothing. He waved over a boy with a tray. "Have you tried the fried hare livers, Sejanus?"

Apicata jumped up and down and smiled at her father. "May I? May I?"

Her father smiled. Apicata could always melt his heart. "Only one and don't share with Perseus!"

The serving boy lowered the tray so she could reach for the liver but not so low that the jumping puppy could steal treats for himself. She snatched a morsel and popped it into her mouth. I knew what she tasted, a sublime mixture of textures, the crispy breaded exterior and the smooth, sumptuous richness of the liver itself. The combination is unexpected. When I first introduced the recipe, it immediately became a family favorite.

Apicata turned to Sejanus. She did not appear to recognize him from the market. "Oh, you must try! These are my favorite!"

"If you say so, I must try!" Sejanus reached for the tray. He took a bite of the liver and surprise registered in his eyes.

Sejanus reached for another liver. "Where on earth did you find your cook?"

"Baiae." Aelia reached for her own sample. "Thrasius's cooking is always exceptional. Wait until you try the hyacinth bulbs!"

"Hyacinth bulbs are one of my favorites." Sejanus ran his fingers affectionately through Apicata's hair as he talked.

I stared, wondering what his intentions were. My right eye began to twitch.

Apicius nodded at Passia to come forward and collect Apicata and her puppy. The girl went begrudgingly and only after Sejanus had planted a kiss on her forehead and promised he would visit again soon.

"There are rumors your father will be named consul," Sejanus said to Aelia.

"I have heard the same." Octavius joined the conversation. He carried a napkin full of sausages. His mouth was full and the corners of his lips were slick with grease. "Aelia, you must be so proud!"

"It is well deserved," Aelia said. "He has worked hard to be a good senator and it's wonderful to see him rewarded."

"Have you seen him much since you came to Rome?" Sejanus asked. He already seemed to be acquainted with Octavius.

Apicius spoke up. "He dined here last week, with Seneca the Rhetorician and his wife."

"Did anyone tell you about Corvinus?" Octavius shook a sausage at Apicius.

Aelia spoke up before her husband could. "Is he all right?"

Octavius licked his lips. "Oh, he's perfectly fine. In fact, he's decided it's time to retire."

I wondered why Fannia hadn't mentioned it to Apicius when she'd talked to him earlier about Corvinus. I could see a surge of excitement rush through Apicius and knew he was thinking through all his clients to determine if he could call in favors with those who held sway with

Corvinus and could recommend him. The spark of hope died in his eyes with Octavius's next words.

"While he's heading to his farm in Tusculum, I'll be taking on his work for Augustus. Now that I'm back from governing Egypt, Caesar wanted to make sure I was kept busy." He stuffed another sausage in his mouth and chewed.

"Splendid news," Apicius managed to say. But it was not splendid news. To have Octavius win the coveted adviser post was the worst news imaginable. I was sure Apicius wanted nothing more than to go throw himself into the Tiber.

"Congratulations," Sejanus said, but he raised a knowing eyebrow at Apicius. Apicius did not return the look, and only continued to smile pleasantly at Octavius.

"Thank you," Octavius said, his point having been made. "Oh, Apicius, I heard about that nasty business with your mother."

Apicius froze.

"What a she-devil you were spawned from!" The insult in his voice was clear. "I'm sure you were right to exercise your paterfamilias with that woman." He smacked his lips.

"You are out of line!" Aelia spoke up. I was surprised at her audacity, to assert herself so to one of Apicius's guests.

"Aelia . . ." Apicius warned, glaring at her. Deflated, she stepped back a pace.

"Now, now, Octavius, we should stay out of the affairs of others, don't you agree?" Sejanus said pleasantly.

Octavius didn't respond but he dipped his head in deference before walking away to talk to a cluster of senators who stood nearby.

"It must be good to be close to family again," Sejanus said, turning the conversation. "I, for one, am glad to be here. Just as Rome was becoming a bit of a bore, my dear cousin and her husband come and throw a party!"

Aelia beamed but Apicius said nothing, only gestured for a servant to refill their wine. He tilted his glass in a toast, then downed it fast, as though he hoped the wine would wash everything away.

Despite that bitter moment, the rest of the party was lovely. My cherubs and nymphs wove through the crowd with trays of food and glasses of wine cut with water by Trio, whom Apicius had asked to be the Magister of Revels. The highlight was Ovid. He was a striking man with sandy-brown hair framing a boyish face, despite his middling age. It was no wonder all the women in Rome fell at his feet.

Ovid cleared his throat and a hush fell upon the garden. "I have heard my host has a young daughter with a hound by the name of Perseus."

Aelia cried out in excitement.

"I am working on a book of the great tales of all the gods. I am not far along, but I can tell you this story, of the great Perseus for which Apicata's pet is named. This portion of the poem occurs right after his triumph over the monstrous gorgon Medusa. Perseus asked Atlas for a night's rest but Atlas, wary of an old prophecy that said the son of Jove would overthrow him, refused."

Ovid took a sip of wine and began, his voice rising above the clusters of guests standing around the garden.

> But Atlas, mindful of an oracle
> from Themis, of Parnassus,
> recalled these words, "O Atlas! mark the day
> a son of Jupiter shall come to spoil;
> for when thy trees been stripped of golden fruit,
> the glory shall be his."
> Fearful of this,
> Atlas had built solid walls around
> his orchard, and secured a dragon, huge,
> that kept perpetual guard, and thence expelled
> all strangers from his land. Wherefore he said,
> "Begone! The glory of your deeds is all
> pretense; even Jupiter, will fail your need."

Thus Perseus was forced to fight the great Atlas, and realizing he could not win, he brought the gorgon's head forward and turned Atlas to stone, fulfilling the prophecy.

I thought back to the reading Apicius had received the day he purchased me. For some reason, it seemed to be a marker for my master, a prophecy of a sort. I wondered if, like Atlas, it would become a self-fulfilling prophecy. "Ultimately, you will be judged in the Underworld by how our world and the world of the future perceive you." I'd often heard

Apicius repeating that last line. In the years since the reading he had shaped his life in relation to those words. He was obsessed with creating a life that would render him memorable to all.

I peered across the garden to where Sotas stood in the shadows. Sotas might be able to protect Apicius from all outwardly harm, but I doubted anyone could protect Apicius from himself.

PART IV

4 C.E. to 5 C.E.

PATINA OF PEARS

Core and boil the pears, pound them with pepper, cumin, honey, passum, liquamen, and a little oil. Add eggs to make a patina, sprinkle with pepper, and serve.

—*Book 4.2.35, Compound Dishes*
On Cookery, Apicius

CHAPTER 10

Now that we were in Rome, Apicius became more focused on public appearances, enlarging and redesigning his villa, including expanding the snow cellar at great expense. He gave me funds to purchase additional slaves for the kitchens in both Rome and Minturnae to accommodate the larger parties we hosted. His name was bandied about among Rome's finest. That summer he hosted many influential patricians, including the governors of Egypt and Carthage, who were both in Rome for the ceremony honoring Caesar's adoption of Livia's son, Tiberius, as heir.

When I could, I continued to work on the cookbook. The task was harder than I'd first imagined. Sometimes one recipe would take me weeks to perfect. Only then could I inscribe the recipes onto the page. Fortunately, Apicius took to the idea of a cookbook like snails to milk.

"Only the best, Thrasius, only the best," Apicius said one afternoon, nearly a year after I first showed him all the recipes. He clapped me on the back as I unpacked a crate of wine just delivered from Greece. "This book will make many a new chef into demigods of their masters' kitchens, but none of them will be able to truly re-create what I am doing, Thrasius. No one else will have this wine, or the same pine nuts from Sardinia. Or the same green walnuts, gathered in the moonlight during the feast of Fortuna! Their wine will be plonk, their pine nuts from the trees in their backyard, their green walnuts fallen and dark. They will think they are tasting a bit of Elysium, but only diners at my table will know true ambrosia!"

I had to bite my tongue when he talked like that, as though the recipes were his doing, not mine.

"You are his," Passia told me matter-of-factly one afternoon when I was ranting about my master's claim to the recipes I had so painstakingly researched. "Therefore the recipes are his." She stroked my hair, soothing me. "Until you have your freedom, all you do is his. You have what many would sell their souls to Pluto for. Take your happiness where you can. Do not whine like a child over that which you cannot change."

She was right. Apicius treated me well and he gave me great freedom to explore what I loved most—cooking. Few slaves had such opportunities.

We began to travel every few weeks, seeking out the best ingredients for the recipes. At first the trips were an adventure. I missed Passia very much, but I was also secretly pleased that my master felt such dedication to the recipes I devised. We went to Egypt, where we found a recipe for bottle gourds; in Sicily we learned an old olive relish recipe; in Byzantium we discovered salted tunny fish; and in Syria we purchased huge jars of the juiciest dates I have ever eaten.

Still, while I freely admit that I enjoyed access to such luxury for my cooking, I worried about my dominus's obsession, mostly because it rarely went well for those around him. Apicius spent great amounts of time and money on luxuries that did not turn out to be what he thought they would. Which is what happened the time we went to the northern coast of Africa.

We were in Minturnae, spending a few weeks near the shore, when I learned of the trip. It was time for the salutatio and Apicius had seen only a handful of his clients. Apollo's chariot was not even high in the sky and already the heat was unbearable. I was looking forward to taking a few moments to stand in the snow cellar to cool off.

Apicius grew more impatient with his clients as the morning wore on. After a time, he leaned over and whispered in my ear, "I don't have time for this. I'll see one more, then send the rest away."

I swallowed the anise seeds I'd been chewing to freshen my breath. Why was he so anxious to end the salutatio? Was he thinking of returning to Rome early? The family had arrived in Minturnae only a few days before, and aside from being able to celebrate Neptunalia in our old home, part of the reason we'd come was to influence the votes of his clients. The governor of the province wasn't convinced it was necessary to extend a crucial road into Minturnae, and as a result, it was going to a regional vote. The road, Apicius had argued to his clientele all morning, would bring more trade to the town. That was true, but Apicius had a different motive—he wanted Caesar to purchase his unused marshlands to transform them into a raised road leading more directly into Minturnae. Such an agreement would be lucrative indeed.

I cleared my throat and read off the next name on my list. "Numerius Priscus Mato will receive the last audience of the day," I said to the men standing in the atrium. "The rest of you may partake from the tray of honey cakes and apples as you leave."

The named client, Mato, was a pale freedman who stood hunched over, much like many older ex-slaves who had once worked on the salt flats beyond Ostia carrying heavy slabs of salt day in and day out. Apicius wasn't fond of the man, who had gotten drunk at one of his cenae a few years prior and had broken a costly amphora of wine. Although it took more than a year, Mato, without having been prompted to do so, paid back the cost of the wine. It didn't matter. Apicius's opinion of him had permanently soured; he had little love for drunkards.

I felt bad for the man. He'd made a mistake and had worked hard to fix it. It bothered me that the effort went unnoticed by my master.

"Priscus Mato, what favor do you seek this morning?"

Mato kept his eyes downward. "It's my son, little Mato. He's very ill. I fear for his life."

"I'm sorry to hear that. You should make an offering to Asclepius," Apicius said, raising a hand to wave Mato away.

"That's why I came to you, Apicius. I'd like to take him to the Asclepeion in Rome but I need money for the trip and the offering. Please, will you help us? I will do anything you ask, vote for anybody you say, give you anything in my power."

Apicius idly ran his fingers across the jeweled goblet that held his morning wine.

Mato dropped to his knees. A flash of sun from the opening in the atrium shone directly into his face and he squinted, forcing tears from the corners of his eyes.

"Get up," Apicius said sharply. He had never liked displays of womanly emotion.

Mato struggled to get to his feet. Sotas stepped forward to help the man but stopped when Apicius snapped his fingers. After a moment Mato stood and wavered unsteadily. Desperation shone in his eyes.

Apicius crooked a finger at his client. "If I give you the money for the trip and for a box of snakes for the temple offering, you must agree to give me your boy as a slave when he has been healed."

I exchanged a worried glance with Sotas. This was unprecedented cruelty on the part of our master. To pay for such a trip and the sacred snakes would be but a trifle, a few denarii at best. To ask for the life of the man's son was hardly a fair exchange. I did not like this dark side of my dominus. Worse, it had come unbidden. I could not fathom what drove Apicius to be so callous.

Mato's mouth fell open at Apicius's proclamation. "You know not what you ask of me, Apicius," he said in a low voice.

Apicius stood. His chair was on a raised platform, and the added height, although slight, gave Apicius the appearance of towering over his client. "I do know what I ask, Priscus Mato. I ask for the life of your son in exchange for the money I will give you to save it."

The blood visibly rose in Mato's face. He trembled but his voice did not shake. "I suffered at the hands of men like you, Apicius. For thirty-five years I toiled and bled for the doings of others. I scraped together my meager peculium to buy my freedom and the freedom of my sons. Death would be better for him than slavery."

"Very well, death may be what he will receive." He flicked a finger at Sotas. "Have him removed."

Sotas gently led the man toward the door. My heart lurched with each step he took.

Apicius snapped his fingers at me as he stood. "Come, Thrasius, accompany me to the library." I followed, deeply concerned about my master's cruel mood.

"Dominus—" I began as we left the atrium. He didn't break his stride when he cut me off.

"I don't want to hear it, Thrasius. If you say one word to me about that drunkard, I will take away your time with Passia."

He heard my sharp intake of breath.

"Don't think that it's escaped me just how much that girl means to you. You would be wise to keep that in mind."

If I had held real knives at the time I might have released them without thinking, so great was my anger. I glanced at Sotas and he gave me a warning look—a look that said I should keep my mouth shut and agree to whatever Apicius wanted. Of late I had been seeing more and more of that look from the big man. My dominus's moods were becoming increasingly unpredictable and extreme and no one understood why.

When we reached the library, Apicius crossed the room to the open window facing toward the ocean. The morning sun made the sea sparkle as if it were covered in flecks of gold. "A beautiful day to sail!" His voice held no irritation. Instead he sounded joyful.

I was flabbergasted. "You've been preparing to sail?" I managed, struggling to hide both my anger and my disbelief. "Where are we going?"

"To Libya! You recall the Carthaginian governor bragging last week about the size of prawns there? Even better than those here in Minturnae, he said. Bigger. Sweeter. I decided to find out. I'm going to hire a ship this morning." Apicius smiled, no doubt thinking of the baskets upon baskets of crustaceans that would accompany his return.

I grunted, angry about everything that had happened that morning. And now, to top it off, I would be spending more time away from Passia.

"Have Rúan prepare a special cena for my return. I will be anxious to share my find with my best Minturnae clients. I also want to ship a few barrels down to Baiae. The gods know those vacationers can afford higher prices for shellfish than the citizens here in Minturnae."

I plastered on my best smile, determined not to let him see my true emotion. His mood was too quick to change and I wanted none of the lash. "Of course. How long do you expect we'll be gone? A week? What about Neptunalia?"

"Yes, a week, give or take a day. The winds are perfect. And Neptunalia is the most auspicious time to set forth over the sea. Why stay here when our fortune lies elsewhere?" Apicius extended a hand toward the ocean beyond the villa.

I followed the motion with my eyes but was already running through the pantry in my mind, thinking about what to make for the cena. "I'll have Rúan begin preparation on the sixth day and everything will be in order when we return."

"Perfect." Apicius started to turn toward the door but stopped. "Oh, could you take a tray to Aelia this morning? Then meet me at the port."

"Certainly. I'll meet you there in an hour." I left, fuming and think-ing of all the things I needed to do in that small space of time.

When I arrived in the kitchen, Rúan was instructing the staff on cleanup from the start of the breakfast duty. Sotas had already sent a slave ahead and told them to stop the preparation for the gustatio, and to pack for the trip; baskets with bread, cheese, olives, and early-summer apples, as well as several amphorae of wine from the cellar. He must have known before the salutatio, I realized.

I talked over the upcoming cena with Rúan, then sent the staff on a day's vacation, for which they were overjoyed. Normally they had days to themselves only on certain slave holidays, so this was a rare treat. I assumed that Apicius wouldn't even notice, and if he did, taking in that wrath was little compared to what he had done to Mato that morning. If I had to, I would endure it.

When I brought breakfast to Aelia's rooms Helene greeted me with a puzzled look. "Domina is still asleep," she whispered. "Why did you bring a tray?"

"I'm awake, Helene, it's all right," Aelia spoke up from inside the room. Helene waved me in, following behind to open the shutters, let-ting light and the ocean air filter into the room. Aelia sat up in bed, still dressed in her sleep shift. She wore her hair in one long braid draped over her shoulder.

"What's this?" She squinted at me. "I was planning on joining my husband for breakfast after the salutatio as I always do. Wait, some-thing is amiss. Where is Marcus?"

I paused. "You mean he didn't tell you?" Nervously, I set the tray down on the table next to the bed.

"Apparently not."

"He is sailing for Carthage this morning. He's excited about a new sort of prawn rumored to be better than those here in Minturnae." I watched a cloud of displeasure change Aelia's sunny features into a dark glower.

My heart sank even further. There was nothing worse than when Apicius had me do his dirty work. Aelia blinked to keep her tears at bay. "He'll be gone for days," she said, her voice quiet but measured.

I couldn't look her in the eye. "Yes, I suspect we'll be gone for seven or eight days. He wants to hold a cena on the day he returns."

Aelia sat silently for a few moments, smoothing the bedsheet methodically with her hands. I stood patiently, awaiting her command, my eyes fixed on the green finch on the bush outside the window. She swung off the covers and jumped out of bed, frightening the bird with her sudden movement. Helene was ready with a robe but Aelia shrugged it off. She went to the window and looked out over the sea where Apicius's ship would soon be sailing.

"Oh, Juno!" she exclaimed, looking skyward. "Tell me why you saddled me with that man?

"This is your fault, Thrasius. Your food and that blasted cookbook. Where will it be next? Numidia for snails? Ebuso for figs? Attica for honey? Tell me, Thrasius, where does he have his sights set on next week?" Her voice rose as she spoke. She picked up an expensive Egyptian wineglass from a nearby dressing table and dashed it on the tiles near my feet. The glass broke into tiny specks of pink, blue, and green.

I jumped to avoid the spray of glass. I had never seen Aelia so angry. "I do not know, Domina, I swear. I didn't even know about today until we had already made dozens of sweet cakes for this morning's salutatio." I began to back toward the door, slowly, head down and eyes on the tiles, desperate to be away from the tempest in front of me. This wrath was new to me and I did not know what she might do.

"Helene, send for Passia and Apicata. We have a lot to do today."

I reached the door and looked back at her. Furious, she waved her hand at me.

"Be gone, Thrasius! Sail away to whatever damned country you desire. I want nothing to do with you or my husband."

I hurried away, my heart in my throat.

The merchant vessel was of medium size, meant for carrying both cargo and passengers. It was a new ship, having sailed only a few times. The wood still gleamed with fresh oil and there wasn't a single chip to be found in its paint. Dozens of men worked to ready the boat to sail.

The captain greeted us on deck. "I heard you wanted to see me?" He leaned against a thick beam and eyeballed Apicius with distrust. The captain was younger than I would have expected of someone of that rank, with fine chiseled features and muscles like those you might see on an experienced gladiator.

Apicius raised a hand to shade his eyes. "You are sailing this morning?"

"Yes. For Greece."

"Cargo or passengers?"

The captain hesitated. "Both. Why do you want to know?"

"I need a ship to take me to the coast off Carthage. I want to leave today, as soon as my men bring supplies. I hear you are one of the best captains in port right now."

"You've heard right, but this boat has already been commissioned. I can't take you." The captain turned away but Apicius called out before he had gone more than a couple of steps.

"I imagine your patron cannot beat the price I'm willing to give you."

The captain paused. "And how much is that?"

"I'll double what he's giving you."

The captain waved over one of his deckhands and whispered something in his ear. The boy ran toward the stairs leading belowdeck and disappeared.

"Let's see what my patron says."

Together we waited in silence, looking toward the dark aperture in the deck where the sailor had disappeared. Eventually he poked his head into the sunlight, followed by a tall man with short cropped hair and a scroll in his hand. As he neared I realized it was a rolled-up map.

I recognized the man. It was Publius Octavius's head steward, Buccio, whom I always seemed to run into at the market. Before the slave could reach us, Apicius touched the captain on the shoulder.

"Forget what I said before. I'll *triple* whatever price that slave is authorized to give to you," he said in a low voice.

The captain's expression shifted from shock to wonder.

How much had Octavius commissioned the ship for? It must have been a large sum to begin with—the vessel was brand-new.

"Master Apicius," said the steward in a stern, less than cordial greeting as he approached. "Captain, you wanted to see me?"

"Yes, Buccio. This man wants to commission my ship for Carthage. I imagine Octavius might have authorized you to negotiate costs if the situation demanded?"

"He did indeed."

The young sea captain could barely contain his excitement. "He's offered to triple the price you have given me."

Buccio gasped at Apicius. "Triple? Do you even know what has been paid?"

"It's of no matter," Apicius replied, sliding a heavy purse full of gold aurei into the captain's hand. "Take this. I've already sent for the money changer to authorize credit for whatever the rest might be."

"Are you mad? That's nearly one hundred thousand denarii!" Buccio blurted out. "You could buy the whole boat!"

Apicius sneered at Buccio. "Slave, were you questioning me?"

Buccio dropped his head, anger and shame tinting the tips of his ears red. "No, Dominus Apicius. I was not questioning you. Nor do I have the ability to meet your price. Take the boat. We will return to Dominus Octavius. I'm sure he will want news of this changed commission right away." The slave didn't wait for a response. He backed up a few steps and moved toward the bowels of the ship to gather the rest of his men.

Apicius gazed toward the sky. I heard him whisper a prayer to Fortuna, for being able to purchase passage, and to Mercury, to bring the news swiftly to Octavius that his rival had stolen the ship right out from under him.

At the end of the third day after we left the harbor, I stood next to Apicius and watched the long fishing boat draw up next to our ship. It had one tall sail and held a dozen or so men, two of whom were playing some sort of dice game while they waited. Heaps of netting were piled on each end of the boat, and in the center, two large, pitch-sealed holding tanks held a variety of fish and prawns in a few feet of seawater. The men were all dark-skinned Libyans, tall and reedlike. There was something beautiful about the way these people moved, about the rhythm of their strange language and their laughter, as clear as the bright sea. Unlike my dominus, they seemed to be in no hurry.

An African man shouted a greeting in a language I did not know.

Apicius gestured for one of the ship's slaves to translate for him. "Ask them if they have any prawns." A youth leaned over the deck to talk to the sailors.

"They have prawns. They say you will not be disappointed."

Apicius rubbed his hands together in anticipation. "Excellent. Have them send a basket to the deck."

The young slave shouted down the instructions. In just a few moments a basket the size of Sotas's head appeared on the hook that the slave had reeled up from the other ship. Apicius hurried toward the basket, excited to see if the prawns lived up to their reputation.

I followed, still amazed that we had spent the last few days on that wretched ship all for the want of a few shellfish. The basket contained a wide-mouthed clay jar filled to the brim with seawater and a dozen or so of the little creatures, still squirming, struggling to climb out of the container.

Apicius reached in and lifted one of the prawns out. He held it in the palm of his hand. "Not very big, are they?" he said to no one in particular. He paused, flipping the prawn over. "By the gods! These are no good. Not any better than the prawns in Minturnae. Have them send up another basket, of the best selection they have."

In due time another basket appeared and the ship's slaves pulled it onto the deck for inspection. Apicius scooped up a handful of the crustaceans, cursed, and threw the prawns over the edge of the boat. He made them send one more basket and then threw up his hands in disgust.

"Sotas," he said, anger rising in his voice like a rushing tide, "go pay those men a suitable fee for their time, then tell our captain to turn the ship around and head back to Minturnae. I'm tired and I'm going to my cabin."

I rolled my eyes, thinking of all the barrels of snow that would go unused in the ship's storage, thousands of denarii melting away.

For the remainder of the trip Apicius locked himself in his cabin with his scrolls, too angry to emerge. I slept most of the time, or played backgammon and knucklebones with Sotas and the other slaves. Always I dreamed of Passia. With every wave that rocked the boat at night I wished she were there, curled into me, our bodies pressing closer together with every pitch of the sea.

Back at the villa I knew Rúan would have started preparing for the dinner on the sixth day. I imagined he'd started by testing the recipes I left with him. To accompany the prawns, I had wanted him to serve black-eyed peas with cumin and wine. The first course would include citron melon, black pudding, and cooked cucumbers. For the third course we had planned a variety of honey fritters, a pear patina, and tiny sips of Roman absinthe. I felt let down that I would have to tell him to cancel the cena. I had been excited, especially about the new sauces, including a pine nut and pepper sauce for the prawns. Lately Apicius had been talking about having me write a separate book, a slimmer volume entirely about sauces. I wanted to surprise him with some of the first recipes for this new book. They would now have to wait.

Rúan greeted us wholeheartedly on our return. I didn't have time to warn him of our master's mood. "Welcome home. We have a marvelous cena planned for tonight. I have slaves ready to run invitations out to your clients as soon as you give the word."

Apicius strode past Rúan toward the bath. Sotas followed behind, looking more enervated than I had seen the big man in past months. He had seasickness much of the trip and I knew he was glad to be back on land. Rúan followed, hesitantly giving us an update on the cena preparations, including the sauce for the prawns.

Apicius cut him off. "The prawns were small. Varus duped us! Varus is governor of Carthage. Of course he would say his prawns were the best. How could I be so stupid? And Publius Octavius. He will gloat to no end when he finds out."

"You didn't bring any back?" Rúan turned to me for confirmation.

"No, we did *not*," Apicius said, slamming a nearby vase from its pedestal to the floor as he continued on his way to the bath.

I jumped to avoid the flying ceramic.

"We can use Minturnae prawns for the dish we had planned for tonight," Rúan offered. "Besides," he continued, "Pilus took down a stag in the meadow yesterday. We have deer steaks; not having the prawns won't be a problem."

"Deer steaks. That sounds delightful." Apicius paused. "Fine. Hurry and invite our guests; the day grows long. Make sure you invite Horatius Blaesus and Claudius Scipio as we have business to discuss. For the rest, pick the worthiest clients. Set up a triclinium for the ladies that opens up toward the sea. That might please Aelia."

At the mention of Aelia's name, Rúan hesitated.

"What's wrong?" I asked.

"Umm . . ."

"Spit it out. What has happened? Where is Aelia?" Without waiting for an answer Apicius stormed off in the direction of Aelia's rooms. Sotas and I hurried after.

"Dominus, please, wait!" Rúan called after Apicius.

Apicius spun on his heel. "Slave, where in Tartarus is my wife?"

Rúan halted a few paces away—out of reach. "She went back to Rome."

I had wondered why Passia had not come to greet me. Now I knew. A wave of sadness washed through me with the realization that I would not see my lover that night.

"What do you mean she went back to Rome?"

"When she found out you had left for Libya, she decided to return to Rome. She packed up and left with her servants."

"The steward let her go to Rome alone?" Apicius was incredulous.

"No, Dominus. I remembered your client Antistius Vetus was going back to Rome—he sent word the night before to let you know he wouldn't be at the salutatio. I told the steward, and when Aelia was packing to leave, he sent a messenger to Vetus asking if she could accompany his family when they traveled. He agreed. Twenty of the house guards went as an escort, with instructions that ten of them should return to Minturnae when she arrived safely in Rome. They arrived two days ago. Aelia and Apicata are both safe at home."

Apicius mumbled a short prayer. "Did she leave a message?"

"I don't know, Dominus, but she left in such a hurry I don't think she would have. I'm sorry."

Apicius stared at the stones at his feet. After a long moment, he spoke, his voice low but full of deep anger. The hairs on the back of my neck rose.

"Sotas, tell the servants to start packing for Rome. I want to be gone within the hour. Thrasius, tell the slaves to distribute what has already been prepared for tonight's cena among my top clients. Then ready yourself to travel."

I hesitated only a moment, but it was enough to further raise Apicius's ire. "Go! Do not tarry! If we are not ready to leave in an hour all slaves will receive the lash."

We hurried to do our master's bidding and were nearly ready to go when a shout rang out across the garden in front of the domus. Everyone stopped to look in the direction of the sound.

"It's that client Mato. . . . Do you remember him?" Sotas said to me, squinting to see the figure making his way toward us.

"The man with the sick boy. Yes, I do."

Apicius appeared in the doorway as Mato neared, his gait halting and awkward. His hair was mussed and his dirty face was lined with tracks made from many tears.

"He looks drunk. Sotas, be prepared." Apicius folded his arms in front of him to stand his ground. Sotas moved toward Mato to keep the man at a distance.

Mato stopped right before he reached Sotas. He dropped to his knees and threw his hands into the air.

"In Jupiter's name I curse you, Apicius!" he screamed toward the heavens. "I curse your family to an early death, like you gave my son. I curse you to doom and delirium. I curse you to a life so terrible that you take your own life and your slaves inherit all you own."

Apicius didn't move a muscle. He watched calmly as Mato made his pronouncements. But when Mato pulled out a long, shiny knife from inside his ripped tunic, Apicius backed up quickly, knocking me over in his haste to get away from the man. I had just enough time to look up from my spot on the dusty ground to see that Mato hadn't stood at all. Instead he held the knife against his throat and, with one fast motion, tore it across his skin. Blood gushed forth in a rush, soaking his tunic. A horrified cry arose from the crowd of slaves. Collectively, we turned our heads, making signs to ward off the evil eye. Mato's body hit the ground with a thump.

Like he had with his mother, Apicius instructed that the body be dumped in the ocean, weighted with stones. He wouldn't come out of the domus until all the blood was gone. He said nothing of the incident after that, but he didn't let anyone ride in his carpentum with him, not even Sotas. I was grateful for the distance from my dominus. A dark melancholy consumed me and I wanted to talk to no one.

We rode through the night and arrived in Rome at daybreak. We stabled the oxen—they were not allowed into the city—and picked up Apicius's litter from storage. It was a long journey back to the villa from the city gates.

Despite the early hour, the city was bustling, preparing for yet another holiday, Vinalia Rustica, the celebration of the year's first grape harvest. The streets leading to the Forum were decorated with ribbons and vines. Vendors hawked painted miniature amphorae to tourists, and troupes of flutists and dancers could be heard practicing in the alleys as we passed.

I loved Vinalia. Every year Passia and I looked forward to the first feast of the three-day festival. Aelia would line up the servants on both sides of the long hallway leading from the front door through the atrium. Together Apicius, Apicata, and Aelia would walk the lines and place a grape on the tongue of each slave and say a blessing to the lady Venus. Then Apicius would have ten jars of his best Falernian wine brought up from the cellar and he would give them to his most loyal servants. I would make sweet curds and honey tarts for the whole household, slaves included, and we would read poetry and listen to music. With Aelia and Apicius on such poor terms, I wasn't sure there would be much of a festival in our villa this year.

When we turned onto the street winding up the Palatine toward Apicius's villa, a young man came running toward our party, shouting, "Apicius!"

Whenever we traveled through Rome, some vendor would race after the litter to sell Apicius some new luxurious food or a special serving dish. These sellers never sold anything worth stopping for. But of course Apicius always stopped.

Sotas stepped forward to block the man from moving closer to the litter, but the man, a wiry Jew, hardly seemed to notice Sotas. He continued to shout and wave his arms as the litter moved farther down the street.

"Apicius! I have silphium! Please stop, I have silphium! I've come from Cyrene and I was told to find you whenever I have silphium!"

I wondered at the man's tale. Silphium had become increasingly rare and costly. The Greeks couldn't figure out how to cultivate it and had to rely on wild sources. Trade was tightly controlled and even the most influential had a hard time obtaining the herb. Where had he gotten it?

The man drew close and, much to my surprise, Sotas didn't stop him. Instead he reached out and gave the man a hearty hug. "Benjamin! It is good to see you. You have silphium? Real silphium, not the stuff from Parthia?"

"Yes! I secured some from a patrician whose life I saved from drowning when I was in Cyrene. I asked for silphium in payment."

I snorted. It was more likely the man had robbed the noble and walked off with the herb.

Benjamin stared past us. Apicius had stopped the litter and disembarked to greet this bearer of herbal gold. I wanted to shake my dominus. Apicius had done nothing for the last twenty-four hours but rant and moan about Aelia. But instead of moving forward, he decided to delay the reunion to buy a plant. I resisted saying a prayer to Jupiter to strike the Jew down into the paving stones.

"Do you truly have silphium? Let me see."

Apicius reached out a trembling hand in expectation.

The man reached into his bag and pulled out a lump of cloth. Carefully he unwrapped it to reveal a thick, reddish-brown root no longer than a finger, twisted and still dirty.

I watched my master scrape the root with his fingernail, then place the bit on his tongue. Apicius closed his eyes to savor what should taste like the bitter pith of a pomegranate with a hint of something spicier.

"Yes, it is silphium! How much do you have? I'll take all of it."

The Jew shook his head. "This root is all that I have. I'm sure you know how rare it is."

"I do know. I'll pay you seventy-five thousand denarii."

I tensed when he named the amount. I thought that after Apicius had offered the captain only a bit more to sail to Carthage I would never again be shocked at my master's extravagant spending. I was wrong. If he was frugal, Benjamin would never have to work another day in his life.

The exchange was made. Benjamin had come prepared with a wax tablet to take down the signed wager and seal mark enabling him to draw the money from the city coffers in Apicius's name. Apicius retired to the litter and we started off again. Sotas and I lagged behind.

I was angry at my master. "What I don't understand is why Apicius couldn't have let me handle that transaction. He would have had his silphium at a fraction of the price and he would already be home to his wife. It's infuriating."

Sotas made a sign to warn against the evil eye. "Why do you wonder about his motives anymore? You know things will unfold as they may."

I understood what Sotas meant. "*For every success, greater failures will cluster to the sides.*' This is the prophecy coming true before our eyes. He has his silphium but at what cost? To his purse and to the detriment of his wife."

"And what of Mato and his son?"

I was surprised. Sotas never spoke critically of our master.

We walked the rest of the way in silence.

CHAPTER 11

As we neared the domus, a surge of adrenaline sliced through me. I recognized the bright family colors of the litter leaving Apicius's villa. It was large and luxurious, with gilded supports and vermilion curtains edged with rich Tyrian purple. A dozen slaves carried the litter, holding on to thick poles wrapped in purple ribbon and capped with golden lions the size of a man's fist. I prayed to Juno that Apicius wouldn't notice the approaching envoy, but as the drumbeat of the slaves' feet came closer, he parted the curtains to peer out. I saw his jaw set hard as he watched the litter pass.

"By Tartarus! What was Sejanus doing in my house?" he cursed when the other litter was out of earshot, bidding his slaves to move even faster toward the villa. Sotas pulled one of the younger slaves aside and told him to run ahead and warn Aelia of their arrival.

Apicius jumped out of the litter before the slaves had the chance to finish setting it on the ground. He waved aside the guards at the front gate to the villa and strode through the courtyard, Sotas and I practically running behind him.

Aelia met us in the atrium. She wore a simple tunica of white and the afternoon breeze played with the edges of her overlying pale yellow stola. She appeared a little haggard, as though she had been crying, and I thought there was a small bruise upon her shoulder. Her hair was pulled back in a hasty bun at the nape of her neck. I wondered if her *ornatrix* was sick; it was unlike her not to have her hair coiffed. She held a small papyrus scroll in her hand. Apicata stood next to her. She held her doll close, as though she were taking comfort in the embrace.

Her seventh birthday was only a few months away and dolls would be a thing of the past soon. I was struck by how much taller she seemed to have grown in the few short weeks since we had last seen her. Helene and Passia stood behind them. I longed to rush across the atrium and caress the cheek of the woman I loved. She looked at me, but her lips held no smile. Instead there was something else in her look—a warning, a plea, that made me desperate to get her alone and see what had happened while we were gone.

"Wife, what was Sejanus doing here?" Apicius stopped a few feet away, not reaching out to embrace her as he usually would after a long visit. "I did not expect you might entertain in my absence."

Aelia appeared to gather her courage. "I have entertained while you were gone. Sejanus is in between campaigns so he visited a few times. Today he brought a gift for Apicata, and last week, we dined one evening with my father and his father—my uncle, if you recall. But he has not been our only guest. Every day my lady friends have come to weave with me and Apicata."

A strange look crossed her face and she moved away suddenly, leaning to the side in order to gaze past us. "Where is your haul, by the way?"

Sotas smiled when I nudged him conspiratorially with one elbow. We too lamented the wasted trip that had brought us nothing but a smaller coin purse and an angry domina.

"The prawns were not as I expected."

"So you just turned back?"

"Yes. And when I returned, I found my wife was no longer there. By Jove, woman! What possessed you to leave without me?"

Aelia looked him square in the eye. "The same thing that possesses you to leave your wife for weeks on end without even bothering to kiss her good-bye."

"You didn't even say good-bye to *me*, Father," Apicata said. Her voice shook and her eyes welled with tears. I wondered at the display of emotion. Apicata was always a little dramatic but this display seemed more so than usual. "Why were you gone so long?"

Apicius fell to his knees, scooped her up, and buried his head in her shoulder.

"My little one, I'm sorry. I didn't mean to make you cry."

Aelia watched the scene between her husband and daughter, her eyes neutral but her chin trembling. She crushed the center of the scroll in her hand with the force of her grip. I wondered at its contents.

Finally, Apicius let his daughter go. He gestured for Passia to take Apicata and depart. Then he turned back to Aelia. "Wife, you are never to leave of your own accord again. I have few rules for you in my house but I will not tolerate disrespect."

Aelia lowered her eyes. "Yes, husband."

"You will not teach Apicata insolence. It is my expectation that as matron of this house you will provide her with a role model befitting our station. You will explain to her how your actions were not appropriate. You will also offer an extra sacrifice to the Penates this evening. You have shamed us and the household gods demand retribution."

"Will that be all, husband?" She sounded more defeated than petulant—we had all seen Apicius in his moods and to provoke him was never wise. A blanket of sadness encompassed her. She refused to look up at Apicius.

"Yes, that will be all."

She left the atrium, a cheerless cloud trailing in her wake. I suspected that by leaving she had hoped Apicius would see how she had been wounded. Instead he meted out punishment. I wished I could run after her and give comfort.

"Come, Sotas, we have much to unpack," said Apicius.

The "we" was not as inclusive as it sounded. Sotas would end up unpacking while his master went to the baths to enjoy a massage and a glass of Falernian wine.

"Dominus?" I raised my voice in question, not daring to assume I too was dismissed.

"Go, get out of my sight."

As I crossed the atrium, I noticed Aelia had crumpled and tossed the scroll she had held. I picked it up from the line of plants where it rested and pocketed it, intending to return it to her when I saw her next. But a short while later, my curiosity won out and I pulled out the scroll.

It was a love poem she had written for Apicius, lamenting the distance between them. It left my heart hurting for my domina.

• • •

It was several hours before I could be alone with Passia. I longed to wrap my arms around her, to run my fingers along her skin. I had been dreaming of her for weeks and I wasn't sure how much longer I could contain this hunger. And yet there was a seed of worry—what had that look she gave me meant?

When Apicata was taking her nap, Passia slipped away and we sought the privacy of my cubiculum.

"Sejanus is a monster," she began as soon as the door was shut. Anger played with her features, wrinkling her brow. My desire dissipated, turning into deep concern.

"Tell me what happened."

"I don't know where to start." Tears filled her eyes and I enveloped her in my arms. She wept into my shoulder.

"Did he touch you?" I could barely ask the question.

"Not me." She choked and fresh tears began anew.

Horror rose in my chest. "Apicata?"

"No, but, but . . ." Again, her tears consumed her.

I led her to the bed and sat with her, comforting her, letting her cry. After a time, she quieted.

"I'm so glad you are home." She wiped her face with the back of her hand.

I smoothed the hair back from her face. "Tell me what happened, my sweet love. Take your time."

"Domina Aelia told true earlier, but she did not tell it all. Last week Aelia's father, Sejanus, and Sejanus's father came to dine with us. They arrived in the late afternoon and the dinner was very enjoyable. You know how I've always liked her father."

I did. Lucius Aelius Lamia had advanced to be governor of Germania and we did not see him often. He was a kind man who doted on Aelia and often sent her gifts from his travels across the Empire.

"They were here for many hours and there was a lot of wine that flowed. In fact, too much wine. Eventually Lamia left for home. He had some things he wanted to finish up before he left Rome to return to Germania the next day. When he was gone, we retired to Aelia's library because Apicata wanted to have Sejanus play backgammon with her.

"Helene and I sat on the slave stools near the door, along with four of Sejanus's guards. Aelia read from Virgil while Sejanus played the game with Apicata. Everything was fine for a little while. Sejanus kept waving to have his wine refilled, which I think I must have done three or four times."

"Let me guess, he didn't want it to be cut with water."

She shook her head and tears rose in her eyes once again.

"At some point, he had Apicata sit on his lap while he showed her how to make more strategic moves on the board. Oh, Thrasius, that's when everything started to go wrong!"

Heat prickled the back of my neck. "Tell me, Passia. What happened? What did he do to Apicata?"

"He, he . . ." She swallowed and choked back her sobs. "He started to rub his hands up her legs and under her tunica, upward. But Aelia saw, and she threw her scroll aside and yanked Apicata away.

"He told her that he was having a little fun, that there were other types of games he could teach her. He grabbed Aelia with his free hand and Apicata slipped away, running to me. I tried to take her out of the room but one of his guards grabbed me and held me back. He held me, with my hand over my mouth so I could not scream. One guard took hold of Helene and another guard grabbed Apicata and did the same. She was hysterical and finally the guard told her that if she didn't stop screaming they were going to hurt her mother. That stopped her, but she was terrified."

"Where were the house guards?" I asked. Besides the regular door guards, there were guards present when visitors came to the house. Apicius had always been somewhat paranoid and demanded it.

"Aelia had dismissed them to guard the outside of the house like they would if we did not have visitors. We all felt safe. Sejanus had his men with him. He is her cousin—she did not think that anything would happen!"

Much as I didn't want to hear what was to transpire, I bade Passia to continue. I held her and stroked her shoulder and her face while she spoke.

"Aelia struggled in Sejanus's arms. He kept trying to kiss her. He ripped her stola to get at her breasts. When she tried to scream, he slapped her."

I swore. Never in my life, even when I had been abused as a slave in times past, or even when Vatia had died by Popilla's mechanisms, had I ever wanted anyone dead so much as I did Sejanus in that moment.

"He was so drunk. I think that was the only thing that saved Aelia. He could barely stand up. After he slapped her, he told her that he had evidence of something very terrible that Apicius had done, that he had tried to murder someone close to Caesar. And that it would destroy Apicius and his entire family if Sejanus shared the evidence."

Her eyes pleaded with me. "Oh, Thrasius, do you think it is true?"

Reluctantly, I nodded. "Yes. It is. It is better that you do not know."

She paled.

"Did Apicata hear about the murder?"

"I don't think so. The guard had made her promise to not scream if he took his hand off her mouth. She was crying and praying aloud to the gods most of the time. But she did hear Sejanus when he made us swear on our lives that we would never speak of what had just happened. If he found out we had, he would expose Apicius and we would all be put to death. That really scared her and the guard had to put his hand over her mouth again."

Passia paused, her tears beginning anew. I let her cry for a few minutes, then bade her to continue.

She gathered her courage. "He told Aelia that if he ever decided he wanted her that she would comply. And that if he ever decided he wanted Apicata that Aelia was to make sure it happened. If not, he would turn the evidence of the murder over to Caesar."

"Then he pushed her aside and she fell to the floor. He staggered away and left us there, in a heap, storming out with his guards in tow."

I poured her a glass of water from the pitcher I kept near the bed. She gulped it down.

I remembered the litter that had passed us as we returned to the villa. "That was last week, correct? Why was he here today?"

"It was as Aelia said. He brought Apicata a gift, a pair of earrings that are quite costly for a child. Aelia wouldn't let him see her to give Apicata the earrings himself. Before Aelia let Sejanus in, she made sure that there were ten of the household guards lining the atrium, which he smirked at when he strode through the door.

"'Dear cousin,' he said to her. 'I came here to be nice, but I see you don't trust me. No matter. Just remember, I own your family. I own you, and I own your husband. Therefore, I own your daughter. Someday, I will call upon your family to deliver what is mine. Now be a good woman and keep your mouth shut about our little secret. Remind your daughter and your slaves. It will be nothing to me if Apicius is put to death, but I imagine it will be a bit more traumatic for you.'

"Before he left he walked over to me and put a hand on my breast and told me that taking me was still in the stars for the future."

Anger consumed me. I picked up the jug of water next to the bed and smashed it against the wall. The terra-cotta shattered in a hundred wet, orange shards that spiraled across the floor.

"Thrasius, stop." Passia threw her arms around me from behind. "Everyone will hear you. They will think we are fighting."

I stood. "We must tell Apicius."

Passia grabbed at me and pulled me back down to the bed. "No! You cannot! If Apicius shows any sign that he knows, any at all, then I fear what Sejanus might do!"

I pulled away and stood once more, unable to sit still.

"May Jove curse Sejanus! I have to do something. When he is here again, it is possible something he eats will make him quite ill."

"You can't poison him."

"Why not?"

"Thrasius, you must be careful. We are slaves. This is a fight that is not ours—it is that of our masters. If something befalls them, it could mean worse for us."

She rose and I held her, brushing her hair away from her face with my fingers. She looked deep into my eyes and for a moment I thought I could see the spark of her genius flickering in her pupils.

"Thrasius, please think. If you make one wrong step, you would be sacrificing yourself but dooming me to a life without you."

In my anger, I had not stopped to consider what would happen to the woman I had grown to love beyond all others. I wiped her tears away with the pads of my thumbs. Oh, by the gods, she was beautiful.

"Tomorrow we will take care of Sejanus," I said, a plan suddenly forming in my mind. "Aelia too. It's best if she joins us. You will need to talk to her."

"I don't understand."

"Tomorrow night, at midnight, we will do what is required."

She let out a small sound of understanding. "You want to curse him."

"I do." A sense of purpose filled me. "If I must be careful, I can at least start there. And perhaps it will bring Aelia some ease."

She nodded, her chin moving against my chest. I blew out the lamp and held my lover, stroking her arm with my hand until we both fell asleep.

The next day was strained. Aelia and Apicius barely talked and Apicata was sullen and listless. I made the little girl all of her favorite dishes, and carved her little animals out of vegetables to adorn her plate. When she saw them, she ran to me and gave me a giant hug and told me how much she missed me. I hugged her for a long time and said nothing when I saw she was trying very hard not to cry.

When I went to the market that day, I bought a honey cake from the temple of Ceres, paying extra for a protection blessing from the priestess. I gave it to Apicata with her afternoon meal, and while surely she had seen temple protection cakes and knew what they were, she ate it without a word.

Passia took Aelia aside and, after much discussion and help from Helene, convinced our domina of what would be the one course of action she could take as a woman, and which we could help her with as slaves. I am sure she did not like the idea of me knowing what had happened, but she did not act ashamed when she was around me. I felt proud that she trusted me with knowledge so close to her heart.

I enlisted Sotas to accompany us. It was one of his few nights off duty and he wouldn't be required to sleep at the foot of Apicius's bed. He knew where the tombs were and I wasn't as sure. Plus wandering around Rome at night was never a safe thing, and knowing that we would have a man like Sotas at hand gave me comfort.

Telling Sotas was not easy. Before I told him the story, I asked if he would swear to keep the truth from Apicius. He refused, saying it would break the oath of loyalty he had with the goddess Fides. Ultimately, I convinced him that this was the type of situation that warranted secrecy precisely to protect Apicius. Only Sotas's faith in the friendship between us swayed him. I had never lied to him before nor would I ever want him to break his oath, so he agreed, and I told him about the wrong against his domina.

Rarely had I seen the man as angry as he was when I revealed what had happened. I was glad that we were in the garden when I told him, and not near any of Apicius's priceless statues inside the house. While I know he has deep loyalty to Apicius, he bore genuine love for his domina and to have her come to harm enraged him.

That night, I slipped a little poppy juice into Apicata's wine before she went to bed. Passia didn't want her to wake and find her gone. The little girl had been having nightmares since the evening with Sejanus. Passia found a fellow slave to sleep in the room with her in case she needed comfort from night terrors.

I did the same for Apicius as an extra safeguard. Aelia had her own rooms in the house so could slip away undetected, but I did not want him to wake and decide to seek her out in the night.

When the water clocks ran a little past *sexta*, we slipped out of the house. Aelia seemed surprised to see Sotas with us, but said nothing. She, Helene, and Passia all wore dark cloaks of the type that a slave would wear.

Even during the blackness of night the city seemed loud, with small groups of people walking through the streets, prostitutes offering their services, and city workers hauling vats of urine to the toga cleaners to be used for bleach. Despite all the activity, and the occasional breaks of light through open windows, the darkness was unnerving. I hoped that Sotas's huge size would make a thief think twice before sneaking up on us to try to score a purse. Aelia had to have been scared, but when I could catch glimpses of her face under the heavy cloak, she appeared stoic.

It was a long walk to the Appian Way leading out of Rome, where the Aelii family tombs were located. In general, slaves could not leave Rome without a note with the seal of their master, but the guards at the city gates gave us little issue once a few denarii and a basket of pastries were placed in their hands. An orgy in the fields beyond Rome never hurt anyone, we told them, and the guards, happy for the treats, ushered us through the gate.

The Appian Way is a strange and sinister road at night. The cobbles are lined for miles with hundreds, perhaps thousands, of gravestones and elaborate multilevel mausoleums rising at varying heights. That night the moon was only a slim crescent, giving us just enough light to discern our surroundings and to enable the stones and buildings to cast their shadows on the ground, creating a supernatural atmosphere down the length of the street.

The tombs of the gens Aelia were grouped in a cluster about a quarter of a mile outside town. A large rock wall marked the group of carefully constructed and artfully carved mausoleums. We slipped through the wooden gate. Aelia led the way once we reached the tombs. She stopped in front of the elaborate mausoleum where her family rested. It was decorated with colorful tiles and symbols of the dead. She pulled a key out of her pocket and opened the lock, letting us into the tomb. The first floor housed dozens of urns of the Aelia family, tucked into niches chest high along the tiled walls. We climbed the short flight of stairs to the second floor and lit the oil lamps. We sat in a circle around the ornate feasting table where, once a year, in the spring, the ancestors of the Aelii would throw a big party to commemorate the dead.

I pulled several objects out of my bag for the ritual, the most important of them being a poppet half the size of my hand and made of clay. I'd spent the evening before forming it into the shape of a human body. It was still semisoft and ready for the spell that we were about to invoke.

"What is that?" Aelia whispered.

"Yes, why do we need a doll?" Sotas asked.

"When I lived with Maximus, there was an old woman who took care of the chickens. She was from Greece and she taught me many things about my country. One of the things she taught me was the ancient practice of using magic with poppets. That's what this is." I held up the clay doll.

"How does it work?" Sotas's features seemed unusually dark and menacing in the lamplight.

"I'll show you."

I placed the poppet on a small cloth on the table in front of me. It was shaped like a man, with a featureless face, but included carved locks of hair, nipples, genitalia, and even a navel. The hands were bent behind the figure's back, as were his legs. The feet touched the hands at the small of the back and its head was twisted sharply to one side. Goose bumps rose along my arms as I studied it.

"Ready?"

My companions grunted their assent. Their faces gleamed in the weak light, full of both hope and fear. In that moment, the weight of what I was about to do hit me and I took a few deep breaths to calm myself.

When I held up the poppet its smooth body shone. "This is the body of Lucius Aelius Sejanus. We now prepare to bind him to our will and to the will of the gods." I picked up the nail and, with the tip, inscribed Sejanus's full name sideways across the belly of the doll. The clay gave way easily and I flicked away the specks displaced from the grooves made by the nail.

I picked up my knife and pricked my finger. I let a drop of blood fall onto the poppet's head. I took Aelia's finger first, then did the same to Helene, Passia, and Sotas.

There was a noise above us then, a racing sound across the top of the tomb. We held our breaths.

"Just squirrels," Helene said, and we all relaxed, recognizing that sound to be true.

I smeared the blood across the poppet, covering as much of the clay as I could with the shimmery fluid.

"Aelia, would you read this?" I handed her a piece of parchment.

She took it with one hand and with the other she wiped her eyes of tears. Her voice shook as she read the Latin.

"With my blood and the blood of my slaves, I call down the powers of the gods against the man Lucius Aelius Sejanus. I call forth the di Manes of the Aelii who will revenge the shame of a family member brought by another family member. I call forth Hecate, who will power this spell with the magic of ancestral ghosts. I call forth Nemesis, who will seek revenge for wrongdoing brought by Sejanus. I call forth Averna, goddess of the Underworld, who will beckon to Sejanus every day of his life with her siren song. Finally, I call forth Mercury, who will bear the soul of Sejanus to the depths of the Underworld, bringing him to the feet of Pluto himself."

I felt Passia shiver beside me. It was as though the spirits were pressing against us, hovering around the lanterns, ready to whisper in our ears.

I took up the nails. "With this nail I bind and curse Sejanus. May any harm he seeks to bring down upon the Gavia or the Aelia family harm him back tenfold." I plunged the nail into the top of the clay figure's head. I repeated the curse with each nail I placed, in both eyes, in the mouth, ears, chest, belly, genitals, hands, feet, and anus. I bound the poppet carefully with the bronze wire before setting it aside and picking up the blank sheet of lead.

"Now for the most important part." With another nail I inscribed a curse deep into the lead tablet, backward, starting at the bottom of the tablet and working carefully up the page.

The lanterns flickered. I told myself it was just a draft of wind through the cracks of the tomb but a part of me could feel the spirits swirling around us. The hairs on the back of my neck raised and my skin grew cold.

I passed out more pieces of parchment, each inscribed with the curse. Together we read it aloud, our voices rising with each word.

"Oh gods, curse Lucius Aelius Sejanus! Hear our plea!
Together we commit Sejanus to the gods, to the di Manes of the
    Aelii,
to Nemesis, Averna, Mercury, and Hecate.
As this clay is cold and powerless,
also cold and powerless is Sejanus,
cold in knowledge, thinking, and memory!

"As the dead are powerless and still,
just so powerless and still will Sejanus be,
his feet, hands, and body!

"Just as this image will break and decay,
Let Sejanus likewise break and decay,
and perish all his seed and property!
Oh gods, curse Sejanus! Hear our plea!
Together we commit Sejanus to the gods, to the di Manes of the
    gens Aelia, to Hecate, Nemesis, Averna, Mercury."

The air seemed to hum when we finished the last word. One of our lanterns flickered and sputtered out.

I folded the lead sheet three times. Again I pricked each of our fingers and smeared the blood. I hammered the final nail into the center of the lead tablet.

"With this nail I bind and curse Sejanus. May any harm he brings down upon the Gavia family return to him tenfold."

I bent the nail against the tablet with the hammer and bound the tablet and poppet together with the bronze wire. My hands shook as I spun the wire round and round. When I was done, I worked the wire and the poppet full of nails into the lead tin. I pushed the lid down on the tin and handed it to Sotas. "Now we bury that damned thing and let the Aelii ancestors help the gods take care of Sejanus."

In the sparse light of the remaining lanterns we made our way down the steps to the outside of the tomb. At the foot of the door we dug a deep hole, dropped the poppet in, and covered it back up.

We stood back and stared at the smooth dirt where the hole had been. Passia wrapped an arm around Aelia to comfort her. Suddenly, the wind picked up and a strong gust blew out one of the remaining lanterns, leaving the other to flicker almost out before sparking back to life.

"I think the di Manes have spoken," Aelia murmured.

My heart hammered like a mallet pounding meat. While I wanted the help of the gods, I wasn't sure I was comfortable being in their presence.

A pack of dogs barked in the distance. The sign of Hecate! I took Passia's shaking hand. "Let's get out of here."

The five of us ran away from the mausoleums, not looking back until we reached the gates of Rome.

CHAPTER 12

"I still don't think it's a good idea," Aelia said as we disembarked from the litter in front of Tiberius's vast villa on the other side of the Palatine Hill from our own domus. "Everyone knows Thrasius is your coquus. It doesn't make any sense that you would bring him along with us today."

The night before, Tiberius's son, Drusus, had married his paternal cousin, Livilla, who also happened to be Tiberius's niece and Livia's granddaughter. It was a twisted sort of arrangement, confusing to all of Rome. The marriage was meant to keep an heir in the family, but many talked of how it smacked of the same arrangements that the old kings of Italy once had. Apicius and Aelia had been invited to the wedding party, and despite Aelia's concerns, he insisted on bringing me. They had been arguing all morning about my presence at the event. I too had tried to convince Dominus of the folly of bringing me along, especially when both Livia and Octavius would be in attendance. It was like flaunting his defiance in front of them. Despite our protests, Apicius would not be swayed.

A slave greeted us at the door, checked our names off the tablet he held, and led us forward.

"I myself don't understand why he brought me," I whispered to Sotas as we entered the wide courtyard. I kept step with him and with Helene as we followed behind our masters. Sejanus had been sent to war not long after that night on the Appian Way, a sign that we hoped meant our curse was working. But I suspected that Sejanus's absence did not mean that all of Apicius's enemies had been swept away.

"He's nervous going places without you," Sotas observed.

"I'm more of a steward than a cook these days," I muttered.

"You are his good luck charm. He thinks it will be auspicious for you to be present if he speaks with Caesar," Helene whispered.

"Ridiculous."

Apicius glanced back at us with a withering stare. I doubted he could hear our words but he hated it when his slaves whispered around him. Chastised, we followed Apicius and Aelia through the villa in silence.

I stared at the back of Apicius's head. At thirty-three, he had just started to show the signs of baldness, mostly hidden by his thick hair. An errant piece had fallen, exposing a slice of pale skin. He scolded Aelia, a sign that he was nervous. All the way to Tiberius's palace he'd talked about how desperately he wanted to make Caesar's acquaintance, but he didn't know how he could without Livia being present. Despite the passing of nearly four years, none of us believed she would have forgotten Apicius's refusal to sell me. Bringing me was dangerous. In the time that had passed since that day I realized that the danger lay not in Apicius's rivalry with Octavius, but in that of Livia still wanting to exact revenge against Fannia for sleeping with her ex-husband. Apicius was caught in the hazardous middle.

The slave left us with dozens of other guests in a vast central garden decorated with a multitude of brightly painted statues, pots spilling with flowers, and fountains spluttering in small ponds stocked with fish. The walls were decorated with frescoes filled with such detail that the people and animals appeared almost alive. The doors were under the surveillance of tall, stern Praetorian guards, Caesar's personal army. More than a hundred patricians and their wives milled about. Tall boys stood throughout the garden, fanning the hot June air above the visitors with their long-poled Egyptian-style fans. The guests wore a thin wreath of laurel and ivy about their necks or upon their heads and the smell of flowers permeated the midsummer air. The drinking portion of the wedding reception wouldn't commence until after the traditional speeches by the patron throwing the party—in this case, Caesar Augustus and his newly appointed heir, Tiberius. Sotas and I stood a pace behind our masters and watched the party unfold.

"Tragic how Gaius died, don't you think?" Fannia said, joining us.

Apicius jumped at the sound of her voice. Aelia leaned toward Fannia in response.

"Tragic! And so far from home! I feel terrible for poor Livilla, being forced to marry Drusus. It's not even been a year since her husband died!" she murmured behind a cupped hand.

Gaius Caesar was one of Caesar's two now dead heirs, and had been married to Livilla. He had died under what some said were strange circumstances in a military campaign in faraway Lycia.

"And so soon after his brother Lucius died from that odd sickness! Don't you find it curious that both of Caesar's heirs are no longer? The poor girl. In some ways it's probably good for Livilla that they took so long to recover Gaius's body from Lycia or she would have had to remarry even sooner." Fannia shook her head. Today her hair was blond, braided, and piled high around a small but elaborate gold and jewel-encrusted headdress.

"At least they are the same age," Aelia offered. "Drusus is handsome and charming. I suppose she could do much worse. I hope he will be kind to her."

"How did you manage an invitation?" Apicius asked Fannia. I had been wondering the same thing.

"Thankfully, Livia didn't have anything to do with the invitations." Fannia peered toward the flowered entryway where Caesar and his wife were due to arrive. "Agrippina asked me to come. She knows how much I adore her son. Drusus will be pleased I came, but I'm sure Livia will be furious when she sees me here. She wouldn't dare throw me out in front of all these guests. It wouldn't be a good omen for the new couple."

Apicius smiled. Fannia was right; throwing out a guest would not be auspicious. The wedding had been, as tradition dictated, a small family affair, but the reception was turning out to be quite the opposite.

Aelia jerked her chin toward a small cluster of patricians. "Octavius and Gaia are here. I know you don't want to talk to them but I should thank Gaia for the flowers she sent to me when I was sick last month. Excuse me, husband. I'd like to bring them greetings."

Octavius waved in our direction and Apicius waved back politely. I suspected that my dominus was happy to have Aelia fraternize on his behalf. Aelia and Gaia were not oblivious to the contention between their husbands, but they never seemed to let it deter their friendship.

"Ahh, my favorite friend has arrived," Fannia said in a sardonic whisper as three *tubicines* appeared in the sunlit entryway, their straight gold *tubae* sounding one long note signifying the entrance of Caesar and his wife, Livia. After sounding their horns, the men stepped to the side with a practiced march.

A small tremor reverberated through my belly as I watched the Imperial couple walk through the doors, flanked by the newly wedded Livilla and Drusus Julius Caesar.

Tiberius drew up the rear, looking both tired and uncomfortable. The gossip was that he had reluctantly returned from his villa at Rhodes to which he had retired several years prior. Apparently his new appointment as heir to Caesar had been enough to make him reconsider. Upon the recent deaths of his grandsons, Lucius and Gaius, Caesar had moved quickly to adopt Tiberius in order to ensure a successor. The plebeian masses had rumbled about the adoption for the last few weeks, concerned about the idea of the dictatorship passing to yet another heir, just as a crown might pass to kings. Augustus merely declared several public feasts (with freely distributed food) to commemorate the event, which quelled the rabble. As for Tiberius, bets had already been placed on how long it would be before he retired once more to his island retreat.

"They look happy," Apicius said to Fannia. "But Tiberius looks as though he ate a bad piece of meat."

"Maybe the wine will cheer him up." She pointed at the long line of amphorae gracing one wall. "Caesar is far too conservative, denying women wine at his parties. Women should be able to partake of wine just as the men do."

"It makes women wanton," Apicius teased.

"Of course it does!" Fannia laughed.

Caesar began speaking, his commanding voice loud enough to be heard even at the back of the garden. He stood between the new couple while Livia and Tiberius hovered in the background, eying the crowd.

"She saw me." Fannia lifted her semicircular gold-painted fan to hide her lips as she spoke.

"I worry about you." Apicius shifted so another patrician blocked Livia's view as he spoke. "This rivalry is dangerous. Fannia, there is talk she may have had a hand in Lucius's death. I heard she paid one of Gaius's soldiers to make his murder look like a battle wound!"

"Rumors, rumors!" Fannia chuckled softly behind the fan. "Besides, you should talk. You are the one who keeps avoiding her for fear she may seek retribution for refusing Octavius's purchase of your coquus. And you dare to bring him here today!"

Apicius shrugged off her criticism. "Fannia, she is staring at you, not me. You shouldn't be here. What *if* those rumors are true? You do not want to be in the sight of the gorgon. And if you are in her sights that means I am too. Sometimes I wonder how much of a liability you are to me."

"I see." She seemed annoyed. "Well, too late now." Indeed, Livia was staring at Fannia—directly, with the intensity of a vestal flame. Despite the burning gaze, she remained composed, her face still beautiful at sixty-two years. She wore barely any jewelry, as was her practice, and her white stola was adorned with a bright red sash. Her gray hair was cropped close in a simple but elegant cut, with dozens of curls circling her barely lined face. Her lips were stained red, the same color as her sash. After a few moments of looking directly at Fannia, she raised her hand in a slight wave, a movement driven purely by the need for public protocol.

Fannia smiled sweetly and tipped her fan in response.

Caesar's speech was ending. I had been so absorbed in watching the exchange between Livia and Fannia that I hadn't heard a word. It didn't matter; wedding speeches were always the same. Good luck, happy life, gods smiling down, et cetera. I glanced at Aelia. She stood next to Gaia and Octavius, smiling at Livilla and Drusus, her face aglow with the moment.

A flock of white doves flew over the garden, predictably, at the close of Caesar's speech, circling twice before landing in an orderly huddle on the roof overlooking the party. It bothered me that the rulers of Rome had always danced with the favor of the gods, faking such displays to puff themselves up for the plebs. No wonder so many of them came to ominous ends.

"What fortune will come to them with so many doves!" Aelia had returned and was beaming. "Apicata will be sad to have missed such a sight."

"Come now." Fannia took Aelia and Apicius by the elbow. "Refreshments are in order." She propelled them toward the front of the garden, where the slaves were distributing wine to the men and juice to the women. Sotas and I followed behind, nodding our brief hellos to other slaves we recognized as we passed.

Throughout the garden, plush couches and chairs were nestled in nooks shaded by bushy palms. Many of the women began to congregate in these cool gossip pockets while others laughed gaily as they watched their husbands line up to be chosen for a drinking game.

Fannia stopped a young slave girl with a tray of glasses. "Here's your first taste of Caesar's finest." She handed Apicius a glass of golden wine, taking a glass of honeyed water for herself and one for Aelia. Apicius lifted the goblet to his nostrils and took a deep whiff.

"Apples, pepper, and cloves." He sipped. "This would have gone well with the pork *minutal* Thrasius prepared last night." He didn't look at me. It made me wonder all the more why he brought me because he acted as though I were not there. With slaves that was standard, but his insistence on my attendance made it seem strange to me.

Apicius was tipping his glass up for another sip when something slid down the folds of his toga and hit his toes before bouncing off into the grass. I saw it was my silphium carved amulet—the one he had given me the day Octavius first tried to purchase me. I instinctively reached up to the spot where the amulet normally rested against my breast. It had gone missing a few days before. I'd assumed it lost, not taken. He must have had someone remove it from the table near my bed when I slept.

Sotas stepped forward and retrieved it for him. I stood in shock, trying to process how I felt at him taking the amulet without telling me. I dared not say a word. In truth it was his amulet—he could take anything of mine at will, but why did he? And why have it taken so surreptitiously?

Apicius took the amulet from Sotas. I watched, my heart beating as fast as a dragonfly's wings. "Hold this for me, Fannia dear?" He handed her his glass and tucked the disk into the folds of his toga.

"Certainly," she said, glad for the opening. While Apicius rearranged his toga, she looked around to make sure no one was watching and took a slug of his wine. Aelia gasped but a look from Fannia silenced any admonishment that might have been forthcoming. Apicius recovered his wine from Fannia and took a sip.

"Aelia," a voice called from behind.

Fannia made a small, panicked noise. Apicius jabbed me in the side and I quickly realized he wanted me to step back and find some way to become inconspicuous. I wasn't sure how to do so but I slipped in behind Sotas and Helene, hoping Livia wouldn't notice me.

Livia came near with Drusus and Livilla. Caesar's wife held out her hand and Apicius leaned down to touch his lips to her ring. She turned to Fannia and Aelia to do the same. Fannia relaxed when it became clear that Livia hadn't noticed her transgression with the wine.

"May the gods smile upon your new union," Aelia said to the new couple.

"Many thanks. I hope this marriage will be as long as that of Caesar and my dear lady." Livilla inclined her head toward Livia. I wondered if there was an underlying meaning in her words. Her previous marriage to Gaius had been short and the rumors about Livia's desire to have Tiberius as heir at any cost, even that of Livilla's previous husband, had circulated widely. Livia remained impassive, betraying nothing.

Aelia smiled, oblivious, and clearly delighted to be in the presence of such beautiful, famous people. Livilla was more alluring up close than she had been from afar. Her black hair, worn in an elaborate jeweled headdress, shimmered in the sunlight.

Drusus was barely eighteen, but already aiming to be a great military man. He smiled at Aelia. "I have word of your cousin, Sejanus."

My ears perked up.

"You do? Oh, tell me he is well," Aelia said, giving no hint at her true feelings. I marveled at her composure.

"Yes. He vanquished another band of barbarians in Germania. There is much for the gens Aelia to be proud of in their adopted son."

My heart sank and I'm sure Aelia's did as well.

"I hear Sejanus is a very brave soldier," Livilla added.

"I'm sure that you are quite brave, Drusus." Aelia adeptly changed the subject. "I hear that you have the makings of a fine soldier yourself."

"I do love swinging a sharp sword about, true. I will be joining Tiberius in the north in a few months. I'm sure a few barbarians will meet the edge of my steel."

Livia pointed a long finger at Apicius's wineglass. "Perhaps you should join the drinking game, Apicius. You know wine better than so many others, I suspect." Her voice was like honey, sticking in my ears. I knew it took everything for Apicius to smile at her words, as though they were the most welcome he had heard all day.

"Fantastic idea! I'll stand in line," he said, bowing his head. I was sure he was desperate to get away from Livia before she asked him anything, before Fannia said something that might implicate him, or, the gods forbid, before he developed sudden nausea, which might manifest itself on Livia's sandals.

"Drusus, will you join me?"

The young man chuckled. "A drinking contest? I have a secret that will help us." He reached into the folds of his toga and pulled out a little pouch. "I came prepared! Five or six of these bitter almonds should keep us sober. Lead the way, Gavius Apicius."

Apicius indicated that Sotas should remain with Aelia, then raised his glass in salute before the two of them turned toward the line of men waiting to be chosen for the game. I took my cue from Sotas and didn't move.

"Oh, I didn't get to tell him thank you!" Livilla exclaimed. Her arm reached out toward Apicius, as though to beckon him back, but he was already out of earshot.

"Thank you for what?" Livia asked with a sniff.

"For the delightful dish of stuffed pumpkin fritters he sent for our wedding meal last night! I have never tasted anything so wonderful," she said, her eyes rolling up toward the heavens.

"I wondered who'd sent those," Livia said in a quiet voice. Then she saw me. She wrinkled her brow as though puzzled at my presence. My heart jumped like a bean in a hot pot. I lowered my eyes, praying to the gods that she would lose interest in me.

Aelia touched Livilla on the arm. "I'll be sure to tell Apicius you liked the fritters. Did you also receive the pepper?"

Livilla took Aelia's hand in her own and clutched it excitedly. "Yes! What a thoughtful gift and, I have to say, the little jars in which it came were my favorite part of the gift. Such bright colors."

Livia had lost interest in the conversation and was staring in the direction of the game, watching Apicius as he went to sit on the long padded bench next to Trio and Drusus. Twenty patricians lined the benches to partake in the game and the slaves had already begun filling their first of eleven glasses. The winner was, quite simply, the one who could drink the most. An intricate crown of laurel leaves would be placed upon his head and a generous purse from Caesar would be placed in his hand. "I take it the fritters were good," Fannia said, testing the waters with Livia.

"They were." Livia tore her eyes away from the game and turned to Fannia. She flashed a smile at her rival.

"I know an easy answer to your dilemma."

"My dilemma?" Livia sounded unsure if she should be angry or amused.

She flipped a thumb toward me. "You want his food in your kitchen, do you not? Simply convince Caesar to give Apicius the position he desires, that of gastronomic adviser. You win and he wins." Fannia shifted her fan to better hold her glass. She glanced over to Apicius and the game. The group of men had downed their first glass and were being handed their second.

What was Fannia doing? I suspected that the wine had made her tongue loose.

Livia's nostrils flared at Fannia's suggestion. She turned her attention back to the drinkers. Her head lifted slightly as the men tipped their heads back to down the next glass of wine. She closed her eyes as though savoring the idea of the wine. Her voice was soft, but clear. "Fannia, you are a stupid cow. Pluto will visit Apicius in the Underworld before your friend ever steps foot in Augustus's home as an adviser. Why you think I would help anyone connected to you is beyond me."

Fannia did not have time to reply. Livia called to Livilla and strode off before the new bride could even say her good-byes to Aelia.

When she was gone, Fannia warned me and Sotas, "Tell Apicius nothing of this. Swear to me. Swear by the gods!" We swore.

"Good. Good." Fannia turned her attention to the game but her brow was wrinkled deep with worry.

I glanced at Sotas, hoping for some word or look of comfort to combat the churning in my stomach, but his face was a mask of stone as he stared ahead, eyes on his master.

On the drinking couches, the twenty patricians were readying themselves for glass number three. I was sure that Apicius could keep up for at least eight or nine glasses, but I didn't know how he would manage the last few. We watched as the Magister of Revels cut the wine with water and the slaves once more went to fill the glasses. At first I worried

Livia might try to poison him, but when I saw the wine was directly from the lot of unopened amphorae along the garden wall, I relaxed.

The poet Ovid appeared beside Fannia, leaning over to kiss her cheek in greeting.

"What a delight to see you here!" She beamed.

Aelia held out her hand in greeting and blushed to her toes when he kissed her cheek in welcome.

"Why aren't you participating?" Fannia asked.

"I'd never make it through the fourth drink!" He tipped his wineglass toward us in a mock toast.

As I suspected, glasses three through five were no problem for Apicius to drink down in one long slow draft, as was required by the rules of the game. Other rules included no burping, no falling off the bench, no declining a drink. None of the participants wanted to be disgraced in front of Caesar. At glass five, one of the city's more prominent lawyers—and one who had begun drinking long before the party started—fell off his bench. The crowd laughed heartily. Caesar didn't smile. A wave of his hand brought two burly men over to pick up the drunkard and carry him unceremoniously out of the garden, his worried wife in tow.

Everything went sour after that. Octavius stood with the Imperial couple, talking with Livia while Caesar was occupied with Tiberius and other patricians. Octavius and Livia held their eyes on Apicius. Then Livia said something to her body-slave, who dutifully trotted over to the slaves serving the wine. Subsequently, on the sixth glass I could see that they had stopped watering down Apicius's glass. And I couldn't do a damn thing about it.

Apicius tipped the glass, and as the drink touched his lips he almost sputtered, but he caught himself before he breached etiquette. As he realized the wine was undiluted, I could almost hear his internal dialogue of worry.

I stepped forward to let Aelia and Fannia know. Aelia let out a small cry that Fannia stopped with a tight grip on her arm.

I knew my master struggled on the bench. Apicius could barely keep the alarm from showing on his face when the seventh goblet arrived and he discovered it too was undiluted. He stared at Aelia, to give him focus, I suspected. Why on the Seven Hills hadn't anyone else noticed?

My master hesitated at the eighth glass, likely unsure of how he was going to keep the thick spiced wine in his stomach. He drank it as slowly as he could manage without breaking the rules. Drusus leaned over to him, and they had a short conversation that culminated in Apicius nodding his head vigorously. Whatever was said, it appeared to give my dominus resolve. But when Apicius passed the glass to the servant, he almost moved forward too much—at this point the slaves had been instructed to stand farther away as a challenge for the drunken men, to see who might fall off the bench. Apicius wavered at the edge, and then finally held the glass to the slave.

"We've got to get him out of here," Aelia said to Fannia. "I fear what Marcus might do if he humiliates himself in front of Caesar. It would ruin all his plans."

Fannia lifted the fan in front of her lips. "Agreed. It won't be long before he won't be able to walk out on his own two feet. You're going to have to play sick. Stagger forward a bit and faint. I'll do the rest. Try to fall convincingly and don't move, don't blink, until I nudge you. Can you do that?"

"I'll try." She looked at her husband. Apicius was starting to turn a bright shade of pink. His wreath hung crookedly on his head and the look in his eyes was imploring. Drusus was sitting closer to him, seemingly bolstering him. I thought I saw him jostle Apicius a few times in such a manner that would keep my master from falling from the bench. Perhaps he realized that Apicius's wine was undiluted as well?

"Sotas, Thrasius, attempt to help but let us manage the situation until it is clear you need to step in."

"Yes, Domina," we said in response.

"Ovid, dear heart," Fannia said in a low tone. "I'm going to need your help. I'll take care of Aelia, you take care of Apicius. Help him when the time is right. I'll explain later. And I promise you, it will be worth your while." She trailed one finger along his bare arm. The poet nodded and smiled without question.

"Now." Fannia nudged Aelia as a slave placed the ninth glass in Apicius's hands.

Aelia stumbled toward the long line of patricians on the bench, clutching the fabric of her stola as though her chest hurt. After she'd taken a few steps and a hush fell over the crowd, she "tripped" and with a cry pitched forward. Fannia and Apicius called her name as she fell. Her body landed on the soft grass, her eyes closed and a blank look upon her face. Sotas and I tried to reach her as did many others in the crowd. Fannia reached her first but it was Livilla's voice that rose above the others, shouting for her slaves to attend Aelia.

For a few minutes the garden was filled with chaos. We could not get near our domina—there were too many trying to help her. The drinking contest fell apart as several of the participants raced to Aelia's aid when they saw her fall. Apicius tried to move toward her, but there were too many people and the wine had clouded his senses. Drusus had thrown an arm around him to hold him up. Apicius called his wife's name over and over as he struggled to reach her side, drunkenly pushing through the knot of senators and slaves, with Drusus helping to part the way. I left Sotas and followed Ovid, who was also making his way toward Apicius.

"Come now; let us move out of the way. Aelia will be fine." Ovid's voice was quiet but commanding. Apicius lifted his head and blearily recognized the poet. "Drusus is a good friend to help you."

"But he knows nothing about bitter almonds," Apicius blurted out.

Drusus chuckled a little at the jab. "I feel fine, Apicius."

"Well, I don't. I am drunk."

"You certainly are," Ovid said, steadying him with a hand to the shoulder.

"You look different." Apicius lifted a hand to touch the poet's face. Ovid pulled his head away and Apicius's hand fell into empty air.

Ovid smacked him across the face. I looked around to see if anyone had noticed, but everyone was attending to Aelia. "Apicius, I need you to stand up straight. Pretend you are sober. You must make us all believe."

Drusus took his arm away to see if Apicius could stand.

Apicius, to my surprise, straightened, just as the sea of people parted. Livilla and Fannia held up a weary-looking Aelia. Two slaves appeared at their sides, frantically waving sizable palm fans to push away the humid air. I saw Sotas standing in the crowd behind them.

"There you are," Fannia said loudly to Apicius. "This is no time for games—we must get your wife home to bed!"

"It's all right, you will be fine. They'll take you home," Livilla kept saying to Aelia. "It's too hot, I know. Look, here's Apicius. He'll take you home!"

Apicius managed to walk a few steps without staggering. He pulled Aelia close to him and they wavered a bit. Drusus reached out a hand to steady Aelia, but I knew the effort was made to bolster Apicius.

I was amazed at how Apicius managed to rally to the situation. "Is there a litter?" he asked loudly. Drusus started yelling for the guards to find a litter, taking away some of the focus from my master.

The crowd parted and Caesar appeared with Livia and a tattooed barbarian slave at his heels. Tiberius was behind him, his face etched with annoyance. Octavius followed up at the rear. I thought my heart might leap out of my throat. *Oh, Apicius! Do not falter now!* He had always desired an audience with Caesar but this was not how either of us had dreamed it—drunk, with his wife feigning an illness in the Imperial gardens.

"Are you all right?" Caesar asked Aelia.

"Yes, it's the heat, I'm afraid. I think I need to sleep for a while."

"There are guest chambers where you can rest." Tiberius waved to his slaves. "Dear lady, please accept my hospitality. My slaves will make sure you are comfortable."

"Thank you." Aelia bowed her head. "You are very generous, but I think . . ." She trailed off. If she suggested she return home it could be seen as an insult to both Tiberius and to Caesar.

Ovid came to Aelia's rescue. "I think what she is trying to say but is far too polite is that sometimes, when one is ill, the best medicine is your own pillow, your own surroundings, and your own medic there to administer to your ills, with your own masseuse there to rub your feet. With your permission, I would be pleased to see them home. I could read to her. I know you understand how the power of words can ease the soul."

Tiberius nodded. "I do understand. It's up to you, dear lady, but know you are welcome to all the comforts of my home and the expertise of my doctors."

"Again, thank you," she said, feigning weakness. "I believe our poet may also read minds. I do long for the comfort of my own bed."

Apicius spoke up, but his speech was slow. He was trying not to slur his words. "Thank you, honorable Caesar. But I ask your permission to depart for home as my wife desires."

"Permission granted," Augustus said. "May the gods bring you swift healing." He waved at the slaves to bring the litter, and left with Livia in tow, I noted with no small measure of relief. Octavius lingered, staring at me with a scowl. Then he snapped his fingers at his body-slave and followed Tiberius, Augustus, and his wife.

Livilla and Fannia kissed Aelia good-bye. Drusus and Ovid helped Aelia and Apicius into the litter and we departed, Sotas, Helene, and I walking behind, feeling strangely useless and grateful for it, all at the same time.

PART V

7 C.E. to 9 C.E.

LENTILS WITH CHESTNUTS

Take a new pan and put in carefully thoroughly peeled chestnuts. Add water and a little soda, put it to cook. When it is cooking, put in a mortar pepper, cumin, coriander seed, mint, rue, laser (silphium) root, pennyroyal, and pound them. Pour on vinegar, honey, liquamen; flavor with vinegar and pour it over the cooked chestnuts. Add oil, bring it to heat. When it is simmering well, pound it with a stick as you pound in a mortar. Taste it, if there is anything lacking, add it. When you have put it in the serving dish, add green oil.

—Book 5.2.2, Legumes
On Cookery, Apicius

CHAPTER 13

"Tear it all down." Apicius waved his hand toward the cluster of insulae standing before him. Finding land in the center of Rome was not an easy task, but if you were willing to pay money for prime real estate it was easy to convince a landlord to displace his tenants. Apicius had done just that, looking for the right property, then propositioning its owner. He had been determined to build in the small valley between the Palatine and Caelian Hills, near where the majority of his friends and clients lived and where it would be a short walk from his own villa.

The block was one of the more crowded along the Vicus Cyclopis, the long winding street between the hills that gained its name from a grove said to hold Cyclops many years past. Several tall buildings rose upward in a mess of rough boards, rickety balconies, and torn curtains flapping in the windows. The insulae had been cleared of occupants but remnants of them remained—a tunic left hanging to dry in a window or a child's ball in one of the doorways. I wondered what had happened to the families who'd lived in those apartments. Housing was difficult to come by in Rome, especially so close to the center of the city. Although it had often been talked about in the Senate, to date there were no laws governing the way occupants were treated when there was a sale. That made it likely Apicius had forced many dozens out of their homes. I winced at the thought.

The foreman to whom Apicius spoke was a sturdy middle-aged man with a big hooked nose and the hint of a country accent. He seemed unfazed by the task before him. "What would you have us do with all of the wood and material from the buildings?"

Apicius shrugged. "I don't care. Do with it what you will."

I couldn't believe what I was hearing. "Dominus, that's a lot of marble, brick, and wood. The profit—"

"Not worth worrying about," he said curtly. "Just tear this mess down as quickly as you can so we can begin building."

I regarded the buildings in dismay. Not only did he just eliminate the living spaces for dozens of families but he was throwing away thousands of sestertii in building materials. I understood none of it. Granted, the gods had been kind to Apicius when it came to money, but when he ruined lives and squandered his money, I felt nothing but anger toward my master.

"I'll return in four days to check on your progress."

I was sure that when we returned the foreman and everything on the city block would be gone. Doubtless the foreman would run as far and fast as he could with his profit before Apicius realized how much money he had given away.

Sure enough, when we returned at the end of the week the insulae were gone and all that was left on the land was some rubble from broken concrete walls. It was a large piece of land and without the buildings it looked even more expansive, just a vacant slab of dirt in the middle of the city.

The architect, named Hippocrates, met us a little past noon. He rolled out several sets of papyri showing how the building would be constructed. He was from Greece and rumored to be one of the most talented designers in the whole Empire. He appeared to be twenty-five at most. The man's foot was twisted to the side and he used a cane to walk.

"This is an ambitious project, you understand?" Hippocrates surveyed the plans and gazed back over the land.

"Yes, I do. I will pay you well for your efforts."

"I know what you suggested in your letters to me but, respectfully, I must disagree. I don't think we should make the entire building two stories. Now hear me out," he said, halting Apicius's protest with his hand. "I think the areas where there are stoves and fires should be one story, with ample ducts for the flames and air to escape. I think it would be dangerous if you put rooms above this area. Instead, let us take only one quarter of the building and make it rise upward. You could have three floors for your lectures and for housing for the school's slaves. In the rest of the building, which would be only one floor, we'll place the kitchen and storerooms. What say you?"

Apicius studied the plans as the architect spoke. "Interesting. Where do you see the entrance?"

"Look here." Hippocrates thrust a dirty finger at the drawing. I leaned in for a better look. "I propose we have a large walled garden at the front of the building where you could hold outdoor parties. There would be a gate at the entrance with a walkway and a series of canals and fountains leading toward the doors of the main building."

"What do you think, Thrasius?"

It was the first time that I could recall Apicius asking my opinion when we were in front of others. I could barely find my voice. "It sounds incredible." And it did. There were no organized school buildings in Rome. Most of the wealthy hired private tutors and those who couldn't sent their children to attend classes in the streets where many teachers held lessons. This would be a different school indeed—there had never before been a place where students would learn how to cook. Despite my trepidation, I felt a great excitement blooming within me.

"I don't want travertine or marble for the columns." Apicius lifted his chin in the direction of the Roman Forum. "You will use porphyry, regardless of the expense."

I sighed. The purple stone was expensive to import and usually reserved for temples built by the wealthiest of patrons. A cooking school was hardly a temple—how did Apicius expect to recoup any of these costs?

The architect nodded, as though requests like this were common, as though building a cooking school were, in fact, common. "You will have your school in one year, Marcus Gavius Apicius." He lifted his cane and shook it in warning. "That is, if you stay out of my way and let me get the work done."

Apicius was silent for a few moments, unaccustomed to such insolence. Eventually he asked, "Do you think I will be in your way?"

Hippocrates smiled for the first time, a wide, yellow-stained grin. "Of course you will be. Patrons are good at finding methods to get in my way and slow my work down or change it from the grandeur of my vision. I dare not hope you will be different, but in the event you might be, I ask you to place your trust in my hands. If so, I will build you a school that will be the talk of the Empire."

"One year?"

The architect grew serious. "Yes. One year and you will have your school."

"And you promise me it will be the talk of the Empire?"

Hippocrates began to roll up the papyri. "Yes, by Apollo, I promise."

I shook my head, wondering if this promise would be like that of the foreman of the last villa Apicius had built, in the Alban Hills beyond Rome. The man had promised a vast estate, but while building it had asked for greater and greater sums of money, half of which went into the use of inferior materials, and the other half he pocketed. Still, there was something about Hippocrates that made me believe he was true to his word. It also helped that he was quite well known, and if he cheated Apicius it would be more damaging to his reputation than it might be worth. Sotas cracked his knuckles; it was as though he knew what I was thinking.

Hippocrates turned at the sound and grinned. He understood the gesture.

"One year, Master Apicius. I promise you, it will be magnificent."

A few days later I was going over a cena menu with my dominus when we were interrupted by one of the door slaves.

"Publius Octavius is here to see you," the boy announced.

Aelia reclined on a long chaise next to us, reading Homer and basking in the afternoon sunlight filtering into the garden where we sat.

"I'll be there presently." The door slave hurried off. Apicius waved the lyre players entertaining us to silence, and dismissed them with a flick of his wrist.

"What could he want?" Aelia snapped her fingers at Helene to hand her a glass of honey water.

"I know not, but I'm sure it isn't good. Come, Thrasius. I want you to wait in the corridor and listen." He gave Aelia a peck on the cheek before stalking off in the direction the door slave had gone. Sotas, who had been standing at his post along one wall, fell into step with me.

On the way to the atrium, we encountered Passia heading toward the kitchen with a tray holding the remainders of Apicata's midday meal. She bowed her head as she attempted to pass but Apicius stopped her with a firm hand on her shoulder. "Have some Falernian wine, grapes, and olives brought to the atrium." He paused and considered her. He brought a hand to her chin and she gawped at him, her eyes widening at the strange, intimate gesture. "On second thought, bring it yourself." He let her go and continued on.

She saw me and a look of shame crossed her face. I stopped as I passed and leaned down to kiss her brow. She sighed.

As slaves we all knew our bodies were not our own, but this was the first time Apicius had crossed into territory that he himself had set when he "gave" Passia to me. I clenched my jaw tight, determined not to let my anger show.

When we reached the atrium I waited in the corridor with two of the other house slaves. I could see and hear everything well but it was dark enough that Octavius would not be able to pick me out from the non-descript forms of the slaves waiting in the shadows.

"Octavius!" Apicius said jovially as he crossed the atrium. "How good it is to see you!" He clasped hands with the man.

"It's good to see you as well." Octavius surveyed the room. "I must say, I love what you have done with this atrium. It reminds me of Livia's chambers in her villa," he observed. Each wall was part of a large garden scene, decorated in great detail with olive trees, bright feathered birds, and a sky of vivid blue.

"Yes, Aelia admired that room when she attended a gathering Livia had arranged, so I hired the same painter." I had heard the story many times before. He loved to boast about the commission.

"I thought so. You should see his new work." His eyes continued to wander over the images in the frescoes. "I hired him last month to design my baths and to decorate the walls of all my slaves' chambers. I anticipate keeping him very busy for the next year!"

Apicius ignored the one-upmanship. Slave quarters were often painted, but never by someone with such esteem.

"Come and sit. Enjoy some wine with me," he said instead. Octavius followed Apicius's lead and sat back on one of the plush couches. Sotas, without prompting but knowing his dominus well, took a spot so that he was standing not far behind Apicius, in large opposing view. The two rivals chatted about the weather, news of the war, and other trivial things. After a short while, Passia swept by me, her arm brushing against me on purpose. She came forth with the tray of wine and food and set it on the small tripod table in front of the men. The front of her tunica dipped down, affording Octavius a glance at her shapely chest.

"Thank you, Passia." Apicius dismissed her with a nod.

"Beautiful girl," Octavius remarked, licking his lips. He stared at her as she left and Apicius smiled with satisfaction. I fumed, thinking about Sejanus and how he had desired my lover as well. It was then I realized what my master had done by introducing Passia. He was flaunting yet another unattainable purchase in front of Octavius.

"Now tell me, Octavius, what brings you here?" Apicius reached forward and took a cluster of grapes.

Octavius lifted his glass to his lips, closing his eyes as the wine went down. After savoring the taste for what seemed to be an inappropriate amount of time, Octavius responded, "I hear you are building a cooking school?"

"Where did you hear that?" Apicius forced a smile.

"Gossip is always easy to find in this city." Octavius waved a hand to indicate Rome's expanse. "I do not recall. At the baths. Are you? Building a school?"

"I've considered it."

"Well, if you have only considered it, why are you breaking ground at the foot of the hill? You tore out an entire block of insulae. What for?" Octavius popped an olive into his mouth and spat the pit out onto the floor for the ancestral gods.

"Ah, that." Apicius took a sip of wine.

"Do you really need so much space for a school?" Octavius pressed.

"Does it matter?"

"Just curiosity, my old friend. I was surprised when I heard the news and saw how much space you have planned. Do you truly think you will have so many students?"

Apicius paused. I had said the same to my master on several occasions but I found he always gave more weight when such observations were made by others.

"I said, 'considered,'" Apicius reiterated with a little too much force.

"Well, what are you building, then? A shrine to Edesia?" Octavius laughed at the reference to the goddess of feasts.

"You will have to wait and see."

Octavius leaned forward, his smile gone and the many folds of his chin stretching out as he elongated his neck. Darkness slipped into his voice. "I would advise you against such a school."

"And why would that be?" Apicius was struggling to keep his composure. His fingers were playing with the edge of his toga; it was a gesture I knew all too well.

"I am trying to keep you from wasting money." Octavius's chin and lips jiggled. "Who would send their cooks to such a school? Who among us patricians wants our cenae to come out the same?"

"Some patricians could use a cook with skills," Apicius replied. "Take Oppius Velius Justus, for example. You've dined on his couch, drunk his plonk, and complained wholeheartedly to everyone afterward."

Octavius lowered his glass. "Perhaps." He didn't deny the claim. "However, I'm also not sure Caesar would approve."

"And why wouldn't he?"

Those words convinced me that Octavius was scared of the cooking school being a success. Caesar couldn't care less about such matters.

"He would never want his parties to fall short of another's," Octavius managed, but it sounded like he was floundering.

"I doubt that could happen with you at the helm." Apicius sounded as though he were beginning to enjoy the conversation. "If I were to build such a school, Caesar would have nothing to worry about. No one would dare outshine him."

Octavius winked. "Except you and me," he said conspiratorially.

Apicius paused, clearly unsure if Octavius was trying to lure him into a conversation he didn't want to have. "I heard you were in Cyrenaica," he replied instead.

Octavius pressed forward. "Yes. I went to meet with my silphium supplier."

I suppressed a snort of derision. How many times was Octavius going to try to trump Apicius during this conversation? Apicius didn't waver. "And how did you fare?"

"Better than I hoped." Octavius picked up the last cluster of grapes. "My supplier stumbled on a few precious plants along the coast. All for me."

Apicius had grown weary of the discussion. He set his glass down on the table and tapped the edge of the couch idly with his fingertips. The tap was an indication to Sotas, who signaled the serving boys waiting in the hallway next to me.

"Really? And he sold them only to you? Impressive." Apicius smiled broadly as he flattered his guest.

"Four little hillocks full, no less!" Octavius started to elaborate but paused when one of the serving boys who had been standing with me emerged from the shadows to whisper in Apicius's ear.

"My apologies, Octavius. It appears I am late for an engagement with a client. I must prepare. Sotas can see you out." He rose from the couch and leaned forward to clasp Octavius on the shoulder. "Thank you for your visit. I promise to consider your words." He gestured to Sotas and hurried out of the atrium, taking me by the arm as he walked past.

When we reached the garden, Apicius collapsed on the divan across from his wife. I took up my spot on the stool next to him.

"Bastard," he muttered as he lay back.

I didn't say anything.

"What did he want?" Aelia asked, not looking up from her scroll.

"He warned me not to build the school. How did he know?"

"You know how slaves talk." She winked at me, then turned to her husband. "Maybe you should listen to him."

"Listen to him?" Apicius was incredulous. "Me? Listen to Octavius? You can't be serious, wife! I would sooner eat a pile of fresh sheep dung than listen to that man."

"I know." Her voice softened. "He has his own reasons for making such a suggestion, I'm sure, but I've been thinking, and, well . . ."

"And what?" He looked at me as though expecting me to back him up. I'm not sure why; it was not my place to speak up in such matters.

"I'm concerned about how it may fare."

"Explain. What do you mean, wife?"

I closed my eyes and wished I were in Baiae, sitting on the beach, looking at the water, with Rome and its intrigues a hundred miles away.

"Now, don't be upset. Think for a minute. What if no one sends their slaves to the school?"

"They will!" he roared, sitting up. "What do you think, Thrasius?"

I opened my eyes. "I'm not sure, Dominus. I do know we have had many requests for me to teach other cooks."

Apicius's lips pressed into a thin line. "I know they will," he said again, with less enthusiasm.

"How can you be sure?" Aelia asked.

"My clients, for one. They will send their slaves if they want to continue to have room on my couch!"

Aelia raised an eyebrow. "Are you sure it wouldn't only be under duress?"

"Is that what you believe, wife?" He sprang to his feet, unable to contain his anger. It bled into his words, lending his voice a screechy quality. "You know how they talk about me in Rome! Even the plebs gossip in amazement about how marvelous my parties must be! My clients are already asking me for advice and to have Thrasius train their slaves. There is no duress."

"All right, but consider this. Once their slaves are trained, who will want seats on your couch?"

I groaned inwardly, wishing Aelia had not opened up this jar full of worms. I hated being with them when they argued, which was often.

Apicius took a sharp breath. "Then tell me," he hissed at Aelia, "why would Octavius threaten me if he wasn't scared? He knows this will be a success."

"But, Marcus, where will your new students come from? How long do you think it will run before people start laughing and calling you a fool?"

"Wife, you are out of line." Danger rode on the back of each word.

Aelia pursed her lips. She rolled the scroll downward to the next stanza of her poem. "Of course, husband. I should not have spoken."

"No, you shouldn't have." Apicius stared at her for one long moment, then abruptly rose and left. Sotas followed behind.

"You are dismissed," Aelia said to me, her voice catching.

As I left the room I heard a sob escape from my domina.

CHAPTER 14

It was just as Hippocrates said—the building of the cooking school took a year, almost precisely to the day.

Apicius burst into the kitchen to tell me. There was sweat on his brow and a broad smile on his face. It had been many weeks since I had seen him in such a good mood.

"Today is the day, Thrasius!"

I pushed aside the meat I was chopping and washed my hands. The water was cold against my skin. "What do you mean, Dominus?"

For the entire year Apicius had been obsessed with building his cooking school. He wouldn't let me see inside, telling me he wanted it to be a surprise. I even tried to get the guards to let me in when I walked by on my way to market, but they had been instructed to let no one in unless the foreman or Apicius was there. And the foreman knew me, so I was equally thwarted on that front.

Apicius brought his hands down against the counter with a heavy thud. He smiled broadly and exclaimed, "My school is done!"

"Already? I thought it was weeks away from being finished."

Apicius grinned, pleased with himself. "I brought in extra workers. I was tired of how long it was taking to build. Come now; let's do what we have talked about doing." He glanced toward the stoves where Rúan was helping the slave boy tie a pig to a spit above the flame.

"Rúan! Come here!"

Rúan approached and looked askance at me, confusion flaring in his green eyes. From that look, I knew my assistant feared the worst. Apicius had become increasingly difficult to read in the past year. Rúan had been on the receiving end of Dominus's anger all too often in recent months, usually for no reason, just for being in the wrong place at the wrong time.

Everyone was watching us, but Apicius winked at me and, without warning, picked up a wide pan and slammed it down upon the counter several times. Then there was no doubt everyone was listening.

"Today is a day for celebration!" Apicius gestured at me with one ringed thumb. "Your coquus, Thrasius, will be assuming duties as head of my brand-new cooking school!"

A murmur of surprise and disappointment rose among the slaves, sounds from those who doubtless assumed Apicius was granting me my freedom (which, despite my growing peculium, I didn't believe he ever would). There were grunts of confusion from others. My face reddened from both the heat and the intensity of being under the gaze of all the staff in my kitchen.

A voice rose from the crowd. "A cooking school?" No one had ever heard of such a thing.

Apicius ignored the question. "Tell him!" The tone of Apicius's voice was giddy, like a child opening presents on the first morning of Saturnalia.

I raised my voice. "Rúan, I am giving you full control of this kitchen. Today Dominus Apicius and I hereby bestow upon you the title of coquus of the Gavia household. From here forward, all servants of this kitchen will take their orders from you."

Apicius bobbed his head with approval. "You will give Rúan the same respect you gave to Coquus Thrasius. If not, then you will be subject to both his lash and mine." He sounded as though he would be delighted at the prospect. A few slaves shuddered at the warning.

I smiled at Rúan, even though there was a deep sadness reverberating within me at the words I was expected to say. When I came to the Gavia household nine years ago I never thought I would be in such a position.

Rúan knelt. One knee slid a little on an errant parsnip peel when he kissed Apicius's sandaled foot but he didn't show any discomfort. "Thank you, Master Apicius. I will serve you well as coquus."

Apicius put a hand on Rúan's shoulder, gesturing him to stand. He looked out on the kitchen again, raising his voice in command. "Make no mistake. Thrasius will remain superior in this kitchen and in all my households. You will heed his words when in his presence."

I leaned against the nearby table, hoping for an anchor to steady me. I loved that kitchen. Those people, huddled around stoves as hot as the fires of Vulcan, were my family. The thought of not seeing them every day saddened me more than I ever anticipated it would.

Apicius seemed infused with the light of the gods. I had seen him this happy only on a few occasions, usually at the height of a cena going particularly well.

My master waved an arm grandly as he spoke. "Tonight we will celebrate such a glorious day! All of us! Rúan, cook us a grand feast and the entire household will partake together this evening. Cook whatever you want. I'll even let you open a barrel of Falernian wine for the slaves. What do you say?"

Rúan grinned, plainly excited at the prospect. Normally the staff was relegated to eating simple foods in the kitchen between the meals the Gavia family was served. What Apicius suggested was a pleasure usually reserved for Saturnalia.

"Yes, Dominus. With pleasure!"

Then Rúan noticed I was standing there in a daze. He gave me a light cuff on the shoulder. "You will be an excellent teacher. You have taught me well all these years. And all of them too." He waved an arm at the servants. They cheered and clapped.

Balsamea came to me and threw her bony arms around me. "I am so proud of you, Thrasius," she said in my ear.

The blood rose to my cheeks as the cheering in the kitchen grew to thunderous levels. Apicius often praised my work but my servants never did; they did their work, they seemed to respect me, and they never talked back. It had never occurred to me to consider how I affected the people I worked with every day. A curious mixture of happiness and sorrow blended within me. I was proud to have become more than a cook, but leaving the kitchen behind, even if not completely, would be difficult for me to do.

A few minutes later, I stood with Apicius and Sotas in front of the high-gated wall I had passed countless times on my way to market. It was the same gate from which the guards had always turned me away. Apicius posted the guards to watch the school after the second episode of graffiti. Someone (both Apicius and I suspected Publius Octavius was involved) had been marring the walls with profanity and images of fat, gluttonous men and women eating mountains of food or doing lewd things to one another. You couldn't trust slaves for such a job so Apicius had been forced to hire a private guard. The first time I saw the monthly fee written in Apicius's account books, I almost choked on my wine.

The door he led me to was no longer the drab wooden door I had passed by each week. Instead it was newly painted in red and bright yellow with the Latin words *Apicius School of Cooking* carved in careful letters. It was impressive.

"Well?" Apicius asked, his voice gleeful. I was reminded of Apicata after she had built houses of sand on the beach at the Baiae villa and was waiting for approval. Was Apicius looking to me for reassurance?

"I have not seen inside, Dominus." I wasn't sure what to say, or how to react. My stomach felt like the gods were playing marbles with my innards. I did not want to admit to my master how excited I felt about the school.

Apicius didn't notice my discomfort. "Come!" He placed the key in the door. It swung inward to reveal a wide courtyard filled with a number of fountains and several mosaic platforms where dining couches could easily be erected. Garden slaves were hard at work tending to the pathways and watering the many plants. To one side a small amphitheater was nestled between two small stands of trees. At the opposite end of the courtyard, marble columns rose in front of a long reflecting pool. Apicius pointed at the door standing between the central columns.

"See that door?"

I nodded, still reeling from the idea that my dominus intended me to run the school. I suspected that not only would I be teaching but I would still be putting on elaborate cenae.

Apicius was still pointing at the door. "That, dear Thrasius, is the door to your future." He strode off toward the building.

The gardens, extravagant as they were, were nothing compared to the interior of the new school.

The first thing I noticed was the floor, a mosaic of various gods eating foods from the histories. "The staircases go up to the classrooms and the slave living quarters." Apicius gestured to steps on each side of the hallway. At the end of the hall, he swung open the door with a flourish and stood aside to let me pass. He told Sotas to wait there and stand guard.

"What do you think?"

When the next door opened, I took in the scene with hungry eyes. It was the largest kitchen I had ever seen. Or kitchens, for what lay before me was not one large kitchen but half a dozen stations, each complete with a hearth, a trough with flowing water, and a large cabinet for pots and pans. Additionally, each work space had a vent in the ceiling to filter the oven smoke upward. Slaves, none of whom I recognized, bustled about the kitchen or waited along the walls for commands. There were more slaves here than I had in my entire kitchen.

But it was the counters that made me gasp. They were made of high-grade porphyry that glistened with a red shine. Seeing the precious stone made me stop in my tracks. How much would the cooking classes have to cost in order to make a difference in paying for building the school? Would they be able to? I didn't think they would.

"Well? Do you like what you see?" Apicius asked me again.

"Yes," I said, but I was torn between glee and despair. What would happen if I could not make it viable? What sort of new trick had the gods played on me?

I walked to the first station and placed my hand flat upon the surface of the shiny stone.

"Look." Apicius moved past me to a series of shelves on the wall. He pulled down a basket of knives, spoons, and other kitchen utensils. "And look over there." He waved a hand at another row of shelves.

I still didn't know what to say so instead I walked across the tiled floor to reach the shelves. Three slaves rushed to help me reach the higher shelves, upon which were dozens of sets of serving ware, silver platters, glasses, and plates.

Apicius let me look only briefly before ushering me toward a central door along the side of the kitchen. He opened it to reveal a massive banquet hall with a multitude of dining couches, some for seating as many as eighteen people.

I gaped. "This rivals anything Caesar could imagine!"

"Shhh, you might insult Publius Octavius!" Apicius chuckled.

"I don't know what to say, Dominus. It is truly magnificent." I ran my fingers along the door frame. The plaster was intricately shaped with small birds carrying grapes and berries in their beaks.

"Say nothing. Instead, start planning for your first class." Apicius motioned for the slaves to close the banquet door. He turned to leave.

I started after him. "Dominus, when will the first class be? How will people know? What should I charge?" The words came out in a rush.

All trace of amusement was gone from his eyes. "Next week. We will tell our clients first and they will help us build a following. You will charge each student ten denarii for four classes a week."

"Ten denarii?" I stammered, unable to believe the paltry cost Apicius was asking. "Dominus, I mean no disrespect, but how can we recoup the building costs if we don't charge higher fees?"

"That is of no consequence," Apicius muttered. "What we want, Thrasius, is students, as many students as possible. I want households all over Rome cooking my food." His pace quickened and I had to jog to keep up with him. Apicius stopped when he reached the door to the front gardens, where Sotas waited.

"You'll find a furnished apartment on the second floor if you should choose to stay here some nights." He nodded at Sotas, who pulled a thick bronze ring with a short extruding key off his finger and handed it to me.

"I still want you to advise me on affairs at the domus, however," Apicius continued. "I expect to see you every morning and for you to be there on days when you do not have classes. Come to me in two days with your plan for the school and together we will inform my clients."

I couldn't speak. The smile returned to his face and Apicius clapped me on the back. "Familiarize yourself with the school now but I expect to see you at the domus for tonight's celebration. This is a glorious day, Thrasius! The gods are smiling on me!"

"Yes, Dominus. Thank you. I will be there." I hoped I sounded sincere. Sotas smirked at me. He knew my mind. I slipped the key ring onto my ring finger but it was too big. I tried my thumb and it fit, but barely. I would have to find a cord to wear it around my neck or with which to tie it to my belt.

"Good! I will see you tonight." Apicius waved to Sotas and turned to leave.

I watched the door slaves close the doors after my master left. I put my hands down on the gorgeous, cool red counter. I wanted to laugh nearly as much as I wanted to cry. Running a kitchen was one thing, but, oh dear gods, a cooking school? The students, the lesson planning, the ordering of ingredients, the promotion of the school to the world. The amount of work ahead of me was more than I wanted to think about.

The school was initially successful. I decided I would start with a series of classes on sauces, on preparing fowl, and on planning and organizing small cenae. They filled instantly. Apicius's clients were desperate to have their slaves learn how to serve such incredible food. We turned many hopefuls away at the door the first month. I had several stops and starts, but after the first week I started to settle into a comfortable pace.

We also decided to hold a few large banquets to help teach students how to run them successfully. Initially, I tried to staff these events using only students from the cooking school, but it took only one disastrous banquet for that to change.

It was the third feast we hosted at the school. The first two banquets were well attended by many of Rome's most prominent families, despite caveats that the cenae were for teaching purposes and ensuring quality and service would be near impossible, especially on the level some of the attendees were accustomed to.

On that night, Herod Agrippa, the future king of the Jews, and a friend to Tiberius's son, Drusus, was in attendance. I had not been informed that he would be a guest, and the majority of the food that was served he couldn't eat.

Tycho brought the first dish back to me, a platter of pork meatballs. "Herod Agrippa can't eat this, Coquus." One of the other boys appeared behind him with a bowl of pork stew.

"Or this," he added, setting the bowl down with the other dirty dishes.

"What *can* he eat?" Tycho asked me. Over the last few years, he had gone from being a simple serving boy to my trusted attendant. At seventeen, he was no longer the cherub who used to flit about Apicius's courtyard. Now he had a scruff of beard and dark curls framing his golden face.

I thought about the menu. "He should be able to have the Numidian chicken. And maybe the beets. Make sure they are brought out to him right away."

A short time later, one of the serving girls came running into the kitchen, tears streaming down her face.

"What is wrong, girl?" I asked after she had collapsed onto a stool in the corner of the kitchen, cradling her face in her hands. She sobbed, choking on her words. "I spilled wine on Prince Herod." Blood ran from a split lip, hindering her speech even further. "Drusus was angry and hit me."

I swore. I left the girl there and rushed out to the triclinium with a fresh carafe of wine and a clean towel.

I bowed when I drew near. "Prince Herod, I heard what happened. I have brought you a towel and fresh wine."

The prince smiled at me, his dark eyes shining. "Thank you," he said, taking the towel. I poured the wine, careful not to spill a drop. He had the smallest circle of wetness on his sleeve.

"Are you the coquus?" Drusus asked me.

I bowed. "I am."

"Your cenae are renowned through Italy. What went wrong tonight? I have been humiliated in front of my friend." His voice held a dark warning in its tone. Drusus was long rumored to have a terrible temper.

"I give you my deepest apologies. This is a school, Dominus. Many of our students are still learning how to serve with the finesse that someone of your illustrious stature deserves." I prayed to Pax that my flattery would keep him calm.

Herod put a hand on Drusus's arm to still him. "Now I understand, my friend. We should be patient with these slaves. They will learn from their mistakes if we school them on how to improve."

Color had risen to Drusus's cheeks. He was furious. I spoke before he could.

"Thank you for the kindness. I am having some chicken sent out to the table in a few minutes."

Herod nodded his approval, then abruptly changed the topic of conversation with Drusus, asking him about one of our Roman customs. I backed away from the table. When I reached the kitchen, I saw that the Numidian chicken was ready to be delivered.

The skin was not as dark as I would have liked. I stopped Tycho before he was to take the chicken to the table and asked him to check it for doneness. I watched as he took a knife to the leg and separated it from the chicken's body. The juice did not run clear.

I thanked Jupiter for watching over me and sent the chicken back to cook a few minutes more. Under no circumstance would I allow another mishap that day.

"You should have them all whipped!" Apicius raged that night after the feast when he heard what had happened.

"Dominus, these are slaves owned by others," I argued. He was within his rights to have the slaves disciplined in the way he desired as they were acting on his behalf and on his property, but there were political ramifications he had not considered, which I tried to explain.

"What about the fact that I was embarrassed in front of a man whom Tiberius has taken under his wing? He dotes on Herod as if he were his own son and we treated him as though he were garbage, giving him bad food and throwing wine all over him. My reputation has been sullied by these students!"

"Herod Agrippa was very understanding. He was very kind to the servants, knowing that they were there to learn."

Apicius's jaw was set. "Fix this, Thrasius. If this ever happens again, it will be you who are whipped within an inch of his life. I will not be embarrassed by you, or by the students of this school." He stormed out of the room and I collapsed into the chair behind me, grateful that he hadn't decided to punish me there and then.

From that point on, I brought in slaves from Apicius's villa to help the students during feasts.

After several months of classes, when I thought most of the major problems of the school had been overcome, a new challenge emerged. I began to suspect that one of the students might be a spy for Publius Octavius. He was a freedman who took to disrupting courses by asking frivolous questions, being belligerent, and provoking or belittling me in class. I did my best to be patient.

In the end, I sent for Tycho. I gave him instructions to follow the troublemaker after class that day and report back to me and Apicius.

I hoped that the man wouldn't show up for my class on cooking grains and cereals but, sure enough, there he was, at his usual station in the front. My resolve hardened.

The students gathered close to my counter. "Today we will learn how to make several different lentil and pea dishes. I'll demonstrate, then you'll make your own." I picked up a large terra-cotta jar and removed the lid to show it was filled with fresh lentils. I scooped out a few handfuls and added them to the bronze pan in front of me. I added a little water and took in my fingers a bit of white powder from a tiny jar I kept on the side of the counter. I raised my voice so the students could hear me over the sizzle of the water hitting the pan. "Add a pinch of soda and some water, then set it on a low fire to cook." I stirred the mixture around before setting the pan on the fire. I waited as the students took notes on their wax tablets.

It wasn't long until the troublemaker spoke up and began to harangue me with questions. Fed up, I kicked him out of the class, despite his protests about how his patron was going to be furious with me and with Gavius Apicius. I nodded at Tycho and he set out to follow the man, as I had instructed him to.

That evening, back on the Palatine, Apicius and I were going over notes for the sauce book when Sotas ushered Tycho into the room.

"What did you find out?"

"I tracked him to the domus of Publius Octavius."

"Damn him to Tartarus!" Apicius stormed across the room to the window and slammed his hand against its edge. "How dare he?"

He stared down at the dimly lit Forum below. "How many of those shadowy figures in the streets are spies of Publius Octavius? Will I never be rid of him?" He swallowed hard, took a deep breath, and seemed to collect himself. He considered Tycho, who was standing near the door, a look of abject terror on his face. "Boy, Thrasius will see to it that you receive an additional fifty denarii added to your peculium."

I inhaled sharply at the same time as Tycho.

Apicius continued, "Now go. Tell no one of this or I'll take back the money and beat you within a heartbeat of your life."

Tycho nodded vigorously and bumped into Sotas as he tried to back out of the room. The big man let the youth go and watched him run down the hallway beyond.

Apicius turned to look out the window again. He tapped the sill with his fingers, drumming them in thought. "So Publius Octavius wanted my recipes but couldn't bear to let me know that he was sending a slave. No more niceties from me." He raised his voice but did not turn around. "Thrasius, tomorrow you will throw that spy out. Tell him his master can take up any grievances with me personally—which I doubt will happen. And moving forward, we will not accept any student into the school unless I have met the patrician who is sending him."

"Yes, Dominus."

CHAPTER 15

That year I finally finished the book of sauces. Between the school and Apicius's ever-growing entertainment schedule, we barely had time to breathe, much less test all the recipes to make sure there were no errors. We hired several scribes to help us make copies, expecting it would sell well. I assumed most of my students would ask their masters to purchase a copy for them. Fannia had also spread the word to her friends. We also sent a copy to Ovid, who had been recently exiled to the isle of Tomis for writing a poem that supposedly incited Augustus's daughter, Julia, to plot to overthrow her father. Despite his banishment, Ovid's influence was strong, especially among wealthy families in the pleasure towns along the coast. He told us he wrote many letters to friends in far-flung places and we should expect requests for copies. Apicius, of course, planned on giving many of his clients scrolls for free. Doing so made him feel generous but it didn't pad the coffers.

At least there was no sign of Sejanus. I often forgot about him for weeks at a time. Every once in a while we would hear word of him conquering some Germanic tribe or another, but there had been no direct reports of him. I held hope that such news would arrive on a cart containing his coffin. But no such luck.

A few weeks before the annual Saturnalia festival at the end of December, I steeled myself to go ask Dominus Apicius for a large favor—to marry Passia. It was bold. While formalizing marriage among slaves was common in many households, Apicius had not previously condoned the practice. Or was it that no one had ever dared to ask? I tried to look at the sunlight side of the situation—that I was in good standing with him, and more and more he treated me almost as a friend, if a man like him could have a friend. He did not think of me as he did the other slaves and he didn't treat me the same. As he grew older he became crueler to his household slaves but kinder to me. He regarded my opinions as valuable and gave generously toward my peculium. But never did he speak of my future unless it entwined with his own.

I was very nervous on the day I went to Apicius. I hadn't asked him for anything in the ten years since I joined the household, and because of that, I was doubly unsure of how he would react. I paused outside the massive library doors and wiped my brow of sweat. I was saying a prayer to the gods when Apicius spoke.

His voice was wary. "Who's there?" He must have heard the shuffle of my sandals outside the door.

Sotas poked his head out and waved me in. I willed myself to move forward and enter the room. "It is I, Dominus."

Apicius stood. I was worried he might be in a foul mood, as he often seemed to be in those days, but he was jovial. "Just the man I wanted to see. Sit and tell me of the school!" He indicated the ornate beechwood chair across from the desk where he sat.

"You are teaching classes on Saturnalia banquets, correct?" he asked as I eased myself into the chair. I curled my hands around the carved lion's paws of its arms and forced myself to smile. The candelabras sputtered as a slight breeze flitted through the window.

"Yes, Dominus. We have more students in this week's classes than last. But shouldn't it be the patricians who come to my Saturnalia classes?" I joked, referring to the ages-old custom of masters and slaves switching places during the weeklong festival.

Apicius smirked, but not unkindly, to my relief. "Possibly. But I doubt my slaves will want to eat the food I make! They are used to your fine fare."

He cocked his head, taking greater notice of me. "But that's not why you came here, is it, Thrasius? You are sweating, my boy. Out with it, what is troubling you?"

I froze. I had hoped to ease myself into the question, to gauge how Apicius was feeling and then take the plunge.

"I, uh . . ."

Apicius seemed more concerned than angry. "Thrasius, this is unlike you. Tell me, what is wrong?"

In my nervousness it all spilled out.

"Dominus, I have never asked you for anything, and I know what I am asking might be too much, but, please, consider my request. It has been eight years and I . . . I want to marry Passia."

Apicius opened his mouth to speak but before a sound slipped past the bar of his teeth, Aelia's voice cut through the awkwardness.

"Why, yes, Thrasius! Yes, you must marry that girl! I'll help plan the wedding!" My mistress swept into the room, her peacock blue stola fluttering around her. She came up behind me, hugged me tight, and addressed Apicius. "Of course he must marry her, am I right, dear husband?" The look in her eyes warned Apicius that he dare not say no. Oh, how I loved Aelia in that moment! Her gesture was one of the kindest anyone had ever made toward me.

Apicius wrinkled his brow as though he were deciding whether to be angry. He shifted the scroll beneath his hands. The silence was unbearable.

Finally, he spoke, but did not look up. "No, Thrasius. I must say no. You may not marry her."

My breath caught in my throat. An hour ago I had prepared myself to be disappointed, but in the moment, hope had won out when Aelia spoke on my behalf. And now his refusal was like a vise on my heart.

"And why ever not?" Aelia asked, echoing my own thoughts. Disbelief made her every word rise in pitch.

"Because I said so. Thrasius does not need distraction." His voice was hard. He ruffled through the scrolls on his desk, refusing to look his wife or me in the eye. "You are both dismissed."

I stood there, slack jawed, until Aelia took me by the arm and walked me out of the room. Sotas gave me a look of sympathy before he closed the door behind us.

"Do not despair, Thrasius!" She put her hand on my shoulder. "I will keep trying. I do not know why his heart is so cold. You are his world."

It was evident in her voice although she did not say the words. I was often more important to Apicius than she was. May the gods bless her, save that one morning before we took the ship to Carthage, she had never expressed jealousy, only care, for me and for Passia.

"No, Domina, it is you who are his world. I just raise his pedestal on this earth a little higher."

She smiled kindly at me. "Have you asked Passia? Will she be sad to learn this news?"

I shook my head. "No, I would not be able to bear her disappointment as well. I did not tell her I was asking Apicius today, but we always dream about truly being wed."

"Keep your dream. Together we will change Marcus's mind." She hugged me again, tightly, before turning to go. Helene, whom I had not noticed, but of course was always where Aelia was, swept past me to follow her mistress.

I returned to my cubiculum, where I could gather my thoughts. I did not want Passia to see the sadness and anger that enveloped me like a blanket. Why would Apicius deny me? Without me he was nothing. In the last ten years I had toiled endlessly on his behalf. He would have no clients if it were not for me, no school, no cookbooks, and no claim to any fame. He was nothing, absolutely nothing, without me.

When I had closed the door, I ripped off my slave plaque and dashed it against the wall. A large piece of fresco came off and fell to the ground. I would likely have to pay for the repainting myself but at that moment I cared not. I wanted to tear apart my room, but I refrained, not wanting to have to explain my actions to Passia. So I left the clay lamps alone. I did not tear the pillow to shreds. I briefly contemplated dashing my little effigies of Edesia, Hestia, Fornax, Fortuna, and Jupiter against the wall, but their wrath was bound to be much worse than that of Apicius. Instead, I lay on my pallet and stared at the ceiling, wishing the sky would open and dash my dominus to pieces.

The next few days passed in a blur. I had several classes to teach and there were many preparations to make before Saturnalia. The holiday was one of the biggest of the year, a week of great feasting and gift giving. It was even legal to gamble. The slaves were, with the exception of flagrant disobedience, exempt from punishment, and we all wore freedman's caps. The previous year, Caesar Augustus had attempted to shorten the holiday from seven days to three, but all of Rome rioted. People threw stones at the Forum when the Senate was in session and took to burning effigies of Augustus in front of the temple of Saturn. Augustus was forced to concede and that year he promised to distribute an extra grain ration to the plebs.

I worked hard with Rúan in the kitchen in the days before the holiday—if we could prepare much of the food ahead of time, it meant less work for all the slaves during the week. While the reversal of the master and slave roles was one of the highlights of the Saturnalia, we still had to make ready the grand banquet and the dinners, even if we were allowed to also sit at the tables and partake. Apicius, Aelia, and, that year, Apicata would serve the main dishes to the slaves, but we still cooked all the meals.

On the afternoon of the first day of Saturnalia, I was in the kitchen sitting on the tiles with Balsamea, Passia, and Apicata, helping them wrap presents, when Tycho burst through the door, out of breath.

"Master, you must . . ." He gasped for air. "You must hurry."

I jumped to my feet, knocking over a box of clay knucklebones Apicata had made as a present for Rúan.

"What's wrong?" I reached out and put a hand on Tycho's shoulder.

"I'm not sure. Fannia arrived and she is in a panic. Sotas took her to Apicius but she sent me to bring you to them. She said it was urgent."

Apicata stood up to come with me. Balsamea took her hand. "Stay with me, Apicata."

"I'm old enough to know what's going on! And you can't tell me what to do."

"Stay, little bird. Please. I beg you." At eleven she had begun to realize that, as we were her slaves, she had the right to demand whatever she wanted of us. I was glad she didn't then.

"Fine," she said, pouting. She picked up the knucklebones that had scattered across the floor. I exchanged a worried glance with Passia, then darted after Tycho down the hall.

When I arrived in the atrium, Fannia waited, wrapped in a thick wool cloak. Her hood was still up and I could not see her face. Two slaves were dressing Apicius to go out, wrapping his legs with woolen strips to keep him warm beneath his toga before putting on the red shoes denoting him as a patrician. Another handed me a cloak and a pair of boots.

"Put those on, Thrasius," Apicius commanded. Anger tinged his words.

Puzzled, I complied. Questions that I did not dare voice swirled through my mind in a flurry. Why was he wearing his formal toga and shoes? Why had he given me his clothes to wear? Was it me he was angry with? Where were we going?

We didn't leave by the front doors. Instead we hurried through the slave hallways to one of the back entrances.

He gave stern commands to the guards outside. "No one leaves or enters this villa and no one is to know we have left. If anyone comes to the doors you will tell them I am ill and am not seeing visitors, even if it's Caesar himself. If I find that anyone, and I mean *anyone*, has disobeyed me, I will put to death the guilty party along with every other slave in this household. I will buy all new slaves when their blood runs across the tiles. Do you understand?"

Apicius turned and glared at me, and I realized I had let forth an audible gasp. To suggest death for nearly a hundred of his slaves seemed rash and I was taken aback. Apicius's stare ripped into me and my heart began to pound. If he was angry enough to kill slaves and a cadre of his guards, what would he do to me if I were to anger him?

"Yes, Dominus," the guards said in unison. The head of Apicius's personal guard accompanied us through the halls and vowed he would convey his words to all who watched the house.

In moments, the three of us were sitting in Apicius's litter rushing across the back roads of the Palatine down toward the Forum. I was glad I was given a heavy cloak to wear. December had proven much colder than usual.

In the litter, Fannia and Apicius ignored me. Fannia pulled off the hood of her cloak to reveal a blond wig full of thick curled ringlets piled up along the sides of her head. She seemed like a woman trying too hard to look young.

"Are you sure, Fannia? Very sure?" Apicius held the edges of his toga in his hands and wrung the fine wool between his fingers.

"My spy is trustworthy. Remember, that's how I knew about the death of General Varus at the Battle of the Teutoburg Forest before the rest of Rome heard the news." Fannia pulled her cloak tighter around her shoulders.

I was desperate to ask questions but dared not.

Apicius tightened his hold on the folds of his toga. I could see his knuckles turn white. "I don't understand. Why now?"

"It's my fault. I saw them at a party last week. I was stupid. I taunted them, boasting of that dinner you held for Claudius. I gushed like a child opening a Saturnalia present about all the food and how marvelous every dish was. I gloated about my place on the couch. I should not have, Apicius, I know. I know."

My heartbeat quickened. Who was she talking about?

I couldn't hold my tongue any longer. Terror filled me—that I might never see Passia again.

"Please, tell me what is happening." My voice sounded disembodied, as though someone were speaking into a long hallway and I stood on its other end.

"I can't believe this." Apicius buried his face in his hands. I thought he must not have heard me. Fannia did, but only gave me a sympathetic look.

I risked a peek between the curtains. We had reached the Forum and Sotas and the other slaves were running the litter along one of the side roads—a curious choice. We always took the main road through the center of the Forum. Apicius always wanted all of Rome to see he was passing.

After a short silence Apicius sat up, bracing himself as the slaves carrying the litter jostled us across the stones of the Forum. I let the curtain fall. His gaze fell upon me.

I saw fear in those eyes. Fear I could not understand. Fear that seemed to find its center in me. When he spoke, his voice shook.

"Livia intends to demand your purchase for the Imperial kitchen."

It was as though a spear had pierced my breast. I fell back against the pillows behind me, unable to comprehend the words I had heard. If Caesar's wife demanded my purchase, Apicius would have no choice but to comply. I would be forced into service in the Imperial kitchen, subject to the whims of Octavius, Livia, and Augustus. I would never see Passia again, or if so, only in stolen moments that would endanger my life if I took them. I might not see Apicata or Aelia or Apicius again. I would likely never earn my freedom, or have any semblance of it.

"Can she do that?" My voice cracked. I already knew the answer.

"Right now she can," Fannia asserted. Despite her answer she seemed optimistic.

The litter came to a stop and Sotas parted the curtains for us. He helped us out and when I had adjusted my cloak I saw we were in front of the Curia Julia, the meetinghouse recently completed by Caesar. It was the center of many judicial activities of the Forum.

Apicius placed a hand on my shoulder and led me into the building, Fannia and Sotas following behind. Both Apicius and Fannia kept looking over their shoulders, as if anxious that we were being followed.

The interior of the Curia Julia was both austere and beautiful. Dim winter sunlight slid into the room through large windows high up on the building's walls. Torches lining the perimeter gave the room further light, flickering off the shiny purple and yellow marble floor and its intricate design of cornucopias and rosettes. At the end of the hall was an altar adorned by a large marble statue of Victoria, goddess of victory, who stood atop a globe. One long arm and delicate hand extended a carved wreath. In front of the altar was a table behind which a magistrate held court. The benches in front of the balding judge were full of people clapping their hands—for what reason I could not discern.

Apicius hurried to the front of the benches. To my surprise, Trio, Celera, and one of their patrician friends, who was familiar to me, already waited there. Fannia and Sotas hurried away to sit next to them, leaving me to stand, confused, with Apicius.

The magistrate's assistant, the lictor, a strapping young man with unusual sea-blue eyes, came forth and whispered in Apicius's ear. Apicius's response was hushed. He withdrew a large money pouch from the folds of his toga and handed it to the man, a bribe to move us to the front of the line. He bade us follow him to our seats near the front of the room. The lictor walked to the table and leaned over and spoke briefly to the magistrate. The magistrate rubbed his bald head with a gnarled hand as he listened.

The crowd in the room was unusual, a mixture of patricians, equestrians, and numerous slaves occupying the benches. Suddenly it dawned on me why we were there. My heart began to pound so loudly I thought Apicius might hear it. I had dreamed of this day my entire life, but never did I expect it to unfold the way it did.

The magistrate beckoned us toward the table. When we reached him, the judge picked up a long smooth stick, the *festuca*, and handed it to his lictor. My suspicion was confirmed. My knees went weak.

The magistrate indicated that I should face Apicius. I turned toward him, praying to Libertas that my legs would not give out from under me.

The lictor moved into position behind me.

He laid the festuca on my head, pressing the heavy stick against my hair and speaking loud enough for all to hear. "I declare this slave a free man of Rome—*vindicatio in libertatem*—a citizen who is free to earn a living, own property and slaves, and take a wife under the full spirit of the law of our Caesar, Augustus. What say you, patrician?"

Apicius hesitated. Conflict played across his face. The silence was unbearable.

When he finally spoke, his voice held none of the worry I'd heard in the litter. "I, Marcus Gavius Apicius, declare my slave, Thrasius, *vindicatio in libertatem*. I also give him his peculium, which he has earned through years of service in my household. It is my desire that he continues to work for me, under salary, within my accommodations, as a loyal freedman."

He spun me around and said the words that gave my freedom finality: *"Hunc hominem liberum volo."* To complete the ritual, he pushed me gently away from him and toward my freedom.

I stepped forward a pace. The magistrate's voice rang across the Curia. "I declare this man, Marcus Gavius Thrasius, to be registered in the census as a free citizen of Rome." My skin tingled with the words. I was free! I could now earn my own money, travel, vote, and do nearly anything I wanted. I had never known such wonder to fill my heart.

The lictor tapped me on the shoulder and I turned around. He pointed at the plaque around my neck. "You won't need that anymore."

I pulled it off my head and stared at it, hardly believing I would never have to wear the nameplate again. In all my years, save sleep or the bath, it had rarely left my person. The lictor handed me my new pileus, the soft, felted gray, conical cap signifying my status as a free man. I stared at it in wonder.

"Put it on!" Fannia urged from her spot on the bench.

I did. And then I understood why all the people were clapping when we'd come in. This time, the clapping was for me.

• • •

It was over before I had any chance to process what had happened. We signed all the paperwork; Trio, Celera, and a friend of theirs had come as witnesses. Apicius paid the court my peculium, thus buying my freedom. Then he whisked Sotas, Fannia, and me into the litter and we hastened toward the villa.

"Thank you, Dominus," I said as soon as we were settled into the pillows. I was overwhelmed and not sure what else to say.

My former master smiled at me. "You'll have to break that habit, Thrasius. Call me Apicius!"

Fannia cackled at my discomfort. "What a wonderful Saturnalia present, right, Thrasius?"

"I am honored. It was unexpected . . . Apicius."

Apicius seemed pensive. "I had always planned to give you your freedom, Thrasius, but I have to admit, not like this."

Fannia patted my knee twice. "You must know that Apicius is being selfish. Livia can't buy you if you're a free man!" Her words were teasing but the truth within them left both Apicius and me feeling awkward. Apicius averted his eyes from mine.

I realized I had the upper hand but I found I had no desire to press it. "I would like to continue working for you, but . . ."

"Of course, of course, I'll pay you four hundred denarii a month. You'll also have your apartments at the school, and I'm sure there is a country cottage in my holdings somewhere that would suit you as well." He gesticulated wildly with his hands while he spoke.

I tried to keep my face impassive. As always, what he suggested was far beyond what was necessary. The salary alone amounted to what Caesar paid his Praetorian guards! I felt guilty accepting such a figure—I knew better than anyone how much he spent versus how much he brought in. But I also delighted in the thought of having so much money. Money I could perhaps contribute to Passia's peculium.

"Thank you. That is very kind—"

He broke in again, desperation in his tone. "And a monthly amphora of Falernian wine."

Fannia winked at me. Surely she must have known how outrageous his offer was. "What about his first toga?"

Apicius clapped his hands. "Yes! Your first toga, Thrasius! I will buy you a fine one indeed! Perfect. It's settled!"

The first night of Saturnalia—and my freedom—was one of the most memorable nights of my time in the Gavia household. Ironically, since I was free, it meant I had to help Apicius, Aelia, and Apicata serve the dishes during the Saturnalia feast. Passia delighted in this new development.

"Slave, my hands are sticky. Come, wash them. Bring the perfumed water." Passia waved at me with a finger slick with honey. She was radiant, lying on the couch next to Helene. Both were dressed in new stolae that Aelia had gifted them for the holiday.

I grinned and rushed forward with the basin and a towel. "Permission to speak," I asked her as I took her sticky hand in mine.

She smirked. "Permission granted."

I slowly ran the damp towel across each slender finger. I kept my voice low so only she could hear. "Later, my dear Domina, I would be delighted to wash you in private."

She raised an eyebrow at me. "I think you will have to prove yourself first, boy."

I bowed in front of her, my head on the tiles. "I will do anything you require, Domina."

"Good. Now fetch me some more honey fritters. And you will clean my hands again, when I call for you."

I winked at her. "Yes, Domina. Anything for you."

That night our lovemaking tasted sweeter than all the honey in Iberia.

Apicata found the situation confusing. "Why doesn't my father grant Passia freedom too?" she asked at the cena on that first evening, when she was helping Aelia and me load up trays with dishes for the second course. Apicius was in the triclinium serving as the scissor slave to Sotas and Rúan.

Passia glanced at me, bemused. Aelia looked alarmed and took hold of the situation.

She put her arm around her daughter, who had grown tall in the last year. "Thrasius has done a great deal to advance your father's interests among Roman society, my treasure. Freedom comes to slaves at different times. Passia is bound to have her freedom someday. But for now, she's happy here. If she had her freedom, both Thrasius and Passia might move away, and you wouldn't want that, right?"

Aelia had touched upon the crux of the matter. It pained my heart to think of it. As long as I was important to his success, Apicius would never sell Passia nor would he grant her freedom.

"That's ridiculous." Apicata snorted, raising an eyebrow at her beloved slave. "Passia would never leave us, would she?"

I couldn't help but chuckle as Passia gave her a reassuring hug. The girl's certainty was refreshing. In moments like those I always felt such a deep outpouring of love for our little domina. She was right. This was our *familia*. How could we ever leave?

I wasn't prepared for how Sotas would take the news. For most of Saturnalia, he was cold toward me, refusing to sit near me on any of the couches, to break bread with me, or even to have more than a cursory conversation. He took the gift I offered him, a new pair of fine leather sandals, but did not thank me or even try them on.

"Sotas, talk to me," I said to him one day while the family was playing knucklebones with the slaves in the atrium.

"I have nothing to say."

"But what did I do?" I knew it wasn't what I did, but what I had become. I was a freedman and he was not.

"Nothing," he grunted.

"You do realize that I am not entirely free. I will still be his cook. And his adviser."

He would not look at me. "You can leave whenever you want."

"I cannot. Where would I go? And how could I live without Passia?"

The big man shrugged and wouldn't say anything more.

On the last day of Saturnalia, Apicius asked me to accompany him to the library. When we arrived, he dismissed Sotas, who did not even look at me, then walked over to his desk, picked up a large, thick parcel, and handed it to me.

"My promise to you."

I eyed the parcel, wondering what sort of promise could be within.

"Go ahead, open it."

I ripped the large wax seal on the parcel and opened it up. It was the toga Apicius had promised me. I didn't unfold it—there was no way I would know how to fold it again. It was made of expensive off-white linen. I knew how much it cost—I had purchased many similar togas for Apicius to give as gifts to his friends.

"I don't know what to say."

He smiled. "Say nothing. I am sending my dressing slaves to your cubicle to help you get into it. Make sure you ask one of them to show Tycho how to wrap a toga—you'll need his help every morning from now on."

The thought of wearing a toga every day was one of the few things about having my freedom that I didn't look forward to. They were hot and cumbersome.

"Thank you, Apicius. Thank you for everything."

"Go on now. Happy Saturnalia!"

I repressed a bow and went to subject myself to the strangeness of having someone else dress me.

That night we held a very big banquet, with all of Apicius's slaves from both the villa and the school. It was a night of great festivity, with games of dice and knucklebones taking place across the villa. Togas were shunned in favor of the synthesis, colorful, casual dress that was never condoned at dinner. There was an amphora of wine free flowing in each of the common areas, food was in great abundance, and Apicius was especially giving to all his slaves and clients. At the salutatio that morning, many of Apicius's poorer clients received a very generous gratuity that many of Rome's richest took honor in giving at Saturnalia and one that the clients relied upon to buy gifts for their families.

We were in the triclinium listening to the slaves give little speeches, mocking the mannerisms and tones of the nobility. Helene had us all in stitches with her speech pretending to be a patrician woman attending an unfavorable play.

"And those miserable wretches in the chorus!" she intoned with a stereotypical voice. "Who do they think they—?" Helene broke off as a door guard ran into the atrium shouting.

"Empress Livia is here! Dominus, Empress Livia is here!"

My heart lodged in my throat. Passia folded herself into me, trembling.

"Oh, mighty Hera, do not let her take my love from my arms," she whispered.

Livia swept into the room before anyone could react. She had with her a small entourage, which included, to no surprise, Publius Octavius. She didn't wear a wig and the gray in her hair was whiter since I'd last seen her. She looked old. Old and determined.

Apicius bowed his head, then stood up tall. He seemed to be drawing on power I had never seen before. Confidence covered him like a blanket.

"My dear Livia, what brings us the honor of your presence on such a special Saturnalia evening?"

Livia was not swayed by the reminder that it was a sacred holiday. "I have come to buy your cook, Apicius. This time I will not take no for an answer."

Apicius smiled, retaining his jovial demeanor. "Rúan, come forward." He extended a hand toward my friend, who stood a few feet from Passia and me. "The empress has come to purchase you."

Rúan stared at me, horrified. My mouth gaped open, shocked at Apicius's words.

Octavius pushed his way past the slaves flanking Livia. His face was as red as a beet. "That's not his cook!" His gaze landed on me. "He is!"

Livia looked at Apicius, anger deepening the lines around her eyes. Her voice held the heat of the vestals' flame. "Are you trying to deceive me?"

Apicius squinted his eyes and curled his lips, looking puzzled. "Why, no. Rúan is my cook. The man Publius Octavius is pointing at is my friend."

"That's the slave, it's him!" Spittle flew from Octavius's lips. He waggled his finger at me like a teacher would at a schoolboy. I thought I heard Fannia snort from where she stood at the side of the atrium.

Apicius smiled and patted the shoulder of his rival. "Ahh, my dear Octavius, now I understand the confusion." Octavius jerked his shoulder away.

"My dear lady, this man used to be my slave and my cook. That is true no longer. He is a loyal freedman and a citizen of Rome." Apicius snapped his fingers in Sotas's direction. "Get me the papers."

Sotas left to get the copy of Apicius's set of papers—mine were tucked away in my cubiculum.

Passia clutched me so hard I knew I'd have bruises on my rib cage. Octavius's eyes skimmed across me. I realized he was looking for my slave plaque or an identifying tattoo that had not been burned away with my freedom. Thank the gods Apicius hadn't branded me, as some slave owners did!

Livia folded her arms across her chest. She was not amused. I suspected Octavius would receive an earful when they left.

"You freed him?" Octavius said in disbelief.

Apicius nodded. "Why, yes, of course. I reward those who are loyal and work hard."

Sotas returned. He handed the papers to Apicius and returned to his place.

Apicius passed them to Livia. "You'll see they're in order. We went to the Curia two days ago; I wanted to surprise him for Saturnalia."

Livia glanced at the papers, then handed them to the wrinkled old secretary who had accompanied her. He looked them over and gave them back to Apicius. "They are true documents, signed by the required number of witnesses."

While the secretary had been going over the papers I observed Livia staring Fannia down. There was darkness in her eyes.

Aelia stepped forward to join her husband. "Empress Livia, we would hate if your visit here was for naught. We would be delighted if you and Publius Octavius would join our Saturnalia feast today if you are able."

"Oh, our trip today is not for naught." Octavius waved a hand at Rúan. "I trust three thousand denarii will be enough?"

Apicius shook his head but kept his smile. "Now, Octavius, you know the worth of a cook from my household. I cannot take less than eight thousand denarii."

I thought Rúan might faint. Passia stiffened next to me. Apicius was playing a dangerous game, bargaining with Livia and Octavius.

Livia did not look pleased but she agreed to the bargaining. "Six thousand and no more."

"That is acceptable. May he remain with us today for our Saturnalia feast? He is well loved in my house."

"Very well." She was angry but resigned. "I'll send my slave tomorrow to draw up the papers and fetch him." Livia waved a hand at her secretary. Regaining her sense of protocol, she took Aelia's hands in hers. "Thank you for your generous invitation but we must be going."

I think I took breath again when I saw the last sandaled heel of the slave who brought up the rear of her group. Passia relaxed her grip on me.

Everyone except Apicius looked stunned. Rúan seemed on the verge of tears. He kept smoothing back his red locks with one hand, a habit he had when he was upset. Balsamea rubbed his arm, trying to reassure him.

Apicius clapped his hands together and the sound reverberated through the room. "What do you say, everyone? Should we break out the Falernian wine?"

Most of the slaves began to cheer. Apicius nodded to me to go with Rúan, a kindness that surprised me. Balsamea, Sotas, Passia, and I steered him toward the hallway that led to the gardens, where we proceeded to spend Rúan's last night at the villa in great but sad, roaring, drunken splendor.

Sotas pulled me aside later that night. He handed me a fresh glass of wine—a peace offering.

"I did not show you my best face, Thrasius. I offer my apology."

I took the glass. "No need, my friend."

"If you were not free, you would not be here before me. For that, I thank the goddess."

I raised my glass. "Let us thank her together."

And we drank.

PART VI

10 C.E. to 11 C.E.

PARTHIAN CHICKEN

Draw the chicken from the rear and cut it into quarters. Pound the pepper, lovage, a little caraway, pour on liquamen, flavor with wine. Arrange the chicken pieces in a ceramic dish, put the sauce over the chicken. Dissolve fresh laser (silphium) in warm water and put it straightaway on the chicken and cook it. Sprinkle with pepper and serve.

—Book 6.8.3, Fowl
On Cookery, Apicius

CHAPTER 16

Rúan's absence made life difficult for all of us in the first months after that fateful night. Not only did I lose a constant friend and trusted assistant, but despite my newfound freedom, I was busier than ever. Because I was still, in many ways, the de facto coquus, we had never found Rúan an assistant. That meant while I was in charge of running the school, with Rúan absent, I took on many of my old duties in the household. By the end of every day I was exhausted.

The better part of a year had passed and we still hadn't found a cook to replace Rúan. Or rather, we hadn't found a cook to satisfy the high standards both Apicius and I had. There were a few slaves we purchased for the task, but in the end, they were always relegated to other parts of the kitchen. So it seemed that while I was free, I was still not free. At least now I was well paid, far more so than I could ever be if I were to leave and be on my own.

One morning during the salutatio a messenger arrived at the door of the villa. His tunic was muddy, as though he had come from a great distance.

"I come from the family of Numerius Cornelius Sulla," he said, presenting the scroll to Apicius. He waited while Apicius read the note.

I wondered at the contents of the scroll. Sulla, of the great gens Cornelia, had been betrothed to Apicata several years ago. Of late Apicata had been asking more about her future husband. She found it hard to fathom marrying someone almost four times her age, despite his wealth and his position as a general in Caesar's army.

Apicius waved the messenger off. "No reply." The man left as quickly as he came.

Apicius handed me the scroll. "He's dead."

"What happened?" But Apicius did not respond. He walked past me to return to the seat where he greeted his clients, irritation wrinkling his brow. I opened the scroll to discover that Sulla had died in the early part of October at the hands of robbers when he was returning to Rome from Germania after a shoulder injury discharged him from service.

I understood Apicius's silence. He now had the new worry of choosing a suitable husband for his daughter.

Passia told me that Apicata said little about the incident when Aelia gave her the news. However, I noticed a new sense of relief that floated about her in the weeks after the news came to us. I did not blame her— the man had been older than her father.

Sometimes Rúan would come to visit me, usually slipping in the back entrance and finding me in the kitchen or the garden. One golden fall afternoon he found me at the villa tending to our prized pigs. After our experiments with fattening up ducks to make their livers even more delicious, Apicius and I had decided to apply the same principles to pigs. We kept four of them in a slightly smaller pen than the other swine and had been fattening them up with several pounds of dried figs a day. When they were fat we planned to feed them one last meal, letting them gorge themselves on honey wine until the figs expanded, and then get them so drunk they died. I had high hopes the resulting livers would be one of the best delicacies I had created yet.

I had finished dumping the last of the figs into the pen when Rúan arrived. He leaned his pale torso against the fence and watched them eat. Even after years in the Roman sun he had not tanned; his skin reddened so he tended to avoid the brightest parts of the day. I watched him flick a loose piece of wood off the fence and into the pen. "If this is a success, I will be forced to steal this idea, you realize," he said ruefully.

"It won't matter." I hung the bucket on the peg next to the pen. "By the time Publius Octavius gets his hands on the idea, everyone will already know it came from Apicius." I did not want Rúan knowing that

I did have concern—his skill in the kitchen was strong and could out-pace mine if he set his mind to it.

Rúan, fortunately, didn't seem to have the inclination. "I suppose that word does get out fast. But soon Octavius will have me torturing other beasts in an effort to outdo you. I'm not looking forward to that."

Rúan had always had a soft spot for animals. He had some crazy barbarian notion that the gods believed they shouldn't be kept penned up. They should wander the hills and be rounded up once a year before winter. How inconvenient that would be!

"How is it, working for Caesar?" I asked, without envy. Whenever he visited, he had a new tale of Imperial life with which to horrify me.

"For me, not good." He lifted up his tunic to reveal fresh stripes taken from his flesh. "One of my boys failed to adequately debone a pheasant served to Livia. She casually remarked on the tiny bone she found and Octavius let me have it."

"You should ask Balsamea to give you some of the salve she makes for the boys."

"That's why I'm here."

I took a seat on one of the stone benches outside the kitchen doors and gestured for him to take a seat on the bench across from me. Tycho appeared with a tray holding glasses of rose water, which he deposited onto the end of my bench before returning to the kitchen.

"Ahh, the life of a freedman agrees with you," Rúan said.

"I wish I felt freer!" I laughed. "Now tell me, what really brings you here today?"

Rúan sobered. He stared into his water, moving the glass so it swirled up against the sides. "Bad news, I'm afraid. Your curse didn't work. Sejanus has returned."

My anger rose like bile. "Damn him to Tartarus!" I threw my glass and it crashed to the ground. Tycho heard the noise and came running from the kitchen.

I waved him inside. My voice shook. "Has Tiberius returned?"

"No, he's still in Germany. Tiberius sent Sejanus home with a recom-mendation that he be installed as one of the prefects in Caesar's Praeto-rian Guard. The talk is that Tiberius wants to have loyalty in the Guard in the event Augustus dies and he's forced to return to Rome."

"Why couldn't he have taken an arrow to the eye?" I muttered, mostly to myself.

"Only the gods know." Rúan leaned forward, his voice low. "But I can tell you this, Thrasius. You will have to find a way to hide your hatred of him. Your position as Apicius's freedman guarantees you will have more direct contact with Sejanus. He's no longer a regular soldier—a prefect wields much power. Be careful."

A piece of glass had landed on the tiles in front of me. I kicked it with my foot, wincing as the edge poked my middle toe and brought forth a dot of bright blood.

A week later, Sejanus sent word to Aelia that he was planning to visit his cousin and her family the next day. Apicius appeared delighted when Aelia told him the news over breakfast but I knew otherwise. Inwardly neither of them was happy. After she left, he stormed out of the atrium, knocking aside one of the youngest slaves who had come with me to pick up the dishes. Later Sotas told me Apicius had spent the morning throwing things around the library, even breaking a precious Greek vase that had been in the family for more than four hundred years.

Sejanus arrived the next day as he promised, promptly at noon according to the sundial. Apicius and Aelia received him in the main atrium. Passia and I hovered in the adjoining room where we could hear through a window that opened to the atrium that had long been covered by a tapestry. It was the first time that Aelia had seen Sejanus since the assault and I worried about her.

They greeted Sejanus, then settled into the couches alongside the renovated fish pond in the back part of the atrium, not far from our clandestine window. Sotas took up a place near us, signifying his presence by giving us two slight taps on the tapestry to let us know he was there.

"Cousin, it is good to see you! How many years has it been?" Aelia was polite, but the warmth she used to have for her cousin was gone.

"Six years. Always victorious but ever so far away from Rome."

"At least you are returning to a life many soldiers never see," Apicius said.

"True. Though Caesar likes to live sparsely. It is not as luxurious being in the Imperial villa as many would imagine. Although I must admit the cooking has improved since I last dined with Augustus."

"I'm sure it has."

I gritted my teeth. The thought of Rúan feeding Sejanus every day made my stomach roil.

"What brings you here today?" Apicius asked the question we were all wondering.

"Oh, just a friendly visit to my favorite relatives." Sejanus was glib. "Where is Apicata? How old is she now?"

Passia's fingernails dug into my skin upon hearing those words. I clamped her hand flat to alleviate the pressure.

"She's not . . ."

Apicius cut Aelia off. "We'll send for her! She's fourteen, and I know she will be pleased to see you. Helene, fetch Apicata please."

"She will be fine," I whispered to Passia, more to reassure myself than her. I looked at my lover in the dark of the room and while I could not see the definition of her features, I could see her shake her head. My stomach clenched; I feared she was right.

The talk continued, about life at Caesar's villa, about Sejanus's treks across Germania, defeating the Dalmatians and Marcomanni, and how he and Tiberius were fast friends. I wasn't sure I believed all his tales, but, then again, I had little trust for him at all.

We heard Apicata coming down the hall with Helene. As she passed the door to the room we were in I heard her say, "I would rather die."

And then she was in the room and Sejanus's voice rang out.

"Oh, my dear Apicata, how you have changed since we last met!"

Apicata didn't respond, or if she did we couldn't hear her.

"Apicata has been studying philosophy," Aelia said, trying to be conversational. "Apicata, recite for us some Plato, will you?"

I could hear a waver in her voice, although it was slight. I wondered if Apicius could hear it too.

"Yes, Mother." She was as obedient as you would ever hope a well-educated Roman child to be.

She cleared her throat and her voice rang out in a loud, clear tone. "From his *Republic*: 'The man who finds that in the course of his life he has done a lot of wrong often wakes up at night in terror, like a child with a nightmare, and his life is full of foreboding; but the man who is conscious of no wrongdoing is filled with cheerfulness and with the comfort of old age.'"

Oh, I could not have had more pride than I did then. Our little bird had spread her wings and let her voice take flight. I wished I could see the look upon Sejanus's face.

There was silence, then a brief flurry of applause. "Lovely, my dear!" Aelia crowed, clearly pleased with her daughter's choice of words. "Oh, Sejanus, I'm sure you would be even more delighted by her poetry."

When Sejanus spoke, his voice had a warning edge. "I'm sure I would be. All the more reason for me to visit more often. Perhaps next time I can make a special request. Thank you, Apicata. That was admirable."

I couldn't see Aelia, but I was sure she understood the veiled threat. She did not respond.

"May I go now?" Apicata asked in a petulant tone.

"Of course you may." Apicius sounded as though he'd been made uncomfortable by her recitation. Could he have thought it was directed at him and not Sejanus? It was likely. My former master was apt to assume the world revolved around him.

"It must be hard for you to manage both the school and the kitchen, with your other cook gone."

I gave a start. He was talking about Rúan. He didn't give Apicius time to respond. "I think I have an answer for you."

"I don't understand."

"You need a cook so Thrasius can focus on your other needs, am I right?"

Apicius sounded skeptical. "Perhaps."

I peered through the thin crack at the edge of the tapestry. I saw Sejanus tuck a hand into the fold of his toga. "One of my guards is related to a man who was cousin to Maecenas. When Maecenas passed, he willed all his slaves to his son, who has himself just died. This is lucky for you, I suspect."

"Do tell." There was true curiosity in my former master's voice. Maecenas had been cultural and gastronomic adviser to Augustus Caesar and was known for his incredible feasts.

"The son left no will and no wife. All his slaves are going up on the market and the proceeds will pad Caesar's coffers. One of those slaves is a man who served in Maecenas's kitchen. He grew up preparing meals for Caesar and for foreign kings."

"Is he for sale?" I could hear the anticipation in Apicius's voice. He felt desperate to fill the gap Rúan had left, and while I did too, I was not anxious to trust Sejanus.

"He is. He went up on the block today. I remembered you were still looking for a cook so I sent word to the slave master to hold on to the slave until you could look him over."

My former master lauded Sejanus with thanks.

Passia and I exchanged a wary look.

The rest of the conversation was banal, except I learned there was a party planned the following week to celebrate Consul Publius Cornelius Dolabella's new arch erected as a gate on the Caelian Hill. I suspected I would be dragged along. At last, Sejanus left, saying he had to get back to Caesar for evening duties.

The next morning found me with a slip of paper in hand, heading to the market to purchase the cook Sejanus had reserved for us. Was he a relation to Sejanus? I wondered. A spy?

As I walked along the line of slaves I was reminded of the day Apicius had purchased me, more than eleven years gone past. I often went to the market to purchase slaves for Apicius, but it was my first time as a freedman. I felt the same wash of sadness I always had when I passed the slave pens and saw the dirty people in rags and chains. The slave master I was looking for had set up shop along one end of the market, with a line of slaves of varying ages.

"There he be." The slave master jerked a bony thumb at one of the cages. The man huddling there had not been cleaned up before I arrived. His shirt was ripped and I could see large bruises along his ribs.

"You've been beating him well, I see." I gritted my teeth and turned to the slave before the slave master could respond.

"Stand up. Did you cook for Maecenas?"

The man grasped hold of the bars and pulled himself up, wincing. He was an older man, nearing forty, I suspected. His hair was speckled with gray and he had deep lines around his eyes and mouth, lines I somehow knew were from a life full of laughs. Until now the man had likely never seen the inside of a cage.

"Yes, sir." His voice did not hold the weakness his body did.

I glared at the slave master. "He's injured and old. This is not what I expected."

He shrugged.

"How much?"

He turned his head and spat on the ground. "Three hundred denarii."

"Are you trying to rob me? This man probably only has another five years in him! I'll give you two hundred." The figure was ridiculously low in the first place but I was always one for a good haggle. I felt a pang of sadness for the man. We were bargaining for his life with such a petty amount. All those years ago, Apicius had paid a staggering twenty thousand denarii for me.

"Two hundred and fifty. Can't go lower."

"Fine." I handed over the money and he opened the cage door. The man stumbled out, looking at me with empty eyes. The smell wafting from him nearly made me gag.

"Come now, let's get you to the baths."

That's how Timon came to Apicius's kitchen—by way of a cursed man. Fortunately, there was no other connection between Sejanus and the cook he recommended for us. Timon turned out to be more than either Apicius or I had imagined. I could only guess that it was a way for Sejanus to make us feel like he was a nicer, changed man somehow. Or to make Apicius feel more indebted. Regardless, Timon easily stepped into the role left by Rúan and, much to our surprise, he did so with the gusto of someone half his age. In the months following his purchase we collaborated on some of the most elaborate feasts Rome had ever seen. It also gave me time to focus on growing the school, which was enrolling more students with each banquet Apicius gave.

CHAPTER 17

Between the grand dinners and the success of the school, Apicius's name seemed to be on everyone's lips. Except for Apicata's.

Apicata couldn't care less about banquets or the school or her father's affairs. By the time she was fourteen she was nearly as tall as me, with a budding figure that made heads turn. It was hard to believe she was the same girl I used to carry on my shoulders to the market.

The name on Apicata's lips was that of a boy, Leonis Antius Casca, the son of a senator, who was, for all practical purposes, a respectable choice of possible husbands for our girl. His father, Antius Piso, had been a trusted adviser to Marcus Vipsanius Agrippa, who died twenty years past, but was once Caesar's most honored military general and Tiberius's father-in-law. Piso had money, but also the ear of many senators and patricians. Piso's brother had once been consul and state augur and still held great influence.

Piso was a frequent guest to Apicius's triclinium, and in recent months he began bringing Casca along as a shadow. The boy was hardly much of a boy anymore, having donned his manly toga several years before, but he still had a rosy-cheeked look about him that made him seem younger than his eighteen years. He wore his hair closely cropped in the style of Augustus. It made his features all the more prominent; dark brown eyes, chiseled nose, and a slight pout in his lips that rounded out his Adonis-like visage. His father, on the other hand, sported a poorly made black wig that only served to make his lack of hair all the more obvious. Fortunately, what Piso lacked in looks he made up for in smarts—his skills in the courtroom were admired all over Rome.

I first saw the spark between Apicata and Casca at a small gathering held not long after the Lupercalia festival in February. Apicius had invited Trio and Celera, as well as Piso, his wife, and young Casca. The seating arrangement turned out to be advantageous for the youth. Apicata lay next to her parents at the end of one side of the couch, diagonally across from where Casca reclined behind his mother and Piso on the adjacent couch. This afforded Trio, Celera, and me an excellent view of their flirting while their parents remained unaware.

It was a quiet evening, full of gossip and good cheer. There was much talk of the early days of Caesar, when he was still known as Octavian, when Antony was still alive and involved with the great Egyptian queen, Cleopatra. I had heard many of the stories before but never from someone who had spent so much time at Caesar's side. Piso had been with Caesar when he ordered the vestal virgins to hand over Marc Antony's secret will, imagine! He was one of the first to know of the full extent of Antony's treachery!

I was so caught up in the discussion that I almost didn't notice Apicata sneaking shy glances at young Casca. Celera had, however, and was watching with amusement. She winked at me when she saw I had also noticed their interest. As Casca mouthed a sweet nothing to Apicata, Celera seized the moment.

"Apicata, I understand you have begun reading the *Histories* of Herodotus. Tell me, how do you like them?"

She almost choked on her honey water, not expecting to be addressed. Casca averted his eyes when he saw me looking in his direction and both of them turned as red as the cushions upon which we were seated.

Apicata recovered quickly. "I've almost finished them. Father was entertaining Annaeus Seneca and when he heard I had not yet read it, he sent me a copy."

"Have you reached the part about how the Ethiopians bury their dead in crystal coffins?" Casca asked, turning his body to rest his chin on both hands and stare at her directly.

"Oh, yes, I'm long past that! I'm reading about how Xerxes had the waters of Hellespont whipped for not obeying him." Her eyes sparkled.

"Wait till you reach the Battle of Thermopylae. What a heroic story!"

The exchange continued for a few more minutes with additional commentary from the others, who were oblivious to the undercurrent between the youths. I was reminded of the early years of my love for Passia and a pang of anger bit into the memory. It was hard to watch Apicius negotiating the marriage of his daughter when he still denied me my own union.

"They would be handsome together, wouldn't they?" Celera said to me, jolting me out of my thoughts.

"Yes, but I believe that Apicius has his sights on other prospects."

"Much can change in the matter of a few months, no?" Celera purred.

I agreed but at the time I did not believe her.

There were other banquets where Apicata and Casca had the opportunity to speak. I kept a close eye on them when I could and always sent a slave after Apicata when I saw her looking as though she were going to sneak off into some dark corner with the boy. My efforts were for naught.

Passia first found out about their clandestine meetings when she stumbled upon a crumpled piece of papyrus in a corner of Apicata's quarters. The meetings were during the day—with slaves sleeping against Apicata's door at night and guards patrolling the gardens it would have been impossible for her to leave without someone knowing. But during the day she had more freedom, especially if Passia was busy helping Helene when Aelia entertained friends.

"She is already in love with him." Passia and I were lying in bed at my apartment at the school when she told me she had confronted Apicata about the note. "They meet in the gardens down the street. She charmed one of your kitchen girls into sending him messages and helping her get in and out through the servants' entrance."

"Which girl?" I growled, vowing to make sure it didn't happen again.

"She wouldn't tell me."

Of course not. I sighed and ran my fingers through Passia's hair. "Did she promise to stop seeing him?"

She pressed her cheek into my shoulder, her breath soft against my skin. "I agreed I would be silent if I went with her."

"Passia!" I couldn't believe she would assent to such an arrangement.

"Thrasius, she is at the age where I can no longer say no to her. I am, after all, her slave. If I say no to her demands she might turn on me to get what she wants. At least this way she might take my advice and counsel."

I pressed her tighter against me, concerned at this turn of events. "Apicius will not be kind if he finds out you are helping her. He would probably whip you till you had barely a breath in your body. I could not bear to see you bleeding on the tiles at the hands of Sotas. Passia, you can't do this."

She pulled away. "Don't tell me what to do, Thrasius. You're the one person I trust not to order me about."

We stared at the ceiling in silence, the candlelight creating flickering shadows against the frescoed walls of the room. I remembered our days when we used to sleep on my pallet in my tiny cubicle near the kitchen. Now the room was large and sumptuous, a room I had once only dreamed of having.

"She wants you to convince Apicius to let her marry Casca."

I wasn't surprised. "Apicius has other suitors in mind. Consul Publius Cornelius Dolabella and Appius Marius Narses are at the top of his list."

"They're old enough to be her grandfather. Besides, Casca would be a good match. He has connections and his father is well liked in the Senate—he could sway any votes Apicius takes an interest in. It might be possible."

While I was not pleased with the idea of championing Casca for Apicata, I did want the girl to be happy. It was rare when patrician marriages had love. I wanted her to feel that same fluttering sensation in her stomach when her love walked into a room. I wanted her to feel the comfort of strong arms around her, keeping her safe. I wanted her to know the feeling that I had every day with Passia. While I wasn't sure how I could convince Apicius, at least there was a slim chance—thank the gods Apicata had the sense to love a man who had status.

"I will try but only under one condition."

She ran her slender fingers along my jaw. "What's that?"

"That she does not see Casca again until I have asked Apicius and we know the answer. I don't care if they exchange notes but I do not want to see you in the middle. I will meet Casca to talk of this arrangement. Apicius is loath to discipline me, as you know. But he would not hesitate to strip your skin bare, despite my influence on him."

Her index finger traced my lip. "Brilliant idea! I, however, would love to have you strip me bare."

I chuckled. "You're already bare, my love."

"I could dress again and you could strip me . . ."

I grasped her shoulders and rolled her on top of me. "Let's move on to the best part, why don't we?"

She laughed and slid her hips over mine.

The next morning, after attending clients at the salutatio, I walked with Passia to Apicata's chambers. The Roman summer was around the corner and although it was still spring, the cicadas had already begun their song. I was anxious at the thought of making such a bargain with Apicata, knowing it would be against her father's wishes. But when her door slave opened the chamber up to us and I saw Apicata at her writing desk, I knew why I was there. Because our little bird was in love.

Apicata jumped up and ran to us when she saw us enter, flinging her arms around my neck, almost knocking me over. "You'll help me, won't you? Oh, Thrasius, I knew you would!" Her voice was loud in my ear. I pulled back and brushed her hair out of her eyes.

"There is something you need to promise me."

She smiled. "What? Anything. I'll do anything if I can be with Leonis!"

It was unsettling to hear her call him Leonis instead of Casca; the praenomen was used only with intimate family. Passia was right; Apicata was deeply smitten. I thought back to my own youth and when I first laid eyes on Passia. It was a feeling that swept me away too.

I pushed the thought out of my head. It would not do to have Apicata see me as soft. "You have to promise me you won't see Casca until your father has made his decision. Send notes if you must but I will not have any of the slaves taking Apicius's wrath for your follies. Am I clear?"

"What if Father says no?" Apicata asked in a sullen tone.

"He might. And if he does, you will have to live with that. Your father has jurisdiction over you until you are given to your husband."

She turned on her heel and stormed across the room. "It's not fair! Why don't I get to have a say in the matter? It's my life!"

Passia went over to where Apicata stood by the window and put her arm around the girl. "I know it's hard to understand, but this is the way it has always been. And the way it will always be."

Apicata pushed Passia away. Tears tracked their way across her cheek. "No, it's not! You are with the man you love! Why can't I be?"

I felt my heart break.

Passia would have none of it. "Apicata, our circumstances are different. You can hardly compare your life to my life as a slave. Tell me, would you trade places and wait hand and foot on me?"

Apicata didn't answer. Passia carried on. "Besides, I am not married to the man I love. As long as I'm a slave I may never have that. I could be sold tomorrow for all I know. But you, you are the daughter of one of the wealthiest men in the land. You will always live a life of luxury. Any husband you have will be happy to dote on you. Even if your father doesn't choose Casca for you, you will be well cared for."

"I don't care about luxury. I want Leonis."

"Do not despair yet. Let us see what spells Thrasius can work on your father."

Apicata brightened. "Will you try, Thrasius? Father never denies you anything."

I considered Passia, thinking about how Apicius continued to deny me the only thing I truly wanted. "I will, but you must be patient. I will ask him on my own time, when I think it best."

Apicata grinned. "I will be patient, but it will be hard."

It would have to do. I would need to approach Apicius soon or the girl would never give me peace of mind. As the poets always say, absence makes the heart grow fonder. And young lovers more desperate.

"Tomorrow I'll discuss this arrangement with Casca. Write me a note to give to him, so he knows I have true intentions."

"Can I go with you?" She looked at me, her eyes full of hope. It took all my willpower, but I told her no. She opened her mouth to protest, but decided against it.

She told me the details about meeting Casca and promised to bring me the note in the morning. When I left, a flock of crows cawed in the distance. Maybe it was the sound of the gods whispering to me that nothing good would come of this. I shook the thought out of my mind.

· · ·

Apicata had been meeting her lover in the public gardens down the street from our villa. There were many alcoves where young lovers could meet and not be disturbed. It was in one such alcove that I found Casca waiting for Apicata to arrive.

He was there at the appointed time. When the bushes rustled, he thought I was Apicata and called out her name in an eager voice.

"I'm afraid not," I said as I stepped through the flowered archway into the space where he waited.

He stood up, alarmed, scrambled over the bench, and held up his fists. There was no exit in that direction but he appeared ready to push his way through the leaves.

"What do you want? Stay back!"

By Jove, he thought I wanted to beat him up! I chuckled to myself. I was not a fearsome figure by any means, and couldn't he see I didn't carry a weapon? Still, he had good reason to be afraid; meeting with a patrician's daughter without permission was a highly punishable offense. I noted the hedge was made of hawthorn, and as such would be painful should he choose to flee.

"I bring you a message." I reached out my hand with Apicata's note.

He stepped forward and took it warily, keeping his attention focused on me as he opened the folded sheet of papyrus.

I had no idea what it said, but it must have been favorable. Casca scanned the note, tucked the message into the fold of his toga, then took my hands in his and pumped them in gratitude.

"Our lives are in your hands, Thrasius."

I smiled, unsure I wanted to bear the weight of such expectations. I tried to extract my hands from his but his grip held firm.

"Does your father know of your intentions?"

"He does, but he knows Apicius has been talking with Dolabella and Narses. He doesn't believe I have a chance against the current consul or a man so prominent in the Imperial household."

"He may have a point."

"But Apicata's note said—"

I cut him off. "I know, but I cannot promise anything."

In looking at the young man, his eyes desperate and flooded with love, I decided I knew the fastest way to either nip this in the bud or change Apicius's mind.

"You want to marry Apicata? Come now, I have an idea. We have one chance."

He followed me back to the villa, asking me questions that I didn't answer.

When we reached the villa, I led him to a small triclinium the family used for breakfast and which had little traffic during the day. He was uncomfortable being in the house with only my permission and no formal reason for being there, but I assured him he had nothing to worry about. I instructed one slave to bring him refreshment and another to watch the door and make sure Casca was not disturbed until I came back.

I went to find Apicius. He was in his library, going over the results of the day's Senate votes. A messenger brought them to him every day after they closed session at the Curia and then his scribe took dictation, letters of thanks or disappointment to the senators who had a hand in each vote.

Sotas ushered me in. "You're lucky," he said to me in a low voice. "All the votes were in his favor today. And he has other good news which I'm sure he'll impart to you."

Apicius was in an excellent mood. He looked up from his papers and a broad smile crossed his face when he saw me. "Thrasius! You will never guess what happened last night! Publius Octavius tripped at his banquet. Fell right into a servant carrying a pot of soup and it splashed all over Caesar and Livia! Oh, what I would have given to see that unfold!" Apicius's face reddened more with each chuckle.

I didn't like to laugh at someone else's expense, but I have to admit, picturing the scene did give me pleasure. Soon Apicius had me laughing as well, as he made up mocking scenarios of what the apology to Caesar must have sounded like.

I broke in, knowing I had to address the task at hand and remedy the situation of Apicata's poor suitor waiting in the atrium.

"Apicius, I come on other business this afternoon," I said, hoping my nervousness was not apparent.

He grew sober. "Oh, yes, what is it?" Apicius poured himself a cup of wine and offered me one. I declined but let him quaff his portion. He might need it.

"I brought someone to the villa to speak with you," I said, unsure how he would take my news. "He's waiting in the breakfast triclinium."

"Let's go." Apicius motioned to Sotas to follow. "Tell me as we walk."

We left the room and headed down the hallway toward the atrium. "Before I tell you, Apicius," I said, still unused to the taste of his name in my mouth, "I want you to seriously consider what the man has to say."

Apicius looked at me in earnest. "Now you have me intrigued! I have always trusted your advice, Thrasius. But why must you warn me?"

"I'm unsure this man would normally have entered into your plans. I believe he's worthy, however, and I want you to consider his petition in all seriousness."

"Who is this man? Stop speaking in riddles!" Apicius no longer seemed inclined to humor me, but fortunately we had reached the door to the triclinium.

I ushered him in. Casca was sitting on the couch, holding a scroll of poetry Apicata had left in the room after breakfast. For one brief moment when we entered, the look on his face was pure terror. To his credit, he composed himself immediately and stood to greet us.

"Apicius, you remember Leonis Antius Casca? He has come here to speak with you about marrying your daughter."

Apicius studied me long and hard, then addressed young Casca. His voice was laced in ice.

"You want to marry Apicata?"

"Yes, Gavius Apicius, I do." Casca was the epitome of a man of determination. I saw his hand reach into the fold of his toga and touch Apicata's note and I realized it was the strength of Cupid guiding this man.

Apicius walked over to the chair next to the couch and gestured for Casca to sit. I took a seat opposite them both. Sotas remained at his post next to the door.

"Tell me what you can bring to this family. Does your father agree with this union?"

Casca didn't waver. "He does. He has remarked to me many times how much he would like to see our families united."

Apicius responded with an incline of his head and his mouth turned up at the edges in a thoughtful smile. "Explain to me, then, why are you here instead of him?"

"He doesn't have my conviction—that you would find me more suitable than Dolabella or Narses."

I was surprised at the audacity of this young man. Apicius was also surprised. He didn't respond right away, which was unusual. When he did, he sounded amused and—although Casca couldn't know it—impressed. "And why do you think I would find you more suitable?"

"It is quite simple." Casca looked at me, then at Apicius. "I love your daughter. They do not."

Apicius snorted. "Love is not a prerequisite to marriage."

"Quite true. However, I bring to you both power and influence—through my father now, but also in my future as I follow in his footsteps. I will continue to bring you and your family honor, and precious votes in the elections. And what I can do that Dolabella and Narses cannot is assure you I will take care of your daughter with every fiber of my being."

"Go on," Apicius said, intrigued. I was glad I had decided to bring Casca here on such impulse.

"I have watched you with Apicata over these many months. I know how you dote on her, how you hold her close to your heart. She is as important to you as your love for culinary delights," he remarked.

Good, I thought. The boy had a sense of how to stroke Apicius's ego, though I knew the truth that Casca—and likely even Apicius—did not. Food and fame would always be first in Apicius's heart.

"I can promise you that your daughter will have love and laughter. Narses and Dolabella care not for her as much as they do for your money. My motives are pure. Few in this world have the chance to marry for love. Let your daughter be one of them."

The silence was thick, like a sauce with too little water. Apicius did not speak for a long time. Instead, he sat there looking patiently at Casca, his face devoid of emotion.

I couldn't take it any longer. "Apicata returns his favor." As soon as I said the words I knew they lacked the confidence Casca had exhibited. Apicius's silence had caused me doubt.

Apicius set a steely eye on me. I feared he would ask me if the two had been meeting and I would have to decide whether I should lie.

He didn't. Instead he spoke to Casca. "There are other men who would be better suited to marrying Apicata. But I admire your gall. Give me one more reason why I should consider your petition, though it will likely not sway me."

Casca paused, his eyes glancing somewhere in the vicinity of Apicius's knees. I thought he was going to falter but then he lifted his gaze, and when he spoke I knew that if Cupid was not with him, Venus certainly was.

"Apicius, I should marry your daughter because we are meant to be. We are like rose wine and oysters, like truffles and pepper, like lentils and chestnuts or crane with turnip. We belong together like mullet and dill, milk and snails, suckling pig and silphium. You have known these loves, Gavius Apicius. You know the truth of their pairings and it is that truth I hold up to you now. Apicata and I are like spoon and plate. One is worth little without the other."

My stomach fluttered. I closed my eyes as Casca finished, half expecting to see a blinding light around the boy, the protection afforded him by the gods.

Instead when my eyes opened I saw Apicius staring at him, his mouth slightly ajar but with his expression still strangely unreadable.

Apicius headed toward the door. "Sotas," he said, pausing a moment before leaving, "have word sent to Antius Piso. I invite him to dinner to discuss a marriage arrangement between his son and my daughter the day after tomorrow. Thrasius will inform Timon of the dinner details."

Then he was gone, Sotas trailing behind him, leaving Casca and me staring at each other, dumbfounded. I had not expected such a swift response. At minimum I thought Apicius might need some time to think.

"I'll have Passia send for Apicata. You can tell her yourself," I said, unable to keep a broad smile from my face. I stood up to go but Casca caught my arm.

"Thrasius, I will never be able to thank you enough."

"Treat her well, as you promised." I gripped his arm in return. "That will be thanks enough."

In the hallway I ran into Passia. I had barely told her much of what had happened before she threw her arms around me and smothered me with kisses before running off to deliver the news.

I stopped in to see Apicius before I headed to the kitchen to let Timon know he would be planning a celebration cena two days hence. He was back in the library, finishing the dictation of his letters. Sotas stood next to the scribe, helping to seal and pile the letters to ready them for delivery.

Apicius waggled a finger at me. "You'd better be right about Casca."

"I have a good feeling about him." Which was true. I did. It was one of the first important things I thought Apicius had done right in many years.

"I know Piso is not fond of Publius Octavius. Now let's hope he pushes favor more heavily in my direction or this marriage will be for naught." He continued his pacing as he talked. "No matter, we have other things to worry about now."

I deposited myself into the sumptuously padded chair near the window that had a view of the Forum below. It was one of my favorite views from the villa, with all of Rome's most important happenings playing out among the temples, statues, and paths at the foot of the hill. The day was hot and many of the pedestrians walking in the gardens of the vestal virgins carried umbrellas to ward off the Roman sun. It was like watching many tiny butterflies flying in a cloud far in the distance. "What worries you?" I asked, not tearing my eyes away from the view.

"A messenger arrived. Sejanus wants to see me tomorrow."

That got my attention. "Why?"

"I don't know. He asked to see me, not Aelia. He's coming tomorrow morning after I meet with my clients." Apicius stopped his pacing. He stood with his hands on his hips, staring at the elaborate cat and bird mosaic on the floor.

"He wants something," Sotas said.

Apicius rubbed a smudge at the corner of the mosaic with his toe. "Yes, but what?"

I stared out the window. One of the largest statues of the Divine Julius Caesar was casting its late-afternoon shadow. A flock of starlings flew through the shadow, a dark and ominous streak of inky feathers.

CHAPTER 18

When I awoke the next morning it was with a heart full of dread. All night I had tossed and turned, wondering what Sejanus might want.

The salutatio was particularly slow. It seemed all of Apicius's clients had something trivial to whine about.

"Lucius Atticus left graffiti on my house because I would not sell him my best pig," complained Valerius Tiro.

Apicius made the same sort of promise he had been making all morning, agreeing to take care of matters, to protect, to fix, all for the want of a vote.

Taking care of Atticus meant I would arrange for a man to let Atticus know that if the graffiti didn't stop, the result would be banishment from Apicius's banquet couch. In return, Tiro would vote no against reinstating the Lex Sumptuaria, a 171-year-old law regulating the use of luxury items and limiting the display of public wealth. Caesar backed it but the majority of the senators and most of the equestrian and patrician population were against it. Although the plebs were excited about the law, most of them were clients whose patrons would exact the same vote requirements that Apicius did with Tiro. The likelihood of it passing was slim.

Tiro bowed. "Yes, yes, Apicius. I'll cast no, I promise."

It continued from there. "My neighbor keeps stealing melons from my garden!" Licinius Bucco wailed, demanding Apicius send guards to threaten the neighbor.

Sotas leaned down and said in a low voice, "If I had a melon right now, I know where I would put it." I held back a laugh as the next client was ushered in.

The door slave ushered Sejanus into the atrium just as Sotas escorted out the last clients. Sejanus smiled broadly, which made the scar on his cheek tighten and twitch. He was clean shaven and wore a freshly bleached toga over the traditional red tunic of the highest of Caesar's guards.

First there was the typical exchange of pleasantries. Then Apicius suggested they go to his library. I was not invited to attend my former master for the discussion but Sotas nodded at me, signaling that he would tell me of the exchange later.

Sejanus stayed for an hour but immediately after, Apicius left with Sotas to attend an assembly in the Forum. I departed at the same time to go to the school to teach classes, hoping I could walk with Sotas. Unfortunately, Apicius had Sotas join him in the litter as he sometimes did when he wanted to talk to someone as he traveled. As I walked to the school, I plotted in my head all the ways I could end Sejanus.

The day's courses dragged as the salutatio had. I taught a class on sauces, one on banquet preparations, and lectured on the importance of spices in modern cuisine. I was so distracted I even burned my hand on a pot—thank the gods it was minor. A snicker from the back of the class pained my ego more than the fire pained my skin.

That night for dinner, I discovered that Apicius had invited Antius Piso and his wife, Lucasta. I thought it odd. We were supposed to dine with them on the following night, so seeing them there was unexpected.

My elevated freedman status allowed me to dine with the family, but when I saw them there, I hesitated until Apicius waved a hand at me to sit. I took up my spot on the opposite couch, thinking it was odd that Casca and Apicata were not present.

For gustatio, the slaves brought out an endive salad with honey and vinegar dressing, a platter of spicy fried pheasant meatballs, and sliced blood and womb sausages. I was pleased to see Timon had already mastered my recipes. Over the meal we made small talk about the Lex Sumptuaria. It was polite that Apicius talk of the engagement first but he seemed reluctant to do so. So instead we ate and talked politics. The guests reveled in the tastes, and while Aelia and I were pleased with their response to the food, Apicius appeared distracted.

His glass even shook when he talked, a fact it seemed I was the only one to notice. He also ate little, which was unlike him.

Finally, Apicius spoke. "Sotas, please clear the room and pour us some wine." The rest of us watched with some measure of alarm as he ushered the slaves out and shut the doors to the triclinium. Whatever Apicius intended to say, it seemed he didn't want the slaves gossiping about it. I wondered about the wine—it was unusual to serve wine during a meal unless the discussion was grave. Sotas poured out a measure of wine for each of us, watered it down, and returned to his post near the door.

Apicius raised his glass. "Piso, I have delighted in your company over the years and it's my hope our friendship will continue to strengthen over the years ahead."

Piso smiled and his wife patted him on the shoulder from her position on the couch next to him. "This union pleases us too," he said, clasping his wife's hand and squeezing it.

For a brief moment I saw a familiar look in my former master's eyes—the look he had when the haruspex had given him his fortune all those years past, and when Livia intended to purchase me. It was a mixture of nervousness, anxiety, and determination. Apicius took a long swallow of wine.

"The union between you and me is one I plan to make strong. Hear me out, for while that is my intention, I regret to tell you I have changed my mind about the marriage between your son and my daughter."

Aelia looked like she might die of embarrassment. The color rose in Piso's cheeks as he considered the weight of Apicius's words. Piso's wife stared downward in openmouthed shock. My appetite transformed into a ball of anger when I realized who Apicius had promised our little bird to—the very man who would, I knew deep in the core of me, destroy her soul.

Piso's jowls shook when he spoke. "Explain yourself. Why send word to us last night that you had chosen my son, then bring us here today to rescind your offer?"

Apicius fiddled with the purple edges of his toga. I was glad he was nervous. I hoped this decision gave him pause.

But when Apicius spoke he didn't seem nervous. Quite the opposite. I hated how he was able to rally under pressure. "I won't lie to you, Piso, or make excuses. I have been offered a more advantageous match."

"You dishonor us!" Piso's wife sat up, tears flowing down her cheeks, creating thin tracks in her pale leaden makeup. She jumped off the couch and stood there, balling up her fists in anger. Piso pulled himself off the couch and gathered his wife into his arms.

Apicius stood as well. "Please, I assure you my intent is not to dishonor anyone. By dishonoring you I dishonor myself. I have a proposal for you, to make up for my lack of decorum."

For a moment, I thought that Piso might reach across the couch and strangle Apicius. "I'm not sure what you can do to fix this," he snarled.

Apicius looked pained. "Please, my friend, hear me out."

"Speak and be quick. I have no desire to dine with you tonight."

"I'm sorry for that, but let me make this up to you. We have not yet shared the news of the engagement, so we can both avoid public embarrassment. However, I know that does not ease the pain of my actions. To compensate you, I will still honor Casca with a sum equal to Apicata's dowry. Additionally, as a gift to you, I'd like to give you my villa in the mountains near Alba. I'll even leave you a retinue of slaves to further show my goodwill. I do not desire an end to our friendship, Piso."

There was silence for a time. Piso's wife leaned over and said something indiscernible.

"We'd like a moment to discuss this," Piso said.

"Stay here, of course," Apicius said. "Sotas will be right outside the door and can attend to any desire you might have. We'll wait in the atrium."

I followed Aelia and Apicius out of the room and Sotas closed the door behind us. Aelia whirled on her husband.

"How dare you break the heart of your daughter?"

Apicius stared at her, his ears reddening with every word she said. "Excuse me, wife? Were you questioning me?"

Aelia was not going to play the dutiful matron. "I am. I want to know why you broke off the engagement. Who are you planning to marry Apicata to?"

My mouth went dry when I realized that Aelia must not have known about Sejanus's visit the day before.

"Your cousin, Sejanus."

Her mouth dropped open in horror. For a moment it seemed that she was going to say something but then she began to sway. Helene caught her just as she fainted.

Apicius signaled one of the other slaves at the door to assist Helene. "Take her back to her rooms, let her sleep."

After they had departed, I could not keep my tongue still.

"Did I understand you? You plan to marry Apicata to Sejanus?"

Behind Apicius, Sotas nodded, his face grave.

Apicius knotted his brow, seemingly surprised I would question him, then softened. "Yes. Sejanus has better long-term prospects than Casca." He touched my shoulder, propelling me down the hall toward the atrium.

There was something he wasn't telling me. "How so?"

He slowed his pace and paused as if trying to formulate what he wanted to say. "Augustus is old. When he dies, I want to be aligned with the right person who will show me favor. Someone who will help me rise to favor with Tiberius."

I leaned against the frescoed wall, the weight of his words driving into me. Did he really think Sejanus would have the ability to change the influence Publius Octavius had within Caesar's kitchen? More so, did he actually *trust* Sejanus to help him?

"That's only part of it. This is about the evidence that Sejanus has against you, isn't it?" I asked, daring to be bold.

Apicius stared at me.

"You've spoken about it in front of me before. I put the pieces together," I said, not wanting to implicate Sotas.

"If you know, you understand that I have no choice in this matter. To deny him would be to kill us all. And that might even mean you."

I had not considered that possibility. I thought of Passia and my blood ran cold.

"Understood. But how will you tell Apicata she's not going to marry her love, but instead will be marrying someone she hates? It could destroy what love she has for you. If you give Apicata to Sejanus, you'll be handing her over to a monster. Worst of all, you are going to break her heart." Even though I tried to be gentle, it came out cruel.

Apicius's eyes narrowed and his cheeks reddened.

He growled at me. "No, *you* will be the one to break her heart. You will tell her she is to marry Sejanus in June when he returns from accompanying Caesar to Greece."

I could not tell how much of this was true fear about the murder or desire to become gastronomic adviser to Caesar. I imagined that inside his mind Apicius warred with both of those ideas. I kept my face passive. "It doesn't change anything. She'll know who is taking Casca from her."

Before Apicius could respond, Sotas poked his head around the corner of the hallway and indicated we should return. Apicius gave me one last withering look, then stomped away toward the dining room.

Piso and Lucasta stood together next to the triclinium couch. Lucasta's eyes were red but her cheeks were dry. Piso held an arm around her shoulders.

Apicius approached them with open arms. I hung back by the door with Sotas. Anger roiled my stomach.

"Come now, tell me what you are thinking. It pains me that I have hurt you." Apicius placed a hand on their shoulders.

Piso nodded. "I accept your offer, Apicius. We appreciate your generosity. Most men would not bring honor to a broken promise and you have our thanks." He let go of his wife and shook hands with Apicius.

"Good, good. I am glad to hear we have made amends. We still have two more courses, my friends! Please tell me you will stay and it will not go to waste."

Piso turned to his wife. After a moment Lucasta said, "We'll stay."

"Excellent!" Apicius led them back toward the couch, then glared at me. "Thrasius has other matters to attend to so he will say his good-byes now."

I came forward to kiss them on each cheek, both angry and grateful for the dismissal. On the way out Apicius called to me in the same tone he would his lowest slave.

"Fetch the kitchen boys for the next course, Thrasius. And make sure nothing is cold."

I didn't reply. Nor did I intend to honor his command. I eyed Sotas as I left. He understood me.

I wandered through the gardens for a time, needing to be alone with my thoughts. Passia was likely with Apicata so I dared not go find her. I couldn't bear facing our little bird. Oh gods, how was I to share such horrific news? In the corner of the garden I fell to my knees before a gilded statue of Mars and prayed to the god for strength and for some sign he would wreak revenge on Sejanus.

The grass was cold around my legs. The moonlight filtered through the umbrella pines and made the stones of the garden paths shine. It was silent, eerily silent, with only the brief sounds of a clanking pot from the kitchen in the distance beyond the garden. I gazed up at Mars and thought I saw his painted eyes blink. I heard and felt the whoosh of wings near my head as a giant owl swooped by me and came to land on Mars's outstretched sword.

I was empty, devoid of all thought but the glorious, menacing owl. Then dread filled my chest, pressing on my ribs and that space between my heart and my breast.

It was a sign, a dire sign. I knew not what it meant. An owl signified disaster, far-reaching disaster. And it was perched on the sword! Would blood be shed?

I fled the garden, terrified of those golden eyes burning into me.

Sotas was waiting for me in the kitchen when I returned, breathing hard from my run across the garden. He was talking with Timon and eating the remains of his dinner.

He dropped his chicken leg on the terra-cotta plate as I approached. "What's wrong? You look like you have seen a spirit!"

Still catching my breath, I gestured to him that we should speak outside, away from the prying ears and eyes of the other slaves. Timon, who was always understanding, tossed Sotas an apple and the big man followed me back out into the garden.

We didn't go far. I was too nervous that the owl would be waiting for me, swooping overhead in the night. Instead we sat on benches near the kitchen where the staff often rested when the ovens were too hot.

"All right, Thrasius, tell me what spooked you," Sotas pressed me. I told him, although it seemed silly that I'd reacted as I had, with such fear. Sotas wouldn't have run; he probably would have shrugged his shoulders and walked off.

But Sotas did not belittle my response. "A serpent crossed my path yesterday when we were at the Forum. I felt the same as you, full of foreboding."

"Tell me what Sejanus said to Apicius." I was desperate to know what was promised in exchange for Apicata's hand in marriage.

Sotas shook his head. "I know not. Against my recommendation, Apicius barred the door and bade me wait outside."

I was horrified. "What? You left them alone? Sejanus could have murdered him!"

"I tried to convey my concern but he made it clear that if I didn't obey immediately there would be consequences. I tried to listen at the doors but you know how thick they are." Sotas took a bite of his apple, spat it out, and tossed it far across the garden. I hoped it hit the owl.

I cursed. It was I who had suggested the heavy doors, to prevent slaves from stealing our recipes when we worked on the cookbook.

"He forced his hand. It's the only reason that Apicius would turn Casca aside."

Sotas fingered the blue silk rope of his tunica, an expensive accessory that in recent years Apicius began insisting his house slaves wear. "Perhaps, but that seems too simple. Sejanus is cunning. I think he would play with Apicius's desires first. He doesn't need to be forceful. I bet Sejanus is dangling some opportunity with Caesar in front of his nose."

I was skeptical. "But Publius Octavius is there. There is no opportunity for Apicius to do anything at Caesar's villa."

"Maybe it's not here on the Palatine?" Sotas conjectured. "Maybe he wants him to entertain foreign dignitaries? But maybe not."

It didn't make sense to me either. "Besides, Sejanus has returned from the war in Germania. He's been prefect for six months. What kind of pull can he have? Everyone knows he's Tiberius's man, not Augustus's."

"Maybe he promised Apicius that he would push Publius Octavius out when Tiberius comes into power?" Sotas suggested.

"I think—" I started to say, but was interrupted by a movement in the trees to my left. As I turned my head to look, the owl swooped down and landed in the dirt a few feet from where we sat. It regarded us for a second, blinked, then lifted its wings and took off into the darkness.

"By the gods," Sotas breathed.

We sat in silence, unnerved, until Passia emerged from the kitchen, her light shawl blowing in the evening breeze. She was beautiful, her body silhouetted by the light from the door.

"Come, sit, my love." She came to sit beside me and I put my arm around her.

"I asked Tycho to bring us some of your wine," she said. I had several amphorae in the cellars that Apicius had declared mine.

"Good thinking," Sotas said, clapping a hand down on the bench beside him. "We are men in desperate need of wine."

She reached around to caress the small of my back as she often did when we sat together.

I let out a deep breath. "Tomorrow Apicata will learn that she is not marrying Casca."

She pulled away to look at me better. "What do you mean? I thought it was all arranged! And Piso was here tonight!"

The clink of glasses marked Tycho's arrival. We sat in silence as he doled the wine out, not watered down, I noted. He left the jug on the table between us. As soon as he was gone Passia began her questions anew. I rubbed her shoulder with my free hand, feeling her tension.

"Who is she marrying, if not Casca? Dolabella? That old man Narses?"

"You will not like the answer," Sotas said.

"The only answer I will like is Casca. If not the son of Piso, who?" I saw the realization dawn across her lovely face. "Oh, please, tell me no . . ."

"We should have killed him." The words tumbled from my mouth.

"Hush!" Passia clapped her hand against my lips. "Do not say those words where others might hear!"

I pulled away and took another drink. Sotas did too.

Passia stood up and started to pace in front of us. "When is Apicius telling her? Tomorrow?"

"Ha!" Sotas guffawed. "You think he has the guts to tell her himself?"

She stopped her pacing and considered me. "Oh, no, Thrasius. He didn't?"

"He did." The words were bitter on my tongue.

She came back to me and put her arms around me. "We'll tell her together."

It didn't make me feel better.

Telling Apicata was even worse than I'd imagined. I gave her the news in the breakfast triclinium, where, ironically, Apicius had, two days before, told Casca he could marry his daughter.

"Your father asked me to talk to you," I said, choosing to remain standing, despite her invitation to sit. Passia took a spot on the couch next to Apicata.

She turned her gaze on me, waiting for me to speak.

"It's about your marriage."

"Is something wrong with Casca?" she asked, worry crossing her face as she put aside the scroll she was reading.

Passia patted her knee. "No, everything is fine with Casca."

I decided to just spit it out. "You aren't marrying Casca. Your father has arranged for you to marry Lucius Aelius Sejanus."

I had scarcely got the words out of my mouth when she dropped to the floor and began wailing as though someone had died. After a few minutes of trying to console her she sprang up from where she lay pooled in the silks of her robe and ran to Aelia's rooms. Passia and I followed.

Aelia was finishing up her morning repertoire. Helene waited by the door and two slaves stood next to where Aelia sat on a plush red-cushioned chair, putting the final touches on her hair and makeup, pinning the curls of a blond wig to best frame her face. They stepped back as Apicata entered, crying. She rushed across the room, fell at her mother's feet, and clasped her around the legs. Aelia dismissed her dressing slaves, then pulled Apicata off the ground. Apicata began her complaints about marrying Sejanus anew, tears staining the front of her tunica.

"He's a lecher, a filthy man! He hates us. He hurt you, Mother! He hurt you! Please don't make me marry him. He will ruin everything," she wailed. "I hate him! I wish he would die!"

Aelia put on the mask of a true Roman matron, her face as cold as a barrel of snow, and slapped her daughter hard. Apicata raised her hand to her tear-stained cheek, now reddened with Aelia's handprint. In all my time in the Gavia household I had never seen Aelia slap her daughter for anything.

"Casca has nothing but his family name. Sejanus has the power and the favor of Caesar. That means he can destroy us all with a single word. Now pull yourself together and say a prayer to Cupid to rip that arrow from your breast. You have to harden your heart, lock away all your tears, and be the perfect Roman wife. It is your duty."

Apicata was stunned into silence. Her mouth was still open in a little o and while she continued to cry she said nothing. She left, dragging Passia with her by the hand. I was shocked at Aelia's response.

I started to follow but Aelia's voice stopped me. "Wait."

Her eyes were wet. I felt better seeing the emotion on her face—to be so harsh to her daughter was out of character.

"Did Apicius ask you to tell her?" she asked me.

"Yes, my lady, he did."

"Ah." She fell into the chair next to her, as if exhausted. A long curl came undone from her wig and fell across her shoulder.

"It should have been me," she murmured.

"I believe it was my punishment," I said, wishing as I did that I could shove the words back into my mouth.

Her eyes were wet with the glisten of tears. "What do you mean?"

"I told Apicius I didn't agree with his decision."

Aelia wiped her face with the back of her hand. "I see."

"I cannot imagine her married to that monster. I truly wished that Apicata might marry for love," I said.

She stood and came over to me and put one hand on my cheek. Her eyes were full of sadness. "Oh, my dear Thrasius, only slaves and plebs are lucky enough to marry for love." She dropped her hand and turned away.

As I left the chamber, I heard a sob escape Aelia's lips. I could not bear to look back so I kept walking.

CHAPTER 19

Apicata punished us all by trying to starve herself to death. She shut herself in her room and refused food. Apicius was too ashamed to visit and that only intensified her sorrow. Aelia and Passia managed to get her to eat part of an apple every day and to drink some water but we knew it would not sustain her for long.

Her once budding figure became gaunt. Her cheeks hollowed and her skin was sallow. She was dangerously weak and kept to her bed.

I didn't talk much to Apicius. He refused my company at the salutatio and only begrudgingly consulted me about some banquets that had long been planned. I was polite but both of us had only one desire—to quickly depart each other's company.

Finally, I couldn't take it anymore. Apicata's stubbornness had left her dangerously ill. I burst into Apicius's library one afternoon, pushing past Sotas before he could stop me.

"How dare you?"

Startled, Apicius dropped the scroll he was holding. I didn't give him time to answer. "First you crush your daughter's spirit and now you have left her to die. What favor will you find in Caesar's villa if your one connection there is dead?"

He blanched. His mouth worked as though trying to find the words to say. I didn't stop.

"Your daughter loves you above all. You insulted her by not giving her the news yourself. And now you refuse to talk to her on her deathbed. I hope her shade haunts you to the end of your days, you fool. I won't know because I'll leave."

I was shaking. I had never talked to a patrician in such a manner. Such disrespect could mean banishment from the household, or worse, he could arrange for my ejection from the city. I turned to leave.

"Wait." Apicius's voice quavered.

I braced myself for an onslaught of his anger. I was surprised to see defeat in his eyes.

"Tell me what to do."

I realized then that the tide of our relationship had truly turned. Over the years Apicius had always been the one to give orders and now it was he asking me for advice. I did my best to temper my frustration. "Come with me now. We'll bring her food and you will tell her you don't want her to die. You'll feed her and let her know she will always be in your heart."

Apicius hesitated. "Why can't you feed her?"

I threw my hands in the air. "Don't you think I have tried? Every day I have tried. She wants nothing to do with me."

"But what if . . . ?"

I had lost patience. "What if she dies?"

Apicius made a strangled sound.

"She thinks all the men in her life have betrayed her, and you most of all. It's your duty to make amends. Talk to her. Tell her you are sorry."

He was silent. I propelled him out the door, and Sotas followed.

We walked through the corridors in awkward silence until we reached the door to Apicata's chamber. The door slaves moved out of the way as we approached. I instructed one of them to fetch me broth from the kitchen.

Apicata was even paler than when I'd seen her that morning. Her hair lay in greasy tangles around her face. Her cheekbones were pronounced, making her look haunted.

Apicius hurried to her side. I motioned all the slaves out of the room. Passia came to stand with me and Sotas.

"Where is Aelia?" I asked.

Passia didn't take her eyes off Apicius. "I urged her to go rest. She is becoming ill with worry."

Apicius sat on the edge of the bed and stroked his daughter's hair. Apicata stirred and opened her eyes.

"Father?" Her voice was weak.

"Oh, my little one, I am here. I am sorry I have not come to you. You and I are truly bred from the same stock—forever willful and stubborn." I couldn't see his face but it sounded like he was in tears.

"Why do I have to marry him?" She could barely keep her eyes open.

"Sejanus has powerful friends." He continued to stroke her hair. "If I ignore his request to marry you, I fear how that choice would negatively affect our family. Or your beloved Casca."

Her eyes opened wide, the blood suddenly returning to her face. "What do you mean? He would hurt Casca?"

Apicius took her hand. "He might. I think that if Sejanus doesn't get what he wants, he can be very dangerous."

I wondered at Apicius's words. Was he lying? Or had he made a bargain with Sejanus?

Tears fell across her pale cheek, glistening in the afternoon sunlight. "If he is so dangerous, why do I have to marry him?"

"He is not dangerous to those he loves," Apicius said quickly. I marveled at how easily the lie slipped from his lips. "And he loves you beyond measure. He was quite in earnest."

I'll bet he was. I doubted that love was something Sejanus was even capable of.

Apicata knew better. "He does not love me."

"Worry not, daughter. Instead, consider your duty." His tone attempted to inspire. "Marrying Sejanus will make you important to Caesar Augustus and to his adopted son, Tiberius. Your sons will inherit great things and have unprecedented opportunities in life. And you will be secure knowing that the people you love most—your family and Casca—will be safe because of your actions. I wish it were otherwise, but Sejanus has powerful influence, little one. It is you who will determine whether he uses it for good or not."

My jaw hurt from clenching my teeth. I couldn't believe Apicius was putting such an onus on his daughter, using guilt to gain her acquiescence in an unbearable situation.

"But he is an equestrian . . . ," Apicata murmured, one last, final plea.

"Yes, but he is a prestigious and influential self-made man," Apicius countered. "The world is changing, my dear, and those with the wherewithal to create their own destinies will be the ones who anchor their stars in the heavens."

I looked at my friends. Passia shook her head and Sotas shrugged. Apicius did not care for self-made men—like the famous orator Cicero, or Gaius Marius, who was consul six times in Julius Caesar's reign. He thought them cheats, unworthy of such status.

Apicius turned to me, seeking what to do next. Balsamea had arrived with the broth and I indicated she should give Apicius the bowl.

He took it from her and spooned up a small measure. "Please, Apicata, take of this broth. The Gavia household depends on your strength."

Apicata eyed the bowl. "I'm not hungry."

"Please, Apicata, eat something. We need your strength. Please, daughter."

She turned her head toward the opposite wall.

"Apicata, do it for Casca. To keep him safe."

At the mention of Casca's name, Apicata gave a nod. "Fine. I'll eat. For Casca, who is lost to me."

Apicius gave his daughter a kiss on the cheek. "Thank you, daughter. Thank you." Passia rushed forward to help feed her.

"In the future," he said as he stood to let Passia take his place, "our family will be proud of how your courage and fidelity helped build the Gavia name."

Pretty words but I doubted them. Sejanus was likely to choke the soul right out of her.

Apicata took her father's explanation to heart, shoring up her emotions and recovering from her self-imposed illness in less than a week. She emerged from her chambers much changed. Gone was the happy girl who'd made the house sparkle with laughter. In her place was a quieter girl who did as she was asked.

When she was well, Passia took Apicata to the temple of Juno, where they stayed for two days of ritual cleansing and special preparations for her marriage. Aelia bade them to bring five white sows as sacrifice—an exorbitant offering. As the ceremony was for women only, Passia would not tell me what went on in the temple, and as it was not a common rite, there was no general knowledge among the slaves that I could draw upon. But when Apicata returned she was truly a new woman. There was no sparkle in her eyes but the sadness was gone. She was cold, efficient, and polite, the perfect model for how a Roman matron should behave.

"It is as though she were lost to us," I said to Passia the evening they returned. "The fire in her is gone."

Passia was matter-of-fact. "She is lost to us. Sejanus will probably be the death of her."

"You don't know that." But as I said the words, I knew that she was right.

She took a sip of wine. "I do. Somehow, she is marked. But do not worry." Passia reached across the table and stroked my hand. "The goddess will protect her soul in life or in death."

I wished I felt assured.

The wedding took place in June, the most auspicious time of year for marriages. We gathered first in Apicius's villa for the beginning of the ritual that would proceed to Sejanus's house and Apicata's new home.

Early that morning, before the guests arrived, I asked Passia if I could be the one to bring Apicata breakfast. Apicata was pleased to see me. I put the breakfast tray down on the side table.

She took my hands in hers. "I am glad to see you this morning."

She sounded like her mother. Elegant. Adult. "I wanted to tell you how much I am going to miss you." I had such love for Apicata—she was the daughter I didn't have.

"It will be hard to leave you and Passia. You taught me there is love and laughter in this world. And good food!" She squeezed my hands and a broad grin lit up her face in a way I had not seen in months. "Oh, Thrasius, I shall miss your radish flowers and the mice you made for me out of eggs! Promise me that when I visit, you will make them for me."

I laughed. Out of all the things I had made for her to eat over the years it was the finishing touches she loved best. It made my heart sing. "I promise, little bird."

A cloud darkened her eyes and the smile slid away. "I want to tell you how much I appreciated what you tried to do for me and Casca. I will always remember that kindness."

My mouth went dry. I had no adequate words.

"Oh, I have something for you." She went to one of the chests along the wall that were packed with her belongings. When she returned she held the wind-up bird that Prokopton had given her in the market on the fateful day we met Sejanus. "It will be freer with you." She gave me the toy and hugged me tight.

The wedding activities commenced in late morning. Passia and Aelia assisted Apicata in her mother's chambers, waiting for the signal from the slaves that Sejanus was ready to take her as his bride. I stood in the gardens with the hateful groom, Apicius, family members, clients, and assorted invited guests. The sun was well on its pass upward through the sky. Slaves wandered through the crowds with glasses of honey wine and pastries to help tide people over until the wedding breakfast, which would take place after the ceremony.

One of the door slaves called out from his place. The augur had come to determine if the wedding would be propitious. I said a silent prayer to Jupiter that a flock of dark ravens would come to roost on the roof overlooking the garden. Surely that would be a sign worthy enough to call off the union! But I had no faith, and my worry overcame my hope.

The augur strode across the courtyard, and after speaking briefly to Apicius and Sejanus, he took his curled wand and drew the quadrants in the sky; a bright, cloudless patch over the Forum. Then we waited. And waited. The longer we waited, the more elated I became. I was filled with hope at the thought that the birds might fail to fly at all. It meant, at minimum, that the wedding would be on hold till more auspicious times.

I looked over at Sejanus. His toga was bright in the sunlight, his red Praetorian tunic underneath edged with gold trim for the occasion. He stood next to his father, Aelius Gallus, and Gallus's brother and Aelia's father, Lucius Aelius Lamia. The two older men seemed anxious about the lack of birds. Sejanus, however, exhibited none of the worry that the rest of the wedding party did. He gazed calmly over the garden walls where the augur had marked the right quadrant. As I watched, the slight smile on his lips transformed into a broad grin.

"There." He pointed. My eyes—and the eyes of the crowd—followed the gesture. To my dismay, a flock of white doves exploded into the sky from a point on the ground. There were at least two dozen of the unusual birds. Never had I seen so many white doves together. It stank of fraud, of purpose.

"Highly auspicious!" The augur's proclamation rang out over the garden. "White, the color of purity, bravery, and goodness. They fly upward from the lower right quadrant to the skies where Sol will warm them with his rays, shining down his power upon them as he will with Sejanus and Apicata. Their numbers signify many children. Good fortune indeed!"

The crowd cheered. Men clapped Sejanus on the back and women lined up to kiss his cheek for luck. They stopped paying attention to the doves. Even the augur had trained his attention to the platters of hot fritters being delivered from the kitchen.

I was the only one still staring at the sky when the owl, defying the light of day, cut through the lower part of the sky, over the villa rooftops, chasing a sparrow behind the flock of doves and snatching it up between its claws.

I thought my heart would stop.

Apicata had the cold beauty of a freshly carved statue when she entered the garden. She wore her dark hair braided in the traditional six locks, woven with golden fillets and fastened on the top of her head with the traditional iron spearhead. I thought about the irony of that spearhead—it was meant to symbolize the first women of Rome, the Sabine brides, taken by force to the city. And now Apicata herself was being taken by force.

Apicata's *flammeum*, the traditional flame-colored veil, which matched her shoes, fell over her hair and down her shoulders. Her lips were stained red and dark kohl lined her eyes in the Egyptian style popular with Roman women. Her white flannel gown was held in place by a golden girdle, knotted at the waist. Later Sejanus would untie that knot.

Aelia led her daughter across the grass to where Sejanus stood near the central pool, surrounded by all the wedding guests. Apicata carried a basket that held her childhood toys and the carefully folded gown of her girlhood. Apicius stepped forward to greet his daughter.

Apicata handed him the basket, her face devoid of emotion. "Father, I give you the toys and clothes of my youth. I need them no longer as I become a woman today."

Apicius accepted the basket. Unlike his daughter, sadness reflected in his eyes. "I hold your childhood treasures in my hands and commit them to memory. May Juno bless you as you walk forward into womanhood."

Aelia guided her daughter to Sejanus and placed Apicata's hand in his. Apicius handed the basket to a slave for safekeeping, and together, he and Gallus took their place in front of the couple. Apicata and Sejanus bowed their heads in reverence to their fathers. Apicius and Gallus stepped aside to let the augur stand between them for the ceremony.

I surveyed the crowd. Several guests had arrived late, including Fannia, who stood to the left of the couple. Her black wig was in a straight Egyptian style adorned with gold beads. She watched the ceremony, her face passive. She had no love for Sejanus.

Publius Octavius had also arrived late, likely invited by Sejanus. There were two men with him whom I didn't recognize. The folds under his neck jiggled as he talked.

Passia appeared next to me. She looped her arm into mine and clutched my elbow tightly with her other hand. We watched the ritual unfold.

Sejanus and Apicata faced each other and held hands. They stood in that position for a moment longer than was comfortable. Apicata seemed frozen, her eyes locked somewhere in the distance beyond Sejanus. Finally, she seemed to realize her place and she said the traditional words. "Where you are Gaius, I am Gaia."

Sejanus smiled at the words. "Where you are Gaia, I am Gaius."

The augur gestured for one of the slaves to bring forth a white sow for their sacrifice to Juno. The couple watched as the augur said a few words and, in a frighteningly quick motion, slit the animal's throat with a jeweled dagger. Blood flowed across the garden tiles. The slaves took it away and the augur circulated through the crowd to collect the appropriate number of witness signatures for the wedding contract. It was an extra blow to know Apicata's wedding contract would bear the signature of Publius Octavius.

The wedding prandium was an all-morning affair. The guests retired to couches in the atrium to eat the most elaborate breakfast I had ever devised. I couldn't bear to sit with the crowd and instead helped Timon deliver course after course of dormice in honey, more spiced fritters, platter upon platter of fried anchovies, flatbreads with goat cheese and pepper, medallions of wild boar, and individual bowls of hazelnut custard. Each dish was served on a golden tray. The guests were given gold spoons and napkins dyed in Tyrian purple—lavish gifts they could take home. In between each course, barely clad serving girls showered the guests with rose petals and helped them wash their hands.

It took three hours. I paid no attention to any conversation. Apicius was out of sorts as well, barking orders at me as though I were still his slave. I was grateful—I did not want a seat on the couches. I think Apicius was himself jealous that he could not join me in hiding in the heat of the kitchen.

Apicata was stoic. The times when I glanced over to where she reclined she seemed neither happy nor sad. She offered up no conversation but politely responded when spoken to. She laughed in all the right places. I wished I could have whisked her away to Minturnae, turning back the clock to times when she was full of laughter, playing in the sand with her dog.

Perseus rested on the floor near her feet. He was old now and walked with a limp. He would be heartbroken when he discovered he could not follow his mistress to her new home.

The time came, all too soon. Sejanus and three of his friends, soldiers by the hardened looks of them, slipped out of the atrium and into the hall. I thought I recognized one of them from that day in the market so long ago. As they disappeared, three boys entered, nephews of Fannia's, who would escort Apicata to her new home. They wore white togas belted with a red sash and, like the other guests, wreaths of laurel and marjoram. It was the part of the day I dreaded most of all—the traditional reenactment of the stealing of the Sabine brides.

Sotas emerged from the house. In his hands was the *spina alba*, a torch that had been lit at the villa's hearth and would be carried to Apicata's new home. Sotas handed it to the tallest of the boys.

At most weddings the procession was the most celebrated part of the event—everyone joined in the fun. I had no desire to do so at this wedding.

The boys moved away from the door in time for Sejanus and his friends to return to the atrium in a loud rush, yelling and screaming war cries.

Sejanus ran to the bridal couch and made to pull Apicata off the cushions and drag her away. Apicius and Aelia immediately locked their arms around their daughter to prevent the "kidnapping." Apicata screamed.

"Don't take my daughter from me! Please, sir, don't take my daughter!" Aelia shouted. The guests thought she was teasing, as she was supposed to be feigning resistance. It broke my heart to watch. Apicius joined in, "You can't have her!" He had a mad look in his eye and there was a note of anger in his voice. Apicata stared at him in alarm, seemingly recognizing that perhaps her father did have misgivings. Sejanus's friends pulled her parents away and then Apicata was in Sejanus's arms.

"No, don't make me!" Apicata's screams were shrill.

The guests laughed. Everyone thought it was part of the play but I knew Apicata wasn't playing.

"Let go of me, you oaf!" She pushed Sejanus away and unwittingly fell into the arms of his friend, who offered her up to Sejanus. He snatched her up by the waist and picked her up. She beat her hands on his chest, hard enough that I could see his face contort with annoyance that she seemed to be taking the play act too far.

He carried her out, flanked by Fannia's nephews holding the hearth fire. The guests followed, filing out of the atrium and out of the house. Passia joined Aelia and Apicius in the procession, carrying the spindle and distaff symbolizing Apicata's domestic role as Sejanus's wife, who would keep him clothed. Sotas marched behind, his bald head bobbing above the crowd.

I didn't follow. I didn't want to see the procession—how the guests would tease Apicata and Sejanus with lewd remarks as they went down the streets of the Palatine. I didn't want to watch Apicata rub the doorway of Sejanus's home with fat and oil, then wreath it in wool to demonstrate her place in the house as a homemaker. It pained me to think of her running that villa, thrust into the violent world. She was just a child!

I didn't want to see Sejanus carry her over the threshold, to see her touch fire and water, to see Aelia take her into Sejanus's chamber to pray and undress her and offer sacrifice. I didn't want to see Aelia leave the room and Sejanus enter. . . .

PART VII

13 C.E. to 14 C.E.

MILK-FED SNAILS

Take the snails, wipe them over with a sponge, take off their membranes so that they can come out (of their shells). Put them in a pot of milk and salt for the first day, and in milk alone for the remaining days, continually removing the waste matter. When they are so well fed that they cannot go back in their shells, pull them out and fry in some oil. Serve in oenogarum. They can also, in a similar way, be fed on porridge.

—Book 7.16.1, *Luxury Dishes*
On Cookery, Apicius

CHAPTER 20

It rained the day Apicius sent me to the immigrant section of Rome, the Trans Tiberim, a crowded part of the city with a mishmash of insulae and middle-class domus tumbled together along the Tiber. It was there, among the loud call of the butchers, bakers, laundries, and stone masons, that I found Glycon, the astrologer whom Fannia had recommended to Apicius.

I waited, peering again over the railing to watch the children. I thought the whole escapade to be foolish. Fannia had been trying to get Apicius to hire Glycon for years and finally she had worn him down. In true Apicius style, and against my recommendation, he was eschewing the occasional visit that Fannia preferred and intended Glycon to live within the villa and be on hand for everyday consultations. I hoped that the astrologer would turn Apicius down. I believed in the stars, as anyone should, but found it hard to believe that someone who was not a devoted priest or priestess of a god could possibly know the path that those gods charted.

Glycon lived on the fifth floor of an insula that couldn't possibly have met the building codes designed to protect Rome against fire. As I climbed the wet, rickety stairs, I prayed to Neptune to protect me against an earthquake. I found it unlikely the building would stay upright if there were a tremor. I prayed the wood beneath me wouldn't give way and drop me to my death.

My destination was a door painted on the upper portion with a crude picture of the eye of Horus. A long coiled cobra was painted on the lower half. I pondered the symbols, wondering why Apicius had sent me on this fool's errand. How he could believe in such nonsense was beyond me. I knocked.

A long moment passed—enough time for me to peer over the edge of the railing. I was afraid to touch it for fear it would fall away. The rain had slowed to a fine mist. Despite the damp weather, several children played with an inflated calfskin ball in the muddy courtyard below.

When the door opened, it was only a crack. "Yes?" said the voice, a woman's. I couldn't see anyone. Only a sliver of darkness greeted me through the crack in the door.

"My name is Thrasius. I come on the request of Marcus Gavius Apicius, who requires the services of the astrologer Glycon." I passed the thin papyrus scroll from Apicius through the crack. The woman snatched it from my hand.

"Wait," said the voice, and then the door closed.

When the door opened, a tall man stood there, dressed in a traveling robe. He was of such pale countenance, I wondered if he had ever stood in the sun. He wore his silvery hair long, drawn together with a leather thong about halfway down his back. His eyes were dark, with a rim of green that gave him a godlike quality, as if he were touched by Cybele herself. Four men stood behind him, carrying two large trunks between them.

"Thrasius, is it?"

"Yes."

He smiled. I was surprised to see how straight his teeth were. "Three ravens perched on the roof this morning, heralding the change that would bring me to your master's house. The stars are aligned. You, my good man, will take me straightaway to Gavius Apicius, where I will guide him as to the wishes of the gods."

I wondered if it was the three ravens or the three hundred sestertii promised in that letter that had aligned his stars. I led the group down the shaky staircase. I disliked astrologers but had to admit I felt a strangeness following me, heralding change. I couldn't find it in my heart to believe it would be for the better.

When we reached the villa I instructed Glycon and his attendants to wait in the coolness of the pergola, then sent one slave to fetch Apicius and another to bring honey water to the newcomers. They drank the sweet refreshment as though it were the first water they had ever had.

When Apicius arrived, he clasped hands with Glycon as though they were old friends. It made me angry that Apicius held no reservations about a complete stranger coming to live within his walls.

"Thank you for coming. Sotas will lead you to your rooms and we will talk when you are rested," Apicius said, motioning to my big friend, who waited by the door.

"Very good. Would you like for me to attend you at dinner?"

Sotas gave me a funny look. This was the first step—the request for a dinner invitation, which would extend to a permanent parasite spot at the foot of the couch, then on to other favors, and eventually, as Glycon realized how easily he could work Apicius into a frenzy, he would be ever present. I wondered how long before the man dictated nearly every step Apicius took.

"Tonight you will meet with me, Aelia, and Thrasius," Apicius said. "But on most nights you will take your meals in your chambers or elsewhere in Rome, whichever you prefer. I have a full schedule of entertainment and there is not normally room on my couches. However, this evening you may dine with us."

Glycon seemed surprised at Apicius's dour tone, but did not comment. "Certainly. And my slaves?"

"There is a cubicle adjoining your chamber where they may stay. They can dine in the kitchen at the specified hours. Timon, who runs the kitchen, can give them the schedule. They are to keep to the slave areas—I don't want to see them in the living areas of the villa. You have permission to use the rest of the house—the baths, the garden, whatever you need, with the exception of the wing where the library and our private rooms are."

"Understood. Will I have access to the roof, where I may set up tools to help me better watch the stars?"

Apicius faltered, surprised at the question. He could not know the answer, having never seen the roofs to know if there was a suitable spot.

He motioned to me. "Certainly. Thrasius will make those arrangements. By tomorrow we shall have readied a place suitable for you."

Glycon tilted his head in acceptance. It was a patient, sage movement, as though he were a wise old priest with much knowledge. I didn't believe it.

"Tonight over dinner we will discuss the various factors that will enable me to divine the future for you," Glycon said. "There is much the heavens have to say, but I need to understand where your place in the stars lies."

Sotas led Glycon and the slaves through the villa. I went along, still curious. We wound our way through the long central atrium, past the deep blue pool, through the long hallways, beyond the smells of the kitchen, and to the back of the domus, where Sotas gestured toward a midsized room flanked by a small unused cubicle. The slaves set down the trunks and immediately began the process of unpacking. One trunk appeared to hold many tools, compasses, and charts, while the other held Glycon's personal effects.

Sotas turned to leave with me but Glycon touched him on the shoulder, stopping him. A strange look had overtaken his features, turning up one side of his mouth in a slight smile.

"I see you are marked by a golden goddess."

Sotas stared at Glycon, clearly disturbed, but said nothing. He took a deep breath and backed out of the room.

What did those words mean to Sotas? I was determined to find out.

That evening, we met in the triclinium for an informal dinner. Apicius had not invited any clients, reserving the time for Glycon. I took my seat on the couch and Sotas was offered a place sitting at Apicius's feet. Passia and Helene were allowed to stay as well, Helene at Aelia's feet and Passia at mine.

While Apicius still refused to let us marry, I was pleased that he allowed me to keep Passia close. When a child of a patrician married, she was often allowed to bring her body-slave and other personal slaves with her. Apicata had refused to take Passia, saying that she would not be someone to break love in two. It was the most precious gift our little bird could ever give me. Apicius seemed to recognize the gesture. For the last two years, he had been generous, letting Passia share duties with Helene as Aelia needed. Sometimes she helped me at the school or in the kitchen.

Timon had made an egg patina of sea nettles and my favorite dish of pheasant meatballs, accompanied by green beans in a cumin sauce, hot pumpkin fritters, and slices of roasted venison. When the scissor slaves had cut our food and left, Glycon began asking questions.

"First, I need the date of your birth and those of your wife and child." He held a stylus in one hand and a wax tablet in the other, ready to take down the answers to his questions.

"And Thrasius," Apicius said, inclining his head toward me.

I didn't want to know my chart. I spoke up, hoping to get out of the obligation. "I am afraid I do not know the date of my birth. I know the year, but not the date." I wiped my napkin across a glob of sea nettle sauce on my chin. I made a mental note to mention to Timon to adjust the proportions of sauce to the vegetables.

"Unlucky, but no matter. Answer me these two questions and I will tell you."

I was skeptical that anyone save my unknown mother would have any true way of knowing the date of my birth, but on account of Apicius, I forced myself to look eager.

Glycon cocked an eyebrow at me. "In dreams, in what season do you find yourself the most?"

My dreams were always seasonless, devoid of any indicator of the exterior setting. I dreamed mostly of people, of places inside the villa, and, most often, the kitchen where I spent my time as a child learning my trade.

"Harvest." It was my favorite time of year if not a true reflection of my dreams.

Glycon made a scribble in the wax before leaning forward to pluck a meatball from the tray in front of him. He popped it into his mouth, chewed, then spoke while his mouth was still full.

"How old were you when your voice began to change?"

Passia stroked my ankle with her finger and I almost jumped.

"I was thirteen," I managed.

Glycon began to write on his tablet again. "Your day of birth is on the nones of October."

I tried to appear impressed. It was hard not to let loose a chuckle of my own. For all I knew I could have been born on the ides of Martius. Despite my ever-growing misgivings, I didn't dare laugh—Apicius took astrology and divinations very seriously.

Apicius broke in before I could say anything. "I was born twelve days before the calends of Julius, Apicata on the ides of Febrius, and Aelia was born three days before the nones of Ianuarius."

Glycon recorded the dates. "Good, good. Now I can begin a more thorough examination of the stars to determine your outcomes. But we can begin with some general observations."

Apicius waited for Glycon to continue. I knew he was doing his best to be patient but patience had never been easy for him.

"Start with me." Aelia smiled sweetly at Apicius, a smile laced with petulance and dissatisfaction. Earlier I had heard them arguing about Glycon coming to live in the house.

Glycon looked to Apicius, who nodded his reluctant assent.

"Certainly, my lady. Three days before the nones of Ianuarius? Ahh. What a good date. You love people and love to see people happy. You are honest and helpful and, above all, affectionate. When you love, you love deeply. I must tell you to take care of your ankles as they may be prone to sprains or breaks."

"Aelia, be sure to tie your sandal straps tight," Apicius said, anxious to move the conversation along. The look he gave Glycon said as much.

"I cannot tell you more without consulting the ephemeris—my star chart." The old man set his plate aside.

"Very well," Aelia said, understanding the underlying exchange. "Husband, I look to you for dismissal. I am tired this evening." Helene stood quickly to help her up. She waved her away and rose gracefully to stand in front of the couch, where she awaited Apicius's response.

"Thank you, wife, for joining us tonight," Apicius said formally. I watched her leave, her yellow stola hugging her lithe body as she walked.

Apicius signaled for the wine to be brought. "Now, Thrasius." I looked up in surprise. With his desperation to hear the astrologer's predictions, I was shocked he wanted to hear about me first.

Glycon looked across the couch at me. "You were born under the scales, a sign auspicious for butchers, cooks, and bakers alike. Venus rules your sign and you have a love for beauty and pleasure. You entertain with elegance and style."

"All true!" Apicius said eagerly. I looked at him and at Sotas, who bobbed his head. Apicius's unsightly ambition was peeking out from behind the purple-striped toga he wore. All reason departed when Apicius heard divinations about food, me, entertaining, and how those three things would comprise his future. Despite the type of divination, be it at a temple to Fortuna, at the hands of a marketplace augur, or even at last year's pilgrimage to the Oracle of Delphi, the outcome was always the same. Apicius was bound to ignore the bounty before him and the warnings of its potential loss. With each new diviner I found my pity for my former master only grow.

"So, my future?" I was already tired of the exchange.

"I will need to read more of the stars before I can tell you much, I fear. But I know you will soon have a child, born under the sign of Taurus or Gemini."

The world seemed to slow. I gripped the edge of the couch. When I felt Passia's hand tighten on my ankle, the world began to right itself.

Passia and I had long differed on our position about children. She wanted them, as did I, but I did not want to bring a life into a world of slavery. Until Passia was free, any child she bore would be owned by Apicius. And as judicious as he was toward me, he was not so about Passia. He saw her as the key to keeping me here. And if we had children? None of us would ever be free. To that end, I paid dearly for the concoction of wild carrot and artemisia Passia took to prevent pregnancy. I even took a great risk in "borrowing" a tiny pinch of silphium from Apicius every so often to infuse a jar of water for her to sip from each month. How had she conceived? She was also not young, at twenty-nine, which was worrisome. I had heard of women giving birth in their thirties, but they often did not make it through the pregnancy. I pushed the thought away.

Apicius was the first to speak. "Passia, is this true?"

She hesitated. Her eyes said everything—the truth, her fear, her hope. A surge of love for her pushed through me.

She drew a breath, her words slow and careful. "Yes, Dominus, it is. It is likely the child will be born in June."

Apicius didn't congratulate either of us. He was too taken in by the accuracy of his new astrologer. "Well done, Glycon, well done! Now tell me, what is my fate?"

I was elated, scared, and disappointed at the same time. Why hadn't Passia told me?

My lover trembled next to me and worry filled her dark eyes. My resistance melted. I could not be angry with her. Passia's hand rested on my leg and I reached down to squeeze her fingers in mine. Damn this astrologer! This was news that should have been shared between us, in private.

Glycon started coughing, tearing my attention away from Passia.

"Excuse me. In the winter I tend to congest with phlegm."

"You have had too much water," Apicius admonished. "You need to dry that humor out. I'll send a slave with a tincture later. Now tell me, what do you see for me?"

Glycon smiled. "Marcus Gavius Apicius, I see the stars aligning for you within the next three years. It will be a time of great prosperity. However, it appears—"

Apicius cut him off. "What sort of prosperity?"

I sighed. Apicius never wanted to hear what came after "however."

"The stars are never specific, but I see wealth and recognition heaped upon you. But I must warn you, there will also be as much sadness as there is success."

"I am prepared for that," Apicius remarked, taking a sip of wine. He had heard it before—the warning—in one form or another.

"Do you see any ghosts around me? My mother, perhaps?"

I was surprised to learn that Apicius still worried about Popilla. It had been years since her death.

Glycon raised an eyebrow. "I am not a priest of Pluto."

Apicius waved a hand at him. "Yes, yes, I know, but surely the stars can tell if there are any ghosts who may hinder me?"

The astrologer nodded. "Ahh. I understand. No. I do not see any influence of that sort. I think you are free of her."

Visible relief passed through Apicius.

A commotion at the door caused us all to look in that direction. One of the door slaves was whispering to Sotas.

"Gallus is here, Dominus. He says he has a shipment for you from Iberia. He is awaiting payment."

The almonds and honey we'd ordered last month had arrived. Apicius jumped up from his place on the couch. Most men of his stature would leave the receiving of goods to the housekeeper, but not Apicius. He was obsessed with looking over each order himself. I rose to follow but he waved at me to sit back down.

"Finish up with Glycon, then attend me for inspection." He departed, leaving Passia and me with the strange old man.

I seized the brief moment, feeling suddenly compelled. If he was right about Passia, perhaps there was some merit to the man. "What do you see about Apicata?" We saw her rarely. When she visited she was reserved, and often I thought I saw bruises under the edges of her stola. She spoke little of her life with Sejanus, instead turning the conversation toward Apicius's trips or food, or toward Aelia's excursions to the market or temple visits. I wanted to ask Glycon about Sejanus but it was too dangerous; the man was becoming more powerful all the time and I knew not where the astrologer's loyalties lay.

He glanced down at the tablet where he had scrawled her birth date. "I need to consult my charts. I am unprepared to tell you anything other than the general qualities for her sign. Let me compare her moon sign and I will let you know what I find."

I motioned to Tycho, who had been lingering in the hallway with the serving slaves. "Please make sure this man is taken care of. Bring food to his chamber and show him the roof as we discussed." Tycho bowed and departed.

"Why didn't you tell me?" I asked Passia as soon as we were alone.

"I was nervous. I didn't know if you would be angry with me." She kept her eyes averted.

I cupped her chin in my hand, turning her face to look upward at me. "My treasure, you should never fear me."

"I know we shouldn't have a child. But it seems the Fates have another plan for us." Tears caught at the corners of her dark eyes. I brushed them away with my thumbs.

"We'll have to figure out a better plan to buy your freedom." I took her bronze neck plate in my hand. "And when we do, we'll melt this down and make it into an amulet for the babe." I smiled.

"I do not think Dominus will ever let me go. He fears losing you too much."

I pulled her close and kissed her softly. "Then we'll have to figure out what he might fear more."

• • •

In the morning I went to the school as I always did. I was exhausted. Passia and I had lain awake late, talking, making love, and planning for the child to come. It was a night of deep emotion that felt right at the time, but as I walked to the school, I began to regret staying up all night. Even worse, as the hours of the day wore on, my attention started to drift. I found myself staring out the window when the students practiced how to wrap pork in a pastry crust, now a dish I was known for. I struggled to keep my eyes open when I realized the room had gone silent.

Someone behind me cleared his throat.

I jumped, not expecting to be interrupted from my reverie. A burst of energy rushed through me when I realized it was Apicius who stood before me.

"Master Apicius!" I realized as soon as I said the words that the title was unnecessary, a habit of the past. My face grew hot at the mistake, knowing the students were watching us intently.

"Continue!" Apicius waved a hand at the class. Reluctantly everyone turned back to their dough.

"To what do I owe the pleasure?" I said, hoping my voice didn't reveal my nervousness. Apicius hadn't come to the school in more than a year, trusting me to manage it entirely.

"Let's step into your private rooms and talk." He looked serious, his brow wrinkled, as if he were pondering a difficult problem.

I left the class in Tycho's trusted hands. I followed Apicius out of the kitchen and down the hall to my room, where I worked on the cookbooks and wrote out the recipes I had tested in the kitchen.

Apicius walked over to my desk and picked up one of the wax tablets with one of the latest recipes for our cookbook on meats. He scanned the words, put the tablet down, and leaned against the desk.

"It's time, Thrasius." Apicius looked at me gravely, fingering the purple edge of his toga.

"Time for what, sir?" The end of my employment? To sell Passia? To take a trip? Expand the school? What on earth could warrant this visit?

He reached into the folds of his toga and pulled out a small papyrus scroll. The red wax seal indicated it was a legal document. My heart leaped so high I thought it would escape my body and soar toward the sky. Oh, Jupiter! Was he going to give Passia to me?

Apicius handed me the scroll with a broad smile. I rarely saw joy in him anymore. He spent much of his time and energy on how to convince Sejanus to come through on his promise to lessen Publius Octavius's influence in Caesar's villa, especially now that Caesar's health was failing.

"Open it!" he urged. I was reminded of Apicata as a child, wanting me to read her a poem.

I unrolled the scroll. It took me a moment to register the contents. When I did, a bolt of disappointment as wide as the hand of Jupiter slapped me to earth.

It was the deed to the school.

"Well?"

"I don't know what to say, sir."

Apicius took my surprise for pleasure. "There are two caveats."

"And they are?" I squeaked, still staring at the scroll. I scanned the page for the fine print, which I found as he spoke his next words.

"The school keeps my name and I continue to receive ten percent of the proceeds."

It took everything I had not to burst out laughing. The school barely broke even! My heart sank. How on earth was I going to manage the costs of the school on my own?

I didn't have the heart to show him how disappointed I was. "Thank you. I am without words to express my gratitude at this gesture." I forced a smile.

"Good!" He clapped his hands on my shoulders and pulled me in for a rare hug. "You deserve this more than anyone I know."

Indeed. But why did this seem more like a punishment than a reward?

Then I understood. "Did Glycon put you up to this?" I asked.

Apicius chuckled. He squeezed my shoulder again. "Only partly. He suggested I take a look at my investments—that some would be better in another's hands than in mine."

How gullible could he be? Of course Glycon would want a say in Apicius's investments! I started coughing to hide my dismay.

"Careful there," Apicius admonished, clapping me on the back.

• • •

That evening Apicius and Aelia were away, dining at Trio and Celera's villa down the street. To my dismay, Glycon was holding court in the atrium when I arrived. He was lounging on a chaise, eating a bowl of grapes and entertaining questions from Passia and a handful of other slaves. A curtain of irritation fell across my mood.

I sat down next to Passia. "Leave us," I said with a wave to the other slaves, who immediately scurried away.

"He's a trickster," Balsamea hissed as she shuffled by. Her health had been failing and it pained me to see how slowly she moved. "He is bad news, bad news," she muttered as she left the room, leaning on her cane.

Glycon never heard a word. "Thrasius! I hear you are a lucky man today!" He waggled a jeweled finger at me.

"Apicius gave me the school," I explained to Passia. There was no joy in the admission.

She, however, thought it was wonderful. "That's fantastic, Thrasius!"

Tycho entered, bringing me a glass of wine from my stores. I took it, grateful that he was so intuitive. I sipped the wine, willing myself to stay calm. Glycon had turned my life upside down and I wasn't happy about it.

The astrologer seemed to recognize my discontent and changed the subject. "You asked about Mistress Apicata?"

Passia perked up beside me. "Please, tell us what you know of her stars."

As the words slipped from her mouth I realized there was a part of me that did not want to know.

"Her stars are tangled. They darken and shade the planets. She will have more babes but I fear they may not live to see the age of their grandfather Apicius."

"What do you mean? They will be stillborn?" Passia placed a hand protectively on her stomach.

"No, my lady. They will grow, but, alas, I do not see how their paths will lengthen as she becomes older."

My patience had run out. "Stop being cryptic, old man. Be frank. You might want to sugarcoat it for Apicius but don't for me."

Glycon stared at me, saying nothing, just stroking his damn beard. I did not break the stare. Eventually, he nodded. "Apicata leads a troubled life. I see a difficult marriage for her. She will have two more children but I cannot see their stars in Apicata's future. This could mean several things. It could mean they will die. It could mean they will be sent away, or it could merely mean they will be insignificant. The stars are not precise."

Oh, Jupiter! I prayed that my first impressions and Balsamea were right, and the astrologer was a sham, but it was hard to have conviction. He knew about our babe and he knew something that had disarmed Sotas.

Unease crept over me. I suspected it would be a long while before it departed.

Over the next few weeks, Glycon began spending every midday meal with Apicius and sometimes in the evening he would be invited to dine on our couch. I took on extra students to help raise more revenue to keep the school afloat, so when I wasn't helping Apicius manage his clients or working with Timon on plans for a banquet, I was at the school teaching. I had two motives: to stay as far away from Glycon as I could, and to raise enough money to purchase Passia.

One morning after the salutatio, Sotas—who had a rare day off—walked with me to the market even though the brothel was his ultimate destination.

"What did Glycon mean when he said you were marked by a golden goddess?" I asked. It had been bothering me since that first day when the astrologer had become ensconced in the household.

Sotas looked at me, eyes wide, which prevented him from seeing the branch in his path. He stumbled. I caught him by the arm to steady him. "It's the biggest ones who fall the hardest."

That earned a hearty guffaw from Sotas. He became more serious. "You took me by surprise, that's all."

Few ever took Sotas by surprise. "He was right?" I asked.

"The astrologer was referring to something no one knows about," Sotas said in a voice unusually quiet for him.

Curiosity overrode my decorum. "Something from your childhood?"

Sotas hesitated, which filled me with shame. If he had never discussed it before, why assume he would share the secret with me?

"I was fourteen." Sotas kicked a stone with his sandal and it skittered ahead. "Marcus Gavius Rutilus had just purchased me for Apicius. On the second day of my new service Rutilus took me to the temple of Fides on the Capitoline. When we arrived we first went to make a sacrifice, but as we knelt at the altar, a priest tapped me on the shoulder. He told me the goddess wanted to speak to me."

I almost laughed aloud but saw how solemn Sotas was and bit my tongue.

"I followed him and he brought me to the goddess's chamber and told me to wait. I knelt on the mat in the center of the room. I have never known such fear as I did that day."

"I can imagine," I said, hoping I sounded sincere.

Sotas slowed his pace. We were nearing the stairs that led down toward the Forum Boarium at the base of the Palatine Hill. I could hear the lowing of cattle and the sounds of the auctioneers rattling off the prices of the livestock.

He kept his eyes averted as he continued, instead looking out over the market below. "I waited for a long time. When I thought I could wait no longer, a bright light appeared at the top of the stairs behind the throne of the goddess at the far end of the chamber. A door opened and sunlight poured in, temporarily blinding me. When I could see again, the figure of a woman was coming down the stairs and across the chamber toward me. She was the most beautiful woman I had ever seen, even more beautiful than my mother. She seemed to shine like gold in the sunlight coming from the doorway and the tiny windows around the room."

I knew what was coming. Stories like this were common, yet Sotas was so wrapped in this memory, so full of reverence, I dared not burst his bubble.

"She came to me and blessed me with a kiss to my lips. I thought I would faint. She told me I had one task in life—that she had gifted my life in service to Master Apicius, and if I served him well in my life I would be rewarded richly when I went to Elysium."

Inwardly, I sighed. It wasn't a common practice so it didn't surprise me that Sotas had not discovered the deceit. He was in such earnest I could not tell him that meeting Fides was likely a sham, a result of a contract between Apicius's father, Gavius Rutilus, and the temple. Sometimes if a slave owner wanted to deeply embed loyalty or fear into a young and impressionable slave, he would pay for one of the priests to appear as the god delivering a message. When Maximus owned me, I once overheard a priest of Juno telling the story of how they performed this service—at great cost—to willing patrons.

It explained a lot to me about Sotas, in particular, why he rarely expressed a negative opinion about Apicius. I had asked him before but he would always divert the conversation. I never understood. Other body-slaves I knew were not so content in the service of their owners. Rutilus was a shrewd man, gifting Apicius with a slave who would be loyal to him until the day he died.

"How did Glycon know?" I wondered aloud.

"Maybe there is more to the stars than we thought." Sotas began the descent into the market. I followed, musing to myself about the more likely possibility that Glycon knew about the ritual.

For the first time in many weeks there were no guests at cena. I was pleased; the quiet family meals were the ones I tended to enjoy best. Timon made our favorite dishes, which somehow were always the ones that were most simple. That night it was fig cakes, sweet wine biscuits, Parthian chicken, lamb and almond meatballs, and soft plaited bread made from olive oil and goat milk. Aelia was unusually lively, clearly delighted to have us to herself. Sotas was the only figure missing for me. Instead, another of Apicius's bodyguards took his place while he enjoyed the night off.

When the first course was being cleared, Glycon strolled in casually as though he had lived in the villa forever and need not attend the dining table unless it suited him. He lay down on the couch next to me and took up a strand of grapes in one hand. "Don't let me interrupt the conversation, please," he said with a wave of his hand. The mood of the table immediately soured.

Apicius was even more irritated than Aelia and I were. "Need I remind you, Glycon, that you are under my pay, under my roof, eating my food, and subject to my rules and invitations? And I do not recall extending an invitation to you for dinner tonight, or for last night, or for the night before. At least, if you have the audacity to crash my dinners, you do so on time."

Glycon's mouth opened in shock. Clearly he thought he held the upper hand. He set the grapes down. "My apologies, Apicius. I did not mean to be late."

"I'm starting to tire of his nonchalance, husband." Aelia's voice was as cold as water in winter.

Apicius picked up his glass of absinthe, fresh from a batch I had made the previous weekend. "Tell me, Glycon, what do the stars tell you today? Make yourself useful if you plan on being here tonight."

Aelia and I exchanged a glance. I suspected she was fuming as much as I was—Apicius was never so lenient with slaves, clients, or his freedmen. If I had strolled in late for cena he would have kicked me out of the room in a heartbeat, and I was one of the closest people to him.

"It's good you asked, Apicius. It's why I was tardy this evening, in fact." Glycon picked up the grapes again, his confidence visibly returning.

Oh, he knew how to make a good recovery.

"Explain," Apicius said loudly, to be heard over the clanking of dishes as the next course was served to us.

"The stars were particularly clear tonight. The moon is in Gemini, which is good for your ambition. You will need to have patience. If you do, I see things changing for you. As you know, Caesar is ailing—I checked his stars and I do not see his health lasting for more than a year or two—and Tiberius may take his place soon. Then there will be opportunity for you. And with the star Cynosura controlling your fortune over the next five years . . ."

"Five?" Apicius said, aghast.

"Yes, do not worry! It is good. It means you will have the opportunity for great success over the next five years as Cynosura moves through this portion of sky. If Caesar does not last beyond the next year, you will have the chance to make your move when his household staff changes."

"Excellent." Apicius drained his wineglass. "Thank you. I'll send for you tomorrow."

Glycon stopped chewing the morsel of lamb he had popped into his mouth. He swallowed the meat, gathered up his robe, and stood. "Yes, Apicius."

Before he had the chance to leave I stopped him with a touch to his arm. I decided to take a chance. "You look familiar, Glycon, and it just occurred to me why. You remind me of someone I used to see when I would visit the temple of Fides every year for the goddess's October festival."

Glycon smiled despite his abrupt dismissal. "Ah, yes. I was a priest there for many years. You have a good memory." He turned back to Apicius. "Good night."

Good night, indeed.

CHAPTER 21

My son, Junius, was born on the ides of Junius, after Passia endured a short labor with no complications. I had prayed heavily to the goddess of childbirth, Juno Lucina, for the safety of my lover, and praised the goddess that she answered my pleas! I repaid my debt by naming my son after her. Everything about Junius was perfect. All his fingers and toes intact, his dark eyes shining, the wail healthy and strong. I did not know how I could be filled with more pride, save if my son had been born free.

Apicius showered me with gifts when the boy was born. He took an instant liking to the child and seemed to delight in playing with him, trying to make him smile. It surprised us all—I had never imagined Apicius being friendly with any child save Apicata, and certainly not a tiny babe. Aelia told me wistfully once that he was not even so loving to Apicata when she was that age.

From the beginning Junius seemed to be a talker, making all sorts of gurgling and cooing sounds. By the time he was two months old, I was convinced he was trying to emulate our words, although Passia assured me it was my wishful thinking.

"Perhaps he'll be a famous orator, or a poet like Virgil," I mused to Passia one morning as we lay in bed cuddling while she suckled the babe at her breast.

"As long as he doesn't become an actor!" Passia joked.

"No!" I was horrified at the thought. Actors were base and full of vice. "We will raise him better than that."

I rubbed my boy's little toes, marveling at their perfection. "Did you hear about Glycon's latest prediction?"

Passia stroked Junius's head, already growing thick with dark hair. "What now?"

"Do you remember how Caesar Augustus saw the eagle at the census ceremony at the Pantheon last week?"

"Yes. How the eagle landed in the *A* of Agrippa's name?"

"Right. He was terrified of the import and Tiberius finished the ritual for him. Well, it seems Glycon took it as a sign too. Last night at the cena he predicted Caesar would die within the month."

Passia snorted. "That's not much of a prediction! Anyone can tell Caesar has not long to live. Before Junius was born, when we were at the games for Apollo, I remember thinking it was a miracle of the gods he was able to stand on his own two feet!"

Together we laughed until Junius was smiling along with us.

One day, a few months after Junius's birth, I began my morning by heading to the Forum Piscarium to see what fish I could feature as the centerpiece for the evening cena. Apicius had invited Sejanus and Apicata, and everything needed to be as impressive as possible. As he was wont to do, Apicius planned on haranguing Sejanus about making the right connections with the Imperial palace. I was dreading the evening as much as I looked forward to it. I wanted to see Apicata desperately. We saw little of her despite the fact that she lived only a short walk away. Aelia visited her frequently but it would not be seemly for me to try to visit. Seeing her healthy would calm my soul.

The market was busier than usual. Several ships had docked at the same time, their sails making the Tiber seem like it was swarming with butterflies. The stink of fish was heavy in the air and the market was loud with men yelling out the prices of their catch. Colorful awnings kept the sun off the marble-topped tables where the fish were laid out on display. Some fish were still alive in big jars of seawater sitting alongside the tables. Occasionally a fish would jump up and create a splash or would tumble off the side of the jar onto the pavement, where it would flap wildly until the fishmonger swooped it up and threw it back into the jar.

At the far end of the market two dozen soldiers had gathered around a merchant's booth where some of the larger fish were sold. As I came closer I realized they were bodyguards for the tall man who looked over the fish on the table. It took me a moment to realize it was Tiberius. I hadn't seen him in nearly ten years, since Drusus and Livilla's wedding. He had been away for so long, and when he was home he preferred to stay out of the public eye.

Caesar's heir stood taller than most of the crowd. He had broad shoulders and handsome features, with short-cropped dark hair starting to show hints of gray. He wore the traditional garb of a Roman general and his sword hung against his thigh. One of his men carried his red feathered helmet. Why was he at the market?

When I neared and could hear the conversation, it made more sense. Tiberius seemed to be checking on permits. There was always corruption among the stall owners, who often rented out their tables for a profit and failed to give the proper tax to the Empire. Every few months Caesar would send his men to enforce what was due. Tiberius probably came to help put the fear of Augustus into them all.

I edged closer until I could see the fishmonger and the swath of fish on the table in front of him. He was a small man, of slender frame and dark eyes. He wore a thick apron and a broad hat to keep out the sun.

"Glad to see everything is in order."

I recognized that voice. Sejanus.

Sure enough, as I pushed closer to see, he moved into view. He shook the fishmonger's hand and walked the length of the stall, Tiberius at his side.

"What a beautiful catch this morning," Tiberius remarked. He paused to look over the fish. "And look at that fat red mullet! Someone will be happy tonight. I'll eat my hat if that mullet isn't bought by Apicius or Publius Octavius!"

"It's a very fine mullet." The fishmonger held it up for better viewing. "It's the largest you will find, at four and a half pounds."

Tiberius nodded his approval.

As Sejanus turned to look at the mullet he caught my eye in the crowd.

"Look, here's Apicius's man now!" He waved me forward.

I came close, my heart pounding. I had never been surrounded by so many soldiers before nor had I ever been so close to Tiberius, the man destined to be the next Caesar.

"Apicius will be glad of that fish for his supper, I expect!" Tiberius gave me a grin and nod of the head.

"In truth, I'll be glad of that mullet tonight." Sejanus laughed. "Considering I'll be dining on his couch!"

"Well, in that case"—Tiberius waggled a finger at the fishmonger—"sell this man your mullet!"

The fish was bigger than any mullet I had ever seen by at least two hands. It glistened red, its scales reflecting the light. Its gray eye was wide and dull but somehow seemed to be looking right at me.

"How much?" I hoped my nervousness didn't show.

"Fifteen sestertii." The fishmonger grinned.

No wonder he was smiling. It was an exorbitant price despite the fish's size.

I started to say "Fine," but was cut off.

"I'll give you twenty-five sestertii." The voice, stern and deep, came from somewhere behind my right ear.

I looked over my shoulder. A man had pushed himself through the guard and now he came to stand by my side. Buccio. Why did he have to show up now?

Sejanus called out over the crowd, "And here's Octavius's man!"

"Ha! What are the chances?" Tiberius chuckled.

I couldn't let Buccio outbid me or Apicius would have my head. "One hundred sestertii." It was six times what I would normally have paid for a fish of that size.

"Two hundred fifty sestertii." Buccio looked smug.

My nervousness was turning to anger. I could not justify spending so much on a damn fish! "Four hundred fifty sestertii." I barely managed to push the words past my lips.

"Eight hundred sestertii."

A crowd had begun to gather, both to gawk at Tiberius and to see what bidding madness was taking place.

I hoped that if I greatly upped the price Buccio would stop bidding. "Two thousand sestertii." The crowd went wild. My stomach was churning. I'd paid that much for a pair of new donkeys last week.

It didn't work. He smiled at me sweetly, as a man would at a child.

"Five thousand sestertii."

I looked at Tiberius and Sejanus, dumbfounded. Slaves often sold for less. Both seemed to be waiting to see what I would do next. If I walked away, what would be the outcome? Would Tiberius appreciate my sensibility or would he be displeased? What would Sejanus say to Apicius at dinner if I failed to bring home the fish?

The fish had huge smooth pink-red scales. It had been sitting in the open air longer than I cared to think about. The eye gleamed at me.

"I concede. I cannot be such a fool to pay so much for a fish." It came out bitterly but I did not appreciate being humiliated.

Buccio flashed his teeth at me. "Caesar won't think Publius Octavius a fool when he is dining on such a catch tonight, I assure you." He handed the fishmonger a pouch.

The merchant beamed, looking like a boy on Saturnalia morn opening presents. Five thousand sestertii was as much as he was likely to make in a year.

"May Roma leave her blessing upon you," I said formally to Tiberius and Sejanus with a deep nod. I made to leave.

"I will be sad not to dine on that fish," Sejanus said.

I looked back and responded, mostly for Tiberius's benefit, "I promise you a meal far superior, sir."

Tiberius and Sejanus chuckled as I walked away.

I vowed there would be no fish at all that night. Instead I headed for the Forum Suarium. Nothing but the finest pig would fill our bellies.

On the way to my room I ran into Glycon. "How was your day?" He looked at me as though he already knew the answer.

"It has been bad but I intend to make it good." Maybe if I was as cryptic as he was he would leave me alone.

"As the stars said." He gave me a slight, sage smile and walked on.

I stayed in my cubicle as long as I dared. I hated being in the same room with Sejanus, and facing both him and Apicius was doubly bad. When Sejanus visited, Apicius became cruel and said biting things to the slaves and sometimes to Aelia. He was like a two-headed Janus, showing one face to Sejanus, and the other, uglier one to the rest of us.

When I heard the slaves announce Sejanus's arrival I couldn't dally any longer. I ran down the corridors to the atrium, arriving when Apicius did, Sotas in tow.

"I am pleased you and Apicata could join us tonight," Apicius said.

Sejanus held Apicius by the shoulder for a moment, as one would an old friend. I thought I saw Apicius tense up but the moment passed. Sejanus didn't notice.

"My wife is more pleased, I suspect. She has been haranguing me to come for a visit."

"I imagine your schedule is hectic," I said, slipping the words in to make my presence known.

"That is true, especially of late. Thrasius, my man, good to see you for the second time today!"

I tilted my head and smiled, hoping my loathing for him didn't show on my face. I was not his man.

"Second time?" Apicius indicated we should walk with him toward the triclinium.

"We saw each other at the market this morning," I responded, hoping Sejanus would leave it at that.

Fortuna was not smiling down on me.

"I must say, that red mullet would have been a fine meal tonight. Tell me you have another delicacy for us instead?"

I cleared my throat, knowing Apicius would have my head later. "I do. I promise it will be pleasing."

Apicius glared at me. It was a gaze I did not want to be under. "What was wrong with the mullet?"

"It was more money than I cared to spend." I knew it was the wrong thing to say. I should have mentioned how long that fish was out in the sun, but the words were already out of my mouth.

"Tiberius and I were inspecting the Forum Piscarium this morning and we saw the finest red mullet we had ever seen. Tiberius joked that either you or Octavius would buy it up. Then we saw Thrasius standing next to us! Imagine our delight! Then, just as he would pay for the mullet, one of Octavius's slaves appeared with a higher bid! The gods were listening to Tiberius!" Sejanus said.

Apicius was not amused. I could not see his face as he walked in front of me but his tone was dark. "Didn't you counterbid?"

"Oh, yes," Sejanus broke in. "It was a proper bidding war!" He clapped me on the shoulder as though I were a fellow soldier.

"And why didn't you win?" Apicius asked.

Sejanus smirked at me.

Bastard! Sejanus found the situation amusing! If I had still been a slave, I would have already been whisked away to have my back scarred with the lash.

"I could have bought three goats for the price of that fish." I tried to sound assertive, not defensive.

"Yes, but you know expense is not a concern."

In the outdoor triclinium Aelia, Apicata, and Passia were already reclining, a small retinue of serving boys fanning them. Sotas took a spot standing nearby in the trees behind the couch.

"It was brilliant," Sejanus said as we crossed the threshold. "Driving up the price to stick it to him."

I almost stopped in my tracks. Did he really think that? I had merely dropped out of the bidding when I couldn't, in good conscience, pay that much for a few pounds of flesh from the sea.

Apicius didn't say anything else but the warning look he gave me was enough.

We joined the ladies on the couches and Aelia whispered in Apicius's ear as he sat down. He took a look at Passia and begrudgingly gave his assent. As a slave, for her to dine on the couch with guests present was generally unacceptable, but Aelia knew he wasn't going to make a scene in front of Sejanus. I loved her for the kindness. She knew how much spending time with Passia would mean to Apicata.

The serving boys arrived as soon as we took our seats. They wore halos of gold in honor of Sol, whose holiday was the next day. The plates were Apicius's best gold, polished to a brilliant shine. The cushions of the couch were an airy white and yellow. I had found some exquisite sun-shaped lanterns in the market that hung from poles in the earth.

The first trays the boys held were laden with the best of summer's bounty—melons with pepper, dates stuffed with fine Iberian almonds, sweet flower bulbs, and honeyed plums.

"You have outdone yourself, Father." Apicata looked at me and I winked at her.

"Truly magnificent," Sejanus agreed, skewering a bulb with the sharp end of his spoon. "A fitting send-off before my long week away."

"Where are you going?" Aelia sounded tired. I wasn't sure why—

Helene said she spent much of her time sleeping late into the morning and often retiring again in the afternoon.

Sejanus finished chewing the bulb. "Tiberius is traveling to Illyricum tomorrow to formally recognize the province as Roman. Caesar is riding with him to Beneventum, and may stop at Nola."

"Will you ride the whole way?" I asked.

"For some of it. I suspect Tiberius or Caesar will have me ride with them for at least a few legs. But otherwise, yes, a long ride ahead."

Passia shifted against me. She, wisely, had remained silent so far and would likely not speak unless directly asked a question. To do so would be to face Apicius's wrath later. Even when I was a slave and his favorite, I dined on the couch only as a shadow, never reclining like nobility. He tolerated her presence only for Apicata.

Apicius leaned forward on the couch. "How is Caesar's health?"

Sejanus threw back his head and laughed. "Dear father-in-law, you are too transparent."

"I know not what you mean, son." Apicius was doing a good job of looking wounded but I knew the anger that seethed within his breast at the insult.

Sejanus grew serious. "Fear not, good Apicius. I have not forgotten. Your turn will come! But time, my friend . . . It takes time. Even if Caesar dies tomorrow, I still have Livia to contend with."

"I did not mean—"

Sejanus cut Apicius off. "No offense taken, Father. But know this is an issue near to my heart. Publius Octavius is a pompous bastard and, unlike you, I do not consider him a friend."

Apicius smiled but the twitch of his nostrils gave him away to me. He was angry and struggling to contain himself. He was not accustomed to such rudeness from anyone.

Apicata, wise child that she was, saved her father from saying something embarrassing by changing the subject. "Thrasius, tell us about the rest of the meal. I know you must have something delicious planned next."

Apicius directed his attention at me. "Yes, Thrasius. In lieu of the red mullet, what are we eating tonight?"

The tone of his voice wasn't lost on anyone. I ignored the implications. "Instead of the mullet, I purchased a sow that had just given birth.

I think you will be pleased. First you will savor the vulva, in the peak of perfection, seasoned with pepper, liquamen, and some spiced wine."

"Oh, it sounds divine!" Aelia exclaimed.

"I'm impressed." Sejanus nodded in approval. "I've had the delicacy once before, many years ago."

I noted Apicius's expression was beginning to soften into approval. "Then the udder, first stuffed with salted sea urchins ground with pepper and caraway, then boiled and served in a mustard sauce. To finish off the main course, its stomach, stuffed with the pig's own meat and brains, pounded and mixed with eggs, pine nuts, pepper, anise, ginger, and a pinch of silphium before boiling. I've asked Timon to serve that with olive oil, liquamen, and a sprinkling of lovage."

"Much better than any old red mullet!" Seeing Apicius smile lifted a weight off my chest.

Sejanus chuckled. "Apicata tells me mullet is one of your favorites. Is that true?"

"Yes. There is something divine about a red mullet cooked tenderly in its own juices. Next time you dine with us, Thrasius will make sure we have mullet."

He winked at me and I thanked the gods my transgression seemed to be forgiven.

Mostly forgiven. "You courted the favor of the gods today," he said to me after we escorted Apicata and Sejanus to their litter. "You prepared an excellent meal tonight. But, Thrasius . . ."

I looked at him. His face was grave. "Yes?"

"Never put me in such a position again. Do you understand?"

"Perfectly."

"Good." He took Aelia by the arm and led her away, Sotas in tow. I bored a hole in his back with my eyes until the corridor swallowed them up.

Glycon's prediction came true. A week and a half later, Caesar died at the family villa in Nola where his father had died years before.

Augustus was seventy-six, dying a month short of his birthday. He had reigned over the Empire for nearly forty-one years. His body was carried to Rome on the shoulders of senators and soldiers from the area. Tiberius was named his heir and businesses closed for the day of his funeral.

We went to the funeral along with almost all of Rome. The procession was magnificent. First, the trumpets playing dark dirges, then the slaves freed in Caesar's will, sporting their new freedman caps.

The body was laid out in a golden coffin on a bier of ivory and gold, covered in the deep Imperial purple. Slaves carried gold statues of Caesar and his ancestors. The family walked behind, led by Livia in a long black stola and shawl, with a sash of purple. All the senators followed and then the Praetorian Guard, led by Sejanus on a lone, ink-black horse.

Tiberius and his son Drusus gave the eulogy, a stirring speech proclaiming Augustus's place among the pantheon of Roman gods. Their words left Aelia in a mess of tears. Helene had to wipe her eyes lest the kohl run onto her pale cheeks.

The procession wound through the streets to the Campus Martius, where, years earlier, Caesar had built a magnificent mausoleum for his ashes to rest. They lit the funeral pyre in the field before the entrance. The pyre, like the mausoleum and as befitting the deified Augustus, was larger than any I had ever seen or imagined. The flames rose toward the skies and perfumes were thrown onto the pyre. An eagle flew up when the flames were at their peak and the entire crowd murmured that they could see the spirit of our dead leader follow.

A team of gladiators fought alongside the flames. Their blood would feed the ghosts hungering for tribute. "It's beautiful, and terrible," Aelia said through the shawl held over her nose to mask the smell of fire and flesh. Apicius pulled her close.

"It is far more beautiful than terrible, I think." Apicius seemed to glow in the light, the flames dancing in his eyes. "His death marks a new beginning."

"I find it sad that Apicius revels in the death of one who will become a god," Passia whispered to me.

"I too. But if he becomes a god, won't he know?" Even I knew better than to anger the gods with the blasphemy Apicius courted with his delight that Caesar had passed this life.

"What harms Apicius may harm us." She linked her arm around my waist and I clasped her tight.

"I know, dear one. I know."

The wind began to blow and ashes kissed my skin. At home that night we would wash them out of our hair.

PART VIII

18 C.E. to 20 C.E.

DORMICE

Stuff the dormice with pork forcemeat and also with all the flesh from all the parts of the dormouse, pounded with pepper, pine nuts, silphium, and liquamen. Sew them up and arrange them on a tile and put them into the oven or cook them, stuffed, in a covered pot.

—*Book 8.9, Quadrupeds*
On Cookery, Apicius

CHAPTER 22

"Glycon says that it's time Sejanus fulfilled his promise. Good thing, because I'm tired of waiting," Apicius said to me as he climbed into his litter. In the years that followed Glycon's prediction of Caesar's death, Apicius had become more and more concerned about signs and prophecies, much to my chagrin. I was very much his most trusted adviser, and as a result, I spent far less time in the kitchen and teaching. I missed the feel of knives in my hands and dough under my fingernails. Instead I was both sounding board and verbal punching bag for my former master. Apicius expected me to follow him everywhere, in the event he wanted council.

That day it was to Sejanus's villa on the other side of the Palatine, a short distance from Tiberius's Imperial domus.

The "promise" he spoke of was that of Apicius becoming Caesar's gastronomic adviser. When Augustus died, Apicius continued to ask Sejanus to work his wiles on Tiberius Caesar, including sidestepping any of Livia's concerns. Sejanus had ever-growing favor with Caesar and it galled my former master to no end that he was not using his politics to benefit Apicius.

Apicius didn't invite me to ride with him in the litter as he was often wont to do. I was glad. It was a short walk and Sotas was always better company.

"I fear he may do something rash," I said to Sotas.

Sotas chuckled. "And that would be unusual, how?"

"I know. But if it angers Sejanus, it may be bad for Apicata."

"What recourse does Dominus have if Sejanus can't make him gastronomic adviser?"

I shrugged. "I imagine Apicius will stop funneling money to him. Apicata's dowry will likely shrink."

"Is that wise? To cross the new prefect?"

It was my turn to laugh, though it was bitter. "I thought we already established that Apicius was apt to do something rash."

I had sent a messenger ahead about our arrival, and when we reached Sejanus's villa, Apicata, flanked by a Thracian body-slave, was at the door waiting for us. She held her son, Aelius Strabo, who was nearly three, by the hand. She was pregnant again and her belly rounded the folds of her stola.

Apicata gave the child to her slave, threw her arms around her father, then me, and, despite what decorum dictated, even Sotas. "I'm delighted to see you. Please come in."

It had been months since we talked. Aelia visited with Apicata often but she rarely came to our villa anymore, despite the proximity. There were dark circles under her eyes. She seemed far older than twenty-one, with barely any trace of the child I had once known visible in the features of her face.

"Sejanus is waiting for you in the library. Be warned, he's in a foul temper."

Her father's smile only widened. "What I have to say may sweeten his demeanor."

Apicata's eyes narrowed. She looked at me and I shrugged. Rash indeed!

She left the babe with the slave and led us through the corridors of the villa. We didn't speak much along the way; Apicata seemed nervous and Apicius was never good at small talk. The house was smaller than Apicius's abode but as sumptuously decorated, with brightly colored, highly detailed frescoes on every wall. At the doors to the library two guards prevented anyone from disturbing the occupant within. "Announce to Sejanus that his guest has arrived," Apicata said to the taller of the guards. He knocked and ducked inside.

"I must go. I'll wait for you in the atrium to see you before you depart." Apicata kissed her father on the cheek and left.

In a moment the guard returned and ushered us in. Sejanus's library looked like a war room. Maps covered the tables, some littered with colored soldiers carved of wood. Imperial banners decorated the walls. The only scrolls in sight appeared to be letters, not books. Sejanus's body-slave sat on a stool near the door. He was a thin, bald man. His bronze slave plaque gleamed around his neck. Sotas and I took standing positions to one side of him.

Sejanus reclined in a chair in the corner of the room. A small jug of wine was propped up on the table next to him. He wore a red tunic belted with a finely woven white cord and his sandals looked shabby in comparison. It was the first time I had seen him dressed in anything other than his guard uniform. All of our previous meetings had been at state affairs and at formal parties.

"You surprise me with a visit today, Apicius." He did not rise from his chair nor did he offer Apicius a seat. "Let me guess. You think I have forgotten our deal."

"No," Apicius began. "I wanted . . ."

Sejanus cut him off with a wave of his hand. "Patience! You must be patient!" He stood and slammed his hand down on the table next to him."

Apicius did not back down. "I have been patient long enough."

The silence was awkward and uncomfortable.

"Did you forget that I can do you more harm than good, father-in-law?"

Apicius ignored the threat. He walked across the room and seated himself in one of the ornately carved chairs across from where Sejanus stood. "You have been married to my daughter for seven years. I gave her to you under an agreement that the gods were witness to. I came to have you honor this agreement."

"The gods be damned!"

My heart raced and I fought to keep my features impassive. I could not dismiss the gods like he could and I sent my prayers to them now for protection. The only thing I wanted at that moment was to leave that chamber alive.

"I came to discuss the arrangement."

Sejanus paced across the library and looked out the window. "What do you intend? To rethink your daughter's dowry? I warn you, Apicius, that may not be a decision you want to make," he growled.

"On the contrary, my son. I intend to increase it. Not only that, but you need to bring new life to Caesar's couches. What I offer will be highly beneficial for all your business arrangements. You know that Octavius does not hold the culinary imagination like I do."

Sejanus turned away from the window. "Is that so?"

"Yes. But you know what I require."

Sejanus crossed his arms. "How much is the increase you speak of?"

"Sixteen thousand sestertii a year."

Rash wasn't the word for it, I decided. *Stupid* was more accurate. Sixteen thousand sestertii was likely more than Apicius would receive in salary from Caesar if he got the post.

Sejanus looked past us to the body-slave at the door. "Take these men to the atrium to await their master." He pointed at Sotas and me.

Sotas protested in a hesitant whisper. "Dominus, I don't think that is wise."

"Go, Sotas," Apicius said calmly, without emotion.

The slave ushered us out the door. Apicata was waiting to see us in the atrium. She led us to a cozy corner with benches covered in cushions the color of rubies. Sotas waited near the door, anxious about leaving his master alone.

"I cannot tell you how much I have missed you," Apicata said, her eyes full of emotion.

I took her hands in mine. "Please, Apicata, tell me he treats you well."

She closed her eyes for a moment and I realized she was trying to muster courage. "He mostly ignores me, save when he decides he has an obligation to try to beget a child, when he is tired of bedding the slaves, or when he is feeling cruel. Then I am often the target of his wrath."

"He beats you?" Sotas asked. I had never heard such anger in Sotas's voice, low as it was. He paced the tiles, not looking at any of us.

"Sometimes."

I rubbed her hand. I didn't know what to say to give her comfort. Anger swelled beneath my breast. Why hadn't the curse on Sejanus worked?

"He won't let me visit friends. I have only one slave I trust, Niobe." She gestured toward the slave who played with Strabo in the corner of the atrium. "I think he sees other women. I don't mean the slaves, although he has slept with all the ones we own."

"What do you mean, other women?" I asked.

"Sometimes messages will come to the house. An envelope with the scent of perfume or script that looks womanly. The slaves have been instructed to keep them from me but Niobe has shown me a few."

"Who are these women?"

"There are several. But I worry most about Livilla."

"Oh, dear gods!" What good could come out of that? Livilla was Tiberius's niece and daughter-in-law, married to his son Drusus! By Jove, I was at their wedding!

"You think he's seeing Livilla?"

She brushed away a tear. "I do."

I swore. If Sejanus was having an affair with Caesar's daughter-in-law, he was playing a very dangerous game indeed.

Sotas broke in. "Will he let you have friends visit?"

"No, he doesn't even like me leaving the house. Even having Mother visit vexes him greatly. He puts up with it only because he doesn't want the gossip."

"I don't understand . . ."

Sotas did. "Control."

"Oh, my dear little bird." I leaned over and kissed her forehead. "I wish I could take you from all this."

"Little bird!" Her face brightened. "I have not heard that in years!"

Sotas hissed at us. "He comes!"

"I must go. It will be better if he does not see me with you." She gave me a fast hug. I did not want to let her go, but she slipped away just before Sejanus and Apicius arrived in the atrium.

Apicius said his good-byes, then whisked us out of the villa. Like the way there, he chose to ride in his litter alone, leaving me ignorant of what had happened in the library after we left. In the days ahead Apicius said nothing to me of how the visit had ended, but instructed me to have his secretary increase the stipend sent to Apicata every month. Although I wondered why it was only half as much as he had promised to Sejanus, I said nothing.

Three weeks after the visit to Sejanus we were in the kitchen working on a recipe for a new cookbook on delicacies. I had stuffed dates with a mixture of crushed pine nuts in pepper and Apicius was helping me roll the dates in salt. We were ready to fry them in honey when one of the door slaves burst into the room, scroll in hand.

Apicius took the scroll and unrolled it. He read it silently, smiled, then set the scroll into the flames beneath the pan of honey.

"It's done." He picked up a date and dropped it into the salt.

"Pardon?" I moved the pan of honey off the fire before it took on any of the flavor of the burning parchment. I set the pan on a rock slab I kept on the table to hold hot items.

Apicius picked up a few of the dates and tossed them in the pan. They sizzled and we leaned back to avoid the splatter.

"It won't be long before there is a new gastronomic adviser to Tiberius."

I remained silent.

He said no more, leaving me alone to finish the dates and wonder at his words.

That night after the cena, Rúan appeared in the garden where I sat drinking a much-needed glass of wine. He hadn't stopped by in a few weeks and I was glad to see him.

He deposited himself onto the bench across from me. "Publius Octavius is dead."

For a moment, I was dumbfounded. Then it all fell together. "Of course."

Rúan squinted at me. "You already know?"

I took a sip of wine and passed it to Rúan. "No, I didn't. Tell me how."

He drank of the wine. "He fell ill more than two weeks ago. He succumbed to the sickness this morning."

"Ill?"

"I suspect he was poisoned. He had indigestion one night before dinner. I fed him the celery and leek soup you taught me to make, with the pepper and honey, but he did not improve."

"Who attended him besides you?"

"I never saw him. He only let his body-slave, Silius, attend to him. If I didn't know better, I would thank the gods. It means I can't be a suspect." He handed me the cup. I smiled when I saw it was empty.

"Did they question the body-slave?"

"They can't. He's missing."

"Missing?"

"Aye, since last night. No one knows where he is."

I set the empty glass down on the bench beside me, wishing I had brought a flask of wine with me when I left the kitchen.

"It's odd, though," Rúan mused, looking out into the dark garden. I thought I heard an owl hooting in the distance.

"What is?"

He sniffed. "No one seems to care about the missing slave. Livia wanted a further inquiry but the doctor proclaimed there was no foul play. Sejanus told Livia he wasn't going to waste men looking into a murder that wasn't there. That is that."

That was that, indeed.

A few weeks later, I was going through a list of client requests with Apicius when a slave burst through the door of the library without knocking. Apicius and I looked up to see Sotas had snatched the boy up by the back of his tunic.

The boy squeaked, "Caesar is here! Caesar is at the door!"

We sat there, stunned. Caesar at our house?

Apicius sprang into action. "Don't stand there! Let him in! We'll be there straightaway!"

Sotas let the boy go and he scampered down the hallway.

Apicius looked me up and down. "Thank the gods we both look respectable. Come now, we can't keep him waiting."

"Why is he here?" I asked as we walked swiftly through the house.

He didn't answer. My heart was pounding so hard I wondered if Apicius could hear it beating.

How could he be calm? I was terrified. Publius Octavius was dead and Livia suspected foul play. What if somehow the trail led back to Apicius? I wouldn't put it past Sejanus to frame him; it would be an easy way to get Apicius out of his hair, and the gods knew Livia hated him as well.

In the atrium, Tiberius sat on a plush chaise the slaves had brought to accommodate him. He was accompanied by several Praetorian Guard, including Sejanus, who sat on a chair next to him.

Sotas left us at the door, taking a spot at the side of the atrium. Apicius strode across the room, stopped before Caesar, and reached out a hand in greeting. I waited behind.

"To what do we owe the pleasure of this visit to my humble abode?" he asked as Tiberius shook his hand.

Sejanus guffawed, the skin around his eyes wrinkling with amusement. "Humble? Your villa is more extravagant than Divine Augustus's was!"

Apicius still smiled. My heart pounded. *Please, Apicius*, I willed him, *don't say anything stupid.*

Tiberius didn't give him the chance. "But that is precisely why I am here. You understand how to entertain dignitaries, princeps, and kings. No doubt you have heard I am in need of a new gastronomic adviser."

"I heard."

Tiberius motioned for Apicius and me to sit in the chairs the slaves had brought for us. "Sejanus tells me you are the best man for the job. Livia tells me it will anger her to no end to bring you into our service. Two good reasons for you to take on this role for me."

Tiberius handed Apicius a scroll and watched as he opened it and scanned the contents. "Are you interested?"

Apicius looked up from the scroll. He looked as he did after tasting a successful new recipe. Euphoric. "I am!"

Tiberius's gaze landed on me. "And you, cook. I applaud your performance at the market a few months ago. A good man knows when the price is too high. Better to have your dignity *and* your purse intact at the end of the day."

"Thank you." I swelled with pride. I looked at Apicius but he was scanning the scroll again.

"You'll need a salary too, I suppose. I'll see to it."

Tiberius stood and we rose with him. "I'll expect you to do much of my entertaining. I am not interested in pandering to those who desire a pound of my flesh. Still, it can't be helped, so you'll do it for me."

"I'm your man," Apicius asserted.

"Perfect. I'll send an escort to you tomorrow to be brought to the villa." He left, his guards following behind. Sejanus lingered.

"I have fulfilled my part of the bargain, father-in-law," he said to Apicius, barely loud enough for me to hear. "Now it is your turn."

"Yes, as we agreed." Apicius made a small motion to Sotas, and the big man deftly, but politely, maneuvered Sejanus out the door.

Then I understood. Oh, the irony! After all these years, the tables had turned and it was Sejanus who became the paid assassin after all.

Apicius had just been handed everything he had ever wanted. It had come at the expense of a man's life and required debt to the very man Apicius hated above all others. I thought back to the prediction of the haruspex and shuddered. *For every success, greater failures will cluster to the sides.*

Apicius was giddy. "Come, Thrasius! Let us tell Aelia the news. Tonight we celebrate!" He rushed off down the corridor, not bothering to wait for us to follow.

I stood there, jaw open wide, at a loss for words.

Sotas clapped me on the back. "Close your mouth, you might catch a fly."

I stared down the empty corridor, confusion and anger coiled in the pit of my stomach. "Did . . . ?"

"Did Apicius just sell his soul to Sejanus?" Sotas asked, then finished for me. "Why, yes, he did."

I shook my head. "What am I doing here, Sotas? Why do I stand by and watch him play these games? I am not beholden to him."

"Aren't you?" He gave me a crooked smile and turned down the hall-way himself.

I thought about Passia and my little Junius and hated how right my friend was.

The next morning Apicius increased Apicata's stipend by another eight thousand sestertii a month—the other half of the money promised to Sejanus.

We were finishing a bleary-eyed salutatio when the man Tiberius sent arrived. It turned out to be Rúan. After losing him to Octavius, Apicius had been caustic toward his former slave, convinced that he was a spy for his rival. This time he greeted Rúan like an old friend.

Rúan took us to the villa Tiberius was remodeling, a short walk across the Palatine. Tiberius resided primarily in a luxurious villa on the Esquiline, but with so many of his clientele living on the Palatine, he wanted to expand the villa on that hill as well. More slaves than I could count swarmed the exterior, making repairs and adding on to what was once a modest dwelling.

"Be careful." Rúan gestured for us to step around boards and buckets of wet cement. I had walked by the exterior of the villa many times on my way to the temple of Apollo. The entrance used to be only a single marble arch but now several arches opened up into a broad atrium, which had itself been expanded.

Rúan led us through a twisting maze of corridors, some painted with frescoes, some not, the walls bare and the rooms empty with no doors. He showed us two triclinia and an office Apicius could call his own. The kitchen was much smaller than the kitchen at Apicius's villa, with half as many slaves. "Is this all?"

Rúan nodded. "Aye, it is. But do not worry. You won't be expected to do much entertaining here, only when Caesar desires to dine at home with his guests, which is not often. Tomorrow I'll show you the kitchen on the Esquiline, which is more expansive. For the most part, though, you'll be expected to arrange entertainment at your own home or the homes of others. Tiberius will send dignitaries and foreign emissaries to you to take care of. You'll find he won't attend many meals unless it's a state dinner or there is something he can't graciously excuse himself from. He's not fond of politics."

"So I've heard."

Apicius seemed disappointed. Being Tiberius's gastronomic adviser was proving to be more work and less glory than he'd expected.

"You may, on occasion, be asked to accompany Caesar to one of his villas at Rhodes or Capri but it will be rare."

"What of his tastes? What foods does he appreciate?" I asked. "Is he fussy about his meals?"

"No. He will eat anything as long as there is wine. It's the wine that he loves. You've heard that they call him Biberius Caldius Mero?"

I couldn't help but snort at the name, which meant "drinker of wine without water," a phrase that described someone who was rude and acted like a pleb. "I had not, but I'll make sure there is plenty of wine to satiate him."

He led us back to the atrium again, where the gardeners bustled about, planting trees and flowers.

"Oh," Rúan added. "You're expected to throw a *cena publica* that announces your new post and demonstrates Caesar's wisdom in giving it to you."

"Of course." We knew such a banquet would be expected and had talked about it over breakfast that morning.

"I'll secure the guest list for you. Thrasius, send me any instructions you like, any lists of food for purchase. I am at your service."

"It's good to work with you again, old friend. I missed your funny accent." A burst of happiness swelled within me when I thought of bantering anew with him over the preparation of a meal. Although Timon was a master at his trade, I missed the camaraderie I had with Rúan.

"Aye, and I missed your funny talk of all your crazy gods! But I suspect you'll work me even harder than Publius Octavius did."

At the name, Apicius seemed to snap out of his reverie. He cleared his throat.

"Come, Thrasius, we have much to do." He strode off toward home. I waved good-bye to Rúan and followed, knowing Apicius was likely to be in a mood best avoided.

We decided to hold the banquet at the school, in the gardens we had designed for such a purpose. The kitchen there would allow for easier food preparation and we could easily set up couches and tables to accommodate the five hundred people on the guest list.

Fannia, Trio, and Celera joined us for dinner that evening. The discussion that night was the possible theme for the cena publica. "Hold a competition." Fannia was tipsy, delighted that Caesar Augustus was dead and Tiberius had ditched the old decorum that one could drink wine only after dinner and women should drink only when religious ceremonies required.

"A competition? With swords?" Trio was skeptical. "Aren't there enough gladiatorial games without us throwing another?"

Apicius waved a hand at Fannia to continue. "Gladiators are so droll."

"Not a gladiator fight. A competition."

We all looked at her, still uncomprehending.

"A footrace?" Celera offered.

"Drinking? We all know how badly that might end." Aelia smirked at Apicius.

"No, no, no. A competition between the gods!" Fannia said.

"Continue." Apicius tossed the bones of his chicken wing onto the tiles behind the couch to appease the ghosts of the ancestors.

"Imagine. Neptune and Diana competing to prove who has the most delicious bounty—the sea or the forest. The food could be animals of the sea and the land."

"Tiberius could judge!" I mused. It was a brilliant idea.

"Yes, exactly!" Fannia exclaimed.

The fire of this idea roared through my brain. I could barely get the words out of my mouth I was so excited.

"Each course could be dedicated to one of the gods. We bring out the seafood first, then the animals, then back and forth in each course . . ."

"Yes! And the final course will be the pinnacle dish from each god!" Apicius had caught the fire now.

Everyone agreed and a clamor arose as they gave suggestions about the banquet. "Excellent!" Apicius was jubilant, as were we all.

It was an exquisite feeling—a feeling that wouldn't last long.

CHAPTER 23

It took us eight months to plan the banquet. Those months were some of the busiest and most exciting of my life. I spent hours at the market looking for ideas, buying up everything from new napkins to intricately embroidered cushions for the couches. I sent messengers across Italy: to our farms for wood pigeons, dormice, capons, and heaping baskets of grapes, apples, and beets; to the fields beyond Rome for fresh pears; to Nomentanum for amphorae of wine, some more than forty years old; to Praeneste for hazelnuts; and to the plains between Ostia and Lavinium for wild boar and deer. I sent men to Ostia for fresh, salty mackerel and mussels and to Mount Hymettus for the finest honey to dilute the Falernian wine we had on stock at home for the princeps and all the senators. I purchased ginger, nutmeg, cloves, and other spices from India and Taprobane, not only to flavor the food but to present as gifts. I even sent a man to Sicilia for green and black olives and for the olive relish that was a specialty of the region. I reveled in the planning of such a massive banquet.

However, all the planning made Apicius unbearable. Nothing I did seemed to please him and I thanked the gods daily that he was no longer my master and could not whip me like he did the slaves unfortunate enough to be in the way of his whims and rages. Even Sotas seemed on edge. About this time came word of the terrible treatment of the slaves by P. Vedius Pollio, a once-friend of the Divine Augustus and a minor acquaintance of Apicius. A cupbearer broke a precious crystal goblet at one of his banquets and in a rage Pollio cut the slave's hands off and hung them around his neck. The slave was forced to parade among the diners before Pollio mercilessly threw him to his death into a pool of lamprey eels.

"Dominus wouldn't ever do that to Junius or me, would he?" Passia whispered to me one evening as I shed my clothes and climbed into bed. Our son, now four, snored softly from his bed in the corner of the room.

"No, my love. For all his faults he is not that cruel. And he loves little Junius. You know how much he dotes on him." Apicius did love the tot, and that day had even given him a new brightly painted wooden horse on wheels to pull along behind him as he toddled through the villa.

"What about the other slaves? This banquet is for Caesar! Dominus might want to keep up appearances."

"Don't worry. Pollio did not win the kind of notoriety he might have liked by killing off that poor boy. Besides, Apicius is too concerned with his image to have people talking about him for anything other than his food. And he depends upon me too much to hurt those I love."

Passia didn't seem satisfied with the answer but she cuddled up next to me anyway. Soon she was breathing heavily into my shoulder. I lay awake for a while thinking of her question. I was not worried about what Apicius would do if something wasn't perfect at the banquet. I was worried about what Caesar might do.

On the day of the banquet I was up before dawn helping the staff put the final touches on the decorations and helping Rúan and Timon begin the monumental task of preparing the main dishes.

When the water clock showed ten o'clock Sotas came to collect me for the astrology reading. Rúan laughed at me.

"Oh, how you Romans love your divinations!"

I just smiled at him. I had long ago tried to convince Rúan that the gods were powerful and that divination wasn't a load of bunk, but in the end we had agreed to disagree. It didn't stop him from teasing me regularly for what he saw as folly.

We met Apicius and Glycon and went to Tiberius's palace on the Esquiline. Tiberius was still in his morning robe when we met in the garden. He had a handful of guards with him, as well as a bald, smooth-shaven man Glycon seemed to know.

"Ahh, Thrasyllus," I heard the astrologer mutter to himself.

"Good day to you, Caesar!" Apicius smiled broadly. "What a fine day to honor you."

Tiberius looked uncomfortable. "We honor Rome first."

I saw Apicius's eye twitch. He thinned his lips into a long line as if trying hard not to respond.

Sejanus spoke up before Apicius could say something regrettable. "In honoring you, Caesar, we honor Rome, do we not?"

Apicius continued to make awkward small talk with Sejanus and Tiberius, leaving Glycon to slip off to the side to speak with Thrasyllus. A gold pendant flashed at the man's neck, of a moon and stars. Tiberius's astrologer. They talked in hushed tones. I caught a few words of their conversation, none of which inspired calm within me: "stars . . . the consequences . . . actions . . . friend . . . dire . . . we'll tell him . . . yes, yes . . . he'll believe . . ."

Tiberius's voice rose. "Come now, let's get this over with."

Sejanus motioned for Thrasyllus to come forward. Glycon trailed behind him.

"Sir, the stars are most favorable. My colleague Glycon was right in choosing this date for the feast. The moon is full and will give us light beyond the candle. Mars is in the templum of Venus and Venus is in the templum of Saturn, aligning them all to look down upon us in various stages throughout the night. Today is a particularly auspicious time for a feast, dear Caesar."

"Excellent! Now it is time for my bath." He snapped his fingers and his guard came to attention. "Oh, and Apicius, I want my servers to be naked. Stark as the day they were born, understand?" He didn't give Apicius a chance to respond, abruptly walking away, leaving us looking at his retreating figure.

"It seems everyone finds favor with you now." Sejanus smirked. Where he had once been cordial to Apicius, he had diminished into sarcastic tolerance. "Let us hope they still do when the banquet comes to an end." He inclined his head toward one of his guards. "Paulus, see them out."

Apicius snapped his fingers at Sotas, who dutifully trotted over to Glycon, said a few low words to the man, and waited patiently until Glycon gave his good-byes.

"A good reading, Master Apicius." Glycon fell into step alongside Apicius, a sight that was now all too common in our household.

"You are sure this will be a good night?"

"Yes, yes, it will be a fine night!" Glycon's voice was slick, like fresh pressed oil.

I didn't believe him.

The day's preparations flew by, and before we knew it, the first guests began to trickle into the garden, some more than an hour earlier than we expected.

"They want to secure the best couches," Fannia remarked, coming up from behind. She had also arrived early, and was overdressed, as usual, in too many golden necklaces and rings and a garish blue stola one step away from the Imperial purple, a dangerous choice considering the possible insult to be made.

I stood with her, watching as our slaves escorted the guests to various couches. I sent the first group of slaves out with the wine. Fannia stopped one of them and took a brightly painted goblet from the tray. She winked at me.

"So much more civilized this Caesar is! Drinking before dinner! Women partaking without shame!" She lifted her glass at me.

While Tiberius had a more relaxed attitude toward wine, most did not share his views. Fannia didn't care one whit and had embraced drinking in public with great gusto.

"Some guests aren't sure what to do." I motioned toward a group of equestrians and their wives. One couple took a glass and other guests frowned at them. "I know I don't like it. You shouldn't drink before dinner. It dulls the senses and the taste of your food."

Fannia laughed. "Oh, you silly man. That's simply not true! A good wine will enhance the flavors of your food. You are too much of a purist!"

"Hmm." I looked back at the crowd. We had to turn up a good portion of our gardens to be able to set up more than sixty couches to accommodate 540 guests. At the head of the feast was a larger triclinium with cushions of sumptuous red and purple silk set up for the emperor and his most important guests. Flanking the Imperial couches were two monstrous gilded bronze statues, one of Neptune and one of Diana.

I was about to return to the kitchen when I saw Sotas emerge from behind Diana's shining skirt. He lifted one massive arm and waved it to make sure we saw him.

"Apicius sent me to tell you Tiberius and Livia are here," he said when he arrived. "Sejanus sent a messenger ahead."

"Wasn't that kind of him?" Fannia smirked. "It's not often you get fair warning before the Hydra strikes."

I shook my head at her remark and turned back to Sotas. The big man jerked his head in the direction of the couches. "Apicius wants us waiting at the dais when Tiberius and Livia arrive."

"Onward!" Fannia gestured for me to lead the way. I wasn't sure I wanted her to follow. Mixing Livia and Fannia was like mixing oil and water, and, as a result, Apicius had been trying more and more to distance himself from his old mentor. Plus I was beginning to suspect Fannia was a little in her cups.

My former master and his wife waited for us at the Imperial triclinium. Aelia wore a golden-edged white silk stola fastened at the shoulder with a ruby-studded pin of gold. Her *palla*, also edged in gold, was draped lightly over her head and shoulders, obscuring most of what looked to be an elaborate weave of curls pinned to the top of her head. Apicius wore a brand-new toga and sported new gold rings on his fingers, each of which held a large gem in its center. I marveled at how much younger he looked than his forty-nine years—younger than I looked, and I'd been born ten years after him. I suspected it was the extra layers of fat on his body, giving his face a rounded countenance, devoid of wrinkles.

"I'm surprised they are arriving so early." I took my place next to Aelia in the line to receive Tiberius and his company.

"We are too." Aelia squeezed my arm in greeting.

Fannia defiantly took a spot next to me. Apicius glanced over with a look of horror. He motioned to me, as though I would be able to say something to convince her not to stand with us. I shrugged. I couldn't control his friend.

Panic began to fill Apicius's eyes, now wide and staring at me. Horns sounded at the entrance, marking Caesar's arrival. "Thrasius!" Apicius hissed at me in a low tone filled with fire.

The crowd began to cheer and moved to line the aisle in the center of the garden to watch Caesar pass by. I looked away from Apicius and back toward the procession. Fannia was oblivious to Apicius's concerns, her eyes fixated on the Imperial family walking toward us.

Apicius gave Aelia a message to whisper loudly in my ear. "She does know she can't sit with us, doesn't she?"

I whispered back, "We spoke about it earlier. We're seating her in the front, but off to the side, with friends of her choosing."

She relayed the information to Apicius, who looked as though he were about to ask Fannia to depart the receiving line. He hesitated too long, however, and then it was too late. Tiberius advanced toward us, his mother on his arm, and his son Drusus with his wife, Livilla, behind. Sejanus and Apicata followed the Imperial family with several Praetorian Guard in tow.

Tiberius strode past us all and greeted Apicius with a hearty arm clasp. He appeared to be in much better spirits than he was earlier. "My good Apicius! I am a hungry man ready for a feast! What do you have in store for us?"

Apicius launched into a description of the dishes to come, but my attention was seized by Livia, who was greeting each of us in the line as etiquette dictated. That was as far as etiquette went. She did not kiss or hug Fannia, only nodding at her when she passed. Drusus, however, took Fannia's hand and kissed it grandly, causing the old matron to blush. Livia offered a hand to me, which I kissed, noting the blue veins under her pale skin. She kissed Aelia on the cheek and stood back, waiting for Tiberius to finish his conversation with Apicius. Apicata looked radiant and she greeted us all warmly.

Sejanus shook hands with Apicius and leaned in to hug Aelia, who froze when he touched her. As his cousin, a hug would not seem untoward, but I noticed the hand that caressed one of her breasts when he pulled away. Aelia gave away nothing, turning after the hug to make small talk with Apicata. Sejanus smirked and turned away to give his guard and Imperial body-slaves their orders for the feast. I began to run through my head all the foods I could feed him that would make him ill, perhaps deathly ill. Then I saw Apicius talking with Tiberius and knew that I could not do anything to mar this occasion. Instead I dug my nails into my hands, which were curled into fists that I wished could meet with flesh.

Drusus made his way through the line and joined his father in the conversation with Apicius. "I trust you have some cabbage tops boiling up for me, Apicius? I fancy a good bowl of them about now."

Apicius shook his head gently at the man. "No, Drusus, there are no cabbage tops at this feast! It would not do to have the masses see you eating such common food! But, if you like, I'll have Thrasius bring you some on the morrow?"

Drusus chuckled. "Common food? I guess I didn't realize."

"You've been eating with the soldiers more than the senators," Tiberius mused.

Livia sneezed, loudly, with a high-pitched note at the end. *"Salve,"* I said instinctively.

"Salve," Aelia, Apicata, Drusus, Livilla, and Tiberius echoed.

Fannia merely smiled at Livia. Apicius had also failed to say the word and, distracted, continued to tell Drusus more lofty ways to eat cabbage. Aelia seemed unaware of her husband's mistake.

Livia's eyes narrowed. She looked at Fannia and waited for the customary response. I held my breath and willed Fannia to do the right thing. To withhold the word for good health was wishing tremendously bad luck on the person who sneezed.

Fannia smiled sweetly at her cousin. She was not going to budge. Livia looked at Apicius but there was no response there. Tiberius and Drusus didn't notice that Apicius hadn't responded. Aelia seemed to realize the mistake but she was no longer standing close enough to Apicius to nudge him.

Livia took a few steps forward to stand in front of Fannia. She leaned in, looking as though she were bestowing a welcome kiss on her, but I could hear the words that were said. Livia's whisper sounded as papery as her skin had felt when I kissed it. "You and your dear Apicius have insulted me for the last time, I promise."

"Oh, I'm sure there will be more opportunity," Fannia whispered back defiantly. She began to giggle, a sound I had heard all too often after dinner when she had been drinking with Apicius.

Livia paused, as if pondering her words. Then she said simply, "No. Your opportunities have run out."

Aelia squeezed my elbow. I dared not look at her.

Livia turned away and took her son by the arm. "Come, Tiberius, I grow hungry. Let us recline."

As they ascended the steps to the couches, I led Fannia away far more roughly than I should have.

"Take your hands off me," she hissed once we were far enough away.

"What's wrong with you, Fannia? Are you drunk or just stupid?"

Fannia pulled her arm out of my grasp. "You have become such a bore over the years since Apicius freed you, Thrasius. So bossy!" She laughed and waved a dismissive hand at me. "Oh, you think she killed Marcellus? Or Lucius? Or you believe the rumors about Livia smothering the oh-so-divine Augustus? Oh, please. That old bitch has a bark far worse than her bite. She wouldn't touch me."

It was more than possible that Livia had had a hand in the deaths of those men, each of whom didn't quite fit into her plans to have Tiberius become Caesar. I tried again. "Please, Fannia, stay out of her way."

"Don't you worry. Go do what you need to do. I'll sip my wine happily at the couch over there—out of Livia's way." She gave me the same sweet smile and hiccuped.

I sighed and set off for the kitchen, making a note to myself to have the cupbearer water her wine down far more before serving it to her.

When most of the tables had filled up, Tiberius stood and clapped his hands loudly. His toga and golden laurel diadem were bright in the fading afternoon light. Immediately the front tables fell into a hush. The quiet spread through the crowd until all eyes were on Caesar.

"Welcome, my fellow Romans and countrymen! Today we gather to witness a battle which you have never imagined. To tell you about this magnificent battle, I present to you my new gastronomic adviser, a man whom you all know, Marcus Gavius Apicius."

The crowd began clapping and cheering. Apicius rose to stand next to Tiberius, a broad smile on his tanned face. He raised his arms, welcoming the sounds of the people reclining on his couches. His voice rang over the crowd.

"My friends! Caesar told you true—there will be a grand battle today. Neptune, ruler of the seas"—he gestured toward the massive statue to his right—"has challenged the lady of the forest, Diana, to a duel." He waved at the goddess on his left.

"You will be participants in this mighty fight—a fight of the senses, of the most delightful tastes, smells, and sights to cross any mortal's plate!"

It was an arrogant boast and I marveled at his bravado. He was in his element and this was his crowning moment.

"You will taste various dishes of land and sea tonight. Given the bounty of these gods, which foods will we, as men, be able to make the most of? Will it be god or goddess that you bow to as victor?"

Tiberius touched Apicius on the shoulder to indicate he would like to speak. Apicius stepped back.

"To judge these dishes," Tiberius shouted to the crowd, "I give the honor to the new governor of Illyricum, Drusus Julius Caesar!" He waved his son forward.

Drusus was a man Passia had once described as "too handsome for his own good," with dark sandy curls cropped close and sparkling green eyes. The crowd roared, cheering at a volume far greater than they'd given to Caesar.

I looked at Sejanus as Drusus waved to the diners. A dark frown tugged at the corners of his mouth. I wondered about the animosity. Perhaps Apicata was right about Sejanus and Drusus's wife, Livilla.

While the crowd clapped for Drusus, Apicius signaled to me and I passed the command on to my slaves.

The sound of trumpets rang out, signaling the arrival of the first course. A parade of glittering slaves trotted forward, some carrying decorations of the sea, statues made of shells, ribbons of blue and silver, or wearing costumes turning them into fish or mermaids. These slaves wandered among the diners as they ate, entertaining them with music or dances reminiscent of the sea. In the midst of these spectacles were the slaves carrying the food on massive trays covered in snow from the mountains, topped with stuffed mussels, lobster mince wrapped in grape leaves, and sea urchins boiled, honeyed, and served open in their own spiny husks. The air was filled with the sounds of delight from the crowd as the dishes arrived at their tables. I breathed a sigh of great relief.

As requested, the slaves serving Tiberius were naked, except for ribbons in their hair. He toyed with them as they served the food, much to the chagrin of his mother and the other women at the table.

Neptune's bounty was followed by that of Diana. I had staged a "hunt" to take place while the diners ate. Several of the bigger slaves were dressed like bears, and hunters with bows chased them playfully around the couches while nymphs tried to hinder their progress. They ran carefully around the slaves serving trays of pork cracklings, mushrooms marinated in wine, stuffed dormice, and figs soaked in milk and honey.

The next two courses alternated between the sea and the land, and with every course more elaborate spectacles entertained the diners. Things did not run entirely smoothly, but the things that did go wrong—broken dishes, not enough oil for the garden lamps, running out of grapes, having to substitute lesser wine when the good wine began to run out—were not noticed by any of the diners, or by Apicius, who, from what I could tell, was having a perfect time dining on the Imperial couch. Even Livia seemed to be enjoying herself.

The person who seemed unhappiest was Apicata. She smiled and was cordial with her dining companions, but I quickly realized her thoughts were on Livilla, who was seated on the other side of Sejanus. Sejanus and Livilla seemed particularly chatty. I was surprised Drusus didn't take notice. I wished I could have taken Apicata away from there, to wander through the gardens as we did when she was a child, looking for birds and butterflies and not caring a thing about the world.

Unfortunately, I had much to care about that night. After the second course I saw Fannia had passed out on her couch. I instructed our slaves to bring her, as inconspicuously as they could, home to Apicius's villa. I wished upon her a terrible headache when she awoke.

At the end of the meal Tiberius and Drusus stood to announce the "winner" of the battle. I stepped forward with the massive wreath of flowers woven for the occasion. "I hereby offer this wreath to the winner," Tiberius shouted grandly, the crowd clapping and whistling their approval. He waited a moment, building the tension of the crowd, then motioned for Drusus to place the wreath at Diana's golden feet. The lamplight flickered off her gilded skin, making it look as though she glowed with pleasure.

"A perfect cena!" Tiberius proclaimed before he left for the night. He waved at his body-slave to slip pouches of golden aurei into our hands. I was not prepared to feel such weight in my palm.

"Now I know what I have been missing," Livia said to me pleasantly before she took her leave. She leaned in conspiratorially. "Apicius was a fool not to have sold you to me those years ago. Such a costly mistake that was."

"I'm glad you enjoyed the banquet . . ." I was unsure what else to say.

She didn't reply and moved on, leaving me in the company of my dear little bird. Apicata gave me a kiss on the cheek and made me promise to send her some of the leftover sweetmeats for her children. I watched her go, my heart aching.

I left the slaves under Rúan's care to clean up after the feast and rode in the litter with Apicius and Aelia to the villa. I had hoped to tell Apicius about Fannia and also about Livia's words to me.

I didn't have the heart. Apicius was elated. I don't remember ever seeing him so happy. I couldn't bear to break his mood.

"What a night! Tomorrow we will go to the temples of Neptune and Diana and give tribute."

"Tonight we will sleep hard as rocks, I suspect." Aelia patted Apicius's knee.

He smiled and kissed Aelia on the cheek in a rare display of affection. "Tonight we will. Tomorrow, we begin planning another feast, Thrasius!"

I coughed. "We do?" The last thing I wanted to do was go through that exercise again.

"Yes! In a fortnight we entertain King Herod of Galilee." He clapped his hands together joyfully.

"Ahh, Herod, we meet again," I muttered. I hoped that the next banquet for him would be better than the first—the terrible one we held at the school all those years past.

"Yes, Tiberius informed me tonight. No pork and no shellfish at this feast! This will be a challenge, Thrasius!"

I smiled, but dreaming up another feast was the furthest thing from my mind.

PART IX

24 C.E. to 26 C.E.

RELISH FROM BAIAE

Put chopped oysters, mussels, and sea urchins in a pan, add chopped roasted pine nuts, rue, celery, pepper, coriander, cumin, passum, liquamen, dates, and oil.

—*Book 9.11, The Sea*
On Cookery, Apicius

CHAPTER 24

Over the course of the next three years, we saw little of Livia, but her warning still echoed in my mind. I had no doubt the grudge she bore was deep, heavy, and would last longer than the stones of the Appian Way. Apicius and I also found that the parties and banquets we threw were not mandated by Tiberius as much as they were by Sejanus.

"I told you no. I will not let you marry that slave, and that is that, Thrasius. Do *not* ask me again!"

I had been in the service of Apicius for fifteen years as a freedman, but despite all my promises, he still did not believe that I would stay if Passia were free. Legally she was old enough, at thirty-nine, and her peculium was more than enough to purchase her freedom, but she could not do so without permission from Apicius. He freed many slaves, but still refused Passia.

I refused to give up. "Apicius, please, listen to me."

"I said no!" Apicius stormed across the kitchen, knocking over a jug on a counter he passed by.

A flick of the wrist from Timon was all it took to set one of the slaves in motion to clean it up. The rest of the staff quickly moved the breakables out of Apicius's path.

"Marcus, be reasonable." Aelia entered the kitchen.

He whirled on her. "Why are you here? You should have sent Helene." Apicius's words were harsh. I felt their sting from across the room.

"Helene is ill, husband. That's why I'm here, for a remedy."

"I'll buy you another body-slave. Is that what you want?"

Aelia looked up, her mouth wide with shock. "No! She has a cold. Why would I need another slave? I will not replace Helene!"

"Then stop complaining about her."

Aelia faltered, then gathered herself and stood up straight. "Why are you being so mean? Not just to me but to Thrasius? He is your friend. Why do you continue to deny him his request to marry Passia?"

"Wife, you know you are out of line." He pressed his fist to his mouth, his knuckles white.

"My husband, please hear him. And hear me. Passia and Thrasius love each other. I have seen this love in their every action. So few people ever feel Cupid's arrow. The lady Venus has chosen them to be together. Why do you thwart the gods and keep them apart?"

"They are NOT apart!" he roared, causing Aelia to take a step back. "If I wanted them to be apart that woman would be on the first slave caravan to Egypt. In fact, I think I have been very generous."

For a moment, I could not catch my breath. The very thought of Apicius selling Passia was unfathomable.

Aelia tried again and I loved her for the effort. "Do it for me, Apicius. I ask you this as a favor to me. If you love me, please, consider his petition. Do it as a gift to me."

Apicius glared at her. The tension in the room was thick. Finally, he extended his hand toward the door. "Begone, wife! How dare you ask me for favors? This has nothing to do with love. Now go before I strike you and remind you of your place in this household."

The color drained from Aelia's face. She gathered up the edges of her stola and fled the kitchen.

"That was cruel," I said to my former master once she had gone.

"No, that was kind. She needs to know her place."

I seethed.

He turned back to me. "Thrasius, you need to understand. I have other things to worry about without your petty demands."

I shut my open mouth and put my knives into the basket on the shelf below the counter. Apicius looked unpredictable.

He slammed his fists down on my table. "Like Sejanus. May Pluto take him soon. My intentions were to work for Caesar, not the damned head of the Praetorian Guard."

The way that Apicius changed the conversation did not escape my attention. But I knew him. Pushing the issue would only make him more stubborn. Begrudgingly I responded, "If Caesar were involved, the meals would still be the same. The same kings, governors, senators. It might be worse. You've heard of Tiberius's cruelty and debauchery. Be glad he is absent from the meals."

"Sejanus is not any better."

There was nothing I could say. I looked down at my hands. They were smeared with pig grease and blood. I waited for his words. He stared at me, then left. I watched him go, sadness welling within me.

Two days later I took an early-morning walk with Passia and Junius across the Palatine, enjoying the brisk autumn air, fresh after a long rainfall. Our time together was scarce, with all the elaborate cenae Apicius and I planned and Passia's increasing role as one of Aelia's body-slaves. Junius spent much of his time in the company of other slave children. At ten, he was still growing faster than asparagus in the spring. Passia looked beautiful that day. My hand entwined with hers as we walked. I tried not to think of the fact that her hand was still devoid of the ring I longed to give her.

Junius walked ahead of us, kicking around a ball I'd made him by drying and inflating a pig bladder from the kitchen. Apicius had spent time with the boy, helping him paint the ball with bright colors.

Passia waved at one of the slaves from the villa who was returning from the market with a basket of fruit on her head. "Glycon has been making dire predictions to Aelia," she said.

"All his predictions of late have been dire. Rarely does he say the stars are aligned. I get the sense he doesn't really tell us the worst of it."

She looked at me, her eyes dark. "You feel that way too?"

"I do. And you know I don't like to believe the tales he spins. What did he say about Aelia?"

"He told her the end of her marriage is near." Passia slowed her pace.

"By the gods! He told her that was in the stars? Why on earth would he say that to her?"

She slowed her pace so Junius couldn't hear. "She's distraught. He couldn't tell her more; he says the stars don't give—"

"Details, I know. When was this? Does Apicius know?"

"Yesterday. She doesn't want to tell Apicius. She wants to change things. Today she is going to the temple of Juno Viriplaca, hoping the goddess of marital strife will show her favor."

"I realize he's not very nice to her these days, but Apicius won't divorce her. He has no other. He doesn't even go near the slaves anymore. His mind is consumed with food and power. What sort of nonsense is Glycon filling her mind with?"

She stopped me. "You can't tell Apicius."

"Why not? Apicius deserves to know his astrologer is lying to his wife."

Passia picked up the pace, not saying anything for a moment. I walked with her, accustomed to these silences, knowing she was thinking.

"What if he's right?" Passia asked.

"Ridiculous." A lone raindrop hit me on the nose.

"He was right about Junius. And he predicted a good feast for Tiberius last year. And that we'd have good crops on the farms this summer. He's been right about a lot of things. What if he knows something is going to happen?"

"I don't believe it."

The rain started to fall in a rush, soaking our tunics and spattering mud up against our ankles. Junius laughed as he ran by us on the race back to the domus. Passia and I followed him, holding hands like children.

A week later, I was preserving the last of the apples for the winter ahead when I heard the clamor of horns—fire horns—in the distance. I did not think much about this until later, when I could hear Passia's screams ringing through the house.

"They're dead! They're dead!" It took me a moment to register her words and realize the implications. My heart caught in my throat. Passia had accompanied Fannia and Aelia to the market that day.

I flew through the corridors, not caring what I knocked over or who I bumped into. I arrived in the atrium to find Passia on her knees, keening, her hair loose and flowing across her shoulders and face, with strands in her mouth.

I fell to the tiles and gathered her in my arms. She sobbed and I stroked her hair. "Shhh, you're all right, my sweet Passia."

Apicius and Sotas arrived, as did all the other slaves in the house. Apicius dropped to his knees alongside me. He grabbed Passia by the shoulders. "Who? Who is dead? Tell me, woman, tell me!"

Passia looked through the veil of her hair and tears at Apicius. I could almost see the words clumping up into sobs in her throat. Apicius slapped her.

"Tell me, slave! Where is Aelia? Where is Fannia?"

"Dead!" She started wailing again.

Apicius shook her. "What do you mean? How?"

"Fire . . . locked in a shop . . . I couldn't get to them!"

Passia closed her eyes and wailed at the sky. Apicius let her go and she fell against me. I wrapped my arms around her.

Sotas instructed the guards to go find out about the fire. Apicius had curled into a ball on the floor, eyes staring ahead blankly but tears flowing across his face to the tiles.

Sotas broke in and took Passia from me, pulling her up off the floor and half carrying her to a nearby chair. He sat her in it and pushed the hair from her face.

"You have to tell us what happened!"

I moved over to Apicius and helped him sit up. I held him as I would a child, my arms around him, hugging him. He buried his head in my shoulder. "I don't want to hear." He sobbed so softly it reached only my ears. His sorrow mingled with my own and I could not keep the tears from my eyes.

A nearby slave brought Passia a glass of wine, which she drank in big gulps. Sotas sat next to her and stroked her hand till she was able to slow her tears. "My little friend, please tell us."

"We went to the Caelian Hill," she began to say.

"Why did you go there? The market isn't on the Caelian!" I burst out.

Passia started crying again and Sotas glared at me. I nodded my head, chastened. He stroked her hand again until she quieted. "Tell us."

"Fannia came to visit this morning and Domina Aelia came out to greet her when she was getting out of her litter. A boy ran up to them saying that he had a message for Dominus Apicius. Fannia snatched it—you know how nosy she is—read it, and discovered that it was a note about some silphium for sale by a man at the bottom of the Caelian Hill, not far from the cooking school. Fannia had the idea to surprise Dominus. She told Aelia that it would be a gift that would make Dominus love her all the more. She asked me to accompany them." She sniffed and wiped her nose with her hand. "When we arrived at the house a man answered and told us to come inside. He said he had bags full of silphium. I was going to follow them into the house but Aelia told me to go back to a market stall we had passed and get some pretty jars to put the silphium in."

Sotas continued to stroke her hand. "Did he seem dangerous?"

"No . . . he looked nice." She hesitated and sniffed. "I remember thinking he was dressed too well for where he lived."

"Then what happened?"

The words caught in her throat and she took another sip of the wine before continuing. "I bought the jars and returned to the man's house. When I got there . . . Oh, dear Hera! The man was locking the door behind him, and then he ran off. I could smell smoke."

As she spoke, I realized I too could smell smoke wafting in from a distance. Apicius buried his head into my shoulder. "Dear gods, he locked them in . . ."

Sotas was as patient as ever. "Keep going, Passia."

"I yelled at him but he ran away. I tried to open the door but I couldn't. I could hear them screaming inside. Smoke was pouring out from under the door. I ran around to the side to see if I could get in a window but all the windows were boarded up." Passia began her sobbing anew. "I couldn't get to them! Oh, dear gods! The flames were so strong. I kept yelling but no one would help me!"

"There were no *vigiles*?" I asked.

"Not until the whole building and the one next door were both on fire. They could do nothing. Nothing! Oh, dear Hera, they didn't have enough water to put anything out. Even when they used their hooks to pull down the buildings it did nothing but spread the fire. Oh, gods, Aelia! Fannia! They are gone." She put her head in her hands and let the sobs wrack her body.

Thank the gods for Sotas that day. He was the calm in the middle of the tempest. He immediately sent guards out to determine who owned that building and to find out about the messenger who had delivered the message. But I knew. It could only have been Livia.

Then I saw Glycon hovering in the crowd of slaves standing along the edges of the atrium. Rage rose up inside my breast and my face reddened with the heat of my ire. *"You!"* I yelled and pointed. Apicius sat up to see who I was gesturing toward.

All eyes in the room swiveled in Glycon's direction. "Yes, you! This is your fault!"

Glycon looked at me, gaping and startled. He gathered his robes around him and stepped backward a pace.

"What is? I don't understand!"

"You told Aelia her marriage was at an end! You sent her to her death!"

"What do you mean?" Apicius choked, his eyes rimmed in red.

"Yes, what do you mean?" Glycon's voice shook.

Passia pulled herself out of the chair and stormed toward him. She pushed a finger into the old man's chest. "Aelia went to buy silphium to please Apicius—because she thought her marriage was ending." Tears made tracks in the soot on her face. "You told her that her marriage was dead! This is your fault! You should have been the one in the fire!"

The front doors opened and one of the guards burst in. The smell of smoke entered with him, strong and ominous. "The Caelian Hill, Master Apicius! Much of it is on fire. They are sending vigiles from all the hills to try to contain it."

Sotas thanked him and returned him to his post. When I looked back to Glycon, he was gone.

Apicius had also noticed. "Sotas, send guards to find the astrologer. If he is still in the house, they have my permission to kill him on sight." Then he collapsed on the couch.

Apicius made us go to the Caelian Hill. We didn't take the litter—with the fire the crowds were too thick and it would have been dangerous. Instead, flanked by a few guardsmen, Sotas, Passia, and I walked, and sometimes ran, with him, tears streaming down our faces. We couldn't get close to the house where Passia indicated the tragedy had struck. We were stopped a block away from our school, which I could see was ablaze as well, flames licking the sides of the upper floor. I watched in horror, thanking the gods I had been in the habit of bringing my cookbook notes and knives home with me every night.

I felt mixed emotions. I had long since tired of teaching, but oh, how the school had changed my life. A part of me died when I saw the roof cave in and half the school burst into flames. Later I would sacrifice a white sow to Jupiter for sparing the slaves who had been living there, all twenty of them.

A row of soot-covered vigiles kept us from going farther up the hill. Sotas tried to steer us home but Apicius kept repeating, "Please, take me where I can see." We led him to an outcropping on the Palatine that held a good view of the Caelian, barely visible through the darkness and thick smoke. Apicius fell to his knees, threw his arms over the low stone wall, and wept. Sotas, Passia, and I huddled and wrapped our arms around Apicius. The hurt that reverberated in my chest was echoed in those arms and limbs, in the tears that wet our skin, in the ashes that filled our hair.

It took two days for the fire to die down and it destroyed the lower half of the Caelian Hill. There was nothing left of the school but rubble. The head of Apicius's guard was able to recover some ashes from the shop where Fannia and Aelia died and he brought them back in small terra-cotta jars wrapped in swaths of black cloth. I had my doubts about how they could be other than pieces of wood from the wreckage but said nothing. Apicius seemed comforted to have the jars even if we had to pry them from his hands after another long jag of tears.

A few hours after the ashes were recovered I took a walk with Sotas in the garden to the far end where we wouldn't be overheard. Sotas's voice was grave. "The vigiles reported that the shop was owned by one of Livia's freedmen."

"I knew it." I threw my hands up to the sky. "Apollo! Let your arrows fly to that woman's breast and make her pay for all the tears we have shed."

"Homer," Sotas recognized. "It's apt."

I wanted to weep in frustration. "We can't tell anyone about this, can we?"

Sotas shook his head. "No. Even the vigiles told me they were not going to make a report. We can't accuse Caesar's mother."

"She killed dozens."

"I know. But if we make a fuss it will only end in more death. Likely our deaths." He rested his hand reassuringly on my shoulder.

I kicked the nearby fence with my foot. "At the first banquet for Caesar, Livia told Fannia her time was running out. And that she and Apicius had insulted her for the last time."

"Fannia was ever taking risks with her cousin. And Apicius crossed the line by not selling you and later by freeing you."

I ran through all the scenarios in my mind—all the ways I could poison the witch. In her soup, in her drink, in a delicate sauce over her fish. Damn all her tasters!

"I know what you are thinking," he warned me. "Revenge is not an answer. You have a woman and child to consider. Leave Livia's fate to the gods. And don't tell Apicius. He would do something stupid that could likely get us all killed. Nor Apicata—do not burden her further."

I could say nothing. Sotas was right. I could no longer hold it all in and I broke down weeping. The big slave held me and comforted me like a brother.

The funeral was a short affair. As there were no bodies, we could not make the wax death masks or have an elaborate funeral fitting of Fannia and Aelia's station. There would be no procession to take the bodies through the Roman Forum. There would be no eulogy. Aelia's father had been recently appointed a new governorship, of Pannonia, and would likely not receive word of her death for weeks.

Claudius Pulcher, Fannia's husband, sent his regrets that he would not be able to attend the funeral nor did he plan on burying her in the family tomb. Instead, we held a gathering at home for both Aelia and Fannia with a small group of relatives, which, unfortunately, included Sejanus and Livia.

"I don't know if I can bear to look at her," I told Passia and Sotas the hour before the ceremony began and the guests arrived, "much less keep my mouth shut or my hands to myself. I want to kill her where she stands."

Sotas looked at me, his steely-gray eyes stern. "It is simple."

Passia and I both let out an exclamation. Simple? Sotas was not deterred.

"Yes, it is very simple. You will say nothing to her. You will bow your head or kiss her cheek if offered, but with every touch, with every look, with any word, you will think of only one thing."

"And what is that?"

He waved to Junius, whom we could see in the kitchen beyond where we stood, playing a game with one of the slaves. "Your son. Junius needs you in his life. He needs you to be strong, healthy, and, most important, not in a dungeon, or worse, dead."

My friend Sotas, always the wise sage. "Aelia would have told you the same."

He was right. She would have said the same.

There was not much to the ceremony, only the hired mourners singing and the priest of Hera saying a few words over the urns that rested on a table in the atrium. I didn't look at the guests—I couldn't bear to see the faces of our enemies reveling in our misfortune. I fixed my sight on the ground, or sometimes on Apicata's dark veil or on Apicius, who was stone-faced and dry-eyed. He stared into the crowd, and when I looked to see where his gaze was fixed it was on Sejanus, who looked downward. Then I recalled what Sotas had told me about the first time Apicius saw Sejanus after their ill-fated affair—over the coffin of Aelia's mother. I could only imagine what was running through Apicius's mind.

Livia did not stay long, thankfully. She was polite and reserved, paying her respects and leaving as soon as it was through. I don't think she had room for emotion in that dark heart of hers. Sejanus left with Livia to attend Caesar.

When the rest of the guests had departed, Apicius, Apicata, Sotas, Passia, Helene, and I went to the Gavia family tomb. We trudged through the town in a solemn clump, adorned in black, followed only by our guards for safety as it grew dark. Apicius held Fannia and Apicata held her mother. Two of the guards pulled a wagon with the heavy *laudatio* stones, etched with the stories of their lives. Helene, Passia, and I carried wine, incense, and fruit for the inhumation. Citizens saw our funereal garb and quickly parted to let us through. They did not want to catch our bad luck.

The Gavia tomb was close to the gates on the Appian Way, which was typical of wealthy patrician families. It was a massive sepulchre, adorned with statues of the gods and carvings of the deeds of the Gavia family. Apicius unlocked the sepulchre and had the guards open the heavy stone door. We stood outside as Apicius and Apicata entered the tomb and placed our hearts on dark shelves with the other ancestors. Sotas and Helene followed them with the sacrificial items and returned to us immediately after. I could see only the flickering candlelight bouncing off the walls of the entryway but deep inside I could smell the incense and I could hear their cries. I hugged Passia close and she sobbed into my shoulder.

When they emerged much later, the guards helped us shut the sepulchre and lock it. They took to their spades and placed the laudatio. Fannia's stone was simple, as was befitting a woman not from our family but given the honor of burial. I noticed Apicius had not included Pulcher's name.

"Please, Thrasius, will you read the stones for us? I know I should, but . . . I can't." Apicius's voice wavered.

I took a deep breath and began with Fannia. "'*To the spirits of the departed, Fannia Drusilla, of seventy-four years, you who died at the hands of another. Fate bequeaths your friends only sorrow at your leaving. Fannia, you were a dear friend to the Gavia family and to others, a confidante, and a matron of high status, beloved by all. May the di Manes grant you rest and protection.*'"

Apicius choked. He fell to his knees and put his head in his hands. "Please, Fannia, forgive me. I treated you so poorly these last few years, Fannia! Oh, dear gods, please be kind to her, oh, please."

Apicius touched me on the arm. "Let me read for Aelia."

Ceres! Did you hear me? Take pity!

Apicius read Aelia's tombstone through a river of tears. "'*Aelia Gavia, wife to me, Marcus Gavius Apicius, mother to our daughter, Apicata Gavia, friend to all, your life was snuffed like a candle at the age of forty-six.*

"'*We met for the first time in Minturnae. You were shy and beautiful and made my heart sing like a bird. You told me my words were like honey—sweet and nourishing. The day we married was one of the best days of my life. When I carried you over the threshold you told me you would always love me and would always be loyal to me. And you were.*'"

He paused, his tears getting the better of him. He began again, haltingly.

"'Aelia, you were a true Roman matron. You took care of my household, you gave me counsel and nursed me when I was ill. You gave me sons but fate took them from us. You gave me a daughter, Apicata, who learned from you and is now as strong and obedient as you were in life.

"'To the end you were a good wife, dying in flames seeking an item you thought would please me. I should have been the one to go to the grave first, not you, you who outshone us all. Natural sadness wrests away my power of self-control and I am overwhelmed by sorrow. I am tormented by two emotions: grief and fear—and I do not stand firm against either. I am destined to long mourning. You will forever haunt my thoughts, my Aelia.

"'I pray the di Manes will grant you rest and protection.'"

"Aelia! Oh, Aelia! Forgive me, forgive me," Apicius wailed to the heavens. Apicata threw her arms around her father and sobbed.

I wished not for the first time that week that I would open my eyes and find it all a dream.

Sotas had had the wherewithal to arrange for a litter to be waiting to take us to the villa. We rode together, curtains drawn, unable to speak. If we weren't crying we stared into nowhere, drained from the events of the last few days. We let Apicata out at the gates to her home.

When we arrived at the villa Apicius stopped us before we went into the house.

"Helene, Passia, wait." He walked to them and took Helene's hands. "Aelia gave you your freedom many years ago but you stayed and proved your loyalty to your domina. Thank you for your service. I want you to have the villa in Baiae if you would wish it, and all its slaves. Aelia told me how much you missed leaving. She always looked after you and I know she would want you to have it."

Her mouth formed a soft O and her eyes began to tear up again. "I cannot thank you enough."

Apicius turned to Passia and took her hands. "I should have listened to Aelia. I should have freed you many times over, all those times when both you and Thrasius came to me with your hard-earned peculium. I was too afraid. But today I free you and your son and we will go to the lictor to make it so. You have been a dear friend to Aelia and Apicata and I cannot thank you enough for your loyalty to them. I hope you and Thrasius will marry and stay here with me. I can give you money or villas but I hope you would consider . . ."

He faltered, looking at me. "Letting me adopt Junius. In name only, of course. I could never be the father you are to him."

My jaw fell open. What he was offering was monumental. It was not unusual for patricians without heirs to adopt, as only a direct male heir could inherit the family name. It would mean my son would be Apicius's heir. It meant he had an entire patrician world open to him. He could even run for the Senate if he so desired! Passia looked to me and we both indicated our assent.

"Good. Next week we will draw up the contracts." He kissed Passia and Helene on the cheek and hugged me, hard. My neck was wet when he pulled away.

CHAPTER 25

Passia and I did not marry right away. We could not bear the thought of binding our hearts together in marriage when they felt so broken by the loss of Aelia and Fannia. Apicius was true to his word and freed Passia. When we saw Helene off to Baiae, all the house slaves came to see her go but Apicius stayed inside, locked in his room, no longer able to look upon the woman who had been so close to his wife.

When I did marry Passia, many months later, it was a small affair, just Passia, Sotas, Junius, and me at home, before the family hearth. That day was a bright spot in what had been a cloudy year. I felt like all the gods were smiling upon me when I took Passia's hands and we declared our love, almost twenty-six years after we had first laid eyes on each other.

I did not ask Apicius to attend. His heart hurt too much to see our happiness. While we never spoke about it, I know he noticed the gold ring upon Passia's finger.

Apicius became increasingly unstable after Aelia's and Fannia's deaths. He alternated between bouts of extreme sadness and anger, sometimes within a few minutes of each other. There would be times when weeks would go by and I would think he was starting to let go of their memory, and then something or someone would remind him of his loss and it would start all over again.

He managed, for the most part, to put on a good show for his clients and for those who attended Caesar and Sejanus's dinner parties. But inside, I knew he was a wreck. He would come home and fly into raging fits at the slaves, or would lock himself in his bedroom to drink himself into a stupor. It was hard to know which mood Apicius decided to don on any given day.

I have thought often about why I didn't just leave then, when I had what I had been longing for most, my beloved. It was more than Junius becoming his heir. Every time I saw Apicius, my heart broke for him. I had my wife and son, but for friends, he had no one but me and Sotas. We were the only ones who had ever stood by him, at first by force, but then . . . then I stayed by choice. He had become my friend, in a strange, stilted sort of way that one might call another a friend.

A year after the fire, Tiberius asked Apicius why he thought he was free from following the laws of marriage. Apicius was forced to comply, but he did so only under great duress and it was I who took the brunt of his wrath.

"I don't want her here! Pack her up and put her in my villa in Cumae. Get her out of my sight!" Apicius threw his goblet full of wine across the library, where it smashed against the still-wet fresco on the wall. I rushed over to gingerly dampen the stain before it could mar the costly mural.

"Let it run! I told the bastard it was terrible!"

I continued to sop up the liquid, ignoring him. The painter had been back three times in the last month to fix various parts of the fresco Apicius thought unsatisfactory. It was a small scene from when Apicius and Aelia lived in Minturnae. In the center of the fresco were two people walking along the beach with an expansive villa on the cliff above. I had argued with him endlessly not to have it done but he insisted.

"Everything all right?" Sotas poked his head into the room.

"Did I ask for you?" Apicius screamed, jowls shaking. Sotas backed out and shut the door.

I tried to reason with him. "Look, Apicius, throwing things doesn't change the situation."

He kicked the desk, knocking several scrolls to the floor. "Damn 'Divine Augustus' and his ridiculous laws."

"I agree," I said, "but the alternative is worse. Taking a wife is the law and it's a law you can't disobey—if you do it, then other men will want to stay unmarried and Sejanus can't have that. You don't want him breathing down your neck more than he already does."

Apicius collapsed into a chair near the window. "Let him try!"

"You haven't even talked to the woman beyond the few words you exchanged during the ceremony. She might be perfect for your household, to keep it running smoothly."

He waggled a finger at me. "That's why I've got you, Thrasius!"

"A wife lends you a certain status I cannot."

He stood suddenly, knocking over the chair in his anger. "My wife is *dead*!"

I shook my head at him and left the room.

"I think he's right. Better to send her to Cumae. I don't think he's going to come around," Sotas said. I could hear Apicius cursing inside.

"Nor do I. We'll be doing her a favor."

I chuckled ruefully and headed down the hall toward the guest chambers, where I imagined that Flora, Apicius's new wife, was pacing the floor, wondering if her husband would ever exchange words with her. She was barely seventeen and as beautiful as a fresh rose on a June afternoon. I had chosen her for Apicius because of her father's status and because I had hoped that her beauty might be enough to jolt him out of his dreary mood.

"He hates me," she said when I entered the room. It wasn't a question.

"No, he hates the idea of being married to anyone other than his dead wife." I sat down on the chaise near the window and asked one of the slaves to pour us wine.

She sat across from me on the edge of the chair, poised as though she might run away at any moment. "Tell me, was he very much in love with her?"

I thought back to all the times when Apicius had neglected Aelia and been unkind. Then I remembered all the gifts he bought her in every port we visited, and how when we would return from a trip he always made sure to seek her out the moment he set foot inside the villa. "He was. And when she passed, I think he realized how much."

She nodded, her green eyes dark with uncertainty. "What happens now?"

I took a long sip of my wine. "He wishes that I send you to his villa in Cumae."

Flora shook her head. "I am to be exiled from him?"

"No, think not like that. You will have all the luxury you can imagine in Cumae. You'll have a monthly stipend. If you are shrewd, you can make even more money from the villa's fleet of fishing boats and its farms in the countryside. I'll send a secretary with you to advise you on such matters. It will be unlikely that you will ever see Apicius again."

She picked up the goblet of wine in front of her and drank a healthy dose not becoming of a young woman. I said nothing. I could not blame her.

"So I am to be alone all my life."

"Only if you choose to be."

She cocked her head at me, confused.

"Be discreet. Abort any children you find yourself with. What Apicius does not hear about does not concern him."

She sighed with relief.

"We have more pressing things to worry about," Rúan reassured me a few days after Flora had left. "She wouldn't have been happy with Apicius." While it was true that Apicius never again laid eyes on Flora, I saw her occasionally in the years afterward when she came to Rome to visit her family, and I would hear from her from time to time when she needed something. For the most part she was a successful manager of the household in Cumae, upholding Apicius's reputation in the way I had hoped. I knew from a few of my trusted staff members there that she had taken on lovers, but she never allowed her position to be compromised.

As for the law requiring Apicius to be married, I'm sure if Augustus had been alive he would not have condoned Flora being sent away—it defeated the purpose of the law, which was to turn around the Roman decline in population. Sejanus, thankfully, had better things to concern himself with. As long as Apicius satisfied the general marriage requirement, he didn't seem to care, which was fortunate.

• • •

Over the following months it became apparent that Sejanus had big plans. He was growing in power, and often when you heard his name, the word *tyrant* would follow. He began to enact all sorts of laws on behalf of Caesar that were very much to his advantage.

We were in the kitchen at the Imperial villa preparing for a banquet Sejanus was hosting that evening. Tiberius would likely not be in attendance; we rarely saw Caesar anymore. Not since his adopted son, Germanicus, had died six years before from poison at the hands of the former governor of Syria. All of Rome mourned, but no one more than his father, and he retreated in sorrow to a villa in Campania. He avoided Rome and appeared for only the most important state functions.

Rúan handed me the bowl of sardines I pointed toward. "I forgot to mention, Apicata came to see you today. She said she hopes you will come by soon."

I was sad I had missed seeing Apicata. Sejanus didn't let her leave home often but sometimes Livia would invite her to the Imperial villa and she would sneak by the kitchen in the hope she might see me.

I poured a flask of oil over the tiny fish. "Did she have the children with her?" Her brood was growing fast, with Strabo at age nine, Capito at age seven, and four-year-old Junilla.

Rúan shook his head. "No, but she did say Tiberius questioned her at length."

That caught my attention. I set down the oil flask. "What do you mean? Why would Tiberius question her?"

"It was about the old astrologer Apicius used to have."

"Glycon?"

"Yes. He asked her about Glycon and all of the predictions he correctly made. She said he was very insistent on knowing how accurately he read the stars."

I scattered a handful of herbs over the sardines. "Curious. I wonder why."

Rúan shrugged and tossed the last of the parsnips he'd been chopping into a pot. "Apicata said she couldn't figure it out either."

Glycon had given us too many true predictions. He had known of my son's birth, of Apicius's appointment to Caesar's staff, and, worst of all, he had known about Aelia's death. I tried not to think of what he had said that hadn't yet come true—about not seeing the stars of Apicata's children in the later years of their life.

It turned out Tiberius was equally nervous about predictions he could not understand. The following day he released an edict outlawing foreign rites of any kind, including those of the Egyptian cults and also the Jews. All adherents of what he called "superstitions" were to burn their religious clothing and items or they would be expelled from the city or sold into slavery.

Apicius and I learned of the edict at the baths, surrounded by gossiping patricians and senators. Tycho and Sotas had already helped us bathe and their practiced hands were massaging our tired necks and backs.

Trio had joined us as well. "I don't understand how he's going to enforce it." A young slave boy rubbed his back, pounding and pinching the skin. "Does he mean to include the cult of Isis?"

"No, no," one of the elderly senators responded. "Isis is a Roman cult now, not Egyptian. Very different from the cults of Horus and Bast. Dreadful gods those are."

"What about all the Jews in the army? By Jove, he's even got a few Jews as captains. He can't possibly want to reduce the size of his army more than he has to, not with the barbarians in the north still unsettled," said Apicius.

"He plans to send them to Germania!" The same senator chuckled. "Or to other, less desirable regions, if there is such a thing. Why should the Jews be stationed in the best lands?"

"What I don't understand is why he cast out the astrologers," said another man across the room, hidden by the steam.

"Ahh, interesting," I muttered, suddenly realizing why Tiberius had questioned Apicata about Glycon. I was filled with bitter happiness at the thought that Glycon would be forced to flee Rome.

I noticed that Sotas, who had been massaging Apicius's back, also paused at the words. Apicius shrugged for him to continue.

The old senator had the answer once again. "All of them except his shadow, Thrasyllus. He trusts him implicitly. It's all the other astrologers whom he fears. What if one of them predicted his death? Or a revolt in Rome? And it came true? Ironic, isn't it?"

"How so?" asked Apicius.

"He bans other religions for their superstitions and yet he is more superstitious than them all."

"Some of the astrologers are terribly accurate, though. I could see why Tiberius is afraid of them," Trio countered. "I mean, look at how accurate your astrologer was, Apicius. How many things he told you came true?"

Apicius was silent for a moment, then he stood up suddenly, knocking Sotas backward and startling all in the bath. "And how would you know how many predictions have come true?" His voice echoed through the vast chamber, reaching the ears of hundreds of bathers. "You know nothing! Nothing at all! You know only of Caesar's games and of scarfing down all the food on your friends' couches. You know nothing of me or my life."

We all watched, openmouthed, as he stormed out of the bath, naked, his penis shriveled and nestled underneath his big belly. Sotas managed to regain his balance and ran to follow him but slipped on the wet tiles and hit his head, knocking himself out. I cursed under my breath.

I could hear Apicius still yelling, "Nothing! You know nothing!"

I rushed to Sotas's side. "Tycho, fetch our clothes, and fast!"

Trio came to help me, lifting the big slave's head to see if he had cracked it open. I breathed a sigh of relief when there was no blood. "What was that about?" Trio asked me. There was no anger in his voice, only concern.

"Glycon predicted Aelia's death."

Trio drew in a breath that whistled between his teeth. "I didn't realize. I was thinking of how he predicted the arrival of your son."

"Did you see Apicius?" I asked when Tycho returned with our clothes.

"No, but people were talking about a naked man leaving the bath."

"Help Sotas and make sure he sees a physician, please. I'll go find Apicius."

"Yes, Master."

"No, you go with Thrasius," Trio said to Tycho. "I'll bring Sotas to Apicius's villa in my litter." Trio waved us on.

I ran out of the baths, not bothering to put my sandals on. Tycho followed and I was grateful for Trio's kindness in the wake of Apicius's terrible outburst.

I decided to go toward home, hoping Apicius might have headed there. We didn't have to run far before we could hear the jeers of a crowd. When we reached the commotion, my worst fears were realized.

Apicius walked in a slow daze through the crowd, his body still pink from the bath and the scraping of the strigils. He wasn't clean, however. Instead he was covered with dust from the streets and the scraps of vegetables thrown at him. A big leaf of lettuce was stuck to the back of his head.

Children tossed pebbles and handfuls of straw at him, laughing as they circled wide. Women made the sign of the evil eye and turned their heads away. Men hurled obscenities at him.

Nothing seemed to touch Apicius, not beyond the shell of his skin. I rushed to him and Tycho helped me push the people away. He had brought a couple of towels and I wrapped them around my old master, doing my best to shield him from other vegetables still being tossed in our direction. He didn't seem to register that I was there.

"That's old Apicius!" someone yelled. It was a *taberna* owner who waggled a crispy chicken leg at us over the heads of the patrons on the stools of his roadside counter.

A new chant arose. "Pig! Gorger! Glutton! Pig! Gorger! Glutton!"

"We've got to get him out of here!" I tried to lead Apicius out of the frenzied crowd but he was slow and did not want to move.

"Aelia."

I heard him whisper her name just as a flurry of thrown figs exploded against the back of my tunic.

A horn broke through the sounds of the crowd. Nervous that it was one of Caesar's guards, I turned to look.

Trio's litter and a handful of his armed guards cut through the people surrounding us. Taunting a naked old man was one thing. Braving the wrath of a patrician was another. While the chants continued, the vegetable throwing stopped and the crowd parted until the litter came up to us. "Come now, get in," Trio said, opening up the curtains. His slaves helped me lift Apicius into the litter until he sat next to where Sotas lay among the cushions.

Apicius only stared ahead.

"Thank you, Trio," I said once the litter was moving again and I had caught my breath.

"No, do not thank me. I can only hope that if I fall prey to such misfortune someone like you would look after me. It is the least I can do."

Sotas awoke shortly after. "Dominus Apicius?" he asked before he had even opened his eyes. I marveled at his loyalty. We explained what had happened as Sotas sat up. He moved over to sit next to his master. "Dominus? I am here if you need me."

Apicius said nothing. The entire way home he continued to stare ahead, seemingly unaware of his surroundings.

Trio stayed with us at the villa until the physician arrived; then he left, promising to check in with us the next day. The physician proclaimed it to be an acute case of melancholia and advised us to give him opium and to feed him a strict diet of mushrooms and leeks—no meat.

Apicius ate when we fed him but did not speak. He seemed happy when he had opium and he would talk on occasion but it was mostly only to speak his dead wife's name.

"It's been nearly two years. Why now?" I ranted to Sotas the first night of his illness.

His response was matter-of-fact. "He has been cursed."

"But by whom?"

"He has many enemies."

I could not argue with him.

Apicius's illness reminded me much of how Apicata reacted when we told her she could not marry Casca. I remembered it was Apicius who broke through to her. I hoped his daughter might do the same for him now.

On the seventh day I sent an urgent message to her. I hadn't wanted to worry her but now I was afraid she might be our only hope of having Apicius back.

Apicata came the moment she heard the news. "I will help him," she said after the door slaves let her in. She brushed past me toward his chamber. I stood aside and let her enter. She shooed Sotas and the other slaves out, then closed the door behind her.

She remained with him for an hour before emerging. Sotas, Passia, and I waited in the nearby atrium, barely speaking. Sotas paced the corridor along the garden and we watched, holding hands and hoping.

Apicius was with her, dressed in a simple blue tunic and a pair of his fine red shoes. "My father is hungry," she announced. She turned to him. "What would you like, Father?"

"Something other than a plate of damned mushrooms." A broad smile lit up his face. "Thrasius, I think I am craving chicken. What about one of your Parthian dishes tonight?"

I gaped, unable to believe the transformation that had taken place in Apicius's eyes. "Yes," I finally managed. "Chicken. I'll make chicken!"

"Good! I think I'll help tonight. It's been a long time since I was in the kitchen."

He turned down the hall and Sotas and Passia hurried to follow him. I stopped Apicata.

"What did you say to him?"

She smiled and it was a sad, wistful gesture. "I lied to him. I told him Mother had come to me in a dream. And that she was still with us, watching over him, wanting him to move on."

I hugged her, then we walked to the kitchen to help Apicius make a dish of Parthian chicken.

PART X

28 C.E. to 29 C.E.

SAUCE FOR GRILLED MULLET

Pepper, lovage, rue, honey, pine nuts, vinegar, wine, liquamen, a little oil; warm it through and pour on.

—*Book 10.1.11, The Fisherman*
On Cookery, Apicius

CHAPTER 26

"A picius is back! Apicius is back!" Fourteen-year-old Junius's voice rang through the villa corridors. I looked at Passia and grabbed her hand. Together we followed our son to the front gate, where Apicius was being helped out of his litter.

In the last two years he'd traveled to various temples all over the Empire, praying to the gods to bring Aelia to him in a dream as she had "appeared" to his daughter. Neither Apicata nor I had the heart to tell him she had lied about the dream. Every once in a while we would receive a letter brought by a courier telling us of the cities he had visited. He also sent back scores of recipes, costly delicacies, and ideas to further grace Caesar's table during his absence, which I executed, much to the delight of the diners on Caesar's Roman couches.

Apicius was a little more rotund than when he had left and his skin was tanned a dark brown, which made the wrinkles around his eyes and mouth more pronounced.

Unlike his master, Sotas had grown even more muscular, likely from additional exercise on their travels. Plus, if he had to assist in carrying Apicius's litter at all, it would have kept him strong. Like Apicius, he was in his late fifties, but you would not have known it from his appearance.

Apicius was jovial and glad to have returned. There was a light in his eyes that shone in a way I had not seen in years.

He gave us all hugs and a broad smile, but the biggest he reserved for Junius.

"By Jove! Who is this handsome young man? I daresay I know him not!" He winked at my son, clearly pleased to see him.

"I've grown a little, I know," Junius said, smiling.

"A little? It is as though I've grown a statesman in my own house! Pretty soon you'll be running off to the Senate for a vote, or taking to the Forum to argue a case. I can hear them now. 'Junius Thrasius Gavius Apicius, the great orator, is ready to present his side of the story!'"

Both Junius and I beamed with pride. Apicius put an arm around my son and started to walk toward the house, asking him a variety of questions about his studies. "Ready the triclinium for the cena tonight, Thrasius. I think I'd like to see a few old friends."

I was only too happy to oblige.

"I am glad you are hosting cenae once more. We missed you and your wit!" Trio lifted his glass to toast Apicius. It was a warm May evening and we dined outside in the garden under the stars of Rome.

"You went far in your travels, Apicius. You must have seen some amazing places," Celera said.

Apicius beamed. "I did."

"Which was your favorite?"

"It is hard to say! Hera's temple in Paestum is magnificent but it is hard to rival the home of Venus in Heliopolis."

He had told me about the experience he had in Heliopolis, in which the goddess told him in a dream to go home and to "waste not fresh tears over old griefs." I think his experience was more attributable to an opium pipe than anything else; Euripides first said that line several hundred years ago. Still, it was those words that brought him and Sotas home and for that I was grateful.

Apicius smiled as he plucked some grapes from the tray on the table in front of him. "I am glad to share this meal with you as well. It has been too long and Thrasius has become overconfident." He winked at me.

"Oh, Apicius, we haven't even talked about the big news! You must be pleased!"

"Pleased about what?"

Trio's eyes widened. "About Junilla, of course!"

Apicius looked to me for an answer but I could only shrug. I hadn't talked to Apicata in over a week. Junilla was seven—what news could there be?

"I haven't had a chance to see her yet. She sent word that she could not come tonight, but she would see me soon."

"Sejanus managed to convince poor, addled Claudius to engage his son to Junilla."

I wondered at the news. Claudius was Tiberius's nephew and not well liked. He was sickly and had a clubfoot that made him the butt of many Roman jokes.

Trio motioned his slave to him, then wiped the grease from his fingers in the boy's long hair.

"Fetch him a napkin," I said to Tycho, who waited in the shadows.

"No, no, that's what Hector is here for." Trio waved dismissively at his slave, who stepped back to his post along the triclinium wall.

"You must be proud," Celera said. "Claudius's son could be Caesar one day."

"Indeed," Apicius said.

The boy, Claudius Drusus, was thirteen. Because there were already several men of Imperial nobility named Drusus, he went by the nickname Albus, which was a nod to his very pale skin. I marveled that Sejanus was so desperate to hold power in Rome that he would look for such a long-reaching opportunity as to marry Junilla to the boy. What was he planning? Then again, if Albus became Caesar at a young age, Sejanus would be very powerful indeed.

"I admit, I do feel sorry for the girl, growing up knowing Claudius will be her father-in-law," Trio said.

I had been thinking the same thing. Caesar's nephew, Claudius, always seemed somewhat slow and deformed. "I hear he spends all his time locked away in his library, writing histories."

"Yes, when he's not shuffling through the palace playing oaf to young Caligula," Celera agreed. "He lets the boy torment him."

"And that wife of his!" Apicius leaned in conspiratorially. "She looks like a monster straight out of Virgil's tales!"

Apicius laughed with his friends but I saw the glimpse of darkness in his eyes.

In the morning, Apicius had Sotas rouse me early. I didn't need to ask why.

"Why didn't she tell us the news in her message to me?" Apicius said once we were in the litter, with Tycho and Sotas walking along-side beyond the closed curtains. I had retired early the night before and missed any previous tirade.

"The note probably came from Sejanus. He rarely lets her out of his sight. He's ambitious and we are of little consequence. He rarely speaks to me unless he requires me to attend a dinner. He has also kept you from Caesar for many years."

"I am barely a dog to him," Apicius muttered.

We rode in silence until we came to a sudden stop at our destination. The door slaves ushered us into the atrium, where Sejanus met us. He wore a blinding-white toga, so fresh and white I could still smell the chalk in its fibers from a few paces away.

"To what do I owe the pleasure of this visit?"

I thought I detected a sneer in his voice although the smile on his lips revealed nothing.

"We heard news of the engagement," Apicius began pleasantly. "We wanted to pay our respects and bring a gift." He signaled Sotas forward and the body-slave passed Sejanus a small sack of what I assumed were a number of heavy coins meant to help supplement Junilla's dowry.

"That is gracious of you! We are very pleased about the union, of course."

"We'd love to see Apicata and congratulate her," I started to say, but was stopped when Livia and Apicata entered from the far entrance to the atrium. Livia leaned on one of her slaves as she walked.

I froze for a second, then forced myself to relax. It was always an effort to hide my thoughts about Livia.

"Father!" Apicata glided across the room to where we stood. She threw her arms around his neck and enveloped him in a hug. "I didn't know you were coming home! Oh, I'm so glad to see you!" She reached up to kiss each cheek.

It was as I expected, she hadn't even known that her father had returned.

"We came to congratulate you about Junilla." He sounded put off. I sighed to myself, wishing he were better at hiding his emotions.

While this small scene was playing out, I overheard Livia talking to one of her bodyguards, a few words that sounded like "the boy or the girl, either one." I watched out of the corner of my eye as the guard slipped off into the corridor.

I averted my eyes when her gaze turned toward me.

"I sent a messenger days ago," Sejanus was saying. "I never heard back from you."

He was lying. I watched his nostrils twitch as he talked, a trick I had learned from Fannia, may the shades treat her well.

"No messenger came." Apicius turned his attention to Livia. "Livia, it is, as always, a pleasure to see you." He smiled broadly and bowed his head toward her in respect. I inclined my head as well but did not smile. Apicius did not know about Livia's part in his wife's death. But I did and nothing could make me smile at such a harpy.

"I'm sure you are happy to have your granddaughter joined in union to my great-grandson. It seems you are to become part of my family." She sounded about as pleased as a bath attendant at the front counter stuck taking coins all day.

"I hope the two of them will be compatible," Apicius said politely.

"Why don't we go see Albus and Junilla?" Apicata said in an attempt to alleviate the tension. "They are in the back playing hide-and-seek with Capito and Strabo."

"I would love to see them," I said, seizing the opportunity. I knew Apicata was happiest watching her children.

"Yes, let us go to the garden." Sejanus moved in that direction. "Claudius will be joining us presently as well."

We walked through the villa, making petty chat about how beautiful Junilla was becoming and what a fine wife she would make young Albus.

Suddenly a child's scream rose from the garden in front of us. We all broke into a run, bursting from the darkness of the corridor into the bright sunlight of the garden. At the other end of the garden, I caught a glimpse of Livia's bodyguard leaving through the opposite doorway.

Junilla and Capito stood over an unmoving form on the tiles alongside the central garden pool. As we neared, we could see it was the boy Albus. His face was a terrifying purple-red and his eyes were unmoving and open, lined with broken blood vessels. His mouth was stretched wide as though gasping for air. In his hand he held a pear with a large bite taken from it.

Apicata was the first to reach the children, with Livia right behind. "What happened?" She picked up the boy and cradled him in her arms.

Junilla began crying. "We were hiding and waiting for him to find us." Her voice caught on the edge of a sob. "When Albus didn't come, I came out and he was dead!" She turned away, tears staining the front of her tunica.

A young slave woman, dark with long braided hair and green eyes, appeared with Strabo. "Where were you?" Apicata asked, her voice frantic. "Weren't you watching the children?"

"I was hiding with Strabo," she started to say.

"Get the children out of here!" Sejanus spat at her. She jumped, then hurriedly ushered Junilla, Capito, and Strabo away.

"Give him to me!" He tore Albus from Apicata. "He's choking!" Sejanus pulled the boy close and pushed on his chest hard, over and over, until a huge chunk of pear flew out of his mouth. It was splattered with blood.

Still the boy did not move or gasp for breath. "Breathe!" Sejanus screamed at the boy. "By Jove, breathe!" He pounded on the child's chest. I thought I heard a rib crack.

"Sejanus, stop," Livia said calmly. She bore no tears for her great-grandson. She put a hand on his shoulder. "He's gone."

"No!" He continued to pummel the boy with his fists. "He can't die! He can't!"

Apicius stood next to me, with Sotas and Tycho standing behind. We watched, aghast. No longer was this about the death of a child. It was about Sejanus—what madness had overtaken him?

"Sejanus, stop! I command you!" Livia's voice cut through his haze and his hands fell to his sides. Tears flowed freely across his cheeks, something I had not thought him capable of. "Pick him up," Livia said, her voice firm and still without emotion.

Sejanus did not move to pick up the boy. Instead, he stood and backed away a few paces, continuing to mutter, "No, no, this can't happen," not quite under his breath.

Livia indicated to her body-slave to pick up the child and bring him to her. Then, with two fingers she closed his eyes. She pulled her shawl from her shoulders and had the slave wrap it around Albus, covering the purple of his face.

"What happened?" A man's thin voice broke our silence. It was Claudius, flanked by a door slave who had likely intended to announce his arrival. Claudius limped over to us as quickly as his clubfoot would allow.

I expected Sejanus to respond as he should have, being the man of the house. Yet when I looked for him, he was gone.

Apicata collected herself and rose from the grass. She started toward Claudius, who was closing the distance between them. He struggled with the effort to run.

Apicius stepped in front of her. "Let me," I heard him say. She moved aside as Claudius shuffled to a stop.

Apicius held out his hand to touch Claudius on the shoulder. "There has been a terrible accident."

I watched Claudius's mouth work to find the words. "Wh . . . wh . . . wh . . . wh . . . wh . . . wh . . . what is going on?"

It was well known that Claudius had a stutter but I had never been close enough to hear him talk until now. No wonder he was the laughingstock of the palace.

"It's your son," Apicius started to say.

Claudius pushed past him, nearly falling with the effort. "Albus?" His voice cracked.

He collapsed on the ground next to Livia. His clubfoot stuck out beyond the folds of his toga, twisted unnaturally.

"Oh, m . . . mm . . . my boy!" He took his son from Livia's arms. "Wh . . . wh . . . wh . . . what happened?" he asked his grandmother.

"He choked on a pear, Claudius. I'm so sorry."

She didn't sound sorry at all.

Sejanus recovered from his frenzy quickly, insisting on footing the bill for the small funeral to be held. No one had seen the bodyguard leave the atrium but me. No one saw Albus eat the pear—they were all hiding. The body-slave was watching the other children hide and saw nothing. When I asked Livia about the bodyguard, she told me pleasantly but firmly that I was mistaken. I didn't miss the warning tone in her voice. Three years ago Tiberius had passed a law that speaking against Livia would be an act of treason. I had no doubt she would have been delighted if I had decided to do so.

Claudius's son was the first Imperial noble named Drusus to die that year.

We had seen the other Drusus, Tiberius's son and only heir, only a handful of times since the banquet at the school. He had been off campaigning in distant lands as a leader in Caesar's army. Drusus was likely one of the few who hated Sejanus more than I or Apicius did.

Drusus's dislike of Sejanus was well known among most of Rome's elite but I had yet to witness his sentiments firsthand. At least not until the hot June eve of Vestalia, honoring the goddess Vesta and the everlasting flame of Rome. Sejanus had decided to host an elaborate banquet in celebration.

During the meal, Apicius had asked me to fetch Apicata from the garden, where she had escaped alone for a breath of fresh air. I found her on a bench admiring the view of Rome sprawled out beneath the Palatine Hill.

On our return we came upon Sejanus and Drusus in heated conversation in the hallway beyond the triclinium. Apicata and I stopped when we reached the knot of Praetorian Guard that stood behind Sejanus. We arrived in time to see Drusus slam his fist into Sejanus's chin. Sejanus staggered backward into his guards, who seemed conflicted about what to do. They were sworn to protect the Imperial family but I knew they were loyal to Sejanus.

"You deserve more than that, you filthy louse. Jupiter and all the gods damn you! I'm not sure what magic you are employing on my father that he has chosen to invite a stranger to assist in the government while his son is still alive, but I promise you, Sejanus, I will find out."

Sejanus regained his footing. He stood in the face of Drusus's rant and said nothing.

"One more thing, Sejanus. If I find that you are sleeping around with my wife," he snarled, "I will personally make sure that my father has you crucified." Drusus spat at Sejanus's feet, a long, wet gob that splattered against the Praetorian's toes. Then he turned and walked off.

Sejanus pointed to his feet and one of the slaves who stood nearby rushed to wipe off his toes with the hem of his tunic.

"He will rue this day. The gods will find favor with me, not him," Sejanus muttered. He turned away and pushed past the guards, stopping when he caught a glimpse of Apicata behind his men.

"Sejanus!" Apicata, schooled as she was to be the perfect Roman matron, and always trying to stay in his good graces, rushed to her husband. She reached her hand to his bruised face.

"Do *not* touch me!" He pushed her hand away in a rough gesture, throwing her off balance. "What in Tartarus are you doing here, woman?" The look on his face was dark. I was sure he was going to strike her but then he saw me. His visage changed and softened.

"Aren't they expecting you at the banquet? I was on my way to see if you were all right," he said to Apicata with a smile.

My chest tightened and I fought to control my anger. What would he have done to her if I had not been there?

Apicata seemed to realize the danger. She took me by the arm. "We were on our way there, husband. My father sent Thrasius to fetch me. Will you return with us?"

"I have other matters to attend to." He brushed past us, guards in tow.

When they were gone I turned to Apicata. "Is he always like this? He was ready to strike you!"

She began to cry.

I pulled her close. "Oh, my little bird." I ran my fingers through her hair, my heart breaking for her.

"I fear he may divorce me soon," she choked.

"Why would you think that?"

"I just do." She pulled away. "I would welcome it, but . . ."

"He will have the children," I finished. I knew they were her true joy.

Her fingers dabbed at the corners of her eyes in an attempt to keep from crying. I reached my hand to her face to smooth out the smeared kohl around her eyes.

Sejanus had married Apicata to vex Apicius and for the vast wealth that came with her dowry. Now he had power and the favor of Caesar. He didn't need her anymore. I understood her worry about the children, but I knew that my heart would feel great relief when she was no longer under his roof.

"Be strong, little bird. That's all you can do. Hold your head up high and never let him know how much he hurts you."

She nodded and together we returned to the party, our hearts heavy.

That summer Apicius and I began work on a new book, this time about breads and fritters. During his travels Apicius had fallen in love with some of the sweet delicacies of far-off lands and he wanted to share these new possibilities with the cooks for all the best Roman families. One of my favorite treats was bread soaked in milk and egg, fried, and slathered with honey before serving.

I made up a batch of this sweet eggy bread for Apicata and Junilla during one of their rare morning visits to Caesar's kitchen. Junius was there as well. He had inherited my and Apicius's love of food and was there helping me test out some of the new recipes.

"Thrasius, this is my favorite thing in the world!" Junilla declared. She licked honey off her fingers.

"I thought that fried dates were your favorite thing in the world!" Junius teased her.

"No, no, this bread is! When I am old enough to have my own cook, I'm going to have him make this for me every single day!" She put her hands on her hips and jutted out her chin at him. Her green eyes shone with determination.

"I think you might get tired of having this bread every day," Apicata suggested as I served up another batch.

"When can I get married? And not to someone who is going to die before we have a wedding?"

I had just put a piece of the sweet bread into my mouth and almost choked at her words. Children could be so blunt. Apicata closed her eyes, seemingly to keep her composure.

"What happened to Albus was an accident, Junilla," Junius reassured her. "Don't worry. You'll be married in due time. And it will be to someone rich enough to buy you a cook who will make you sweet bread every day."

"You'll be a beautiful bride, Junilla, but you don't need to grow up so fast. I'll make you sweet bread whenever you come to visit. Will that do for now?" I said. Apicata mouthed her silent thanks to me.

"It will have to do," Junilla said in a childish huff. Junius laughed and ruffled her hair.

In September two pivotal things happened. As Apicata had predicted, Sejanus divorced her.

The day Apicata came home was bittersweet. She arrived in the middle of the night, alone and without her children. At her behest the door slave woke me and not her father. Passia and I met her in the atrium and walked her to the room we still kept for her.

"They tore the boys out of my arms," she sobbed. "Junilla kept screaming for me. Oh, dear gods! Why? I was a good wife! Why did he take my children away from me?" She had shredded the front of her stola with her hands and the skin on her breast was wet with tears. Passia brought her a robe to cover herself but she flung it off. "It's that whore Livilla, I tell you! She has bewitched him and cursed me!"

"Shhhh." Passia smoothed down her hair. "You'll wake your father."

She quieted and cried against my wife's shoulder for a long time until, finally, she fell asleep in Passia's arms.

"I'll stay with her tonight." Passia waved at me to go. I did but I did not sleep much, so full of concerns was I about the implications of Apicata's divorce.

The implications became clear enough in the morning. At first light a messenger arrived with a note from Sejanus, addressed to Apicius. Apicius, who did not yet know Apicata was home, accepted it when he arrived in the atrium to receive his clients at salutatio. I joined him as he finished reading the letter.

"What did you do?" He threw the scroll at me.

I picked it up off the ground, confused. I rolled it open and read the official decree. Apicius was no longer cultural and gastronomic adviser. There was no explanation, only a thank-you for his service and a statement that he would no longer be required to attend Sejanus or Tiberius at future banquets and dinners.

"What did you do?" he screamed at me again, then charged me without warning, his bulk slamming into me and throwing me to the ground. His fists hit my face before I could stop him.

"Nothing!" I held up my arms to protect myself. "Sotas, get him off me!"

"Don't you dare!" Apicius screeched at Sotas as the big man came near. "I'll have you lashed if you disobey me."

Between the blows I saw Sotas hesitate. I pushed myself upward, trying to heave Apicius off me. His weight made it difficult.

"Father!"

Apicata's voice rang out across the atrium. "Sotas, get him off Thrasius. This has nothing to do with him."

Sotas pulled Apicius off me, holding his master at arm's length. "I'll have your hide for this," he spluttered at the body-slave.

"No you won't!" Apicata nodded for Sotas to let Apicius go.

"Wait, Apicata, what are you doing here?" Apicius said, suddenly realizing his daughter stood before him in her morning robe.

"Sejanus has divorced me."

"He *what*?"

"He divorced her." I allowed Passia to help me up. I tasted blood at the corner of my mouth. "That's why your services are no longer required."

Apicius stared at his daughter, his mouth ajar. Disbelief shone in his eyes.

"Divorced?" he managed after a spell.

"I'm sorry, Father," Apicata cried.

He looked at me, his face a mixture of emotion. "I'm sorry, Thrasius."

"I know."

He took a deep breath. "I hated the bastard anyway."

His words did not disguise his true feelings. Every part of his body seemed to radiate defeat. "No salutatio today. We will resume on the morrow."

We watched him leave the atrium. Apicata fell to her knees and began to sob.

It was two weeks after the divorce and we were listening to a new harpist in the garden when Tycho brought us the news about Drusus. He'd died in his cups the night before. Few thought it strange; he was known for his heavy drinking. His death left Tiberius without an heir and many assumed Sejanus would be chosen to succeed him.

"Now he can have Livilla," Apicata said when she heard the news. "How convenient."

"You've seen how much Drusus can drink. He just had more than he could handle," I said, trying to ease the emotion of the situation.

"No he didn't. Sejanus had someone poison him."

"You can't be sure of that," I said halfheartedly.

"Yes I can."

"It is too much coincidence," Apicius agreed. "I am coming to believe it will be good we are no longer in his sights. I think he is a very dangerous man to cross."

Apicata fingered the edge of her shawl. I knew that no one understood that fact better than she did. "You are right, Father, he is."

Apicius said what I had been thinking since the divorce. "I think if it were not for your children, Apicata, he would have me killed."

Apicata stared off into the cluster of trees lining the garden walls, her face a mask devoid of emotion. But her head bobbed up and down, a nearly imperceptible movement that said everything words could not say.

I looked across the garden where her eyes were fixed. A crow sat on the wall, tearing apart a mouse. It pecked one last time at the carcass, then tossed it away. It wiped its beak on a wing and then took flight, its black feathers a momentary ink against the sky.

CHAPTER 27

Apicius's paranoia about Sejanus was strong. With nothing to hold the Praetorian prefect in check, he feared for his life. To stay out of Sejanus's sight in the following year, Apicius avoided Rome, instead staying at his various homes in the countryside. I traveled with him, sometimes with Passia and Junius. I continued to write, and together, Apicius and I published another cookbook. The latest had been such a success I'd rented a space in a small shop on the Aventine and employed three scribes full-time to make copies. The book was a massive compendium of recipes to complement any kitchen. It had taken two years to write, and while many of the recipes came from our other books, there were scores of new dishes for the accomplished cook to try.

We made little money on the cookbook, however, because Apicius loved to give it away for free to his friends and to people he met. I tried many times to counsel Apicius about his money—my son's inheritance—which he spent at an alarming rate, but he refused to listen. I was comforted by the fact that he was entertaining less, but also worried about the money that we spent traveling from villa to villa. His latest project was renovating a new villa in Herculaneum.

The villa proved to need supplies and Apicius wanted to purchase more slaves, so we returned to Rome. Apicata greeted us at the gate. She had remained in Rome over the last year to stay close to her boys, even if they could not live with her. Sejanus never forced her to remarry, and for that I think she was glad. He, on the other hand, had tried to marry Livilla after sufficient time had passed from his divorce and from Drusus's death. It was said that Tiberius had thrown a glass at Sejanus and told him not to under any circumstances, and that Sejanus had overstepped his bounds. While I held little respect for Caesar Tiberius, I liked him more after I heard the story.

Nine-year-old Junilla pulled back the curtain of the litter and jumped out. She ran to Apicius and hugged him, then threw her arms around my waist, seemingly not aware of the road grime that coated my clothes and skin. I patted her head and hugged her tightly. "It is good to see you, Junilla. Do you bring your brothers?"

She shook her head, which was not unexpected. Sejanus eventually let Junilla live with her mother but Sejanus rarely let his sons out of his sight, save for short, occasional supervised visits with Apicata.

"No, they are with Father. But look what Strabo gave me!" She held up a straw doll complete with a tiny tunica and a flower tucked into her straw hair. She was almost too old for dolls, but was clearly pleased to have a gift from her brother.

I smiled. "Strabo loves you very much, I suspect."

"He does," Apicata said as she neared. My heart caught in my chest. I could have been looking at her mother's shade.

Apicius hugged her close and praised her beauty. I kissed her cheek but did not hug her for fear of leaving dirt on her stola. "We came to pick up some supplies and I missed Passia and Junius," I said.

"We'll be here for just a few days," Apicius said.

We walked up the path to the villa, Junilla running ahead to find Junius, whom she admired. I watched her race up the walk.

"When you return, I think we should come with you to Herculaneum. It might be a good idea," Apicata said.

"What do you mean, it might be a good idea?" I asked.

She looked at me, an incredulous look in her dark eyes. "By the gods, you haven't heard the news?"

"What news?" Apicius asked.

"Livia is dead."

I stopped in my tracks. "Dead?"

"Finally? You are sure?" Apicius was equally incredulous. Livia had been ill more than once over the last decade and there were many times she had almost died.

"Yes. She died on the ides. I've seen the body. When I left, the Senate was still waiting for Tiberius to come for the funeral, but he says he cannot, that he is otherwise occupied."

Five days had passed since the ides. I couldn't imagine what state her body would be in when Tiberius returned.

"I don't understand. Why would her death make you want to leave . . . ?" It dawned on me then. Without Livia, Sejanus would run unchecked.

"He rules Rome by striking terror into all. I fear him. And now that the boys are older, he lets me see them less and less."

My chest tightened.

"Yes, yes, daughter, you must come with us to Herculaneum," Apicius agreed. "We'll gather supplies tomorrow and leave the day after."

"Let us go find Passia." I took her arm and wrapped it around mine. Apicius fell in step on her other side.

Apicata squeezed my arm. "Tell me about the cookbook! I heard all the senators have bought a copy!"

"I sent three copies to the library in Alexandria and two more to the library in Athens." I was proud of this fact for it meant our book would be part of the historical collections.

She chuckled. "The rumor is that after they bought your book, three of the new senators hired tutors to teach their cooks how to read!"

"That is good news!" Apicius said. "Now, if only we could convince the rest of the senators to do the same!"

We found Junilla and Junius in the atrium playing ball around the burbling fountain. Junius tackled me when he saw me, which sent both Apicata and Junilla into peals of laughter.

Apicius and I played with them while one of the slaves went to fetch Passia. Apicius stood in one place and threw the ball, not very well, and the rest of us teased him when we had to run after his errant throws.

When Passia emerged from the interior of the house I thought my heart might burst with the happiness of seeing her. Oh, how I hated being away from my beloved wife.

After I had lifted Passia off her feet and swung her around, covering her in kisses, she broke free to embrace Apicata. "I know you live close but I wish we saw each other more often."

"You'll see more of her now."

Passia looked to me, then to Apicata. "What do you mean? Is everything all right?"

Apicata patted Passia's hand reassuringly. "Yes. But with Livia gone, I think I may take Junilla and join my father in Herculaneum."

"With you and Junius," I asserted, moving closer to my wife and draping my arm around her shoulder.

She tensed. She knew that if I wanted her to leave Rome it was because I was afraid for my family. For as much as we hated Livia, we knew that she was one of the only reasons Sejanus hadn't become a real Roman tyrant.

"He leaves me alone because of the children but I fear what he might do to you and Father. Out of sight, out of mind, would be best for all of us," Apicata urged.

"I can take care of myself, daughter," Apicius said, although his voice belied the truth.

I never thought I would need to move my family from Rome, but Apicata was right. Sejanus stood to gain a lot if he accused Apicius of treason and demanded his fortune be handed over to Rome—or essentially into coffers he alone had access to. And if Apicata was afraid, it meant we should be doubly careful.

"Will you stay for cena?" Passia asked.

Apicata smiled and shook her head. "My neighbor Gratius Stolo is celebrating his eldest son's name day. His wife invited me to join. I thought you might accompany me."

"Is that the son who is campaigning for a Senate post?" Apicius asked.

"It is."

Apicius waved a hand. "Go and enjoy yourself. Take the Guard with you to accompany you home. Junilla can stay here for dinner and tell her grandfather stories."

I smiled. "She does love to tell tales! And when she and Junius are telling stories together, Comus himself would fall over laughing," I said, referring to the god of comedy.

Apicata hugged me. "Thank you, Thrasius! Come, Passia, let's figure out what you should wear!"

I kissed my wife and Apicata and I watched them scamper off, giggling like young girls. It made me glad to see Apicata smiling. Her smiles were few and far between.

• • •

Much later that night, after I had purchased a score of new slaves for the Herculaneum villa, negotiated for furniture made from dark black pine to be sent, hired several new guardsmen, and shared a light meal with Apicius, I collapsed onto a couch in the garden. I began reading a scroll of the *Aeneid* Passia had left on a nearby table but it wasn't long before I passed into sleep. I awoke hours later to a slave shaking me.

"Dominus Thrasius, hurry," the girl was saying. It was one of Passia's maidens.

I jolted awake. I tossed the scroll aside and followed her through the house to the bath, where I found Passia and Apicata. Apicata sat on the edge of the bath wrapped in a towel, crying. Passia combed her long hair between comforting hugs. They had sent all the other slaves from the room.

I rushed to their side. "What happened?"

Apicius appeared then, wrapped in a loose robe, Sotas following and taking a place next to the door.

At the sight of her father, Apicata put her face in her hands and began weeping anew. Passia hugged her close. "It's all right. Tell them what happened."

She sniffled. I saw she had several bruises on her arms. Fingerprint bruises.

"Who did this to you?" I tried to keep the anger from my voice.

Apicata couldn't answer. She took in big gulping breaths of air between her sobs.

Passia looked at us, her own eyes wet with emotion. "Sejanus."

"What? How?" Apicius came to his daughter's side and put his arm around her.

Apicata wasn't able to talk so Passia told us what she could. "He came to the party. I don't think he was invited, but Gratius Stolo didn't dare turn him away. Livilla was with him. He was high on opium and staggering drunk. He had his Praetorians arrest the one man who dared to comment on his condition.

"I was talking to one of Stolo's daughters when he came in the door. I saw him first, but by the time I found Apicata so had Sejanus."

Apicius cursed. I felt as though my blood were thickening in my veins.

"I ducked into the closest room, a huge bedroom. Livilla wasn't with him; she must have gone to greet Stolo. I heard Sejanus in the corridor talking to Apicata, telling her how much he missed bedding her. Right before he pulled her into the room, I hid under the bed and curled up against the wall so they wouldn't see me."

Apicata seemed to regain herself. "I was glad to find that Passia was there. Now someone else will believe me."

"Did he rape you?" Apicius asked, his voice soft.

She nodded, tears falling off the edge of her golden skin. "It was much like our marriage."

I clenched my fists and wished I had something—no, someone—to punch.

"But that wasn't the worst of it."

"Bloody Apollo, how could it get worse?" Apicius gripped the edge of his robe so tightly that his hand was turning white.

Apicata dried her eyes on the towel. "Tell him, Passia."

"When he came into the room he sent all the slaves away and told them to bar the door. He had at least ten guards with him. I knew if I tried to help Apicata they would kill us both. I stayed under the bed. It was awful."

I put my hand on her shoulder. I would have rushed to the river Lethe if its waters could have erased the memory from my wife's mind.

"Apicata was brave. She didn't fight him and she didn't cry. Afterward, when he lay spent, she was very bold and asked him to tell her the truth about Livilla."

Apicata kicked a foot in the water, making a big splash. "When he drinks heavily he becomes boastful. It was the same then as it was during our marriage. Sure enough, the bastard told me everything. That he slept with her regularly, that he'd divorced me for her, and that he would see Tiberius dead for denying his marriage to her."

Apicata rarely cursed and it startled me despite the circumstances.

"He told Apicata to tread lightly, that he had killed Drusus and he could kill her too," Passia said.

I couldn't believe what I heard. "By the gods! How did they kill him? Poison?"

"Yes." Apicata wiped her eyes with her fingers. "I told him I didn't believe him . . ."

"I thought he would strangle her then and there," Passia added.

"I thought so too, but instead he told me how he and Livilla had done it," Apicata continued. "They had his cupbearer put something in his drink one night and paid off the doctor to make sure he declared it death from drinking. One moment he was giddy with how brilliant he thought the plan was, and the next minute he was angry Tiberius still thwarted his marriage to Livilla."

"Why didn't he kill you after he told you?" Apicius asked what I had been thinking. I couldn't understand why he would have let her live after spilling such a secret.

"He passed out. I gathered myself together and Passia and I left as quickly as we could. On the way out, to my horror, Livilla stopped me. She had no idea what had happened, thankfully."

"She was horrible," Passia said. "She told Apicata that she would never win Sejanus back. That he loved only her."

"As though I would ever want to be with that monster again. I wanted to tell her that her husband had just had his way with me, and that I knew the truth about Drusus, but Passia pulled me away before I could say something stupid."

It was terrible news. And more terrible because Apicata knew the truth about how Caesar Tiberius's son died. If Sejanus remembered that he had told Apicata, he would most certainly have her killed.

Apicata saw the realization in our eyes. "Oh, Father, what should I do?"

I had already been thinking of the answer to her question.

"I have an idea. Get dressed and meet us in the library. Apicius, come with me. I think I know what to do." I kissed her on the forehead and hauled Apicius to his feet.

We stopped at Tycho's cubicle to wake him. My slave was an excellent scribe and we would need his help.

When we reached the library, I told Apicius of the plan. He only nodded his head and went to work. I know not how much time passed before Apicata and Passia appeared, but Apicius was dictating the last sentence on the sixth letter when they arrived. He gestured for them to sit.

"What are you planning?" Apicata's eyes were bloodshot but dry. She wore a thin gray stola and her mother's favorite sandals, so old and tattered, Aelia had worn them only around the house.

"It's quite simple." Apicius brought the letters to the table in front of them and fanned them out.

Apicata gasped. "What if this backfires?"

"I trust each of these men implicitly. It will not backfire."

Tycho chuckled. I smiled, knowing what he was thinking. He had been scribing the letters and knew the contents and to whom they were addressed. "Of course it helps that we know a secret about each of them they would rather not have others know. All those years on Apicius's couches have paid off."

Passia looked at me with approval. "Blackmail within blackmail. By Jove, dear husband, I knew you were brilliant but I had no idea how much!"

Apicius gathered the letters up. "When dawn breaks, Apicata, we will send a boy with a note for Sejanus to meet you here. I suspect he will be here faster than you can blink. If he isn't, it will be because he doesn't remember any of it."

"What if he comes here to kill me?"

"He will have to go through me first. And Sotas. Now go, try to sleep. Have Timon make you some poppy juice if you need it. I've got to get some messengers on the road."

In the morning I had Apicata pen a note to Sejanus, barely hinting at his words the night before, in case his memory was poor. I sent my fastest messenger off to his house.

Sejanus arrived within the half hour. His memory wasn't poor.

Apicius and I were waiting for him in the atrium. When he arrived, he stormed through the front door, not bothering to wait for the guards to announce him. "Where is she?" he snarled when he stopped in front of us.

"She is resting. I understand she had a bad night," Apicius said. Behind him, Sotas grunted.

Apicata and Passia were in the nearby cubicle where they could hear.

"What else did she tell you?"

"Enough that I think you should guard your tone with me." Apicius sounded bold but I knew he was shaking inside. What if my plan wasn't enough to stop Sejanus?

Sejanus laughed, his golden armor clanking as he threw back his head. He had taken to wearing the formal Imperial armor more often now that Tiberius was ensconced in Capri. Tiberius likely wouldn't have approved of such ostentation.

"*You* are the one who should guard your tone with me! Guards!" It was a fatal command, one that left no doubt as to what he intended the guards to do to us. Six burly Praetorian guards drew their swords and moved forward.

"That would not be wise," Apicius said. His voice projected no fear.

The guards did not stop their advance.

"Go ahead!" he shouted. "Kill me and find out what happens to you! Kill me! Kill me and all of Rome will know about your treason!" He threw his arms upward as though welcoming their blades. I did the same, as did Sotas, each of us on either side of Apicius. I wondered how long it would take for me to die when the first blade passed through my body.

The words gave Sejanus pause. "Halt." The guards stopped but did not lower their weapons. I heard the sounds of slaves coming to the atrium to hear what the commotion was about. Several guards broke off to attend them. A few waves of their blade points sent the slaves scurrying into the depths of the villa.

Sejanus advanced until he stood a few inches from Apicius. He pulled a jeweled dagger from the leather sheath strapped to his arm and held it to his throat.

"What could you possibly have to say that would make me reconsider killing you?"

"If you kill me, or Apicata, or harm any member of our families or our households, six letters telling the truth about Drusus will be sent out from different parts of the Empire."

"Letters? You are bluffing. There are no letters." The knife bit into his skin and a bright drop of blood surfaced.

"But there *are* letters. To Tiberius. To the Senate."

He laughed but it didn't sound as convincing. "Letters that will never reach their destinations."

"How can you be sure? You know not where those letters will come from, nor when or how they will arrive."

The knife bit deeper. "Nothing goes in or out of Capri without me knowing."

"Ahh, but you, of all people, should know anyone can be bought for the right price. You are not in Capri. How can you be sure?" I gave thanks to Jupiter for his boldness. It seemed to be enough to put some caution into Sejanus. He pulled the knife away and stepped back.

"And if I do nothing to any of you, nothing will happen?"

"Exactly. Leave us in peace. You do nothing and we will do nothing."

He stepped forward again, waggling the knife. "You cannot be trusted. Your mind is not always clear."

"I've heard the rumors," Apicius said, deadpan. "But I assure you, I am quite clear about this."

"How do I know they will not share the contents of those letters anyway?"

"They won't. Unlike you, I know my friends are loyal. This decision is yours, Sejanus. You are, as ever, in control."

Although we both knew Apicius was the one directing this play.

Thick tendons stood out in Sejanus's neck and his face had grown purple. I had never seen anyone so angry. He stared Apicius down for a spell before turning on his heel. The guards sheathed their weapons to follow him. At the door he looked back at us.

"If one of those letters gets into the wrong hands, I swear to the both of you, the following will happen." He looked at Apicius. "I will kill your daughter, then I will take all of your lands, and all of your money, kill your slaves, cut out your tongue, remove your hands, and leave you penniless in the streets of Rome."

Then he turned to me. "I will hunt your wife down and rape her till she bleeds. I will do the same to your son. Then I will, while you watch, cut away every part of their faces, cut off every limb and feed them to my dogs. After, I will have you crucified."

He left, his men in tow. When the door shut I nearly fell onto the bench behind me. Tycho ran to our sides. "I'll fetch the wine."

Apicius nodded. "Thank you, Tycho. A bottle of my finest, I think. We all deserve it after that." Apicata and Passia emerged from their hiding spot and threw their arms around us. Unfortunately, the outcome of the encounter did not lessen their fear.

• • •

Apicius retired immediately to the bath. "I need to think," he said, but I knew that what he meant was that he would be actively not thinking by taking a heavy dose of opium.

"Sejanus will find a way to kill us." Apicata began to pace the floor, wringing her hands with each step.

"I don't think he will chance it," I said, somehow convinced this was true.

Passia collapsed on the bench beside me. "I pray to the gods you are right."

"I will never let him touch you. You would die at my own hands before you would ever die at his."

She pressed herself closer against me.

The next day we departed for Herculaneum. It took us two days with one stopover at a roadside inn. I had guards keep watch to make sure we were not followed by Sejanus's men. We saw no one on the way, nor did we receive word of any trouble.

As soon as we arrived, Apicius sent Sotas to all his clients in the area, inviting them for dinner. I cursed when I heard the news. Although I had purchased an experienced cook for the kitchen, I always felt like I needed to be the overseer for such events. We decided to make it an evening highlighting the bounty of the sea, with an overabundance of oysters, mussels, sea urchins, prawns, lobsters, and little fishes. I sent some of the new kitchen boys to the shore to pick up seashells to adorn the flower wreaths and, if large enough, to serve as small plates.

After a long, tiring morning of travel and an afternoon of preparation, I finally fetched Passia for dinner. She looked radiant, as always, dressed in a pale green stola adorned with an elegant gold pin in the shape of a dolphin that Apicata had given her for Saturnalia the previous year.

"The sea suits you," I murmured, pulling her close and nuzzling her neck with my lips.

"I have missed the sea," she admitted. "Everything is freer here. Rome is such a den of vipers."

• • •

The viper den was our main topic of conversation at dinner. Everyone had heard the news of Livia's death and everyone had an opinion.

"What sort of man doesn't come back for his mother's funeral?" one patrician raved.

"A man who hated his mother," another said.

One of the men, a rich local merchant, popped a plump mussel into his mouth. "Did you hear about Agrippina? The first thing Tiberius did when Livia died was to send guards to arrest her and her sons for treason."

Agrippina was Tiberius's niece and the widow of the great general Germanicus. She had been very vocal against Sejanus of late and seemed to disagree with much of Tiberius's politics.

"Livia hated the woman—arresting her seems to be Caesar's parting gift to his mother. Word is they will banish her," said the merchant.

"I doubt they will banish her sons." Apicius dipped a prawn in the thick sauce on the seashell plate before him. "Likely they will just kill them. Though Tiberius seems to have taken a liking to Caligula. It's possible he will escape prison."

"Sejanus is behind this. Once he found out Agrippina had joined with the senators opposing him, he started to get scared. She has become popular since Germanicus died and Sejanus fears her influence. I'm sure that he asked Tiberius to arrest her." The merchant said the words others were thinking but not sure if they should say them aloud. Sejanus had become a powerful man and Tiberius had given him great leeway to run much of the Empire. It was thought he had spies everywhere.

"There are new gilded statues of Sejanus all over the Roman Forum," Apicata said, wiping her mouth with her napkin. She had said little that evening. I knew the conversation was distasteful to her in every way but she was ever the dutiful daughter and Apicius wanted her there.

I posited the question that had been bothering me for many months. "Do you think Tiberius will finally appoint him heir?" I couldn't imagine the world with such an evil man ruling the Empire.

The merchant grunted. "Perhaps. Or perhaps he will come to his senses and realize Sejanus is overstepping his bounds."

Apicata stood and surveyed the diners. "He grows stronger every day. He will not stop until he is Caesar." She put her hand on Apicius's shoulder. "Father, I am tired from the journey. Please excuse me."

He patted her hand and smiled. "Yes, yes. Rest up. I thought to buy a boat tomorrow. We can go sailing."

Apicata only sighed.

PART XI

31 C.E. to 38 C.E.

PIGLET IN SILPHIUM SAUCE

Pound in a mortar pepper, lovage, caraway; mix in a little cumin, fresh silphium, silphium root; pour on vinegar, add pine nuts, dates, honey, vinegar, liquamen, prepared mustard. Blend all these with oil and pour on.

—From the *Extracts of Apicius* by Vindarius
30 recipes collected by a man in Imperial service,
separate from the book Apicius, *but with recipes*
that still bear his name
On Cookery, Apicius

CHAPTER 28

Sejanus kept his word. While he was ruthless and cruel to senators, patricians, and anyone who crossed him or spoke out against him, he left Apicius and Apicata alone. Earlier that year Tiberius had appointed him joint consul, rendering him even more powerful to do whatever he wanted in Rome. Most lived in fear of finding out what that might be.

Passia and Junius remained on the coast, spending their time in Apicius's villa in Herculaneum. I visited them as often as I could. Yet with Apicius as my son's adoptive father, and my friend, I didn't want to leave him, especially as his moods and manners changed with melancholy, age, and time. He grew stubborn and refused to leave Rome entirely, so I stayed with him. Apicata avoided Rome, returning only when an event required her presence. She rarely saw her own sons.

The fateful night when everything began to unravel centered on an elaborate cena. Apicius, emboldened by Sejanus's seeming lack of interest in him, had started spending more and more money on parties he threw for guests and this time was no exception. It began with the gifts, elaborate toga pins of ruby-studded gold and finely inlaid wooden boxes filled with pepper or dried apricots, a fruit still new to Rome. The most precious gifts of all were the intricately woven, self-cleaning asbestos napkins. You simply threw them into the fire and all the particles of food burned off, leaving the surface clean and white. Apicius loved showing guests how they worked. I didn't love the price tag; each napkin cost half as much as a young goat.

The meal itself was equally elaborate and expensive. It began with sea hedgehogs, fresh oysters, mussels, and asparagus with mustard sauce. There were fattened fowl: roasted duck and chicken, stuffed pheasant, flamingo steaks, boiled teals, ostrich meatballs, fried songbirds, and roasted peacock presented with its feathers rearranged in full display. Apicius also had me arrange another gift: slave girls adorned only in a small swath of fabric, white feather headdresses, and draped luxuriously with golden chains. Their sole task during the meal was to gingerly place food in the mouths of the men who wished to partake of such intimate service.

I sat as Apicius's shadow that night, at his feet on the end of his couch, a position with which I was content. The group who dined with Apicius was opinionated and I dared not voice my concerns with such members of the elite, whose views were controversial. They were all of a faction that mostly opposed Sejanus, but I thought it wise not to share my hatred of the man in such company. Interestingly enough, Casca's father, Antius Piso, was in attendance that night. He and Apicius had long since patched up their differences, and seemed to have bonded over their equal dislike for Sejanus.

"I have never been so well fed!" Piso exclaimed as he beckoned to his girl for more fried squid. "You have outdone yourself, Apicius." He had fallen into deep conversation with Apicius, leaving the other diners to socialize among themselves.

"I should have camped on your couch long before now."

Apicius gave him an oily smile. "I promise your next visit will be equally memorable."

A weight descended upon me at those words. I didn't know how we could keep doing these parties. They left me tired, and despite the blackmail pact we had with Sejanus, they placed us more and more in his sights, sights that had been deadly for many of Rome's most wealthy. Worst of all, I could see my son's fortune dwindling. Apicius had spent more in the last two years than he had in the five previous.

"Tiberius should never have let you go as gastronomic adviser," Piso said.

"He's a fool." Venom laced Apicius's words. "It won't be long before the mob turns on him, or worse, he ends up like Divine Julius, bloodied on the Senate floor."

The slave placed another tidbit on Piso's tongue. He crunched loudly.

"That time might come sooner than later, I think. You remember Satrius Secundus?"

"Sejanus's man? The one who turned in that historian, for treason?" I asked.

Piso nodded and indicated with a finger that he would continue after he finished his mouthful of food.

"That was, what, six years ago?" Apicius squinted, as if trying to remember.

Piso swallowed. "Yes, one of the first Sejanus had executed, I think. At any rate, I have stayed friendly with Secundus over the years, not because I like the fat bastard but because I prefer to keep my enemies close. Yesterday I ran into him at a popina. After a few drinks, he mentioned that he knows how Sejanus is plotting against the emperor."

Apicius snorted. "Ha! Of course he is. Who doesn't know that?"

Piso shook his head. "No, I mean, he seemed to have proof. Documents."

"Do you believe him?" I asked.

"I do. I think he tells true."

It was as though all the wind had filled my lungs to bursting, my excitement was so great. Proof Sejanus was treasonous?

"Why doesn't he go to Caesar?" Apicius asked as he dipped a meatball into the sauce on the plate his slave girl held.

Piso chortled, spitting a chunk of food onto his slave's arm. She grimaced as she wiped it off. "He can't get an audience with Caesar! Even I couldn't think of a soul who could help him. I don't dare implicate myself."

Apicius shook his head thoughtfully. "It's impossible to get past the watchful eyes of Sejanus. You can count on one hand the number of people who can get a message past the guards he has posted to watch Caesar on Capri."

My elation deflated like a sheep's bladder split open. He was right. Few would be able to penetrate Sejanus's security and Tiberius seemed to trust him implicitly.

I found I could no longer concentrate on the conversation and excused myself, much to Apicius's displeasure. I would hear it from him later, but I didn't care.

• • •

My thoughts in turmoil, I decided to take a walk. It had been an unusually warm autumn and I was glad I didn't need a cloak. I slipped out of the villa and wandered the quiet roads of the Palatine, racking my brains trying to figure out how to get a message to Capri. I knew no one who would betray Sejanus. I hated the feeling that encompassed me— the answer was so close, and yet terribly far away.

I was almost at the villa when someone behind me called my name. A figure emerged out of the darkness. I knew the voice.

"What are you doing wandering around in the night?" Rúan asked as he caught up to me.

"I could ask you the same. Have you come to drink my wine?"

"I work for Caesar. Do you honestly think your plonk can compare?"

I laughed wholeheartedly at this. I knew the quality of our wine exceeded that of Caesar's but that did not need saying.

A noise on the path alerted us to a tall beast of a man walking toward us from the direction of the villa. I'd recognize that shadow anywhere—Sotas.

"What brings you out here tonight, big boy?" Rúan said, looking up at him as he neared.

Sotas came to a stop before us. I could barely see his face in the dark. "Apicius was feeling generous and gave me the night off. I'm heading to the brothel. Join me? You look like you could use a good poke."

"Ha! I'm not a body-slave. I don't have to watch my master screwing. I have my nights to myself and I fancy I see far more action than you can imagine."

Sotas guffawed, his laugh ringing particularly loud in the night.

"Why *are* you out here?" I asked Rúan, glad for his company regardless.

"I needed to get out. Your abuse is preferable to that of Sejanus and his guards."

We laughed, but I was compelled to share my news. I lowered my voice in case there were others unseen in the gardens we passed as I told them of Secundus. "We could be close to ending his power."

"They read all the mail that goes into Capri," Sotas said.

"Not all," Rúan said.

"What do you mean, not all?"

Rúan leaned in and Sotas came a few steps closer. "Antonia. His sister-in-law. Claudius's mother."

"And Livilla's mother! Why on earth do you think Antonia would ever say words against her?"

"You know those women I have bedded?"

"The ones you wished you had bedded, you mean?" Sotas countered with a playful cuff to Rúan's shoulder.

"Well, one of them is Antonia's scribe. She writes all of her letters and I can tell you two things. One, because she's Livilla's mother, Sejanus trusts Antonia and doesn't have her letters to Tiberius read. And two, she is not happy with her daughter and the rumors about her ties to Sejanus, and the rumors that Livilla's sons are not born of Drusus. Apparently they have come to words about it. Antonia once even threatened that if she ever finds out the gossip is true she will expose Livilla to Caesar."

"Are you certain about this?"

"The lovely lass who shared these secrets was certain."

"And you trust this girl?" Sotas sounded as skeptical as I felt.

"Aye, I do. She has slept with me nearly every night for the last year." I smiled, glad to hear Cupid had once again pierced Rúan's heart.

"I must get him an audience with Antonia," I said, already thinking of how I could do so without her rejecting my request.

"Who is this man?" Sotas asked.

"Satrius Secundus."

Rúan coughed. "Isn't he Sejanus's man, loyal to the core?"

"Not based on what I have heard tonight."

"Antonia wouldn't believe Secundus, even if there was proof. She was a staunch supporter of that historian that Secundus turned in to Sejanus for treason years ago. What was his name? Cordus? At any rate, I doubt Antonia would even take an audience with Secundus. He was the one who got her friend killed. You need something else—no, someone else—to back it up."

Then it hit me. "I think I know who."

And I told them.

• • •

When I shared the idea with Apicius, he was wary but agreed. He would take any chance he could to end Sejanus's power. The next day I had Tycho trail Secundus and alert me when he went to the baths so I could "run into" him. After some skepticism (and anger that Piso had betrayed him) he agreed to let me buy him a cup of wine. I explained my plan and the burly man agreed.

Then Apicius and I met with the linchpin to my plan: Apicata, who had come to Rome for a friend's wedding. She agreed without hesitation and Apicius sent a messenger to Antonia.

And so it was that Apicius, Sotas, Apicata, Secundus, and I found ourselves at Antonia's door on the last morning of September. Antonia, daughter of the famous Marc Antony, was one of the most respected matrons in Rome, and even more so since Livia's death. My heart pounded as the door creaked inward and the slaves admitted us. Sotas immediately took up a post by the door.

While I saw Antonia often at state affairs or at the Imperial villa, I had spoken with the revered matron only once, briefly, at Aelia's funeral. She had been close with Aelia's mother and knew her as a child. I remembered Antonia had been very gracious, kissing my cheeks and telling me how Aelia once told her how much she loved the honey fritters I would make her for breakfast. She had made me cry.

Seven years had passed since that day and age had not marred her visage. Her hair was a bit grayer and it was tied back conservatively as was befitting her stature. Her skin was remarkably smooth and only a few lines framed her striking green eyes. The blue stola she wore gave her face a vibrant glow, making her seem far younger than the sixty-seven summers she had seen. I wondered what magic she must have employed to maintain such a youthful appearance.

She had been friendly to me at the funeral, but this time she had no kind words of greeting.

"What is *he* doing here?" She pulled back after kissing Apicata's cheeks and seeing Secundus standing beyond. "He killed my friend and is not welcome in my home."

"My lady"—Apicata put her hand on Antonia's shoulder—"he has information I think you should hear."

She sniffed. "Apicata, Thrasius, welcome. And you, Secundus," she said, pointing a long finger at him, "better have a good reason to be standing here, or my guards will throw you out and loose the dogs."

"I think you will find his news of great import," I said as we seated ourselves on the benches she indicated. Antonia's house was decorated more sparsely than most, with few plants lining the *impluvium* pool in the center. The paintings on the wall were of a style forty years past, with dark paint and small scenes of country life framed by thin columns painted on the wall.

"Antonia, please know I would not ask you this question if it weren't of the utmost importance, but do you trust your slaves?" Apicata cocked her head in the direction of the line of slaves along the nearby wall who awaited Antonia's command.

"I repeat, I hope this information is worth my time." She paused for a moment, considering. "Irene, you stay. The rest of you are dismissed."

The slaves, save for a young dark-haired woman, filed out of the room.

"Now tell me why you have brought this evil man into my midst."

I felt Secundus tense beside me. "He's here to make right the actions of his past," Apicius said, nudging him.

Secundus didn't strike me as the type of man who would be nervous, but his thick hands shook and he would raise his eyes to Antonia only for a moment before turning them back toward the atrium tiles.

"I cannot take back Cordus's death, although I wish I could," he said, already swerving from the script we had discussed. I looked at Apicata. Her body was as tense as a runner in the blocks at the games. Secundus continued, "I doubt all the deaths of recent years—that any of the men Sejanus has put to death were traitors. Or if they were, I know now that they had only the best interests of Rome in mind. Sejanus is a poison to us all and I am living proof of such rot."

To my surprise, Secundus sounded truly contrite. And by the gods, there were tears in his eyes. Antonia's mouth had opened a little, as though she wanted to counter him but couldn't.

"Livilla, she has moved from the Palatine to the Caelian into a new villa, yes?" Secundus asked.

Antonia nodded.

Secundus drew a thin stack of papers from the pouch he carried. "Sejanus asked several of his men to help her move. I was one of them. It was late in the day and we got caught in a downpour. The wagon hit a bump and one of her chests went flying and landed in a puddle. It broke open, ruined some of her clothes, and we lost some jewelry in the mud. This packet of letters also fell out. I was able to snatch it up before the rain ruined it."

He handed the packet to Antonia, who took it gingerly, as though she were afraid there was poison on the pages.

Secundus's voice quavered. "When we reached the villa and placed the furniture, I remembered the packet. It was wrong, but I could not keep my curiosity at bay. I read the letters and knew I couldn't return them. When we gave Livilla her clothing and the muddy contents of the chest, I told her that her papers had been ruined in the rain. I muddied a few pages to satisfy her, letting the ink run so she would believe me."

Antonia thumbed through the letters in her lap. Her eyes widened and one hand flew to her breast, her fingers pushing into the skin as though it might hold in the horror. "Oh, Juno, my dear lady Juno," she breathed.

She read a few more pages, her eyes filling with tears. "My wicked, wicked daughter."

Apicata got up and sat down next to her on the couch and put a comforting arm around the matron. "There is more, I'm afraid."

Antonia choked on a sob. "What could be worse than knowing my grandchildren might be bastards and my daughter is a treasonous whore?"

Apicata had started to cry herself. "Sejanus . . . one night at a party, he, he became intoxicated on opium and wormwood wine. He . . . he took advantage of me and told me, oh gods . . ." She gulped, struggling to say the words.

Apicius finished for her. "He confessed to murder." He leaned in and touched Antonia's hand, hoping to give her comfort. "Sejanus and Livilla killed Drusus. They planned it and had her eunuch do it."

"Oh, Juno!" Antonia buried her face in Apicata's stola. "Drusus! That precious man, he did not deserve to die at their hands!"

She sobbed for a while and we sat uncomfortably while Apicata comforted her. Antonia's tears left streaks in her leaden makeup, erasing the illusion of her youth. At last, she sat up and wiped her eyes.

"What do I need to do?" She looked at us.

I seized the moment, thanking the gods she had been swayed. "Write to Tiberius. Send him some of these pages. We know yours are some of the only letters Caesar is allowed to read without censor."

"I believe that to be true. If it's not . . ."

"We have to try." Apicata dabbed at her eyes with the corner of her shawl. "Sejanus is tearing the fabric of Rome apart. He shames the Aelii and the Antonii families with every move he makes. He's accused fifty-two people of treason, Antonia. Fifty-two! He must be stopped!"

As one of the elders in the Antonii gens, Antonia would be very keen to protect her reputation. I smiled inwardly, proud of my little bird for knowing the right words to say.

"You are right. I cannot let my daughter drag us all through the mud." She turned her attention to the slave who leaned against the wall. The girl straightened when she saw Antonia's eyes fall upon her. "Irene, fetch my scribe. Speak to no one on your way there and back. Not one word, girl, or I'll cut your tongue out!"

Irene bowed her head, her long dark curls falling into her eyes, turned on her heel, and slipped down the dark corridor.

Antonia wiped at her face, smoothing her makeup into place. "I will tell Tiberius of the treachery contained in these letters. I cannot tell him of Drusus." She looked at Apicata. "That is for you to tell. Were you alone when he confessed this?"

"No. Thrasius's wife, Passia, was hiding in the room. She will testify," Apicius said.

Antonia sighed. "Is Passia a slave? She will have to be tortured for the evidence. I offer to do it . . . I will be kind."

A shiver of relief passed through me, raising goose bumps on my arms. "No, thank the gods. She has been manumitted." By law the only way a slave's testimony would hold true in court was if it had been obtained by torture. I could not imagine Passia undergoing the trials of torture—burning, removing fingernails or whole digits of the hand.

"That is fortunate. I will leave it to you to inform Tiberius of Passia's account. I recommend you wait until we find out the reaction to my letter first—in case we need more fuel for this fire."

Apicata exhaled. I don't think she had planned to bear the news of

Drusus's murder to Tiberius herself. We had one small hope—if Antonia's letter was enough to condemn Sejanus, perhaps she wouldn't have to.

Irene returned with the scribe, a striking woman with pale skin and chestnut hair who looked to be Iberian. I stifled a smile, which would have been inappropriate given the gravity of the situation. If the slave was Rúan's bedding partner, he was a fortunate man.

"I will write this letter," Antonia continued. "But I must request one thing." She looked to Secundus. He shifted his bulk nervously on the couch. "You remain here. Let Rome think you went missing. I cannot trust you not to change your mind. And believe me, I like it no better than you."

"Am I to sit in your dungeon?"

"As much as I think you deserve it, no. You will stay in my guesthouse. You will have two slaves to attend you and I will make sure you have as many books as you want. But you will not leave. My guards will see to that. Once Tiberius responds to my letter, you will be free to go. This protects both me and you. Sejanus would not be kind if he found out you have betrayed him."

"I will stay." He sounded like a child who had been told to go to bed early. Sad but resigned.

"Good. I will send a messenger to you as soon as I hear anything." She kissed us good-bye and we left, our hearts full of hope.

It was twenty-four endless days before we knew the outcome of Antonia's missive to Tiberius. The word came at dawn one morning when we were preparing cakes for the salutatio. One of the slave boys rushed into the kitchen, his lips trembling with the news.

"Soldiers! There are soldiers surrounding the Senate!" He stopped in front of me, panting. It was one of Timon's prodigies, a lanky boy with hair so blond it was nearly white. A barbarian from Germania, I surmised.

"How do you know?" Timon asked, angry.

The boy, momentarily excited, lowered his eyes to the ground, chastised. It seemed he had been caught dallying on an errand.

And thank the gods he had. "Speak!" I said, taking the boy by the shoulders. "What do you know? Tell me! I swear, there will be no punishment for you for telling me the truth."

In fact, I had already fished a golden aureus from the pouch at my waist. I slipped the coin—more money than the boy had likely ever imagined owning—into the boy's dirty hand. "Speak!"

The child's eyes grew large. "Soldiers are at the Forum! They came to take Sejanus away! A letter from Tiberius, they say, is being read to him and the Senate. But the soldiers wait outside to take him away!"

I pushed past him and ran for the door.

"Tycho!" I yelled on my way through the house. Soon I could hear his sandals slapping behind me.

We passed Apicius on the way to the atrium, where the salutatio was about to begin. "What . . . ?" Apicius began.

I didn't slow. "Sejanus! I think they are arresting Sejanus!"

As I ran off, I heard Apicius tell Sotas to let the guards know the salutatio was canceled and to send for Apicata.

Minutes later Tycho and I were running down the path across the Palatine Hill toward the Forum. We emerged near the temple of Castor and Pollux and ran across the stones of the Forum, pushing past merchants, beggars, and children. We ran until we reached the crowd forming around the Curia Julia, the Senate meetinghouse where I had earned my freedom twenty-two years before.

The crowd milled about, talking in hushed tones, as though not wanting to spoil whatever surprise was waiting for Sejanus when he emerged. A ring of Praetorian Guard circled the Curia, mixed with dozens of vigiles. The head of the vigiles, a hardened man named Gracinius Laco who had once dined on Apicius's couch, stood at the base of the stairs, waiting.

"What's happening?" I asked the elderly equestrian next to me as I struggled to catch my breath.

He squinted in the morning sun, which was shining off the massive bronze doors of the Curia. "They're reading a letter from Tiberius. Sejanus thought it would be more accolades. He was bragging when he went in. But if the letter was accolades, why would there be soldiers waiting for him?"

"How long have they been reading the letter?"

"Nearly twenty minutes—"

He was cut off by the sound of shouts inside the Curia. The doors swung open. A cluster of soldiers led Sejanus down the Curia's short flight of stairs. I recognized the soldier in front, a man previously always by Tiberius's side, a general named Macro who was even larger than Sotas. He towered over Sejanus and the other guards.

Then I couldn't see over the screaming mob. All manner of items were thrown at the traitor. The Praetorian Guard lifted their shields to protect themselves from the flight of rocks and rotting fruit. The vigiles pushed the crowd back to let the soldiers pass.

"Back off!" one of the soldiers yelled. "You'll get your turn in time. Let them by!"

The soldiers swept past us, moving Sejanus through the Forum, the crowd in tow, joined by the throngs of senators leaving the Curia.

I caught sight of Trio in the crowd. He had recently been elected senator and would have seen all the proceedings. I dragged Tycho through the throngs. "Trio!" I shouted, hoping he would hear me and stop.

"Thrasius! Good to see you." He slapped me on the back, as friendly as ever, almost as though we weren't in the center of a mob of people.

"Where are they taking him?"

"The temple of Concord. We'll try him at dusk. I suspect it will be a short trial after the letter we just heard."

"What did it say?"

Trio took me by the elbow and pulled me off to the side to escape the rush of people. "It was a strange letter, praising Sejanus at first and talking about some of the laws we are trying to enact. Then the letter turned and Tiberius appointed Macro as Praetorian prefect! He accused Sejanus of treason, stating that he had evidence that he was plotting to overthrow Caesar. It was magnificent! We couldn't have wished for a better end to that bastard."

"Truly," I agreed, elated.

"We must celebrate. Tell Apicius I expect a grand cena tomorrow after Sejanus's body lies broken on the Gemonian stairs!"

"I will!"

We stopped at the temple of Hecate on the way to the villa to arrange for the sacrifice of a bull in thanks for her help in bringing Sejanus to his knees. Later I planned to do the same for Nemesis, Averna, and Mercury for fulfilling the curse, be it years after it was made.

They were sacrifices I would never make.

When I reached the villa, Apicius was sitting in the peristylium with Apicata.

Apicius seemed to be in shock. When I approached he only said, "I can't believe it, finally I will be rid of that bastard." Then he looked downward to the tiles again, his hands wringing the edges of his toga.

Apicata sat next to him, her arm around his shoulders. Her eyes were swollen from crying.

"Apicata, are you all right?" I thought she would be elated that Sejanus was getting his due.

"They have Capito and Strabo."

Horror overtook me, crushing the breath out of my lungs. How had I not foreseen this? Of course. If they killed Sejanus, they would kill his children and eradicate his bloodline. Oh, dear gods, what had we done?

I had no words to say. After standing there for a space of time, empty, watching Apicata sob against her father's dazed body, I left, unable to bear their heartache.

When I returned a bit later, after meeting with the kitchen slaves and dismissing them for the night, Apicata was still crying. Apicius was holding her with a tenderness I had not seen for many years—years before Aelia had passed.

"Why did we go to Antonia? Why? Why?" she sobbed. The kohl lining her eyes had been reduced to smudges. "My boys! What will they do to my boys? Oh, they will kill them! I know it!"

"Do not fear, daughter. I'm sure all will be well." Apicius stroked her hair but it did not calm her.

"Send another messenger," he said to me when he noticed my presence.

I had already tried. I touched Apicata on the shoulder. "Macro has given orders that no one is to leave or enter the villa. But do not worry, I'm sure that as soon as the trial is over they will be released. By this time tomorrow you will have them in your arms."

Apicata looked up. "Do you think so?"

"Yes, I do," I lied to her. Apicius gave me a knowing look. We were only prolonging the inevitable, but what were we to do?

She sat up and wiped her eyes. "I hope you are right."

Apicius helped her straighten her shawl. "It will do you no good to cry, daughter. We won't know anything until the morrow. I'm sure they are safe. They have locked the doors as a precaution to make sure there are no traitors in Sejanus's house."

Apicata seemed to accept this. Her eyes, now dry, hardened. "I want to watch."

Apicius looked at me. "I think we all do."

I saw Sotas bob his head from his place along the wall. So many years later, our curse had taken effect. Oh, Minerva! And with consequences we could not have foreseen.

Tycho entered with a small scroll in his hand. "Master," he said, bowing as he handed it to Apicius.

Apicius unrolled it. "It's from Trio. They expect that Sejanus will be found guilty. People are already lining up to hear the verdict. He has reserved a place for us to watch at the top of the stairs." His eyes flickered across the scroll and he smiled. "What great news!"

I knew him too well. There was something else on that scroll. His sudden cheer was unnatural. The scroll must have said something about Apicata's children, but I didn't ask. I did not want to know.

Late in the afternoon we headed to the Gemonian stairs, a massive staircase of marble rising from the streets of the Forum up between the Arx—the highest point of the Capitoline Hill—and the temple of Concord and the Tabularium behind it. Traitors to Rome were strangled, then thrown down the stairs, where they would lie for days, usually until the stench became unbearable in the nearby temples. After, they would toss the body into the depths of the Tiber. Sejanus would be thrown down the stairs if convicted, but no one had any doubt of his guilt.

We traveled along the ridge of the Capitoline Hill rather than through the throngs in the Forum, then sent the slaves and sedan chairs back while our guards led us through the crowd on foot. Apicius showed the scroll's seal to the vigiles guarding the coveted spaces at the top of the stairs. They parted ranks and one of the younger guards led us to the top few stairs, where we were told we could wait.

When we arrived there were already hundreds of people lining the sides of the stairs. The top stairs were reserved for senators and their families, and the middle and bottom stairs for wealthy patricians and equestrians. Common plebeians were not allowed on the stairs and gathered at the base and filled the streets of the Forum below. Vendors sold fruit and sips from wine flasks to the milling crowd. The noise filled my ears: the sounds of barking dogs waiting for the body to be thrown, men debating how Tiberius found out about Sejanus's treason, and children yelling as they played tag up and down and across the stairs.

At dusk, a roar broke out from the crowd as the Praetorian Guard—who had been Sejanus's own men up until the day before—led the prisoner up the stairs to the temple of Concord, where the trial would be held. People screamed epithets at him, but the most common cry was "Traitor! Traitor!"

When Sejanus neared the top of the stairs he spied Apicius. He jerked his chains in our direction. "You are calling me a traitor?" he screamed to the crowd. They weren't listening but he kept shouting. "Marcus Gavius Apicius is a traitor! And a murderer! He murdered a friend of Tiberius! You should be trying him and not me! I have proof! I have proof that Apicius is a murderer!"

Sejanus yanked at his shackles and with his bound hands pointed toward Apicius, who stood stock-still. Waves of fear radiated from Apicius. He gripped my arm and I could feel him trembling.

One of the guards kicked Sejanus in the back of the knees and he went down, banging his chin against the marble stairs. Another guard hauled him up and pulled him up the last few stairs. He was still screaming Apicius's name when they rounded the corner of the temple.

Apicius still held my arm and his grip had tightened. No one seemed to have paid any attention to Sejanus's words. Even Apicata did not seem to have registered the import of what her ex-husband had been saying. The crowd likely thought that Sejanus's screams were only the desperate cries of a man about to die and therefore carried no import. At least, that's what I hoped.

With Sejanus gone the crowd quieted. We sat down on the marble and waited, something Apicius would normally never have done, but, of course, it was an extenuating circumstance. All along the stairs patricians sat like commoners, waiting for the spectacle of Sejanus's death to begin. Apicius said little. The pallor of his skin told me everything.

Before long, dusk descended and lamps were lit all along the stairway. Hundreds of torches and lanterns bobbed up and down the streets of the Forum like sparks in the night.

I heard the clatter of swords slapping the thighs of the Praetorian Guard before I saw Macro and his soldiers leading forth the condemned. Sejanus slumped between them, pushed along as though he could barely walk. Then three hundred senators flooded my vision, a wide swath of togas with red stripes filing past to stand with their waiting families on the stairs.

When we could see the top of the stairs again, a mere fifty feet away, Sejanus sat on a rough stool. Two of the largest men I've ever seen stood behind the prisoner, flanked by Macro and the Praetorian Guard.

Trio came to stand next to us. "Can you believe it," he said, leaning in so we could hear, "during his trial he tried to tell the Senate that you murdered a friend of Tiberius."

Apicius made a strangled sound and his eyes went wide.

Trio laughed. "It was like watching a bad play. He was rambling like a madman, accusing everyone he knew of being a traitor, a murderer, an adulterer. He named all of our friends as someone against Caesar. It made it all that much easier to convict him—his lies helped him rise to power, and we were only too glad to make his lies end him."

Apicius gave a deep sigh of relief.

Trio smiled. "Yes, it will be good to end this monster, won't it?"

Senator Pontius Castus came forth to stand at the top of the stairs, a few feet in front of Sejanus. A jolly man with a round belly and speckled beard, Castus had been expected to win the position of consul until the Senate, under great pressure from Tiberius, appointed Sejanus instead. I wondered what ran through his mind as he prepared to read the words on the papyrus he held.

Apicata grasped my hand. She gripped Apicius tightly with her other hand. I looked at Sotas and Tycho, and for a brief moment I knew a solidarity I had never before had. We were equal in one thing, despite all else: our hatred for Sejanus.

Castus began to speak, his voice ringing out like a clap of thunder, hard and sudden.

"Romans! I stand before you today to read the sentence of the prisoner Lucius Aelius Sejanus."

The crowd went wild. A chant went up. "Kill him! Kill him!"

The senator let the chant continue for a moment. Sejanus lifted his head and surveyed the crowd. Even in the face of death he appeared arrogant.

As the chant began to die down so Castus could read the sentence, Sejanus began to yell at the top of his lungs.

"I would have been your god! I would have saved Rome! You say I was a tyrant? Hear me, Rome, I curse you! The next Caesar Rome will know will show you people what a tyrant really is! I curse you, Rome!"

Most of the crowd missed his words over the noise but I would never forget them. They would come back to me often when Caligula took reign.

Castus motioned to the Praetorians who held Sejanus to his chair. One of them shoved a rag into Sejanus's mouth to silence him.

Castus shouted out the sentence, likely knowing his words would be lost just as Sejanus's curse had dissipated in the din of the crowd. "The Senate and people of Rome find Sejanus guilty of treason against Caesar and against all Rome. He is sentenced to death by strangulation and his body to be thrown down the stairs before us."

The voices grew louder. "Kill him! Kill him!"

Castus continued, "In the days to come all whose blood runs on the same side as Sejanus, be it his children, his slaves, or his loyal friends, they too will meet their death."

"No!" Apicata howled. Apicius pulled her back before she could rush up the stairs and pummel Castus with her fists.

"Daughter! Take hold of yourself!" He turned her around and shook her by the shoulders. She struggled to get away, screaming about her children. Apicius glanced around at the crowd, some of whom were starting to look in our direction. He slapped her. "Daughter! You will be quiet!"

She slumped against him, sobbing. He held her tenderly but there was no surprise in Apicius's eyes and it was as I had guessed—the scroll must have read that Apicata's children would be sentenced when Sejanus was sentenced. The traitor's bloodline would not be allowed to continue. My stomach roiled.

The guards pushed Sejanus and the stool forward. He stared at a point above the crowd and across the Forum, not a trace of fear in his face. A hush fell over the crowd as the largest Praetorian pulled out the gag, wrapped a rope around Sejanus's neck, and pulled the two ends tight, slowly strangling him. Sejanus's face grew red, then purple, then his eyes began to bulge and his tongue stuck out as though trying to reach air. A guard handed a large metal hook with a very sharp point on its end to the other vigile, who slammed it into Sejanus's chest with great force, hooking it into him. Blood spurted and the patricians at the top of the stairs scooted backward. The crowd roared its approval.

When Sejanus had ceased thrashing around, the guards unwrapped the rope at his neck and tied it to the hook. A donkey was brought forth from the guards at the top of the stairs. They tied the rope to its saddle and, with a loud yell, the Praetorian slapped the donkey on the ass, causing it to rush forward down the stairs, Sejanus's body in tow. The noise of the crowd was deafening. The dogs held at the bottom of the stairs were loosed and they rushed to meet the falling body. I recognized them. They were Sejanus's own dogs, the same dogs with which he had often sentenced men to their deaths.

The body fell off its hook halfway down the stairs. The dogs bit into Sejanus's flesh and men rushed forward to kick at the body. I felt nothing, only a deep numbness as the blood ran across the marble stairs, so slick that dogs and men alike slipped in the pooling red.

It was done. Sejanus was dead. And yet there was no satisfaction. I watched the body tumble, pieces of flesh separating and flying.

Fifteen-year-old Strabo met the stairs the next afternoon, and thirteen-year-old Capito's strangulation took place the following day. Junilla was next. Beautiful Junilla, who would never know true love, who would never see the crown of her own newborn's head, who would never grow into a young woman. First they raped her—it was illegal to condemn virgins—then they strangled her and threw her down the stairs to rest among the remains of her father and brothers.

Apicius forbade Apicata from going to the executions, knowing that they would not let her near her children, nor their broken bodies once they were dead. She railed against him, slamming her fists into his chest, tearing at his clothes and screaming her rage until Sotas and I had to pull her off her father. I resorted to drugging her wine with opium. Apicius instructed Sotas to guard her and not let her out of his sight.

After the execution of her daughter, Apicata sat on a bench in the atrium, quiet, rocking herself back and forth, her eyes staring at the door. She ignored anyone who sat with her or tried to talk to her. For hours she sat like that, until Apicius pulled up a chair to sit in front of her. He said nothing, only took her hands in his and kissed them, then sat with her, face-to-face, holding her hands, for nearly a quarter of an hour. Eventually, she stood, gave her father a long kiss on the top of his head, then retreated to her room, motioning with a jerk of her chin that I should follow.

She had me sit with her while she penned her missive to Tiberius. She said nothing to me, and I had no words of my own to say. I watched her make each letter with the stylus, intricate and careful but with a flourish that made my heart ache. Her note to Caesar was scathing and sad, about how her only comfort in the deaths of her children was that Caesar's own child, Drusus, had also died at the hands of others—Livilla and her lover, Sejanus. She cursed Caesar, willing him to die in the same way as her sons and daughter, by his very breath being taken from him, forcefully, when he least expected it.

Apicata handed me the note to read, seal, and send to Caesar. She kissed me on both cheeks, held me tightly, and turned away from me, a clear gesture that I should go.

When I had closed the door behind me, I slid to the ground and stared at her door. The world seemed to spin around me. Never could I have imagined that we would find ourselves thus—empty, spiraling into darkness.

We found her the next morning, dead by poison, the tiny pink vial still in her hand. Apicius locked himself in her room and wept over her body, refusing to come out for a night and a day.

When he emerged, his eyes were red but dry. I had waited with Sotas outside in the hall all night. He stared at me for a moment, almost as though he did not know who I was. Finally, he spoke, his voice hard. "Take her from me. I want no funeral. I want never to hear the names of my daughter, my grandchildren, or my wife again. You are to inform my clients and my friends of this request." He swept past me toward the baths.

We spoke of his family only once more during his life, right before he died.

I moved through all this in a daze. Everything around me was gray and empty. My heart ached for my wife and child, tucked safely away in Herculaneum, away from the horrors we had just been through. For that I was grateful.

When Tiberius received Apicata's letter, he sentenced Livilla to death. Antonia requested the right to be the one to punish her daughter and, strangely, Caesar agreed. She locked Livilla in a room in her house and starved her to death. I thought back to the day when Livilla was married, and Apicius had gifted her with the pumpkin fritters and she said it would be the last meal she would ever desire to have. I did not give her that kindness.

In the weeks that followed, Tiberius had Macro hunt down those loyal to Sejanus. The wealthy were quick to accuse one another and many more bodies piled high on the stairs.

It had taken twenty-five years for our curse against Sejanus to take effect. That curse turned out to be the biggest regret of my life. How much of the blood was my fault? It is a weight that presses upon my heart to this very day.

CHAPTER 29

If there was one thing all of Rome had come to know in the last three decades, it was that Marcus Gavius Apicius knew how to throw a dinner party. A month after Sejanus fell, the parties began to happen almost every night. Unlike when Aelia died, Apicius did not appear to mourn. To most it seemed he had hardened his heart, or perhaps his joy at Sejanus's death overshadowed the anguish he felt at the death of his daughter. Many may have assumed he had been ashamed of her connection to Rome's greatest tyrant and that he approved of her suicide.

I knew different. Apicius was pouring his grief into entertaining all of Rome. I poured my grief into helping him.

He became reckless, drinking more than he had before, saying things he was once too reserved to say, and giving more and more lavish gifts to his guests. He also began to refuse my advice when I tried to curb his spending or if I gave suggestions on anything, even something as small as the color of napkins or the number of clients to invite to balance out a party.

Strangely, it was a little boy who set his mind to worrying about his money, or rather, his reputation in relation to money.

It happened on the night that a patrician friend, Gaius Plinius Celer, his wife, Marcella, and their twelve-year-old son came to dine with us. "My son is going to be a historian," Celer said, motioning toward his young son, Gaius Plinius Secundus, whom they called Pliny. The boy had come as a shadow for his first adult meal outside the house. "He's recording events for posterity's sake."

"I'm writing a history of the world and everything important," the boy said solemnly. He was a wiry boy, as thin as a reed.

"Apicius is one of the most important men in Rome!" Marcella gushed. "He's written dozens of cookbooks! You will have to include him in your history."

The boy only nodded but the look on his face was thoughtful. I was surprised to see Apicius frown, as though he were worried what the child might think of him.

"Pliny, you must try the flamingo tongues—they are the most superb flavor! Here," Apicius suddenly said to the boy, pointing at the platter of the pan-fried delicacies. "Once you have tasted them, you will feel as though Venus is smiling down on you from her throne of stars."

A young boy nearly the same age, dressed like a cherub, held the tray in both hands out to Celer and to Pliny. The father closed his eyes as he savored the offered tidbit. "Quite delicious," he agreed, sinking back against the couch. "Please, leave me some more." He gestured for the slave to deposit a few of the crunchy tongues on his plate.

"Make sure you leave some room in your belly," I said to the boy. "There is more to come." He didn't hear me. He had extracted a wax tablet from a pouch hanging from his tunic and was writing. I saw the words *Apicius says flamingo tongues are of the most superb flavor*. I had to smile. Pliny was off to a fine start recording the events around him. After the diners reduced the contents of the plates to crumbs and shells, I signaled for the slaves to remove the appetizers and bring in tray after tray of meats and vegetables. The first dish to arrive was a platter of mullet cooked in its own juice, followed by boiled partridge; chicken in fennel sauce; honeyed mushrooms; roasted wood pigeons; crane in a celery and mustard sauce; lentils with chestnuts; suckling pigs in pastry; and even a beautiful stuffed hare complete with wings I had taken from a dove, a tribute to the magnificent Pegasus.

Pliny continued writing on his tablet as the food arrived. While the scissor slave cut up the meat, the boy spoke up, his voice still high like a girl's. "You spend a lot of money."

It was directed at Apicius but it wasn't a question, just an astute statement. Pliny's father reddened and opened his mouth to say something, but Apicius spoke first.

He was smiling but I could tell he was irritated. He spoke to Pliny in the same voice he often used with his poorer clients—polite but with a hint of disdain. "Because I spend a lot of money you were able to have those flamingo tongues. You liked those, did you not?"

"Not really." I barely choked back a laugh. Only a child could be so blunt. "Someday you might run out of money."

A couple of the other guests gasped and this time Celer kicked Pliny hard in the leg. "No more talk from you. You have been disrespectful and we will discuss this later."

A lilting voice lifted over the crowd, distracting our attention. "Apicius!"

Claudia, one of the other guests, reclined next to Marcella. Apicius turned his attention away from the boy and toward the women.

"I must inquire where you found these exquisite goblets! Certainly you did not find them at any local market. I have never seen such stone."

"Nor would you," Apicius said. It had been difficult to acquire the goblets and he loved to tell the story. "Early last year I ventured to Sicily, where I heard tale of a stone worker who had a talent for crafting the finest items out of opaque stone. I purchased all he had available, which included these goblets and the basin you saw in the entryway. It took the stone worker ten years to make them!"

It took a lot to keep from rolling my eyes. It had taken only ten weeks to make the set but Apicius was forever embellishing his stories. He had become worse in the last few months.

She fluttered her eyes at Apicius. "What a shame. I had hoped to flatter you with a copy on my own table."

"Claudia, you flatter me merely by asking!"

The conversation turned to other things. Apicius leaned over to me. "Have the basin sent as a gift to Claudia on the morrow, will you?"

I squinted at him, puzzled, but Apicius had already looked back toward the other diners. I saw, with some measure of amusement, that Pliny had heard our exchange and that Apicius was watching the boy write furiously on his tablet.

After the diners had left he pulled me into the library. "Have you seen the books lately? Where do we stand?"

I was shocked. For years I had been trying to get my former master to pay attention to the amount of money he spent and now he was asking me because he was worried about what a boy was writing on a wax tablet?

"Why are you concerning yourself about money now, Apicius? You have never cared before."

"Yes, I know. But I have a reputation to uphold. What if young Pliny is right? What if I run out of money?"

I sat down in the chair beside the long desk, still unable to believe my ears. "Why do you care about what a little boy writes?"

Apicius threw his hands into the air, exasperated. "It's a *history*!" He looked at me as though I were stupid.

"Ah, yes, a history." I wondered what Sotas was thinking in the corridor beyond the door. He must have been laughing his sandals off.

I had gone through the books with the secretary just the day before. I pulled the scroll out from the pile on the top of the desk and unrolled it.

"We stand at ten million sestertii. Tonight's meal cost around ten thousand sestertii, a heavy sum, to be sure, but this is nothing in comparison to the cenae you used to give for Tiberius."

"Only ten million?" Apicius paled at the thought.

"Only? It still places you among the richest men in all of Rome."

Apicius didn't see it in the same way. "My gods, so my inheritance is nearly gone? It was one hundred million! Are you telling me my fortune has dwindled to nearly nothing?"

"Apicius, a thousand sestertii would feed an entire plebeian family for a year." I smoothed back my hair with my hand. "You realize," I continued, "that while you were among the vulgar rich before, now you are simply among the very rich."

The irony was lost on Apicius. He began to pace up and down the length of the library, muttering to himself.

"And what about the farms? The school? My pay from Caesar?"

I sighed. "The farms don't turn much of a profit because we use them to feed your dinner guests. The school never turned a profit—we operated at a loss, and we still owe money after the fire. Your pay from Caesar is long gone. You spent most of it on new villas, furniture, and gifts for all your friends."

"This will not do." He continued to pace.

"We can cut back on various expenses," I offered.

Apicius stopped, nearly knocking an array of scrolls off the shelf next to him. "Cut back how?"

"Simple things would go a long way." I rolled up the scroll and knotted it with a cord. "Take, for example, all those geese and pigs you are fattening up in the farm boxes. Stop feeding them the expensive figs and put them back on slop. That alone would save you nearly five thousand sestertii a year."

Apicius sat down on the chaise across from me. He clutched his stomach, wrinkling the creases of his toga. "I cannot. No, absolutely not. Their livers are all the rage among my diners!"

I tried another tactic. "Find a way to philosophize it . . . make it unfashionable. You are the gourmand, not your diners."

"They will see through it. They will know my money is disappearing!"

"Fine. Don't worry about the livers. Even if you served fewer dishes it would curb your expenses. No one would even notice. There is so much waste at the end of every cena. There is no possible way for every dish to be eaten when you serve so much food."

Apicius would have none of this conversation. "No, no, that will not do," he said, standing again. "I cannot let Rome know my current standing. That will never do. They must suspect nothing. I will find another way. That boy will never be able to write about me as a failure."

"What do you intend to do?" I asked, pouring myself a glass of wine from the flagon on the desk. I thinned it with water from the accompanying pitcher.

Apicius ignored the question. "Ten million sestertii? How long do you expect my fortune to last?"

"Maybe five years if you are even the tiniest bit more thoughtful. Far longer if you consider what you should do to start making money rather than spending it."

"That's all?" He started to pace the room once more, muttering to himself under his breath. Eventually, he drew near to the desk once more, having come to some sort of internal decision.

His look startled me. It was a look of determination, something Apicius never exhibited when it came to money. I used his familiar name, which I never had before, hoping it would convey my concern. "Marcus, what are you thinking of doing?"

Apicius poured himself a glass of wine from the flagon, not bothering to thin it down. He smiled and raised his glass to me. "My good man, you will see. I think I have an answer. In a few months' time all will be very different. And that boy? We'll make sure he writes only the most glorious things about my history."

I raised my glass, but there was no joy in my toast. Only worry.

After Sejanus fell and Apicata died I sent for Passia and Junius to return to Rome. I wanted to ease my aching heart, but a part of me also hoped Apicius would take comfort in their company, especially that of Junius, his adopted son and only living heir.

Unfortunately, Apicius barely noticed them, and when he did he was curt to the point of being rude. "That's fine with me," Passia said to me as we were readying for sleep one night. "He's become so mean. I'm not sure how you can stand to be around him."

"His heart is hurting," I replied, but even as the words came out of my mouth I knew they sounded inadequate.

"So are ours. We were closer to both Aelia and Apicata than he ever was, and I don't see either of us snipping at everyone crossing our path."

I slipped off my tunic and hung it on the back of the low chair against the wall. "I think something is very wrong with him," I said, voicing my concerns for the first time. "He's become erratic. He threatens me one moment and in the next he praises me, seemingly forgetting he just told me he was going to make me a eunuch. He has also started to leave the house without guards, even without Sotas."

Passia put down the comb she had been running through her hair. "Without Sotas? But why would he do that? All manner of things might happen to him! He's got more than a few enemies in Rome."

"I don't know. Sotas trailed him yesterday and apparently he went to a knife and arms master, but came out with nothing."

Passia wrinkled her nose. "How strange. But he's been very social lately. More than he has been in a long while."

"Exactly. Which is yet another thing on the list of things that don't make sense to me. And now he wants me to start preparing for a very elaborate convivium next month, the biggest one we can hold here in the house. He wants to spare no expense. None at all. He wants gold plates, jeweled napkins, rubies in the bottom of every wineglass. I'm supposed to buy any silphium I can find, regardless of price. He wants me to source only the best honey, the best figs, the best wine, and the best meat. He wants me to buy new serving boys and girls, only the prettiest, he said."

"But I thought you said he was worried about money."

"I thought he was. And if not, he should be." I pulled back the covers and climbed in. My eyes roamed the saucy painting on the wall above our bed.

"But what about Timon? He's so ill."

"I know. But even if he wasn't sick, Apicius didn't want him to be in charge of this meal. He wants it to be me. He keeps saying this will be the most amazing meal Rome has ever seen, and if so, it means Rome's best cook needs to be in charge of the kitchen. Which I suppose I should be flattered he thinks is me."

"Well, you are the best cook in Rome." Passia climbed into bed next to me, and I marveled at how her body was still so slender after all these years. She leaned over and gave me a peck on the cheek.

I snatched her by the arm and pulled her close. "Good thing you are married to me, then, right?"

She laughed and her hair tickled my face. "I didn't marry you for your food, you silly goat." I felt her hand between my legs.

I smiled and put Apicius and everyone else out of my mind.

The next day was not pleasant. Timon died in the night, succumbing to the fever that had consumed him off and on in the last two weeks. I always wondered how long he would serve us. After all, he was old when I found him. I was doubly upset now, though, for his death left me with such a feat to accomplish in such a short time frame.

Apicius had no sympathy for me. When I asked if we could hold off his party until I found a new cook, he said, "No, we can't. This will be the ultimate party, Thrasius. I know you don't want to miss it. Do it for me this time and I promise that you won't need to cook again in my house unless you absolutely want to. You can wait till after the party to find a new cook."

I groaned, but he had me. I wanted to stop cooking. I was starting to tire of spending so much time in the kitchen, and the thought of doing it without Timon was especially daunting at my age. "Do I have your word on that?" I asked, still wary.

He smiled. "I give you my solemn oath. After this convivium you will be able to decide if and when you want to cook again."

I didn't believe him.

Still, I began the preparations. My initial intention was to cut corners on costs but Apicius hovered over all my plans, preventing me from saving precious coin. I sent messengers on horseback to the farthest reaches of Italy for the goods one could carry back to Rome in a few saddlebags. I spent an inordinate amount of time at the markets, Apicius on my heels, purchasing the most costly spices; reams of opulent silk for pillow coverings; ornate, one-of-a-kind oil lamps; and hundred-year-old wines so thick that only the best honey, lead, and spices would bring them back to life. I buried fish in salt, and sealed plums in spirits and left them to age in the dark. I made Roman absinthe and apple wine. I bought the best suckling pigs and began to fatten them on the most expensive figs. I fed our goats a specially sourced mixture of apples, hay, and clover to give their milk new flavor.

The guest list was the biggest challenge of all. We could fit only two hundred or so people in the house, even if we transformed some of the rooms into additional triclinia. Which meant we had to pare the guest list back by more than seventy-five people.

"We don't have to seat them all," Apicius insisted. "Let them wander."

It was late afternoon and Apicius had returned from the baths, where he had apparently invited several random friends who didn't happen to be on the initial guest list.

"We don't have room in the house, Apicius. We don't have the space we had at the school, or when we could throw parties at Caesar's villa. Maybe we could stretch the list to two hundred but that will be pushing our limits."

Apicius looked out the window down onto the Forum below. "Do what you can. Invite two hundred for now but maybe more will show up." He sounded wistful to me, as though he didn't believe anyone would attend.

"Do you trust me to create the list?"

He glanced back at me. "Implicitly. But I may invite some who aren't on your list."

"Apicius!" I was exasperated. "If you trust me to invite two hundred people, you shouldn't need to invite anyone else. Didn't we just discuss we have no room?"

"That's fine. I'm sure all the right people who need to be at the party will be there." He turned back to the window.

One of his moods crept across him. He stopped answering any of my additional questions, so I left, wondering to myself the very thing Passia had asked me—how did I endure him?

I thought a lot about that over the coming weeks as I prepared for the meal. Apicius tried my patience at every twist and turn. Why, then, did I put up with his mood swings and irrationalities? A sane person would have left long before. Was I insane?

No, I had to admit I did it because Apicius was my friend, my family, and because without me he was nothing; he had nothing. I thought of myself in his place—I would want a friend by my side. I continued the preparations, despite all my misgivings.

I'm not sure what I expected the party to do for him. I knew it wouldn't satisfy his grief, nor would it change Rome's opinion of him. It might make people think he was richer than he was, but it would only serve to worsen the dilemma he faced—how to continue to maintain the appearance of such wealth when in truth it was dwindling.

The last thing I expected, of course, was what actually happened.

On the morning of the convivium Apicius came to the kitchen, a slender box tucked under one arm. I looked up from the pastry dough I had rolled onto the counter. I was surprised to see him awake.

His smile was broad. "What a beautiful morning!" He glanced over my shoulder through the window toward the sunny garden. The pigs were being slaughtered and we could hear their final squeals.

"Yes, it is," I agreed, wishing I were out walking in the sun rather than trapped in the kitchen making pastry animals.

"I brought you something to celebrate."

"To celebrate what?"

He laughed, his jowls shaking. "All the amazing meals you've made for me! You, of course!" He slid the box across the table toward me, careful to avoid the piles of flour.

I wiped my hands on the towel at my waist, curious and a bit dismayed by his gracious speech. The box itself was gorgeous, made from a beautiful piece of citron wood. I was reminded of a table Cicero once bought that had been made from the exorbitantly expensive wood. He wrote that the veins were "arranged in waving lines to form spirals like small whirlpools." It was such a vivid description, I had always remembered it, and now, as I looked at this box, I realized how true the statement was. I could not imagine how much the box cost—and it made me wonder what on earth the contents might be.

"Go on, open it!" Apicius jerked his chin toward the box. A crooked smile decorated his face.

With a deep breath, I opened it. Inside lay two beautiful ebony-handled knives, both made in shapes I had myself personally sketched—Apicius and I had long talked about how to improve our kitchen knives. I had never imagined the designs would have gone beyond our brief conversations, and yet here they were, inventions of my own mind come to life.

One knife was longer, meant for carving, and the other was shorter, designed for smaller kitchen tasks. The metal of each blade contained a beautiful and delicate pattern that looked very much like flowing water. I touched my finger to the flat of the larger blade, expecting to feel a raised impression, but instead found it was smooth. And oh! The blades were very sharp. I nicked my finger with the slightest test.

When I looked up at my former master, I had a lump in my throat.

Apicius clapped a hand to my shoulder. "They're from Damascus. I had them made for you. They should last for centuries. They are unique, truly, as there are no others like them in the world and likely never to be again. Just as you, my friend, are rare and unique. You have been a great source of pride in my life. Thank you."

"I don't know what to say," I stammered.

"Then say nothing! Cook with them today. Cook me the best meal I have ever had. No, the best meal Rome has ever had!"

"I will. I promise you."

And I did. I cooked him the best meal of his life. It was also the best meal Rome *never* had.

. . .

His fellow Romans never partook in the meal because in the moments before the convivium was to start Apicius ordered Sotas to have the guards bar the doors and turn all the guests away. Passia came to the kitchen bearing the news.

"Apicius forbade everyone entry! The guests are pounding on the doors!" She was breathless, having run the length of the house. She had been with the slave girls in the atrium awaiting the guests when Apicius made the announcement.

"I don't understand. He canceled the party? Without telling me?" I didn't wait for an answer, storming past her toward the triclinium.

Sotas stood outside the room, his mouth drawn in a somber line. The doors to the triclinium were, uncharacteristically, closed.

"I take it you've heard the news."

"Mercury's boots! What is going on? I have my slaves lined up with the gustatio, ready to go."

"Don't worry. They will still serve the food."

I noticed Sotas had his sword with him. It lay against the wall, gleaming in the light from the torch in the corridor. I started to ask but Apicius's voice rang out from behind the doors.

"Is that Thrasius? Send him in!"

I had been looking at the door when the shout came. I turned back to Sotas, hoping for a hint of what to expect. What I saw shocked me.

He looked like he was about to cry.

Thoroughly disconcerted, I pushed open the doors. Apicius reclined on the farthest couch, sipping a glass of honey water. His broad smile confused me even further. What was going on?

"Why did you bar the doors? Your guests are banging to get in!" I walked across the tiles to where he lay.

"Ahh, come, Thrasius! Sit with me for a moment."

I sat across from him but didn't recline. I wasn't sure what to think. He looked happier than he had in years, his round cheeks ruddy and hale, and his eyes glittering. I waited for him to explain.

"Today is the day, I decided. I turned my guests away because they should not have to endure what is to happen."

My stomach felt like a stone had been dumped into it. "And what is going to happen?" I asked, although I knew what he was going to say.

"I want you to serve the meal just as you would have if all the guests were here. I want to watch the entertainment, to touch the skin of the girls and boys who serve me. I want to feel the smoothness of a grape on my tongue, experience the flavor of the swollen liver from the pig you slaughtered this morning, know the taste of figs as their seeds scrape against my teeth." He pulled a sheaf of papers from beneath the pillow next to him.

"Take this." He handed the packet to me. "It's my will. I give everything to you and Junius. You are to free Sotas and five hundred of my slaves of your choosing. The rest of my slaves and all of my piddling fortune fall to you and your son."

"I don't understand, Apicius." My words caught in my throat. "Why . . . why, why must you do this?"

"Now, do not be upset. I have my dignity to uphold! It's time to go, before I have nothing left. I want the entire world to know me for the feasts we had—for their magnificence, for the experience you and I have given them that no one else could. That boy Pliny was right. I am running out of money. And it would not do to have that in my history. I want no one to say that old, fat Apicius starved to death!"

I couldn't believe what I was hearing.

"You are still quite rich, Apicius! There is not an equestrian alive who wouldn't still be envious of your fortune!"

He laughed, a jolly sound that grated against my ears. How could he laugh?

"Oh, Thrasius. An *equestrian*! All my life you would have said patrician, but I have sunk and only the world of the plebs lies before me."

I stood, knocking several silk-covered pillows onto the floor. "This is ludicrous!" I was shouting, but didn't care. "Patrician, equestrian, it matters not! You need not do this. Your coffers are still fat and we can do things to bring more money in. We can convert one of your farms into a garum factory. You don't have to give out expensive togas to guests. There is so much we can do!" I knew as the words fell off my tongue that they fell on deaf ears.

"No, no, no. I do not want to worry about such things." He sat up and waved me over with a chubby hand. "Come here, Thrasius."

I took the few steps toward him, my body shaking. "I don't understand."

He stood and reached up to his neck and lifted off the amulet he wore. My silphium carved amulet. I had forgotten about it, that he had stolen it so many years ago. "I believe this is yours," he said as he put it over my head.

"No, it's yours!"

He took my face between his hands. He bent forward and kissed both of my cheeks. Still holding my shoulders, he leaned back to look at me.

"My dear boy, how much you have changed since that day in the market. I remember how much you stank, how much you worried me. And that rotten haruspex . . ." He let me go, a wistful look in his eye.

I had kept the priest's words in my head for decades, always shoving them to the back of my mind, hating that the man had so much foresight. *You will feel the blood of life mingling with the pang of death. Your good fortune will be as a disease throughout your life. The more you work toward success, the more your sky will darken.*

"Please, Apicius, do not do this." I fell to my knees. As though in a dream, I wrapped my arms around his legs as a child might.

He ruffled my hair, making me feel more like a child. "I must, Thrasius. Please do not fret. You have such love in your life. I have so little. Let me leave with dignity."

I held on to him for a few more moments, barely able to comprehend what was happening. Finally, I let go. I scrambled to my feet, even though my legs threatened to collapse from under me at any given moment.

I wiped away tears, trying to regain my own dignity so I could give him his.

"The first course will be out shortly, Dominus Apicius." I tried to keep my voice from trembling. "I suspect you will be very pleased."

He clapped his hands together. "Excellent! Bring out the girls and the boys! Bring out the snails, the apples, the mussels, apricots, and the dormice!"

When I left, Sotas was still beside the door, but he turned away from me as I walked out. He didn't want me to see him cry.

I went through all the motions of the meal, sending out the slaves with the food when the courses dictated. I sent the entertainment in—flutists, harpists, and singers. I sent the girls, the boys, all dressed in ever-amazing costumes, some like birds and animals, some like monsters, some like heroes, and some like nymphs.

And oh, the food was magnificent! I had re-created all the old stories of the gods. Venus carved from a gourd, emerging from her shell. Fantastic Roman triremes made from hollowed cucumbers and holding tiny white carrot men fought battles across an ocean of cold beet soup. A platter of cheese and figs shaped into Cerberus and his double heads. And the dishes! Only the finest delicacies were served, with the pinnacle of each course flavored with the few dried sprigs of silphium I had been hoarding for a year—there was no fresh silphium to be had. Plate after plate of marinated mushrooms, Baian beans in mustard sauce, pork meatballs, honey melons, stuffed boiled eggs, fried veal slices, crunchy duck and flamingo tongues, pork pastries stuffed with figs, pear patinae, steamed lamb, soufflés of little fishes . . . even now my mouth salivates thinking back to that meal. I hope Apicius found great pleasure in those dishes.

I couldn't bear to sit with him while he ate. Instead I remained in the kitchen, tasting only ash and tears.

I wished Rúan had been there to help me when I faltered, because falter was all I seemed to do. I had to send Passia away—her keening was more than I could bear. I put the fear of the gods in the slaves, telling them that if they did not perform their best for Apicius that night I would have them put to death. At one point Tycho took my new knives from me, afraid I would follow through on my threats, or hurt myself.

After the final course went out, one of the boys returned with a message that Apicius was asking for me. He wanted me to bring the finest wine in the cellar.

I walked that long hallway with the heaviest of feet. I had never before known such dread and sorrow mixed together as they were those two hundred steps.

Sotas was not at the door when I arrived. I drew upon all my courage, determined to control my emotions. I pushed the door open and saw Sotas standing behind his master. His eyes were red but there were no tears on his cheeks.

Apicius lay back on the pillows, rubbing his bulging stomach. "Ahh, here he is! Thrasius, come with my best wine!"

I held up the small pitcher, the last of Apicius's favorite Falernian vintage, seventy-five years old. "I mixed it for you too." I was surprised that I could speak, but the words fell off my tongue, my resolve holding.

He motioned for me to sit and he waved Sotas to sit on his other side. "Have a glass with me, you and Sotas."

My shaking hands poured the wine into goblets that should have been for other guests. I handed one to Apicius and one to Sotas.

Apicius reached into the fold of his toga and pulled out a tiny green glass flask. He unstopped it and poured a muddy liquid into the glass. "A very strong dose of opium and hemlock," he explained. "As you know, I'm not one for pain."

I watched him stir the liquid into the wine with the long handle of his spoon. I suddenly chuckled, surprising myself.

Apicius looked at me, the corner of his mouth curling upward. "What's so funny, Thrasius?"

"You are right; you never were one for pain! I remember you stubbing your toe on a rock on the beach at Baiae once. You made us carry you back to the villa!" I couldn't stop laughing and soon both Apicius and Sotas were laughing as well.

"You mean, *I* carried him back to the villa!" Sotas snorted.

"Well, you're a beast! Why should they have expended energy when you could practically pick me up in one hand?" Apicius was crying tears of laughter.

"He can't do that anymore," I managed, wheezing.

"That's your fault, Thrasius," Apicius said. "All those damn milk-fed snails you addicted me to!"

"I don't think it was just the snails." Sotas chuckled.

Apicius did not wait for our laughter to fade. He lifted the glass. "To you, my friends."

"No, Apicius, we raise our glasses to you," Sotas said solemnly.

Apicius laughed again. It was the last time I would hear that bright sound. "Let us raise our glasses—to us!" He knocked back the glass. We followed suit. Sotas drained the contents of his goblet and set it down on the table next to him.

"Oh, my, what a wonderful vintage this is!" Apicius lifted the glass again and downed all that was left. He fell back on the pillows.

"Sit with me, my friends. Tell me stories about the best meals we have ever eaten." He reached out a hand to me and one to Sotas. His grip was tight. He closed his eyes.

Sotas drew a deep breath, and for a moment I thought he would not be able to speak. "I remember the first time you let me try a fried dormouse." He too had closed his eyes in memory. "I was fifteen and Fannia was giving a party. You snuck one out to me as a reward for not telling your father you had been the one to graffiti the wall of the barn. I remember how the bones crunched, how the skin crackled, and the way the juices ran across my mouth. I think it tasted even better because I wasn't supposed to have it and because I had pleased you."

Apicius gave a small grunt of pleasure but said nothing, his eyes still closed.

His grip was starting to slacken in my hand. "I remember the first apricots we had a few years ago," I said. "Oh, what a new taste it was for both of us! Who would have thought the gods could give us something so lush, so full of honey and sunlight. And you were right, Apicius, they did make the most amazing patina, didn't they? I think I will make one for you tomorrow, in fact."

No sound from Apicius. His grip had weakened as I spoke and soon it was me gripping his hand, not him gripping mine.

I moved my hand to his wrist, clasping it, feeling his pulse weaken. The tears came unbidden. Sotas and I sat with him, crying until his pulse was no more.

I pulled three coins from the pouch at my belt. I placed one on each eye and gently opened his mouth to place the coin on his tongue, which would guarantee that Charon took him across the River Styx to the Underworld.

I didn't notice that Sotas had retrieved his sword until he knelt with it in front of him.

"Oh, my friend, no, not you too . . ."

"It's how it was meant to be," he said. "My lady Fides pledged me to

Apicius in my youth. My pledge is complete and now she will take me to Elysium."

"No, no, it's not like that."

He smiled a little. "Yes it is. Good-bye, Thrasius. You were a friend indeed, to both my master and me. The gods will reward you richly, of that I'm sure."

Sotas plunged forward suddenly, falling on the point of his sword so hard it emerged through his back in a spurt of bright blood. He did not cry out.

"No!" I moved forward, knowing that nothing I did would matter. I reached him as he slumped forward, dead.

I screamed my sorrow to the gods until all the slaves came running.

EPILOGUE

Passia, Junius, Tycho, and I came to Athens in March, afraid that Emperor Caligula's greed would stretch its long arm toward us and demand our fortune. We were in especial danger as we were not patricians, but made rich by the inheritance Apicius left to us.

I eventually sold all of Apicius's villas and farms, save the domus in Minturnae, where we first found each other and where so much began. I put the money away for Junius, who at twenty-five has become one of the best orators in all of Athens. He married a beautiful girl with eyes that remind me of Apicata's. She is heavy with child and I feel such pride and hope for my grandchild-to-be.

Rúan came with us when we fled to Athens, bringing with him the beautiful woman who was once Antonia's scribe. I bought them an expansive house nearby, down the street from us on the hill where our villa overlooks the sea. Together, Rúan and I still cook, but now we cook for our friends and our families, sharing our love of food only with those whom we love the most.

I still have my knives and I use them daily. I know not what spell Apicius had them bound with but I have yet to sharpen them. They shine as they did on that fateful morning he gifted them to me. They are sharp enough to slice papyrus and bone with equal measure and the swirl of waves has not faded from the blades.

My memory of him is as sharp as those knives, even now, so many years gone by and so many miles away.

AUTHOR'S NOTE

Though it is likely that there were other gourmands in ancient Rome, Marcus Gavius Apicius is the only one known to us. Historians believe that he lived sometime in the first century C.E., during the time of Caesar Tiberius, and many of the events described in *Feast of Sorrow* are documented in sources dating from that time.

Apicius, who was known to be one of the wealthiest men in Rome, achieved fame as a lover of luxury and fine food. *On the Luxury of Apicius*, written by his contemporary, the Greek grammarian and orator Apion, is now lost, but surviving sources largely condemn Apicius as a spendthrift. In his *Consolations*, Seneca relays the story of Apicius's death—it seems he really did poison himself because he feared starvation when he learned that his fortune had dwindled to ten million sestertii—and asks, "How great must the luxury of that man have been, to whom ten millions signified want?" In reference to his cooking school, Seneca also decries that Apicius "defiled the age with his teaching," a critique commonly leveled against those who displayed their great wealth in a vulgar fashion. In the centuries that followed, Apicius became one of the most iconic examples of such flagrancy and, in fact, the very word *Apician* came to mean "glutton."

Many of the other characters in *Feast of Sorrow*—Sejanus, Apicata, Livia, Livilla, Tiberius, Drusus, Claudius, Antonia, Pliny, to name a few—were also real people whose lives are recorded in the annals of Roman history, and I endeavored to stay true to the historical record as much as possible. In his *Annals*, for example, Tacitus tells us that Sejanus "had disposed of his virtue at a price to Apicius, a rich man and a prodigal." I found that anecdote to be particularly intriguing, as some scholars believe that Sejanus's wife, Apicata, must have been a relation to Apicius given the naming conventions of women during that time. I had to wonder what would compel Apicius to marry his daughter to a former lover. Other details, including Sejanus's horrific downfall as well as Apicata's and Livilla's fates, are well documented, and those scenes are imagined retellings of what their contemporaries recorded. Still others were fabricated to add color and clarification to the text. Claudius's son, Drusus, for example, was not nicknamed Albus; I gave him this moniker to distinguish him from his relatives with similar names, a common occurrence among the Romans.

Parricide, or the murder of a parent, considered the most heinous crime one could commit, was an act punishable by death in ancient Rome. In fact, the Romans devised a particularly cruel and unusual form of capital punishment solely for those found guilty of this crime. The *poena cullei*, or punishment of the sack, which was first documented in 100 B.C.E., typically involved flogging the culprit, sewing him into a leather sack, sometimes with an assortment of live animals, and throwing him into the sea. However, it is not clear with what frequency this punishment was doled out, and some ancient sources maintain that only those caught in the act of murdering a parent faced any penalty at all. Moreover, the very wealthy were often above punishment, and that's the direction I chose to take in *Feast of Sorrow*.

There is no record of the slaves whom Apicius owned, but given his wealth it is probable that he owned many hundreds. None of the slaves in *Feast of Sorrow* were real people, though slaves did often become a cherished part of the household, could earn their freedom, be buried in the family mausoleum, and, in some cases, inherit their masters' wealth.

When it comes to food and feasts, we know that Apicius dined with Augustus's adviser, Maecenas, with Martial the poet, and with several Roman consuls. In his *Natural History*, Pliny notes that Apicius advised Tiberius's son, Drusus, not to eat cabbage tops or any cabbage sprouts because those were for commoners and that he declared that the tongues of flamingos were of the "most exquisite flavor." The scene where Tiberius wagers that either Apicius or Publius Octavius would buy the extraordinary red mullet was recorded by Seneca in his *Let-*

ters to Lucilius. And, in his *Deipnosophistae*, the rhetorician Athenaeus shares the story of Apicius sailing to the coast of Africa to look for prawns.

It is thought that Apicius was responsible for several different books about cooking, including one on sauces referenced by several ancient chroniclers, but none has survived. However, a cookbook that bears his name has survived and, ultimately, it is Apicius's most important legacy. The oldest known collection of recipes, it is believed to have been compiled in the third or fourth century, long after Marcus Gavius Apicius lived, though it is likely that some of the recipes were first developed in his kitchen. While *Apicius* is full of ancient delicacies such as roasted peacock, boiled sow vulva, testicles, and other foods we would not commonly eat today, there are many others that are still popular, including tapenade, absinthe, flatbreads, and meatballs. There is even a recipe for Roman milk and egg bread that is identical to what we call French toast. And, contrary to popular belief, foie gras was not originally a French delicacy. The dish dates back twenty-five hundred years, and Pliny credits Apicius with developing a version using pigs instead of geese by feeding hogs dried figs and giving them an overdose of *mulsum* (honey wine) before slaughtering them.

The best adaptation of this cookbook is *Apicius, A Critical Edition with an Introduction and English Translation*, translated by Christopher Grocock and Sally Grainger (Devon, England: Prospect Books, 2006). In fact, the recipes on *Feast of Sorrow*'s part title pages (with minor changes by the author) are from this book. Sally Grainger's companion cookbook, *Cooking with Apicius* (London, England: Marion Boyars, 2006), offers wonderful modern interpretations of the original recipes. My favorite is the Parthian chicken. I've included a modified version of this recipe, along with several other recipes for ancient Roman foods, on my site, crystalking.com, and I would love to hear from you if you try one!

Buon appetito!

Crystal King

ACKNOWLEDGMENTS

Feast of Sorrow would not have been possible without the support I received from Boston's GrubStreet writing community. It is there that I workshopped early drafts, began teaching, found my writing group, and met my agent. There are so many wonderful individuals associated with this center of excellence that it would be difficult to name them all, but a few deserve a special shout-out: Christopher Castellani, Eve Bridburg, Lisa Borders, Sonya Larson, Whitney Scharer, Michelle Toth, and Michelle Seaton.

At GrubStreet, I met my fellow Salt + Radish Writers, women who have toiled with me for the past ten years on every aspect of this book. Each scene within *Feast of Sorrow* contains a spark of magic from Anjali Mitter Duva, Jennifer Dupee, and Kelly Robertson.

I am indebted to the team at Touchstone Books, who championed this novel from the very moment I came on board: my editor, Trish Todd, as well as Kaitlin Olson, Shida Carr, Leah Morse, Meredith Vilarello, Kelsey Manning, Beth Ireland, and everyone else behind the scenes. I was also lucky to have worked with acquiring editor Etinosa Agbonlahor, who gave me the chance to tell the story I wanted to tell. Her influence and keen insight are woven into the fabric of every page. Everyone at Touchstone has been a joy to work with and I couldn't have imagined a better entrance into the world as a debut author.

I have the great fortune to be represented by Amaryah Orenstein at GO Literary. She believed in the story from my first pitch and has been an incredible collaborative partner in the entire process. Mere words cannot describe the superstar she is to me.

ACKNOWLEDGMENTS

Thank you to my enthusiastic readers and dear friends Leanna Widgren, Melissa Ayres, Linette Gomez, Michelle Morgan, Laura Warrell, Shadra Bruce, and Ryan La Sala.

Steven Bauer of Hollow Tree Literary helped me with some crucial edits along the way. Classicist Emily Hauser helped me with many clarifications to the Latin text and Roman traditions.

I have been extraordinarily fortunate to share the journey to publication with my fellow TheDebutanteBall.com authors: Amy Poeppel, Lynn Hall, Jenni L. Walsh, and Tiffany D. Jackson.

My friend and Italian tutor, Graziella Macchetta, has fueled my love of the history and language of Italy. *Chi trova una amica, trova un tesoro.*

In Rome, Patrizia and Beniamino at Casa Dei Coronari welcomed me with open arms, making each stay more special than the last. They taught me that *Si sei venuto qui cor core 'nmano, tu de diritto diventi già romano.*

Thanks also to my parents, sister, and brother for indulging my childhood stories and encouraging me in my earliest creative years.

I also owe gratitude to historians Sally Grainger and Christopher Grocock for their translation of *Apicius*. Additionally, during my years of extensive research, I found that these particular texts were critical to my work: *Around the Roman Table* by Patrick Faas, translated by Shaun Whiteside; *Empire of Pleasures: Luxury and Indulgence in the Roman World* by Andrew Dalby; *The Classical Cookbook* by Andrew Dalby and Sally Grainger; *Handbook to Life in Ancient Rome* by Lesley Adkins and Roy A. Adkins; *The Houses of Roman Italy, 100 B.C.–A.D. 250: Ritual, Space, and Decoration* by John R. Clarke; *An Introduction to Roman Religion* by John Scheid; and *A Taste of Ancient Rome* by Ilaria Gozzini Giacosa, translated by Anna Herklotz.

And to my husband, Joe. Thank you for the countless hours spent (over thousands of delicious meals) helping me with all the stickiest parts of this book. Of all the time spent working on this novel, that has been my favorite part of all. I could not have asked for a more supportive, loving advocate for my writing process. *Ti amo.*

ABOUT THE AUTHOR

Crystal King is a writer, culinary enthusiast, and marketing expert. Her writing is fueled by a love of history and an obsession with the food, language, and culture of Italy. She has taught creativity, writing, and social media at GrubStreet and several universities, including Harvard Extension School and Boston University. Crystal received her master's degree in critical and creative thinking from the University of Massachusetts at Boston. She lives in the US with her husband and two cats, Nero and Merlin.

This reading group guide for *Feast of Sorrow* includes an introduction, discussion questions, ideas for enhancing your book club, and a Q&A with author Crystal King. The suggested questions are intended to help your reading group find new and interesting angles and topics for your discussion. We hope that these ideas will enrich your conversation and increase your enjoyment of the book.

INTRODUCTION

On a burning hot day during the twenty-sixth year of the reign of Augustus Caesar, Rome's famous gourmand Marcus Gavius Apicius hands over an exorbitant amount of money to purchase Thrasius, a young slave who has turned heads as Flavius Maximus's cook. The slave master promises that Thrasius will make Apicius famous with cooking that will attract throngs of people to his feasts, but the priest that Apicius visits after the purchase foretells a different fate: one of success mingled with failure and darkness. Thrasius shares the story of his time with Apicius and his family. As Apicius grows more obsessed with his legacy, Thrasius falls madly in love with the handmaiden Passia and dreams of their future together. But as Apicius goes to greater and greater lengths to garner the attention that will allow him to take the coveted spot as Caesar's gastronomic adviser, he grows careless and erratic, taking actions that put his family and his slaves in grave danger. Thrasius's tale of the man whose name graces the world's oldest known cookbook gives readers an intimate look at the dark politics and mystical mythology of ancient Rome while posing the timeless question: Is man really the master of his own fate?

TOPICS AND QUESTIONS
FOR DISCUSSION

1. The story begins with Thrasius's account of the day he was purchased by Apicius in Baiae. Why do you think the author chose to
make Thrasius the narrator of the story? How might the story be
different if it was told from another point of view or from multiple
points of view?

2. What significance do birds have in the novel? Why do the characters in the story pay them such attention?

3. What role does food play in ancient Roman culture? Why is Apicius
so obsessed with having only the best food at his lavish dinners?
What position does he hope to secure through his reputation as
Rome's best gourmand? Is he successful? Why or why not? What
effect do these ambitions have on the rest of his life?

4. Consider the motif of betrayal and sabotage. Who betrays or sabo-
tages another character in the book and what is their motivation
for doing so? Would you say that their actions are justified? Why or
why not? Are they ever brought to justice?

5. Examine the treatment of women in the novel. What do the female
characters reveal about the role of women in ancient Roman culture?
What do they tell us about marriage, motherhood, and love? Alternatively, what role do they play in Roman politics, culture, and religion?

6. Evaluate the representation of the master-slave relationship in the novel. Why is Thrasius surprised by Sotas's feelings about his master? How does this relationship compare to Thrasius's own relationship with Apicius? How does the relationship between Apicius and Thrasius change over the course of the story and what causes this? Why do you think Thrasius stays with Apicius even after Apicius frees him?

7. Many of the characters in the novel rely on prophecies and signs to foretell their future. However, in Chapter 6, Rúan says that he believes man controls his own fate. Does the book ultimately support Rúan's point of view or does it support the view that fate is beyond our control? Discuss.

8. Evaluate the theme of fidelity. To what are the characters faithful? Alternatively, what causes them to be unfaithful?

9. How is love characterized or defined within the novel? What kinds of love are represented therein? What does Aelia tell her daughter about the role of love in the lives of the wealthy?

10. What role does marriage play in ancient Roman culture? How does the author characterize Apicius's marriage to Aelia? Why does Apicius refuse to give his permission for Thrasius to marry Passia? Why does Apicius change his mind about allowing Apicata to marry Casca and instead betroth her to Sejanus?

11. What does the book indicate about social mobility during this time period? Are any of the characters able to move beyond the class they are born into? If so, how do they accomplish this? Likewise, is it possible for people of this time to lose their status? If so, how does this happen?

12. What does Apicius want his legacy to be? Is he successful? Why is he so concerned with Pliny, the young boy who attends one of his dinners? What effect does the future historian have on Apicius? Are Apicius's actions that follow surprising? Why or why not?

13. In the Author's Note at the end of the text, King discusses the nature of the historical novel, explaining that while Apicius is a character drawn from real life, some of the characters are the product of her own invention. What elements were fictionalized and what purpose might they serve? How might the book be different without these fictionalized elements?

14. Throughout the centuries, food has been a marker of social distinction between the haves and have-nots, even in today's society. What are the similarities between food/foodie culture of yesteryear and today? How does Apicius or Thrasius compare to today's celebrity chefs?

ENHANCE YOUR BOOK CLUB

1. Research ancient Roman culture during the time period represented in *Feast of Sorrow*. How does King's account fit in with other historical accounts of this time? What rituals and mythology are represented in King's novel? Choose a few examples and research them in greater depth, considering why they were important within ancient Roman culture.

2. Use the novel as a starting place to examine the complex role of women in ancient Roman culture. How are the female characters treated in the book? What roles do they play in politics, family life, and religion? Consider how they were both repressed and revered.

3. Have an Apicius-themed dinner party with your book club. Invite your guests to bring dishes inspired by Apicius's own cookbook or make a few dishes together. Use the recipes printed in *Feast of Sorrow* as a place to begin or refer to the books recommended in the Author's Note at the back of the novel: *Cooking with Apicius* by Sally Grainger (London, England: Marion Boyars, 2006); *The Classical Cookbook* by Andrew Dalby and Sally Grainger, revised edition (Los Angeles: J. Paul Getty Museum, 2012); *A Taste of Ancient Rome* by Ilaria Gozzini Giacosa, translated by Anna Herklotz (Chicago: University of Chicago Press, 1994); *Roman Cookery: Ancient Recipes for Modern Kitchens* by Mark Grant (Northampton, MA: Interlink Publishing, 2008); *The Philosopher's Kitchen: Recipes from Ancient Greece and Rome for the Modern Cook* by Francine Segan (New York: Random House, 2004); and *Around the Roman Table*

by Patrick Faas (Chicago: University of Chicago Press, 2005). You can also visit the author's website and view additional recipes at CrystalKing.com/culinary-delights.

4. Imagine that you are writing your own cookbook. What recipes would you include in the book to be a part of your legacy and why? Have you chosen these dishes because of their impressive gastronomic qualities or because of something you feel that they represent personally or culturally?

A Conversation with
Crystal King

What inspired you to tell the story of the real-life character Apicius, ancient Rome's most famous gourmand? Can you discuss the novel's origins?

I was writing a different book about some fantastical knives and I needed an origin story. During my research I came across a snippet of information about Apicius and how he died. I wrote a scene showing Apicius purchasing the knives to give to his chef, who would then pass them on to his apprentice and the knives would continue being handed down through the ages. But the more I wrote about Apicius, the more I realized that his story was the more interesting one. I wanted to know what would make a man decide to end his life in such a dramatic way. You'll notice, though, that I kept part of the scene in which Apicius gifts the set of knives to Thrasius. The knives may also show up again in the next novel I'm writing.

Why did you make the decision to tell the story from the point of view of Thrasius, his imagined slave and cook?

I struggled with this decision. I began writing the book from Apicius's point of view but quickly realized that if I did that it would be hard to end the book with the same punch. The number one thing I knew about this person was how he died and I wanted to keep the suspense all the way through to the end of the book. I couldn't have done that with Apicius as the narrator. Also, Apicius's life, in my novel, was a series of very tragic decisions. I saw Thrasius as a counterbalance. He is the calm in the storm, the one who holds Apicius together, and, in the end, he is the one who comes out somewhat unscathed.

Since the work is a historical novel, what sources did you consult in order to prepare for writing the book? Can you tell us a little bit about your research process?

After I had the idea for *Feast of Sorrow* I spent nearly a year only reading books that pertained to my research. I read everything I could get my hands on: anything about ancient food; books about ancient religion, culture, architecture, slavery, politics; and a wide variety of books written in ancient times, ranging from Virgil to Pliny to Cato the Elder. The Metropolitan Museum in New York and the Museum of Fine Arts in Boston have incredible ancient Roman collections that enabled me to understand what people may have looked like and how they lived their day-to-day lives. I also spent considerable time in Rome itself, talking with guides and historians about the ancient city, particularly the Roman Forum and the Palatine Hill, walking in the areas where my characters would have walked. When Apicius and Fannia are rushing to the Curia to free Thrasius, for example, I know the path they would have taken because I've walked those same roads. Many of the descriptions of items within the novel are taken from ancient places and artifacts I have viewed firsthand, such as the tomb where Thrasius uses the curse tablet, the paintings that decorated the walls of the villas, or the many different types of glassware described at the parties. I took a lot of notes and a lot of photos. To write this book I had to truly be able to picture the world and how the characters moved within it.

Then, once I had done all the research, I had to figure out the best way to weave it all into the novel. There are many passages that were cut from the novel because, while they were interesting, they just didn't move the plot along. It's also important not to overwhelm the reader with information, which would be easy to do. And at the same time, I had to paint a world that is quite foreign for many readers. One case in point is that most modern Americans understand slavery in the context of African slavery and the world of Southern plantations before the Civil War. Slavery in ancient Rome was much different, and I had to find the right ways to adjust the reader's expectations when it came to the slaves within the book.

What information about this time period found during your research was the most surprising to you? Is there any facet of society or living that you feel has not changed much since ancient Roman times?

At first, I was surprised to discover that Roman society was so advanced. They had running water, personal hygiene, libraries, universities, advanced architecture, factories, mathematics, etc. So much of that civilization was lost and destroyed with the expansion of Christianity, which deemed anything Roman as pagan and thus heretical. I cannot help but wonder where our society would be now if that advancement had continued. There are many reasons why ancient Rome fell, but in my mind, the thread that runs through from then until now is the ongoing disagreement centered on religion—whose god is the right god?

What role does food play in your own life? Is it simply a necessity or do you share Apicius's enthusiasm for food?

I grew up with a very limited palate, with a childhood diet that consisted of hot dogs, Kraft Mac & Cheese, and other sorts of fast, easy-to-make processed food. When I met my husband, Joe, who sold wine for a living at the time, he introduced me to a whole host of foods I would never have imagined eating (mushrooms, artichokes, funky cheeses, foie gras, offal, rabbit, etc.). Now I'll try most any food at least once. From him, I learned that pairing food and wine is, in some ways, a form of art. From there my interest in food and food culture grew. Later, one of my oldest and dearest friends, Greg McCormick, introduced me to the writings of the famous food writer M. F. K. Fisher, and I was hooked. I loved everything about her work. For me, like so many other people, food is emotional. It is comfort, it is conviviality, and it is also a fascinating differentiator in our culture. I've also learned a great deal from the various chefs and bartenders whom I've come to know in the Boston restaurant industry. You could call me a "gourmand," "food nerd," or "culinary enthusiast," whichever moniker you think fits. I find it funny that many people who are food lovers are picky about the word "foodie," but if you want to call me that, go for it.

If you were attending a dinner with a host as enthusiastic about food as Apicius, what delicacies would you most hope to find on your plate?

This is a hard question! One of the most amazing dishes I've ever eaten was at Metamorfosi in Rome, Italy. They make a 65-degree sous vide carbonara egg with crispy pasta, fried pork rinds, and Parmesan foam. It was so unusual and it was such a stunning taste in the mouth—I remember thinking that Apicius would have appreciated the wow factor of the dish. I think that a dinner to rival one of Apicius's would have to be made from the freshest produce and meat, with the finest ingredients, and the courses a mixture of the deliciously simple to the types of foods that would be a showstopper today, like that egg.

Have you made any of the dishes from Apicius's cookbook? If so, what dish or dishes are you the most drawn to or fascinated by?

I've made several dishes from Apicius. The Parthian chicken is one of my favorites. My husband is a great cook and we love to try to re-create the recipes. It's been one of the most fun things about writing about historical chefs. It's fun to make recipes that others have interpreted, but it's even more fun to figure it out on our own. As of this writing we're working on the sweet-and-sour dill chicken that is found in Apicius. Without any real instructions or proportions, the process is a bit of an experiment. We've made it at least four or five times now and I think we've almost perfected the recipe. It would be excellent on chicken wings!

You have already been at work writing a new book about another well-known cook. How did _Feast of Sorrow_ influence or inspire your current writing projects? Has this book changed the way you write?

I'm working on a historical novel about Bartolomeo Scappi, who was the most famous chef of the Renaissance. He was the private cook to several popes and he wrote a cookbook that was a bestseller for more than two hundred years. Both Apicius and Scappi shaped so much of the cooking we know and love today. Yet, what is interesting to me is that very little is known of the lives of these individuals. I love the idea of coming up with stories that are as delicious as the recipes themselves. The second book has been a bit easier to write in that I have a better sense of how to write a book. _Feast of Sorrow_ went through so many edits and I learned a lot about avoiding certain pitfalls the second time around. My second novel won't be nearly so tragic. It's a mystery and a love affair and it's been tremendous fun to write.

As a reader, who are some of the storytellers you find most inspiring and why?

So many authors over many genres have inspired me and my writing. When I was young I loved fairy tales. The Brothers Grimm and Hans Christian Andersen kept me dreaming. I have never lost my love for the fantastical or the speculative and I particularly love the works of Margaret Atwood, Stephen King, Catherynne Valente, Haruki Murakami, and Mark Z. Danielewski. The idea of someone creating an entire unfamiliar world and making it feel accessible is intriguing to me.

But history has also inspired me in many ways, clearly, as I'm writing in the historical genre. And really, what is history other than storytelling? Plus, sometimes history can be just as much fiction as fact. Two of my favorite books are *The Histories* by Herodotus and Benvenuto Cellini's *Autobiography*. Herodotus's book is considered to be the first real attempt to write a book of history. Yet what I love about it is that it is full of hearsay as well as myths and legends that the people of that time believed to be true. And Cellini's autobiography is a roaring embellishment of his life as a goldsmith during the Renaissance. He was a tortured but successful artist. He was put in jail for murder but got out by the grace of the pope. He tells you how he single-handedly saved the city during the Sack of Rome but conveniently leaves out all the times he was jailed for sodomy. It's hard to know what is true and what is not and I love that.

One of the best storytellers I have ever encountered is Chuck Palahniuk, the author of *Fight Club*. I listened to him speak at a writing conference in Boston a few years ago. He told the story of being in Paris to give a speech when he received the news that his grandmother had died. For the entire hour that he spoke I was riveted. My emotions ran the gambit from high to low. When he was finished I realized that I would remember that story forever, it was that powerful.

Can you recommend some of your favorite books about ancient Rome?

Virgil's *Aeneid* is still required reading for most Italian schoolchildren. For centuries he has been particularly revered in Italy as their greatest poet, and if you want to become a little bit closer with Italian culture, start there.

I cut my teeth on Robert Graves's *I, Claudius*, which is a classic. The history is rather embellished in many places, but it's a book that opened up a whole world of interest in ancient Rome for readers.

Other books I've enjoyed a great deal include Kate Quinn's Empress of Rome series, Elisabeth Storrs's Tales of Ancient Rome series, Phyllis T. Smith's *I Am Livia*, Michelle Moran's *Cleopatra's Daughter*, L. J. Trafford's the Four Emperors series, and anything by Steven Saylor, Robert Harris, and Colleen McCullough. David Wishart also has a novel with his take on Sejanus that is a good read.

For pure history, Mary Beard's *SPQR* is a must. Anthony Everitt's *Augustus* is a comprehensive view of the life of one of the most famous men to ever live. And Tacitus's *Histories* and Pliny's *Natural History* are still very accessible centuries later.

The characters in *Feast of Sorrow* are fascinated with fortune-telling and divine signs. Have you ever had your fortune told or are there any mystical signs you pay attention to or look for in your own life?

I had my palm read once, many years ago when I lived in Seattle. The fortune-teller told me that I was going to move to a new place soon and that it would be very beneficial for me. That was true—I moved to Boston about six months later. She also told me that I would have two children, the first of which would come in two years. Nope and nope. However, I do have a good friend who practices astrology and she has read my charts a few times. They've always been accurate, even pinpointing the date that my husband asked me to marry him! I'm not sure I would call myself a believer, but I don't entirely disbelieve either.

I do believe that we have control over our own fates. That said, I have always found that in my life when I am working toward my goals—the ones that truly matter to me—all sorts of doors open up. Synchronicity is a funny thing, and I love when the stars align and everything seems to fall into place.